THE GOOD SISTER

THE GOOD SISTER

DIANA DIAMOND

St. Martin's Press
New York

www.stmartins.com

Library of Congress Cataloging-in-Publication Data

Diamond, Diana.
    The good sister / Diana Diamond.—1st ed.
        p. cm.
    ISBN 0-312-29165-5
    1. Inheritance and succession—Fiction. 2. Sisters—Fiction. I. Title.

PS3554.I233 G66 2002
813'.6—dc21

                                                        2002017137

10   9   8   7   6   5   4   3   2

To Duff
for being so understanding

PART ONE

ONE

Why would I want to kill my own sister? I don't think it was be-
cause I hated her. Hatred *is too strong a word. We fought a lot as*
children. Name-calling, nasty tricks, lies that would get each other
in trouble. But if hatred means wanting the other person destroyed,
then I don't think I hated her. So why would I want to kill her?

Maybe just to get rid of a rival. Rivals *would be a better descrip-*
tion of our childhood: bitter rivals. *We competed for everything. If*
we were drawing a picture with crayons, we'd race to see who would
finish first, then run to our mother to see whose picture was best.
Neither of us would settle for "They're both lovely." We had to have
a winner, so we would demand to know who had the prettiest sky
or whose tree looked best. And we weren't satisfied if one of us had
the best sky and the other the best tree. All we'd do is change the
argument to who had drawn the best barn.

I remember staying awake a whole night because I was sure my
sister was going to sneak into my room and tear up a picture I had
drawn. We were still just little girls, my sister and I. No older than
six or seven. She did a picture in school, and our mother oohed
and ahhed as if it were a Picasso. So I did the same picture, only
better. She was angry because I had copied her picture, and I just
knew she would try to get rid of mine. So I hid it under my mattress,
and then I stayed awake the whole night. She must have known I
was waiting for her, because she never came. The sun was coming
up, and I couldn't stay awake much longer, so I went to her room
and found her picture right on top of her desk. I colored a little
yellow over her blue sky so that it took on a green tint. I rubbed

some black into her blue water. Nothing terrible. Just enough so that her picture looked a little silly. That way, no matter what she did to my picture, hers wouldn't be any better.

All children do things like that, don't you think? But that isn't hatred! It's just sibling rivalry. Silly, I suppose. But certainly not cold-blooded hatred.

There was another time. We had both gotten dolls, so how old could we have been? Certainly not more than first- or second-graders. They were absolutely identical. Curly blond hair. Deep blue eyes that closed when you laid them down. Tiny red lips with open mouths for play nursing bottles. Pink cheeks. The only difference was the color of the dresses. My doll wore pink, and hers wore yellow. The pink was much prettier, but my sister said she liked the yellow best. You can see what I mean about our being rivals. She couldn't even admit that my doll was prettier than hers.

I knew she would try to change the dresses. And if she did, how would we have known which doll was hers and which was mine? I mean, if she started changing the dresses, then maybe my doll would be in yellow and I would think it was her doll. There had to be something I could do so that they couldn't get mixed up.

She was playing outside with a friend from down the road, and there, right in her doll carriage, was the one in the yellow dress. I knew it was hers because I had hidden mine away in the basement where she couldn't find it. So I took the doll into my room and used a pencil to poke out her eyes. The little glass eyes fell into the doll's head, where they rattled around. You could see them inside if you looked through the gaping holes in the doll's face.

My sister had a crying fit when she found her baby blinded, and Mother held her, and rocked her, and promised to have the doll fixed. When my parents couldn't get it fixed, they bought another doll. But the new one wasn't nearly as pretty as mine, so no matter what my sister did with the clothes, I would always have the prettiest doll. That's the way we were! Just rivals. Believe me. If I hadn't hidden my doll, she would have done something to steal the pink dress.

As we got older, our competition moved to other playing fields.

In junior high it was field hockey. Even though we were a year apart, we both made the team, and both of us at the same position. Only one of us could start, and the other would be a substitute. You can imagine how that turned her on! She would have done anything to see me on the bench while she was making all the plays, and I didn't care about any of the other positions as long as my sister wasn't starting ahead of me.

You know what she did? She started sucking up to the coach. How do I handle this situation? When do I pass and when do I shoot? *Dumb questions just so the coach would know she was a serious jock. And it was working! In scrimmages, she was with the starters, and I was with the scrubs.*

We were both going for the ball, each of us with an equal chance. She had her stick ready, and I pulled mine back, legally, no higher than my knee. We both swung, and she was first to the ball. I missed the ball completely, but my stick smashed into her ankle. She went down with a broken something-or-other, so it turned out that I had the starting position and she was on the bench watching me. All her brown-nosing didn't buy her a thing.

Did I cripple her on purpose? Absolutely not! It's just that she was first to the ball, and I had to do something. I couldn't just pull away as if we were playing hopscotch. Field hockey can get pretty rough, and she should have been watching out for herself. Besides, she got all sorts of sympathy. Mom and Dad helped her with her therapy. Teachers let her out of class early. And the kids on the team voted her an honorary captain. She got a lot more out of the season than I did.

But you can see what I mean. We were rivals, just like most sisters and brothers. Kids have accidents. That's not what you would call hatred.

In high school we were rivals over boys. We were close enough in age, just a year apart, so that we were in the same crowd. Sometimes we would talk about the boys we liked and the ones we thought were jerks, and about the other girls who were chasing after them. We knew which guys wanted action and which girls were giving away the store just to get dates. Neither of us had any thought of being easy. We both had high standards that we wanted to maintain, or at least that's what I thought.

There was this basketball player who was coming on to me, a big-man-on-campus type the girls were crazy for. He played the field and talked to everyone, but I could see that he had the hots for me. My father hadn't yet made it big, so my sister and I didn't even have cars. But this guy would manage to be on his way out the door just when we were leaving, and he was always anxious to drive us home. We were all in the front seat, usually with me closest to him and my sister next to the door. But sometimes she'd jump in first and sit between us. He wouldn't say anything. He was too cool to be obvious. And I wasn't going to kick up a fuss. I really didn't care that much about him, and I certainly wasn't going to make the first move.

Then, out of the blue, the two of them had a date for the movies. Behind my back, my own sister had put a move on my boyfriend. I confronted her and demanded an explanation. I mean, friends don't do that to each other, much less sisters. And she played innocent and hurt, just as she always did. She had no idea that he and I were an item. I'd never said anything. Like I'm supposed to tie a ribbon around any man I like. And he just asked her, she didn't do anything to encourage him. That was her answer. A bunch of barefaced lies.

They became quite a pair, with him hanging around her locker and her turning into a gym rat to watch him at practice. They sat alone together in a corner of the cafeteria, away from the rest of us. She even talked him into leaving at different times so that they could ride home without me. "Oh, were you waiting?" she'd say to me. "We thought you had gotten another ride." More of her damn lies!

They were dating every weekend. If it wasn't a movie, it was a concert. And if they couldn't find a better excuse, it would be just a walk in the park. But they always lingered in his car before they said good night, and sometimes good night extended to the living room sofa. A couple of times I walked in on them by accident and found them inside each other's clothes. "Oh, I'm so sorry," I said, when really I was wondering which one of them I should kill first. Him because he had switched to her just to get into her pants. Or her because she had thrown herself at my boyfriend.

She was like that with boys, a pushover, so they were all sniffing around her. Not that I was a prude! I knew my way around the backseat of a car, and I always had a date for the prom. But I drew the line. And you could tell by the way the guys were lining up that she wasn't quite so fussy. So it wasn't really a fair competition. It was like a kid having a birthday party, but everyone goes to another party because that kid is having clowns and a pony.

It was the same way with our father when he left the phone company and started the satellite business. He was traveling all over the world, and we wouldn't see him for weeks at end. Of course we were thrilled when he finally came home, but to see little Miss Goody Two-shoes, you'd think he had come back from the dead. She sat at his feet like he was Jesus, listening to all the miracles he'd worked. This or that company had signed on to send him their video programming. Or he had talked some Greek tycoon into bank-rolling his research. Our father liked to brag, and my sister was a great audience. She'd sit there openmouthed, lapping up all this hype as if she actually understood what he was talking about. And our father fell for it! I mean, I was the one who had the higher grades in science, and even I didn't understand escape speeds and parking orbits. At least not then. But she was some actress. Do you know that she even kept his mailing lists on her computer!

And just like with the boys, it paid off. Daddy always brought us gifts when he came back from a trip. Perfume when he was in France, or jewelry from Italy. Little things, although they became very substantial once his first satellite was up and the money began rolling in. But after a while it was no secret that she was getting the better gifts. I remember when he came back from Central America after one of his trips, he brought us each an Aztec bracelet. Soft silver with very intricate patterns of pre-Columbian figures. And would you believe that hers was much wider? He said he thought I would like the more feminine look of the thinner bracelet, and of course I was gracious and agreed completely. But hers was twice as heavy and you could tell that it had cost a lot more. She played it cool. I remember her telling him how he had picked exactly the right bracelet for each of us. And then she was all ears waiting to hear about his latest miracles.

Then there were the gold chains. He had been to Milan and stopped in Florence on the way back to get Mother a leather bag. In the market, he spotted these gold chains that were in style at the time and brought one back for each of us. But this time we both liked the thinner, more delicate design. Strange that I got the thinner bracelet but wasn't given the "more feminine" chain, don't you think. Instead, he had to flip a coin to see which one of us got to pick first. And I don't have to tell you who won the coin toss.

Believe me, I had no trouble with competition. It was natural that my sister and I would compete for honors, and awards, and even the favor of parents and friends. Someone wins and someone loses, and I can be just as gracious when I lose as when I win. But that doesn't make me a pushover. When people decide to walk all over you, you're not supposed to take it lying down, are you? You fight back, don't you? Does that mean that you hate the other person? Does that make you some sort of psychopath?

What was I supposed to do, just let my sister steal my boyfriends? And turn my own father against me? I had to do something, and that's what the Internet thing was all about. Sure, you can make it sound like I was some sort of fiend for even thinking of such a thing. Now, when we're all older and more experienced, it's easy to make childhood mistakes sound sick and depraved. But back then computers were toys, and everyone was playing computer jokes. It was only a dirty trick. Not the big deal that some people make it out to be.

My sister and this jock were sending each other e-mails before they went to bed. Little "thinking of you" notes and greeting cards that they downloaded from one of those free birthday-card services. I found one of the cards from him in her printer, and the one she was sending back still up on her screen. Then I realized that if I had her password, I could look in on their breathless conversations. That's all it was. Just a bit of teenage curiosity. I thought if he called her something endearing—love lips, or pussycat, or something—I'd let it drop some night at the table and watch her face hit the floor. Or maybe she'd say something equally ridiculous to him, and then I'd get someone to use it in front of him. If she called him "hunky," then I'd get the girls to start calling him that and see how red he'd turn. Childish, I admit. But we really were only children, and a kid's prank is a long way from fiendish hatred.

But I couldn't find the damn password. And when I did find it in her school notebook, all I got were her homework assignments. She had set up a personal address with a separate password for the drivel she exchanged with Hunky! As if anyone would be interested. But she was like that. Secretive, paranoid.

You know, maybe she's the one you should have writing out her life's story. I'll bet it's a lot more warped than anything you're going to get from me.

I tried everything that she might use as a password. Her birthday, his birthday, the day they met, the day I first caught them on the living room sofa, her jersey number, his jersey number. One of the nerds at school had an algorithm that ran combinations of numbers by the hour, and even that didn't work. And then, one day in our bathroom while she was taking a shower, I spotted an ankle bracelet that he had apparently given her. "In love at last" was engraved behind her name. And when I put that into the computer, I had their whole correspondence scrolling in front of me.

Most of it was stupid, even for high school kids. But some of it was very graphic, particularly the Monday exchanges after their weekend dates. As far as I could tell, they weren't sleeping together, but they had pretty much perfected the art of foreplay. Great reading, I thought, for the gang at school, so I spent a few days editing the old stuff and then selectively adding the new material that was showing up every day. In a little while I had a ten-page document that would make them a laughingstock. Once it got around, he wouldn't dare show his face around our house. Heck, he'd probably have to drop out of school. Sure, my sister would guess who had done it. But she could never be sure. Anyone who got hold of her password or his, and knew the address that went with it, could have dialed into their love life. Either one of them could have made a stupid blunder.

So that was it. Just a joke! And maybe a payback for the both of them. As I said, I didn't know which one I wanted to kill first. Both of them had treated me shabbily. I never planned the rest of it. It just happened when my father put up his first satellite, and suddenly we were rich.

It was high school graduation and we both got sports cars. Mustangs! Convertibles that had recently come back on the market. It was the dolls all over again. Mine was red with a black interior; hers was green with a tan interior. No contest, right? I mean, Ferrari red! At last I had gotten the better of her. But wouldn't you know it—she comes up with a book about the great age of English road racing, and aren't all the Coopers and Lotuses painted in her green with tan interiors.

I admit it. I was furious. Probably stupid, because by then you'd think I would have gotten used to her being Daddy's little girl. But as I say, when people are walking all over you, you can't simply lie down and take it. At least not if you have any self-respect. And I couldn't put the doll's eyes out again. If I had keyed the paint or taken a razor to the leather, the insurance would have covered the repair.

That's when I remembered the mailing lists she used to keep for my father. He didn't use them anymore because he had a promotion department now, with much more sophisticated lists than the early ones. But still, most of his important colleagues were still in my sister's file. So I took her panting e-mail correspondence and sent it all out over the list. For weeks my father and his little favorite were the jokes of the business world, not to mention our entire community. One of the business writers even took to calling my father "Hunky."

I know it went too far, but you have to admit that it was a stroke of genius. I got her for pushing me aside to get closer to my father. And I got my father for liking her more than me. And the best part of it was that she took all the blame. The list was in her computer, so it stood to reason that she must have put the wrong address code on the wrong correspondence. For the whole summer you didn't see her smiling when she tooled around town in her racing-green Mustang!

But it wasn't as if I set out to destroy her. As I say, we were just rivals, and one thing led to another, and maybe once or twice things did get out of hand. But I never hated her. That's not why I helped to kill her.

TWO

"*TROIS MINUTES.*" Henri held up three fingers.

Gaspar nodded. "Three minutes and counting," he explained.

Jennifer smiled. She made a show of crossing her fingers. Gaspar took her hand and uncrossed them. "No luck involved. Everything is going perfectly."

Jennifer crossed the fingers again. "It can't hurt," she said, and Gaspar flashed his easy smile.

"I suppose not," and then he crossed his fingers.

There were twenty of them in the bunker, unkempt men in tropical dress, staring at computer screens and babbling French phrases into headset microphones. Each of the screens was filled with columns of data that changed by the second, inspiring nods, grunts, and satisfied smiles.

"*Bon!*" Gaspar said over and over in response to reports called from Henri. He turned to Jennifer. "Absolutely perfect. It's never gone smoother."

She nodded in agreement, even though she couldn't confirm Gaspar's assessment. Jennifer understood just a few of the phrases and even then had no idea of what they signified. But as long as Gaspar kept saying "*Bon,*" she assumed that nothing serious could be going wrong.

Through the small slit windows on the front wall she could see the ten-story *Ariane 4* rocket that was still wedded to a gantry a quarter of a mile away. On top was a dart-shaped pod that held Pegasus III, her company's $200 million communications satellite. Put into a precise parking orbit over an exact point on the eastern coast of Brazil and it would earn back its cost every few months for the next fifteen years. Miss the orbit and Pegasus III would become the latest addition to a growing armada of space junk, flying around uselessly until it incinerated itself in the earth's atmosphere. Even though she didn't know all the rules, Jennifer was definitely playing at the high-stakes table.

"Deux minutes!" Henri announced.

"Two minutes and counting. Everything is go," Gaspar translated. In the distance, the gantry backed away, leaving the rocket a delicate finger pointing at the heavens.

The Ariane team had included her in everything since she had arrived from New York—the technical meetings, the rehearsals, the positioning of the payload, even the dangerous process of fueling the bird. She had sweated her way through the jeans and khakis she had bought for the trip and was now wearing borrowed shorts and a men's T-shirt. At each step the team seemed to defer to her judgment on whether they should proceed to the next task. But it was simply the deference that good business managers show to their best customers. Jennifer had paid for the rocket and was footing the bill for the launch. It was a big bill, already over $120 million, and there were no refunds for failure.

When Martin Pegan had first come up with the idea of a privately owned satellite network, there were no commercial launching companies such as the Ariane group. Rockets belonged to government agencies, and communications satellites were the exclusive property of the international telephone cartel. Satellites should have been the end of long-distance charges. After all, a telephone call via satellite doesn't travel much farther to reach someone across the country than it does to reach someone next door. But telephone companies weren't planning on sharing the savings with their customers.

That was Pegan's big idea, low-cost telephone and video communications from rooftop to rooftop. He had persuaded an American company to build him a satellite. When American aerospace companies refused to sell him a rocket, he had turned to the French at Ariane, who were building a launch center in the old prison colony in French Guiana. His first satellite, Pegasus I, had blanketed North America, carrying telephone traffic, pager messages, sporting events, movies, and business data over private circuits. Pegasus II's footprint spanned the Pacific, linking Asia to North America. Now Pegasus III was hoping to close the loop around the Western world, linking North America, Europe, and the Near East. Once in orbit, it would make Pegasus the world's largest private communications company.

"*Une minute!*" Henri chanted.

Jennifer nodded before Gaspar had time to translate. They were down to the final minute.

Martin Pegan would have groomed a son to take over the business. But there was no male heir. Instead, there were two daughters, Catherine and Jennifer, emerging from college with no particular skills in communications technology and no burning interests in business management. He bribed them both into graduate school; Catherine chose to study business while Jennifer grappled with the rudiments of telephony. Together, he hoped, they might someday replace him at the helm of his venturesome company. But someday came sooner than he planned.

The two girls had just finished their studies and joined the company when a routine physical discovered cancer in Martin's gut. With his wife dead and his daughters still immature, Martin needed to find a way to keep the company together after his death. Take it public, he was advised, and leave each of the girls a fortune in stock. Sensible, but it didn't take into account the bond between the man and the company he had fought to create. Pegan hadn't merely bought Pegasus Satellite Services. He had conceived it, nurtured the concept to life, and then fought governments and global cartels to bring it to birth. Its name was a derivative of his own, its growth the echo of his own energy. He needed a clone of himself to run it.

Those had been his thoughts when he met Peter Barnes, only in his mid-thirties but already making a name for himself in high-tech business. Peter had pioneered new ideas in light-wave communications, outmaneuvered larger competitors, and landed

Pegasus as one of his prime customers. Martin bought the company, claiming he was seeking vertical integration. Actually, it was Peter Barnes he was after. Peter could run Pegasus until the girls were ready to take over.

"*Dix . . . neuf . . . huit . . .*" Henri began tolling the final seconds of the countdown. Gaspar's grip on Jennifer's hand tightened. She felt her mouth go dry, even as she felt the rivulets of perspiration under her oversize T-shirt.

White smoke puffed out from under the missile, replaced instantly by bright jets of blue flame. The control bunker began to tremble, the windows rattling.

"*Ignition!*"

"Here we go," Gaspar whispered.

"*Trois . . . deux . . . un . . . DECOLLER!*"

The rocket began to lift, slowly, uncertainly. Jennifer's breath caught. Something seemed wrong. It was wobbling, more unsure of its footing than anxious to leave the ground. She glanced quickly at Gaspar. His eyes were squeezed shut. "Liftoff!" he announced.

Just barely, Jennifer thought. A few feet at most. All around the room voices were chattering in French. They seemed calm and professional, with no hint of emergency. But still, the *Ariane 4* seemed to be going nowhere.

Martin Pegan had died just two years after hiring Peter Barnes, leaving the company with its single satellite aloft and another scheduled to fit into a slot over the Pacific. Its debts were enormous, but the income from Pegasus I was carrying the interest, and Pegasus II promised to turn the enterprise profitable.

Peter Barnes became president, compensated with a minority share of the business that could make him vastly wealthy. He had promised Martin to grow Pegasus Satellite Services, protect its assets, and pay its debts. But the deathbed commitment he made to his mentor was to nurture Martin's daughters until they were ready to assume full responsibility. And the deathbed advice Martin had given his daughters was to trust Peter completely.

With Pegasus III, Peter would honor his obligation to grow the company to its potential. He had already met his commitment to the daughters. Catherine was now in charge of marketing operations, finding new customers for the company's services. Jennifer was in charge of network operations, expanding and maintaining the satellite system. Both had sharpened their skills and earned the respect of their organizations.

Space appeared under the rocket. The jets of blue flame turned white as they lifted the *Ariane 4* out of the initial cloud of smoke. It gained speed and climbed past the narrow window openings. Jennifer looked down at her monitor. Outside cameras framed the rocket perfectly as it eased past the horizon and accelerated into space.

Then the noise stopped. The bunker was no longer vibrating or the windows rattling. The thunderous rumble that had begun with ignition became a distant hum.

"You did it," Jennifer congratulated Gaspar.

He leaned back in his chair and shook his head. "Not yet. This is just the beginning. Now it has to find its orbit."

She watched the monitor until the rocket had turned into a tiny dot of light. At that point, the *Ariane* had separated from its first stage. The second stage, with its expensive cargo, was two hundred miles out over the Atlantic, fifty miles high, and traveling at almost three thousand miles an hour.

Gaspar left his place by Jennifer's side and walked down the line behind the monitors. He peered intently over shoulders, spoke a few words here and there, and finally arrived at a conference with Henri. He was smiling when he returned.

"A small course correction, already accomplished," he announced.

"Where is it?" she asked.

"Over Africa, directly above the equator. So far everything is right on schedule."

"What do we do now?"

"Just wait. The Seychelles will take over in another minute, and then they'll pass her on to Tahiti. We won't have control again for . . ." Gaspar turned to his computer, tapped a few keys, then concluded, "Six hours. You might want to get some rest."

Jennifer left the bunker and climbed into the Jeep that the launch company had put at her service. She drove the paved road to the housing compound where they had put her up in a two-room suite. She stripped off the sweat-soaked clothes, pulled on a one-piece swimsuit and a terry robe, then drove to the small, stony beach that was part of the Ariane property. She drove to the water's edge, threw off the robe, and without pausing ran headlong into the modest surf. She dove into the first breaker, and when she surfaced, she was out well beyond the waves. She shook the water out of her eyes, gave a strong kick, and then rolled into a smooth, well-trained stroke. In college, her specialty had been the sprints, but she didn't hesitate to set off for a mile swim out to the farthest point of land and then back to the beach. It was refreshing to leave the last week's tensions behind her.

The launch was her responsibility. She had taken the market research from her sister and fitted the satellite's coverage to include the most important markets in its footprint. Not that she had ever run a formula or touched a screwdriver. The aerospace vendor had armies of engineers who specialized in those things. What she had done was develop specifications and evaluate lab predictions, trading area of coverage for intensity of coverage and swapping less important regions for more profitable target markets. There were months of studies, long and angry meetings with her suppliers, and days of patient bartering with Catherine and Peter. Catherine insisted on coverage criteria that Jennifer couldn't always deliver; Peter set cost limitations that she couldn't always meet. They had been difficult partners, just as she assumed each of them would label her a difficult partner.

Then there had been the tradeoffs with the launch-company engineers. Again, she had no useful knowledge of their art, only requirements for a precise positioning to maximize the satellite's design capabilities, an elegant orbit that would prolong its service life, and cost control to preserve her allotted budget. Gaspar, she guessed, would also call her a difficult partner.

But she had done her job well, and despite inflamed tempers and bruised egos, Jennifer knew that she had earned everyone's respect. Catherine, never easy to get along with, had congratulated her in the end. When Peter reviewed her final launch plan, he had smiled and touched a finger to his forehead as if tipping his hat. Then, in the final seconds of the countdown, Gaspar had clutched her hand to steady his own nerves as well as hers. This was where her father wanted her to be, she knew. Right in the top ranks of the company he had built. And she guessed that he probably didn't want her to stop there. Maybe she was ready for the next step.

But for the moment all that was out of her hands. Pegasus III was hurtling around the other side of the globe at five times the speed of sound, losing speed slowly as it climbed to a higher and higher orbit, its momentum gradually coming into balance with the earth's gravity. None of her efforts could succeed until it was carefully throttled back to a speed that would hold it in orbit over a specific spot on earth. And even then, nothing was accomplished until it powered itself up and showed that it could receive a signal from anywhere in Europe and pass it down to the East Coast of the United States, or relay an American broadcast to anywhere in Europe.

Jennifer stroked back through the surf and let a wave push her back onto the beach. Then she lay down on top of the terry robe and stretched herself luxuriously in the tropical sun. "Just five minutes," she told herself. Her indoor complexion, nurtured by long days in the office, would burn very quickly.

She had a nice figure, athletic rather than sensuous, practical rather than fashionable. By Barbie-doll standards, she was two thick in the thighs, too wide at the waist, and too flat across the chest. Yet, in every dimension, she was within an inch of the ideal female of her age. Jennifer didn't mind being seen in a bathing suit, but she was a bit self-conscious in the ladies' locker room.

Her hair was no particular color, a common shade somewhere in the spectrum between brunette and blond. She had never colored it and wouldn't even consider a different shade, at least until she had some gray to hide. She had it razor-cut in a barbershop to keep it short and manageable, and used a brush only after a shower. "Please let me get you an appointment with Nicholas," her sister begged her at least once a month. "You look like you're auditioning for a motorcycle gang."

Jennifer rarely used makeup. An occasional touch of lipstick, usually a pale color, to add definition to a small and purposeful mouth. And maybe mascara to frame eyes that were described on her driver's license as hazel. But foundation, blush, and eye shadow were nowhere in her arsenal.

At five feet six inches, 130 pounds, she was practically the definition of normal, though distinctive in her inquisitive squint, the determined set of her jaw, the intensity of her listening, and the economy of her speech. Jennifer took life seriously, and her appearance was testimony to the fact.

She was on her feet the moment she began to feel the sun burning her legs, and drove the dirt path back to her room with nearly expert shifts of the Jeep's noisy gearbox. She tossed through the laundry that had just been delivered and selected jeans and a man-tailored shirt. She slipped bare feet into tennis shoes, dried her hair and arranged it with a towel, and, in a completely frivolous gesture, tied a colorful scarf around her waist. Then she drove back to the bunker where the station in Tahiti was reporting on the condition of Pegasus III.

"Perfect! Right on trajectory," Gaspar reported. He was clutching a cigar in his teeth, indicating that celebration would soon be in order.

"When can Miami try?" Jennifer asked, referring to her company's uplink on the Florida peninsula. Her people in Miami would be the first to contact Pegasus III and begin routing traffic to European test sites.

Gaspar shrugged. "Another hour. Maybe two." His part of the operation would be concluded successfully once the satellite was parked in orbit. If it failed to communicate, that would be the fault of the satellite manufacturer. It was too early for the satellite manufacturer to be lighting up a cigar, but Gaspar and his Ariane team were very close to success.

Tahiti supplied data that the engineers in Guiana pored over, and then Guiana handled the last details of parking Pegasus III in its permanent home. Henri worried the satellite into its exact parking orbit, then lit a cigar of his own. "Try Miami," Gaspar finally announced.

Jennifer watched data flash over the broadband connection with her company's uplink as each one of the satellite's transponders was addressed and given traffic to forward. Test sites from Finland to Egypt, from the Canary Islands to the Black Sea, reported contact. Slowly, her elation began to fill her smile, until Gaspar was able to offer, "A cigar. Cuban, of course. You can't get these in America."

She shook her head. "Another half hour. And then maybe some of that French champagne instead."

The engineers waited, watching her anxiously, as Pegasus III established its place in the global network. When Jennifer jumped to her feet and held two thumbs up, they screamed their applause. In an instant, corks were popping around the control room, and within seconds, a flute of Dom Perignon was in every hand. The launch was perfect and the satellite fully operational. Another financial empire had been launched, and the two rich little Pegan sisters were richer than ever. Jennifer took a full bottle, raised it to her lips, and then threw her head back. A moment later, she had her first taste of a genuine Cuban cigar.

"Heaven," Gaspar said, throwing his arms around her. "And there's Russian caviar waiting."

Jennifer was laughing hysterically. "Let's not keep it waiting any longer."

They poured out of the control bunker into the waiting bus and sang their way back to the dining hall at the housing compound. Jennifer was still focused enough to notice Gaspar's hand resting on the small of her back, touching her skin under her shirt. But she was too overjoyed to care about the details.

At the party she danced easily in and out of the arms of the engineers, stood atop the piano while she faked the words to a recorded rock-and-roll beat, and laughed her way through a competition that required each loser to down a shot of Calvados. She was more than a bit tipsy when she took the microphone, expressed her gratitude for the skill and dedication of the people who had put her payload into orbit, and bid all a good night. By midnight she was in bed trying to fall asleep, despite the sensation that the room was spinning.

When the telephone began ringing, Jennifer assumed it was the alarm clock and tried all the snooze and sleep buttons before spotting the flashing light on her station button. She dragged the handset into her bed and tried "Hello" three times before she was able to make a sound.

"Jennifer?"

"I think so."

"Are you in bed?"

"It's too dark to tell. Wait while I put a light on."

"What are you doing in bed?" Catherine's voice demanded.

"Aren't I talking to you?" Jennifer responded.

"Why aren't you celebrating? I just talked with someone at the party. It was so noisy I could hardly hear."

"I did celebrate."

"Jennifer, this is the biggest coup of your career. You're in a building with a couple of dozen Frenchmen and a maybe a thousand bottles of champagne. What the hell are you doing in bed . . . alone?"

"What makes you think I'm alone?"

"Because the French male voice I spoke with said that you had left the party at the stroke of midnight. He wondered if you might have lost a glass slipper in your hurry."

"It was getting a bit out of hand."

"That's what a party is, Jennifer. It's supposed to get out of hand."

"Catherine, is this why you're calling me? To tell me to go back to the party?"

"No. I called to congratulate you. Peter left a message at my hotel telling me that Pegasus III was up and working. You could have let me know."

"How? You didn't tell me you'd be traveling. I don't even know where you are."

"In Hollywood, dammit. Don't you ever read my e-mail?"

"Oh, right . . . right," Jennifer mumbled as she searched through her foggy memory. "That Cannes thing, isn't it?"

"Cannes *thing*?" Catherine sounded angry. "It's the Cannes Film Festival, and maybe enough movie traffic to load up Pegasus III and keep it full."

"Of course," Jennifer answered. "That's what I meant. How's it going?"

"Very well, thank you. We're going to be featured at three of the technical presentations, and most of the producers will be guests at our party."

"And the Europeans?" Jennifer questioned. It was the European producers and exhibitors who would make money for Pegasus III.

"Some will be at our hospitality. We have lunch dates with others. We'll just have to make cold calls on the rest. But we should see all the important ones."

"That's wonderful," Jennifer said. "Sounds like you deserve congratulations as well."

"I most certainly do." Catherine laughed. "We can buy each other lunch in New York."

They laughed together before they hung up. It took Jennifer only a few seconds to get back to sleep.

THREE

CATHERINE RETURNED to the guests in her suite and interrupted the piano player to announce the successful launch of Pegasus III. There was a burst of applause, then gushers of congratulations as the party pressed in around her. The richest person in the room had just become much richer, and the Hollywood moguls sensed money the way sharks sense a struggling tuna.

But if Catherine had moved a few notches higher on all the producers' hit lists, the more important of them were in clear focus on hers. Pegasus Satellite Services was about to take a giant step into film distribution, routing live movies through the air in competition with copy prints shipped as freight in heavy cans. The company's satellites could change the way movies got from the studios to the theaters, eliminating dozens of costly and time-consuming printing and duplicating processes. So, as each of her guests fawned over her, hoping to register his name and face, Catherine trained her dazzling smile on the few who produced films in bulk. It was a smile that Peter Barnes often called the company's greatest asset.

Catherine had made herself the exciting persona of a company that was boringly technical, and given visibility to a business that had no visible assets. She had left the technology and the operations in the capable hands of her sister and given herself over completely to the first rule of marketing: Put yourself where the money is. Pegasus was playing for big stakes, she had reasoned, so it had to play with the big players. She had set out to make herself known in all the boardrooms of global business.

First were the charities; she lent her energies to Save the Children, the Fresh Air Fund, Doctors Without Borders, Make-A-Wish, and dozens of groups determined to end the endless hunger of East Africa. She even made the cover of a weekly magazine holding an emaciated Somalian child in her arms. She rubbed elbows with publishers, broadcasters, software gurus, computer mavens, university deans, and television clerics. She was invited onto the boards of a local exchange carrier, a television network, and a publishing conglomerate. Simultaneously, three telephone and data communications companies signed on to the Pegasus network.

Next came the arts. She raised money for symphony orchestras, funded local opera start-ups, patronized obscure painters, and supported urban dance companies. She was photographed with the conductor of the New York Symphony, on the stage of La Scala, and surrounded by the Vienna Boys' Choir. That put her shoulder to shoulder with old money, billions of dollars in residue from defunct steel mills and grown-over railroads. Three financial institutions brought her onto their boards, and she brought financial wire services and private banking networks into the Pegasus fold.

Catherine managed her image carefully. Everything she did projected a keen business mind, a burning social empathy, and nearly imperial stature. She also mixed in a generous glimpse of cleavage and an occasional flash of thigh so that even when she wasn't actively involved in a momentous occasion she could count on making the fashion pages and the gossip columns. She had been flattered when her advertising agency proposed making her the company's spokesperson in television commercials and print ads. But, wisely, she had recognized that turning herself into a commodity was the worst thing she could do. The trick was in convincing everyone she met that he or she had a special place in her life.

Hollywood had required a slight shift in her image. She took her long hair a shade or two lighter and let it blow a bit more freely. Her makeup became a tad more theatrical, with more red in her lip gloss, deeper tones in her eye shadow, and blush to emphasize her perfect bone structure. She slipped her hourglass figure comfortably into a smaller dress size and added bare-midriff jeans to her wardrobe. The result was a younger, more casual version of herself, still intelligent, still sympathetic, still sexually provocative, but definitely less regal. She had moved to the left cusp of the horsey set, where it blended indistinguishably into the entertainment riffraff.

Catherine kissed the cheek of each of her guests as they left, begging off invitations to join one group for a nightcap and another for a sunrise beach party. She had to get packed for her trip back to New York, she reminded them. After all, there was an empire to run. "See you in Cannes" were her last words to the studio heads and important producers. She made it sound like a friendly promise, even though it was really a sales pitch.

Her New York apartment was part of the persona, a two-story penthouse overlooking the East River that had been featured in both *Architectural Digest* and *Interior Design*. Catherine managed the place with telling glances to her housekeeper, a German matron named Inga who ordered about an army of window washers, silver polishers, and cleaning services with Prussian efficiency. In response to a call placed somewhere over Kansas, Inga had laid out Catherine's black business dress and a string of perfect pearls, so within an hour of her transcontinental flight's touchdown, Catherine was flashing by her secretary's desk and into her office.

The office bore little resemblance to a work area. Surrounded by a glass floor-to-ceiling panorama of the New York skyline, it was arranged on two carpeted levels. The lower level had several groupings of modern furniture, minimalist in design so as not to block the picture windows. There was a conference table with half a dozen stern chairs, a grouping of softer, more comfortable chairs and a sofa around a coffee table, and four chairs arranged theater-style in front of a huge television screen. That level was currently taken up with sketches and models of the company's planned exhibit at the Cannes Film Festival. The exhibit, built around the capabilities of Pegasus III, had been in the works for months before the launch, a tribute to Catherine's confidence in her sister's capabilities.

Up one step was Catherine's desk, a glass platform that seemed to float in space with no visible means of support. There was just one chair, a chrome and white leather low-back design in keeping with the minimalist theme, and one desk appointment, a chrome telephone. The design required secretaries to carry work in and out on demand, and those who approached the desk to remain standing. It also served, as Peter Barnes delighted in reminding her, as a perfect showcase for her perfect legs.

Not immediately visible were the other rooms of the office suite. A bathroom with a cavernous shower as well as an oversize Jacuzzi. A wine cellar with two-zone temperature control. A fully equipped gymnasium. A clothes closet with changes that let Catherine dress up or down on a minute's notice. And a small kitchen with a stocked refrigerator and china cabinet. It was, as Jennifer teased her, a decent apartment for a family of five.

Catherine jumped up and rushed across the office to greet her sister, who was still dressed in jeans and a blouse. She kissed Jennifer on the lips, hugged her close, and repeated her congratulations. "The news rocked them in Hollywood," she reported. "I think we did more celebrating than you."

She stepped back to take in Jennifer's attire and reacted with horror. "Oh, for God's sake, we could have put this meeting off until tomorrow. You haven't even had time to clean up from the jungle."

"I got in this morning," Jennifer answered.

"That is her business suit," Peter Barnes said, standing in the doorway. Catherine went toward him with a sisterly kiss.

Peter wandered to the sofa and settled in, his long legs sticking up awkwardly from the low perch. "Both of you returning home in triumph. No Caesar was ever blessed with such generals." He glanced around at the Cannes displays. "I got a glimpse of this when they were setting it up. It looks spectacular."

"It is," Catherine answered. "It's also expensive, to answer the question that you're dying to ask. Way over budget but worth every penny."

Jennifer settled into a chair and stretched her sandaled feet onto the coffee table as Catherine began her presentation of her plans for conquering the Cannes Film Festival. She was interested, but only in the broad brush strokes. She could safely leave the details up to Peter. He had demonstrated time and again that he could digest volumes of information and spot the minutest flaws in the logic. He would sit with a pleased expression as Catherine gushed over every element of the design and justified every event. But before she was finished, he would pin down the need for every meal being planned and the cost of each shrimp on every plate.

Martin Pegan had made a fine choice in Peter Barnes, and the two sisters had come to appreciate their father's wisdom. They were both headstrong, confident, and accomplished, but neither harbored any illusion as to who was responsible for the success of the business. In the final analysis, it was Peter who had made the decisions. Not that he had been arbitrary. As they both came to recognize, he managed by guiding them to the right decisions.

But if they knew his business style, they were generally in the dark as to his personal life, a mystery that he seemed to enjoy leaving unsolved. They knew, for example, that he had been a high-tech nerd, one of the educational dropouts who invented light-wave devices in his garage. But there was none of the sneakered iconoclast about him. He wore well-tailored business suits with tasteful ties, more in the style of a banker than an inventor.

They knew he was a technical genius with a clear understanding of the physics of satellite orbits and the electronics of digital communications. Yet he spoke in simple declarative sentences with hardly a trace of the technobabble that passed as conversation in their industry.

Although he was single, he always appeared at business affairs and at Catherine's social events with an attractive woman on his arm. He was never secretive about who the lady was, or her background and accomplishments. But he didn't give a clue as to whether the relationship was serious or casual. What they noticed was that few of his women lasted through a season. None had ever stayed around for a year.

It was obvious that he was wealthy. They both knew his salary, his bonuses, and the value of his stock. Yet he lived modestly in what had once been a caretaker's cottage and summered aboard a boat tied up at a North Shore marina. He was certainly successful but had never appeared in a business publication, never given an interview on cable, never spoken at an industry event.

They knew he was good-looking, even if his nose was a bit too long and he had developed a habitual squint through his heavy glasses. They knew he was athletic, with a fine tennis game, a low golf handicap, and a successful record in yacht racing. They knew he was passionate about an Italian sports car that seemed perpetually in the shop, and that he was addicted to books on European history. They knew he liked good bourbon and defied convention by drinking it over a single ice cube.

But they had no idea where he'd been born and raised, who his parents were, or whether he had any brothers or sisters. They didn't know where he had gone to school or for how long. Was he always single, or had he divorced? Was he religious or agnostic? Gay or straight? Generous or thrifty? Did he bathe or shower? Wear boxers or briefs? Despite the fact that they were with him every day in an intimate business relationship, their private lives never mingled. Peter offered no insights into his, and they had never caught him peeking into theirs.

They had often speculated. Once they had hired an investigator to look through yearbooks and other matters of public record. Just the essentials, they told each other. Things they really were entitled to know. But they had called the investigator off before he could get started. If they were entitled to know, they should simply ask Peter, they had reasoned. They knew how much they depended on him and couldn't risk driving him away.

Privately, both had wondered from time to time whether Peter might have any romantic interest in them. Catherine, with her public glamour, had a very sensitive antenna for both decent and indecent advances and fielded them skillfully on an almost daily basis. But she had never once detected any personal interest in her from Peter. He complimented her, teased her, and never forgot her birthday. But his manner was always "big brother," personal but never intimate. She had also wondered whether Peter held any particular charm for her. He was a desirable man from any point of view. But in her analysis, he turned out to be too straitlaced, long on reliability and short on excitement. Maybe she had been overexposed to his business demeanor.

Jennifer had a different view. She had spent a bit of personal time with Peter, joining him in road rallies in Connecticut on rare occasions when the Italian sports car was running, and sailing with him in club races on Long Island Sound. She knew he had a great capacity for fun and excitement and had enjoyed every moment she had spent in his company. But she had little interest in intimacy and was generally careful to shield herself from its dangers. Little rich girls, she knew, had to be suspicious of compliments. And in Peter's case, there was an added danger. If she grew too close to him, it might well upset the delicate balance among the three principals of Pegasus Satellite Services. There could be nothing between the two of them as long as Catherine was involved in their affairs. Jennifer had seldom offered Peter encouragement.

"Just a couple of points!" was Peter's opener when Catherine had finished explaining the Cannes arrangements. "You need to spend less time at our pavilion and get to more of the events. The publicity will center on the openings, so that's where you need to be.

"Next, I think you ought to move one of our cocktail parties out of the hotel and onto a private yacht. The change of venue might get us a second crack at some of these guys.

"Third, I think Jennifer should be at our technical display. She's the most knowledgeable person we have to handle questions about Pegasus three."

Jennifer's feet snapped down from the coffee table. "Me?"

"Why not?" Peter said.

"Because I don't do openings."

"He's right," Catherine joined in. "Everyone knows you're the one who put up the satellite. They'll be dying to meet you."

Jennifer jumped up. "Out of the question," she snapped. "I'll line up some of the engineers."

"Our guests won't be engineers," Peter said. "They'll be former furniture salesmen who fancy themselves as artists. Or graduates from film school who think they're producers. Maybe even a few billionaires who really believe that the starlets find them physically attractive. They won't understand a thing our engineers tell them."

"It's a very personal business," Catherine added. "The top people all know one another. And they want to know all the people they're dealing with. They won't spend ten seconds with a technical expert, but they'll spend hours getting to know you."

"You're both crazy." Jennifer laughed. "Can you see me in one of those Academy Award dresses with no top and no back?"

Peter smiled. "That's just the way our Hollywood customers would like to see you."

"You can wear whatever you want," Catherine said.

Jennifer glanced at her with eyes narrowed in disbelief. "Anything?"

"Well, within reason. Give me an hour in one good store. We'll find something that you're perfectly comfortable in. And then another hour with Nicholas . . ." She made a show of inspecting her sister's grooming. "Well, maybe two hours."

They both laughed.

"You know this isn't my thing," Jennifer said to them.

"It's important," Peter responded.

"What's not your thing?" Catherine asked. "A week of partying with Hollywood heroes. Great French restaurants. Sunny beaches. Yacht cruises. What part of that do you find painful?"

"I'm not a . . . celebrity. I don't like to be on display."

Catherine threw up her hands. "I give up. It's not as if we were asking you to dance naked on the bar. All you have to do is put on a tasteful outfit, a few cosmetics, and talk to people. No one will mistake you for a celebrity."

"It really will give us better coverage of our customers," Peter said. "I wouldn't suggest it if I didn't know you could handle it, and frankly, I think you'll wow them. So at least give it some thought before you turn it down."

After a long pause, Jennifer agreed.

"Thank you," Peter said.

"I agreed to think about it," she corrected.

Peter nodded.

"And while you're thinking about it," Catherine tried, "would it be okay if I got you an appointment with Nicholas? He doesn't have to do anything. He'll just make a few suggestions."

"Okay, as long as I can still belong to the motorcycle gang."

"Sure," Catherine said. "But could I see the tattoos before you have them done?"

The next day Catherine took her sister shopping, and Jennifer had to agree that the dresses weren't bad. There was a simple black cocktail dress with straps that crossed over the bustline, leaving a slight V; a more fastidious gown with a lace coat over a strapless sheath; a cruising outfit with low-cut white pants and a sailor top; a bold print with a square neckline and wide skirt for afternoon wear; a pinstriped pantsuit for more serious moments.

"Was that awful?" Catherine teased.

"The clothes were fine. The shoes were ridiculous."

"Don't worry about the shoes," Catherine answered. "Men only notice them if they're the only things you're wearing."

When Jennifer wasn't looking, Catherine stuffed stockings and underwear into a shopping bag. Who knew what Jennifer wore for underwear?

Then came Nicholas, whom Jennifer approached as if he were a dentist. She cowered in the waiting area and kept her distance when he came out to meet her. Then she circled his chair twice before she settled into it.

"Relax, it isn't an electric chair," Catherine encouraged.

"It would be easier if it were."

Nicholas studied her like a cat sizing up a birdcage. He paced, stopped, stared, and used his hands to frame her face. He started toward her and then backed away like a sculptor afraid to take his first cut at the stone. Finally, he decided.

"We'll have to work with the hair. It's too late to try a wig. But with a little coloring . . . some shaping around the ears . . . a more definite part . . . it might just work."

Catherine breathed a sigh of relief. Her sister had just been rescued from the junk heap.

"I'll bring out the eyes and maybe subdue the mouth. The basic bone structure is sound, so we can use that as a foundation." Jennifer resented the way she was being discussed. Nicholas sounded like he was planning to pave a driveway.

"Maybe, here, around her nose . . ." Catherine braved.

"I'm not a plastic surgeon," Nicholas reminded her. But then, with a cheery smile, "I've handled worse problems."

Just turn on the electricity, Jennifer prayed silently.

But she was astonished when, only two hours later, Nicholas spun the chair so that she could see herself in the mirror. It was still her own face. The hair was lighter, streaked to a shade like strawberry blond. And it was freer, hanging down a bit on her forehead and threatening to cover the tops of her ears. The eyes had more color, enhanced by a nearly invisible tone of eye shadow. Her mouth had a bit of pout. And her face seemed thinner, an effect achieved by defining her cheekbones. But still it was her, natural, athletic, and basically unadorned. It wasn't the painted-on expression that graced the covers of most fashion magazines and that Catherine wore to perfection. No one would confuse her with her sister.

FOUR

CATHERINE DAZZLED Cannes the same way she had taken over the opening night of the New York Symphony and dominated the coverage of the first food shipments into Angola. She had more information than the financiers, better taste than the producers, and more style than the stars. She was at the hub of every important conversation, near the host at every cocktail party, and stepping out of a limousine at every opening. The Cannes festival is a movie-industry board meeting disguised as a celebrity event, and Catherine worked both sides of the street.

Her display turned the ballroom of a seafront hotel into a vision of outer space as seen from her communications satellites. Stars turned overhead, comets flashed by, and other orbiting satellites came dangerously close. Space girls in silver suits served cocktails, mingling with wispy aliens that appeared and disappeared mysteriously. Even the special-effects people were impressed.

Her office in the hotel's penthouse was a news center with over a hundred screens displaying every movie, concert, and theatrical event that Pegasus satellites were transmitting around the globe. Visitors were stunned by the sheer volume of entertainment traffic, ranging from a children's show in Japanese to a chamber concert in Italian, from Russian ballet to California porno.

The two hundred guests at her invitation-only banquet were served by six of the world's leading chefs, each spooning out his signature dish. The wines, including bottles thought no longer to exist, were stunning. The place settings were a new Venetian pattern developed specially for the occasion.

By the end of the second day, there were just three topics of conversation. A Chinese film, incomprehensible but incredibly beautiful; a starlet who had taken the final step in fashion by wearing nothing; and Pegasus Satellite Services.

"We'll need a bigger yacht," Catherine said sensibly when told that her seagoing cocktail party was oversubscribed. "We can't turn away Harrison Ford or Kate Hudson, even if they don't buy satellite services."

"There isn't a bigger yacht," her secretary explained. "We've already got the biggest yacht in the harbor."

Catherine's eyes flashed her frustration. "Peter?" It was her appeal for help.

"We'll check the Mediterranean ports and see what's available," Peter answered. "Maybe we can find something close enough to get here by tomorrow night. If not, then we'll have to get a second yacht."

"That won't work, Peter. I can only be on one boat."

"It's not ideal, but as you say, we can't throw Harrison Ford overboard. If we go to two yachts, Jennifer will have to play hostess on one of them."

Catherine rolled her eyes. "Jenny would kill me if I put her on the spot like that." She thought for an instant and then said, "You could take the second boat."

Peter shook his head. "No, I can't. I have appointments all day tomorrow with potential buyers. I have to meet them. That's what all this is about, isn't it? Signing up customers?"

Catherine accepted his decision reluctantly. "Can you be the one to tell Jennifer? You know how sensitive she can be."

He nodded. "Okay, but don't give up yet on finding a bigger boat. There should be one available, and we'll buy it if we have to." Then he asked, "What's the latest we can decide?"

"Noon," she answered. "We can probably wait until two for a new boat to arrive, but we're going to need a few hours to clean it up and stock it."

"I'll get calls going right now. One way or another, you'll have an answer by tomorrow morning."

Catherine thanked him, then turned back to her secretary. "That means you'll need two sets of crew uniforms and two orchestras." The secretary wrote quickly. She was used to insane demands.

Jennifer learned of the crisis when she came in from her morning swim. She had decided on the pantsuit as her uniform of the day and was dressing for an afternoon of greeting guests at the display center.

"Line up someone to fill in for you tomorrow," Peter told her over the phone. "You may have to host half of the floating cocktail party."

"Peter . . ."

"I wouldn't ask if it wasn't essential. We've got a big investment in this week and I don't want any slipups."

He had said *ask*, but Jennifer knew from his tone that he was really telling. If there had to be a second boat, she was going to be on it. And if she was honest with herself, she knew that she could handle it. Her first day of greeting guests had gone better than she could have imagined. In fact, she had enjoyed it.

Most of the visitors, she found, were polite and well informed. The financial people were filled with admiration for the enormous investment that Pegasus had put in place, and had specific questions on costs of taking films from one point to another. Producers were more interested in the technology. How did a film get on her network? How was it safeguarded against piracy? Directors were concerned about quality. How much of the definition and color were lost in transmission? Screen owners wondered how they would tap the network.

Jennifer had answers for all. She understood questions and the concerns behind them and went to great lengths to provide complete information. She simulated satellites with glasses on a table and drew the interlocking footprints on the tablecloth. She led audiences to two theater screens playing the same film and challenged them to decide which image came from a duplicate print and which had traveled around the world via satellite signals. She described encryption techniques that would block theft by all but the most sophisticated and best-equipped pirates. I know this business, she told herself in the midst of one of her presentations. I know it better than our engineers do, because I understand the true impact of the technology. I know it better than Peter, because he's too focused on the money. I know it better than Catherine, who doesn't really care what she's selling. So, why have I spent my career in the basement?

It was while she was congratulating herself that she had seen Padraig O'Connell leaning into the group that surrounded her and heard her own voice lose its cadence. She had seen the expatriate Irish actor in a dozen films and recognized him instantly, even though he was a bit older and a few pounds heavier in person. A signature starlet clung to his arm. When their eyes had made contact, he flashed his screen smile, and Jennifer was aware that she had stopped talking altogether.

O'Connell had lingered as Jennifer's audience disbursed and asked a few questions about the cost of satellite distribution. Odd, Jennifer thought, for an actor who was generally credited with enormous overruns on his pictures. She had teased him about his new interest in economy and he had answered that he was switching to the other side of the table to launch his own production company. "A bit long in the tooth to be hanging out of helicopters," he had allowed. "It's about time I went to work."

He had dismissed his starlet with a playful pat on her rump and given Jennifer his full attention, which she found both flattering and exciting. Even as they talked business, she had enjoyed being so close to a star. O'Connell had come to Hollywood in a serious Irish film that had picked up half a dozen Oscars, and had stayed for ten years in leading-man roles. His melodic voice and cheeky manner had made him a natural as the unflappable adventurer who saved mankind from a series of diabolical plots. The roles received little critical acclaim but, as his producers frequently remarked, they certainly put fannies in the seats. O'Connell's going rate had reached $10 million a film.

His personal life had been every bit as colorful, including rumored romances with several leading ladies, two of whom were tossed out by their husbands. He had also made headlines in auto racing, racking up a dozen arrests for topping a hundred miles an hour on Los Angeles streets in his Porsche Turbo. He had been indicted but never convicted of statutory rape for an affair with a high school cheerleader who honestly believed that she would star in his next film. On several occasions his indifference to shooting schedules and adventurous absences had put his studio on the brink of financial ruin. Which of his misdemeanors and felonies were true character flaws and which had been dreamed up by his press agents was a subject of industry debate. But there was no debate that life around Padraig O'Connell was dramatically exciting.

He had thanked Jennifer for the information and taken a packet of literature but lingered for a few words of small talk. He had complimented her dress, and then her appearance. "Why aren't you in movies instead of sending them into space?" he had asked with a roguish twinkle.

"None of your blarney," Jennifer had countered with her best imitation of his own accent. Then she had asked, "And why would you ever get out of movies just to make them?"

"It's a long and tedious tale." O'Connell laughed. "It would take all night to tell." And then, innocently, "Are you available?"

"Booked solid," she had answered, and then mentioned that she would be hosting the company's floating cocktail party.

"Real liquor?"

"All kinds. Tell me what you like and I'll make sure we stock it."

He had promised to come, a commitment that she didn't take very seriously. And even if he did, it would be Catherine who got to hear his nightlong tale.

———

She was surprised to find him waiting in the ballroom when she started the new day in her hostess role. "My God, who does your tailoring?" he said as an opener. "That suit makes you look like a member of Parliament."

Jennifer did a double take on the pinstriped outfit that Catherine had described as the very soul of chic. "It's suppose to project my responsibility," she told him through a smile.

"The dress you wore yesterday projected your ass," he answered, "which, by the way, is a much more valuable asset." Despite his suggestive tone, Padraig O'Connell quickly got down to business. He had been through the literature and had several more questions about cost and reliability. "I'm planning a completely new production company, and if I'm going to do it, I'm going to do it right. I'll put everything on your satellites if they'll do the job. I've seen the future, and I want to make damn sure that it's me."

They took drinks from one of the wandering space girls and found a table under the red sphere of Mars. Jennifer was amazed at how much this casual playboy knew about the economics of his industry and about the workings of her service. His questions were the most challenging she had heard from anyone at the festival.

He ended the conversation abruptly. "Well, that just about ties it all up. I think it's safe to say that I'll soon be one of your customers." The twinkle reappeared as he slipped his reading glasses into his jacket pocket. "Now, as an important customer, I think I'm entitled to some personal service."

"Only what's in our brochure," Jennifer answered.

"Well, when will it be convenient for me to tell you my tedious tale?"

A dozen ways to refuse the invitation flashed in her mind. But this was too good to believe. A Hollywood star was actually hitting on her. "How about on our cocktail yacht. We can meet on the fantail at eight bells." She decided to see just how far she could take it, although she knew it would end when her Hollywood star got a glimpse of the real star of the family. Catherine, she decided, would eat Padraig O'Connell alive.

Catherine's worst fears were realized. There were three suitable yachts available, but two were in the Greek Isles, too far away to be of any use, and the third belonged to a publishing baron who had no intention of bailing out a competitor.

"There will be two yachts," Catherine told Jennifer the next morning. "Please, you've got to work one of them. I can't do it all."

"Sure, no sweat," Jennifer said instantly.

Catherine couldn't believe her ears.

The yachts were side by side, sterns to the pier in a Mediterranean moor, long curved shapes of seamless white steel. One was 160 feet long, the size of some naval vessels. The other, at 110 feet, was a modest yacht in the local competition. They were European designs, styled more like the wind than in the tradition of North Atlantic working boats. Their interiors combined teak and stainless steel in vistas that were both seafaring and landlocked, nautical adaptations of ancient baronial castles. The only things familiar to the Hollywood types who elbowed their way aboard were the well-stocked bars and the smiling faces of their peers. All of them were looking for profitable marks that they might corner against a railing.

The starlets were out in see-under, see-over, and see-through costumes better suited for the lineup in a bordello. Bankers in double-breasted blazers carefully scrutinized them. Producers tended to more casual dress, white slacks with Italian sports shirts, and a variety of precious chains. The screen owners were in shorts with dress socks halfway up their calves. Established stars were less predictable. Ladies were in low-cut pants with a variety of revealing tops. Naval hardware was everywhere. The men went in dozens of directions, some even clanging about the decks in cowboy boots.

Catherine was at the head of one gangway, sharing a personal recollection with each arriving guest. She wore navy slacks and an imitation officer's jacket with gold stripes on the sleeves. A single brass button closed the jacket over her bare cleavage, giving the impression that she had nothing on underneath. The paparazzi swarmed around her like worker bees. Jennifer was on the other gangway, smiling hellos at faces that she could only vaguely remember. She wore fitted jeans and a light sleeveless sweater, simple, tasteful, but hardly memorable. Fortunately, waiters with trays of beluga were positioned on deck, so no one took time to study her appearance.

Padraig O'Connell appeared on the dock with a willowy, bored-looking model. He studied the two ships for a few moments and then made his way up the gangway toward Jennifer. "Eight bells, on the fantail," he said to her as he shook her hand.

"Eight bells," she answered.

The yachts tooted whistle signals to each other, took in their lines, and slipped out to sea. On the decks, cocktails were flowing, and the bands struck up their dance beats. For the moment, the Chinese movie was forgotten, and the young woman who had made the fashion breakthrough was yesterday's news. For at least this evening, Pegasus Satellite Services was the star of the festival.

Catherine worked the crowd with the confidence that only a billion-dollar trust fund can bring. She managed to be more conservative than the bankers, more daring than the producers, and more glamorous than the actors. The bankers whispered to one another, wondering about her financial connections, while the fashion designers wondered what she really was wearing under her officer's jacket. In a photo with Robert Redford, she managed to make him look short. Julia Roberts was a skinny child beside her, and the headman at Miramax was simply fat and bald. But despite her gleaming smiles and her constant tinkle of laughter, Catherine's small talk was deadly serious and precisely attuned. Electronic communications would remake the entire industry. She and her company were the future.

As always, she managed to project the undercurrent of promise about a romantic future. No list of the world's most eligible heiresses was complete without her picture, which was generally the most provocative on the page. The Norwegian princess was tall, thin, and angular, the Greek shipping magnate had too big a nose, the middle European pretender's daughter was visibly overweight, and the media baroness was suspected of being a lesbian. And then there was Catherine, sophisticated, sexy, and with a fortune that grew hourly out of thin air. Even the industry's heaviest hitters wondered if they had a chance.

Catherine had mastered the art of indicating to everyone that they might just get lucky. A subtle smile for a passing gentleman while she was involved with a group would leave him wondering if the gift had greater meaning. A man drawn aside for a private compliment would wonder if he was the only one so honored. A touch on the arm might be mistaken for the prelude to an embrace or a small aside that might be an invitation to a private conversation. If it was teasing, it certainly wasn't a game. If it was flirting, then the mating call had been raised to the dignity of an operatic aria. But any important man who spent more than a moment with Catherine was certain that he had made an impression and could swear that he had heard her heart miss a beat. There were thousands who thought they were "more than friends," but not one who could explain exactly why. Everyone knew that she had lovers. But no one knew who they were.

Jennifer's performance wasn't nearly as accomplished. She was outgoing, friendly, and interesting. She sought out lost souls and coaxed them into conversational groupings. She spotted empty glasses and pointed waiters in their direction. But nowhere on deck was she the center of attention. Groups greeted her and welcomed her into their circle, then continued with the conversation she had interrupted. Starlets seduced men away from her grasp. Conversations shifted before she had answered the question she had been asked. "Great party," she was told over and over again. "I hope you'll be coming to our affair," she was frequently invited. As she passed one group she heard a knowing voice say, "That's Catherine's sister." At another place on deck she overheard, "I understand she's the real brains of the outfit." By eight bells, when she took a glass of champagne and wandered back to the fantail, she really didn't expect to find Padraig O'Connell. But there he was, holding a full bottle in one hand and two champagne glasses in the other.

"Pack of savages," he said, nodding at the riotous party she had just left. "You're lucky to have escaped with your skin. These people often boil and eat their hosts." He took her glass and casually dropped it over the rail. "Start with a fresh one," he said, and poured two bubbling glasses.

"Where is your friend?" Jennifer asked, referring to the willowy model.

"Long gone. An hors d'oeuvre for one of the producers. I turned my back for an instant, and *chomp!* She had vanished."

"And what have you eaten?" Jennifer wondered aloud.

"I've been saving my appetite."

They made small talk and exchanged laughter that Jennifer found surprisingly genuine and easy. Of all the guests aboard, he seemed the one most real. Outrageous, to be sure, but honest in admitting his own culpability. And, Jennifer thought, surprisingly frank in assessing his Hollywood future.

"I'm near forty," he told her, "but I'm getting less near to it every day. Do you know that they're planning on using a body double for my love scenes?" She spit out champagne in her laughter. "Oh, yes, funny for you. But it's damn humiliating standing on the sideline while someone else's ass bounces on top of the heroine." She found his feigned indignation hysterical and had to hold up a hand to stop his act. "I've got stuntmen doing my fighting, professional pilots doing my flying, and a whole squad of Navy SEALs doing the scuba shots. I'm drinking tea out of wineglasses and water out of martini glasses, and they tell me they're planning on using a telephoto lens for anything that involves frontal nudity. Now stop and think for a second. I'm becoming a creature of special effects. The real me is just an expensive bit of overhead that they'd love to do without."

"You're a star," Jennifer reminded him.

"A brown dwarf at best, and I'm about to be sucked into a black hole."

They talked for nearly an hour, the most relaxed hour that Jennifer had enjoyed since her arrival on the Riviera. O'Connell explained the painful final fade of movie stars who often end up doing cameos on television sitcoms, and he outlined his plans for salvaging his dignity. His production company would avoid the legendary errors of the industry. "Good scripts," he said. "If I have to wait a year to find an original piece of good writing, it will be a year well spent." He would keep low budgets, achieved by shunning the outrageous demands of the top stars in favor of the more modest cost of "real actors."

Jennifer responded, untypically, by talking about herself. She wasn't comfortable, she admitted, in the limelight and preferred her part behind the scenes. Yes, it was sometimes galling to be permanently cast in her sister's shadow, and she often envied Catherine's celebrity status. But in all honesty, she hadn't been blessed with her sister's looks and outgoing personality and couldn't possibly fill Catherine's shoes. "It's really worked out well with Catherine on the outside and me on the inside. As kids we were terrible rivals, but now we each have our own roles. So we don't tear each other's hair out anymore."

"Well, if you don't like clothes and jewelry, what does tickle your fancy?"

"Not much, I'm afraid." She enjoyed her work, she explained, and didn't mind the long hours. She had liked the bit of yacht racing she had done with Peter Barnes and, of course, her few turns in his sports car.

"Automobiles!" Padraig interrupted. "My one true passion. Women are fine, of course. And I am a bit too fond of the grape. But an overpowered car with tires that are barely able to restrain it . . . that's the secret to great orgasms." Then he added, "Would you like to try one?"

"An orgasm?"

"A car. I've been thinking of renting something gorgeous and taking it up to Monte Carlo. I'd like to drive the Grande Prix route. There will be pedestrians in the way, of course, but we could simply run them over. And dodging the other traffic will be part of the fun."

"Are you serious?"

"Of course. There are great roads all through the Maritime Alps. You can spend a whole day without coming across a single straight stretch. And I won't bring a stuntman . . . or a body double."

"I'm not sure—" Jennifer began.

"And that's your most addictive trait. You're not so damn sure about everything. You're wondering whether you ought to take a chance. Well, I say take a chance. What's the worst that can happen to you? You'll be killed doing one-twenty in a brilliant red Ferrari with a handsome leading man by your side. Beats the hell out of dozing off in some old-age home with the oatmeal running down your chin."

She hesitated.

"Please," he said in a tone that suggested he wouldn't waste the money on the gasoline without her.

"Sure. Sounds like fun. Just tell me when and where."

"I'll get back to you," he said.

"And I better get back to my guests."

Catherine was stretched across her enormous bed, wide-eyed, her chin resting in the palms of her hands. "Padraig O'Connell," she said, and smiled at just the mention of his name. "The secret agent from Interpol?"

"That's the one. Except he says that we may have been lusting after his body double," Jennifer said from her place on the floor where she sat with her legs folded and her toes in her hands. They were like girls at a pajama party the night after the prom, sharing their experiences, and neither could remember when they had ever felt this close. Jennifer had finished the day in the Jacuzzi in Catherine's suite and wandered out in a towel only to find her sister coming in from the day's wars.

"How'd it go?" Jennifer had asked.

"Great! Better than I hoped." Then Catherine had delivered a business report as she undressed and slid into her silk pajamas. "How about you?" she concluded.

"Not bad," Jennifer had answered, then added, "I got a date with Padraig O'Connell."

She described every moment of the encounter and repeated nearly all the conversation. "He loved the fact I wasn't sure of myself. He could sense me wondering whether I ought to take a chance . . ."

"He really said that?"

"Pure blarney, of course. Probably a line from one of his movies."

"Maybe not," Catherine warned her sister. "Padraig's come-ons aren't nearly that subtle."

"You've met him?"

"Several times. And I always found him surly and drunk. Except once, when he tried to put a move on me."

Jennifer feared that her bubble was bursting.

"He wasn't quite as tender as he seems to have been with you. I don't remember his exact words, but the gist was that my nipples were showing and giving him an erection, and exactly what did I plan to do about it?"

They shared a laugh and then Catherine went on, "I understand that he's a lot of fun. Outrageous but genuine. Not that he would be a great catch, but don't discount that he may have fallen madly in love with you. At least for a week or two."

Jennifer shrugged. "What's the old saying about rich girls being wary of compliments from men?"

"That only applies to poor men. O'Connell probably has as much as you do. What's he get . . . a billion dollars a film?"

"Ten million."

"He told you that?"

"Yeah, and he's afraid he won't be getting it for much longer."

Catherine sat up and slipped under her covers. "Well, don't run an audit before you let yourself have a bit of fun. You didn't even want to come to Cannes, and now it looks as if you're going to be the star of the show. Don't blow it. You might find you like your picture in *People* magazine."

He picked her up in a red, mid-engine Ferrari rocket with six forward speeds. He held the door until she was safely strapped in and then vaulted over the other door and into his seat. "Did that getting onto a horse once," he said. "Extremely painful, particularly with a western saddle." He ground his way through a few gear shifts, wincing each time the metallic twang sounded, and eased his way in and out of the waterfront traffic. Minutes later, they were on the national highway, heading east around the Nice airport, and on their way to Monaco. At about 140 kilometers an hour, the Ferrari found its throat and settled into a blissful murmur. Padraig made a great show of draping one arm around his woman while he steered casually with the other.

He was truly a rakish figure, red hair ruffling in the wind, steely blue eyes panning the scenery, the first hint of a smile playing across his lips. Indeed, he was on the far side of forty, and there were crow's-feet around his eyes, small skin blemishes, and softness under his chin to prove it. But his expression was one of pure joy springing from a hidden hedonism rather than from any of the virtues. It gave the crow's-feet strength of character and the blemishes an outdoor patina. Even the soft chin could be excused as the very small price of his fabled excess.

"I suppose you've been properly warned to be on your guard," he said over the rush of the wind. "The fathers, mothers, and siblings of all the world's attractive women are in conspiracy against me. Virtue is their goal, lies and exaggerations their weapons."

"Indeed I was," she said, falling into his theatrical Irish cadence. "But I was also told that you might be a breath of fresh air, and that by a woman you once gravely insulted."

"I? An insult? Never, unless she was slow getting out of her knickers."

"It had more to do with nipples," and then she retold Catherine's story.

"I said that?"

"In substance. She couldn't remember the exact words."

"Then it wasn't me. Everyone remembers my exact words."

He turned abruptly onto a side road, downshifted without a clank or a shudder, and aimed the car up a narrow road where no one had bothered to paint a dividing line. A minute later and they were into switchbacks, using just the bottom of the gearbox as they climbed into the mountains. The hint of a smile grew into a wide boyish grin. Each time the back wheels skidded out toward the edge, caught a bit of traction, and fired the car up toward the next turn, O'Connell burst into laughter. "They should break the knuckles of anyone who tunes a car without being Italian," he said. Jennifer could only peer down over the edges and wonder how far the car would fall before it hit the wall of the cliff and began tumbling.

They crested the top and came to a long road that wandered along the seam of the mountain. They could see ahead for at least a mile, where another series of switchbacks would take them up to the next peak. O'Connell downshifted, slowing the convertible until it seemed to be standing still at forty. Then he touched the brake and pulled to the side, a few feet from the edge of the steep slope. "Here, you try it. It will drive you mad with pleasure."

"Me? No way."

"Well, then, we'll have to walk back, won't we? Because my heart can't take another minute. The thrill is killing me."

He bounded over his door into the road and around to Jennifer's door. "Nothing to it, really," he said, helping her out, "once you get used to the clutch."

She opened the door to get in, then adjusted the seat. "How long does it take to get used to the clutch?"

"Maybe an hour. You've probably noticed that Italians have one leg bigger than the other. That's why they walk around in circles." He slouched down in the seat and closed his eyes as if planning a nap.

Jennifer tried the clutch. It didn't go down easily. Then she went through the gears. They were as precise as clockwork, and the lever had to be fitted carefully. She turned the key and tried to settle herself into the sensuous hum of the engine. "Don't doze off, Padraig. If I don't have this down by the time we reach the next switchback, I'm going to start walking."

"Not to fear. By then I won't be able to tear your fingers off the wheel."

She started slowly, shifting carefully up to third, which gave her all the speed she could handle. She eased into the road and steered like she was trying to keep the car on rails. O'Connell's eyes remained serenely closed. If he was anxious, he was a better actor than he let on. She dared a bit more throttle, and when the engine played back a sharp note, she forced the clutch and dropped the gear shift into fourth. Eighty kilometers. Hardly moving for the Ferrari, but breakneck for the road. And the next round of switchbacks was approaching fast.

"Padraig?"

He opened one eye.

"I don't think I can handle these turns."

He closed it. "God," he mumbled, "but you're exciting when you're frightened."

She let the engine run down and tried a downshift. The gearbox growled but obeyed. She steered into the turn and added power to straighten out of it. And then she was gone, through the first gate and on to the next switchback.

"Whee!" She laughed.

"It only gets better," Padraig said. He sat up suddenly and looked straight at her. "Nothing is as satisfying as the face of a woman who feels the excitement building."

"It's terror, Padraig," she answered.

"No, it's not. Not for one moment. It's excitement, and if you give in to it, then you're headed for the ride of your life."

"I'm not sure," she said as she headed into the next turn.

"No one's ever sure," Padraig answered.

She downshifted, tore into the curve, and felt the rear end beginning to drift. Her instinct was to brake, which might have been fatal, so she forced herself to add power. The rear tires chirped as the car fired out of the turn and raced on up the hill. Jennifer broke into a broad smile.

"Okay," Padraig said. "Pull off whenever you're ready. I'll take over."

"No way," she answered. "There's a dozen more turns ahead."

"I knew you'd never give it back."

"It's your fault. You told me to do it."

He slumped back into the seat. "Women are always blaming me, when all I ever do is show them their potential."

"Hang on!" There was another turn coming up.

She drove for nearly an hour, climbing higher and higher, until she reached the turn at the top of a mountain.

"Oh my God!" She braked to a skidding stop, the nose of the car pointing out over the edge. "Will you look at that."

O'Connell was already looking at the Mediterranean coast spread out before them. Below was Monaco, a tiny smudge of activity with the royal palace visible on the edge of a cliff. To the left was the Italian Riviera, behind the industrial waterfront of Genoa. To the right, the red rooftops of Nice. Straight ahead, the cool blue of the Mediterranean, reaching all the way out to a pale blue sky.

"First prize," Jennifer said. "The most beautiful world I've ever seen."

He had turned away from the seacoast and was looking back at her. "First prize," he told her. "You stir feelings of wonder that I wouldn't share even with my psychiatrist."

Jennifer shook her head playfully. "Padraig, you could score in a convent."

"I have," he answered, "but this has nothing to do with scoring." He leaned across the console, took her face between his palms, and kissed her gently, first on the tip of her nose and then on the edge of her lips. He stared at her for seconds that passed like hours and then smiled. Not his signature flash of white, but a soft smile that was almost sad. "Take me home," he said, "before I lose my devilish image."

FIVE

JENNIFER WAS back at the hotel in time to tell Catherine and Peter about her tour of the Maritime Alps with Padraig O'Connell.

"A Ferrari Three Eighty." Peter whistled. "You're in the big leagues of motoring."

"When's your next date with the great Irish bard?" Catherine asked.

"Nothing definite. Not till 'our paths cross again,' as he put it."

"Which will probably be this afternoon."

Jennifer smiled. "I hope so. He's fun."

"That's what all the ladies say," Peter told her.

"Oh, I know I'm just this week's game," Jennifer admitted. "But I'd like to get a full week."

Catherine smiled. "Well, I'll give the devil his due. I've never seen you happier, and it looks as if Padraig O'Connell gets most of the credit."

In the morning, Jennifer went back to the basic black dress that Padraig had said showed off her best asset. She was sure he'd find a reason to stop by the hall, and she had already decided to leave with him when he did. The festival was winding down, and the traffic through the displays was light. Let someone else answer the questions while she enjoyed whatever Padraig had planned for the day.

She stopped short as she exited the hotel's glass doors. Parked at the curb directly in front of her was a bright red Ferrari convertible in showroom condition. Either Padraig had had yesterday's car washed and detailed, or he was starting the day with a fresh model. She looked around anxiously to see where he was lurking.

"Miss Pegan?" The English was accented, carefully pronounced by a middle-aged man in a dark suit. She nodded.

"I'm Giovanni, from Ferrari. The dealership here in Cannes."

"Hi!" She looked over his shoulder, still searching for O'Connell. Then she noticed the key ring that Giovanni was holding in front of her face.

"Mr. O'Connell says that you should take more chances." He dropped the keys into her hand and took an envelope from his jacket. "This is the title and the European Union registration. I offered to take you for a demonstration, but Mr. O'Connell said you already drive better than I do."

She stood openmouthed, bewildered.

"I'll move it for you if you like. This is a no parking zone, and in Cannes even Ferraris get tickets."

"Where is Mr. O'Connell?"

Giovanni shrugged. "I have no idea. He was waiting outside when we opened, but he left after we finished the paperwork."

She scanned once more, hoping that Padraig would step out from behind a bush or from around a corner, but there was still no sign of him. She gave the keys and title back to the auto dealer. "Yes, please, park it for me. And leave the keys at the desk." She walked quickly up the boulevard to O'Connell's hotel.

"He checked out this morning," the desk clerk said, painfully sorry to be giving her disappointing news.

"He can't," Jennifer answered. "He has appearances, commitments . . ."

The clerk held up his hands in despair. "Monsieur O'Connell is . . ." Then he shrugged. Jennifer could fill in *delightfully irresponsible,* which seemed to be the clerk's meaning. Or perhaps there had been other women asking for him and he was trying to let her down easily.

She managed a smile, but she was amazed by how disappointed she was when she turned away.

Then she saw him, crossing the lobby from the restaurant. He went to the bell captain's stand, where he was joined by two bellmen, each carrying two suitcases. Jennifer moved quickly and got to the revolving doors ahead of his entourage. O'Connell showed shock for only an instant and went immediately into his usual character role.

"Jennifer, dear, what a pleasant surprise." The bellmen piled up behind him.

"I wanted to thank you for the car," she said, showing a bit of the anger she was feeling. She pointed to his luggage. "I didn't know you'd be so anxious to avoid seeing me."

"No thanks are required," he said. "The car was made for you."

"Still, no one has ever given me a Ferrari. I think gratitude is in order."

He flashed the stage smile. "I've given away several, Jennifer, although there's no one I can remember more deserving than you."

"Still, at the price of these things, you can't have given away many. So I should be grateful for making your short list."

Padraig waved the bellboys away. He took Jennifer's arm and steered her to one of the lobby's plush furniture arrangements, sitting her in one chair while he took the next one. "Don't be angry with me, darlin'. This was just the kind of ending I was trying to avoid."

"Is that what it is? An ending?"

"There's always an ending, and I wanted this one to be happy."

"A simple goodbye would have been nice."

"Oh, I wouldn't have had the courage for something as easy as that."

"Courage?"

He drew a deep breath, sighed, and reached across the space between the chairs to touch her hand. "Jennifer, if I stay around you, I'll do something very foolish that will destroy the rascal's image I count on for my livelihood."

"Something like . . ."

"Like fall in love."

She felt her jaw drop the slightest bit.

"You see, darlin', in this crazy business of narcissistic head cases, I've never come across anyone quite as fresh and unassuming as you. And there's this streak of honesty in my bones, probably the curse of an Irish childhood, that says I must have you. But in the picture industry, the swashbuckling rogue is obligated to fly like a bee from flower to flower. He can never be still long enough to lose his heart to anyone. If it was learned that I had fallen in love, the young ladies in my fan club would throw themselves into a mass grave."

"Will you please shut up," Jennifer ordered.

He did, showing surprise that he had stopped talking.

"In that whole speech, which I'll bet comes from one of your movies, you said just one thing that made sense."

"It didn't come from a movie. I made it up last night. And then, when I heard how dreadful it sounded, I decided to send the Ferrari instead."

"You said you love me."

He stared at her. "Hopelessly," he admitted. "And you understand why I can't do that."

"Take a chance," Jennifer reminded him.

"I couldn't promise you how it would come out," he said.

"You never know how things are going to come out."

"Most of my relationships have ended in failure."

"So have mine."

He pursed his lips, then showed the gentle smile. "Shall we have a fling at it?"

"Let's. But there's one thing you should know."

He looked puzzled.

"I'm not going to give the Ferrari back."

"Oh dear, then I suppose I'll have to pay for it."

"Every penny!"

O'Connell stood and offered his hand. "Can I drive it every once in a while?"

"Maybe on Sundays."

During the last few days of the festival, they were everywhere together, formally attired at the openings, in T-shirts at the discos, in bathing suits at the beach, where Padraig built her an enormous sand castle. The gossip columnists sensed the story of Padraig O'Connell's latest conquest and warned that one of society's poor little rich girls was about to be fleeced. Paparazzi followed them everywhere, producing yards of film of them holding hands, dancing close together, or climbing out of the sports car.

"She's sleeping with him," Catherine told Peter after she found Jennifer's bed unused. "She didn't come home last night."

"What an unusual thing for lovers to be doing," he said.

"Peter, this a new adventure for Jennifer."

"She's a consenting adult," he said. "You make her sound like an adolescent."

"The guy she's consenting with is a master. She may be overmatched."

"She is. But Jennifer is smart enough to know it. She can take care of herself. Besides, the festival is closing down. O'Connell will be looking for new fish in a new pond."

Neither of them was prepared for Jennifer's news, delivered from behind a napkin at the closing banquet. She wasn't coming straight back to New York. There were roads in the west of Ireland that Padraig thought she would love. They were shipping the Ferrari on ahead and planning to spend a week in his native country.

Catherine and Peter returned to New York, where they totaled up their victories. The festival had been a smash success for Pegasus, and Peter was more than generous in giving Catherine full credit. They had gathered over a dozen contracts, each paying up to reserve capacity on the satellite network. There were two others that began to use the service immediately. Pegasus III was generating income, less than a month after the launch.

Jennifer was calling in every day, keeping on top of her obligations. Her only personal comments were that the West Ireland roads were indeed glorious, and that she and Padraig were having a great time.

"You said he'd be fishing in a new pond," Catherine reminded Peter.

He admitted his mistake. "This seems to be O'Connell's longest commitment to anyone since he dumped his first wife."

"But you're not worried."

Peter took off his glasses and wiped them carefully. "No, I don't think so. I guess I'm still delighted that Jennifer is living a little."

They left the car in a garage at O'Connell's ancestral home. "How long has the place been in the family?" Jennifer had asked.

"Almost a year now," he had answered with his impish grin. He had kissed her goodbye at the airport, to the delight of the photographers who had been trying to keep up with them. Then he had flown to Hollywood while Jennifer had boarded the New York flight. She called from Kennedy Airport to invite Catherine and Peter to dinner. "I've made reservations at Ciro's," she said. "The stuff in my refrigerator is probably growing hair."

At dinner, Jennifer dropped the bombshell. She and Padraig were going to be married.

Peter's expression never changed, almost as if it were set in cement. Catherine mumbled a "Dear God" and lowered her face against the back of her hand.

"I knew you'd be overjoyed," Jennifer teased.

"Married?" Peter managed. Then he added, "Is that really necessary?"

"Only to make an honest woman out of me, for whatever that's worth."

"You've only known him for . . . what? One festival and a couple of weeks in Ireland," Catherine speculated. But almost immediately she got control of herself. "Oh, hell, what am I saying.

I should be thrilled for you. You must be so happy. But are you sure? Absolutely sure?"

Jennifer shrugged. "Who's ever sure? I know I'm taking a chance. But so far all the chances I've taken with Padraig have worked out just fine."

Peter forced down his dinner in near silence. Catherine moved a fish fillet around her plate with a fork and ignored the vegetables. Only Jennifer ate heartily.

It was a week later when Peter summoned the two sisters to his office, opened a bottle of white burgundy, and passed a small file folder to each of them. "A distasteful subject," he announced, "but one that has to be considered." They both looked down at the first page: "Prenuptial Agreement Between Jennifer Ann Pegan and Padraig Aloysius O'Connell."

"Jesus," Jennifer said, and slammed the folder shut. Catherine looked sternly at Peter.

"This, or some version of it, is absolutely essential," he went on. "You're bringing forty-five percent of this company into your marriage, as well as millions in personal assets. Your money is your business, but it's my responsibility to protect the company. Depending on where you get married, Padraig O'Connell could have the second largest stake in Pegasus the moment you say 'I do.' That's because he could own one half of everything you own." He was unyielding, staring across the table at Jennifer, who was just as defiantly staring back.

Catherine felt a need to mediate. "I agree, Peter. Some sort of protection is certainly needed. But does it have to be this? Now?"

"It does have to be this. Prenuptials have the full weight of law. And it has to be now. I doubt Mr. O'Connell will be anxious to sign after the wedding."

Jennifer jumped to her feet. "Is that what you think Padraig is interested in? The company? My money? Open your eyes, Peter. He has his own fortune."

Peter opened his own folder. "A little more than two hundred thousand dollars. And half again that amount in lines of credit.

But he also has debts. He's solvent, but he doesn't have a fortune."

"Where did you get that?" Jennifer snarled.

"It's public information. Our bankers gathered it for us."

"Not for 'us.' For you. I'll have no part in snooping into Padraig's affairs."

Catherine put a hand over Jennifer's, siding with her. "I don't think that was necessary," she told Peter.

"It's a factor in framing the agreement," he answered calmly. "Half of everything he has could well become Jennifer's."

"Well, your figures are all screwed up," Jennifer snapped. "Padraig got ten million dollars for his last movie."

Again Peter consulted the notes. "Actually, it was eight million. He owed a bit to his agent. And seven million of that turned around in three weeks to cover debts he'd run up."

Now Catherine seemed concerned. "But he has more films in the works."

"Very true, but thus far there's no financial backing."

"He's going to start a production company."

"That has no financial backing, either."

"Jesus, he bought me a Ferrari. On a whim!"

Peter turned another page. "He made a down payment and took out a chattel mortgage. That's part of the debt I mentioned. For the time being, the bank owns your Ferrari."

Jennifer glared at him. "You bastard," she whispered. She turned on her heel and stormed out of the room, leaving Peter and Catherine staring at each other.

"Well, that was a hell of a wedding gift," Catherine finally said.

Peter nodded. "I handled it poorly. I just assumed she would have realized that a prenup was necessary."

" 'Poorly' is an understatement. But you're right, of course. I have no interest in having Padraig O'Connell as a partner."

"Will you tell her that?"

"Of course," Catherine answered.

"And maybe you could also apologize for me," Peter said.

"No! That's something you ought to do for yourself." She got up to leave but then turned back to the table. "Do you think he'll sign?"

Peter gathered his papers. "If he loves her, he will."

"Do you think he does?"

"We'll certainly find out."

That night Catherine phoned her sister but was intercepted by the answering machine. "Pick up, Jennifer," she said. "I'm on your side." But the machine beeped and waited to record her message. She tried two more calls, then grabbed her purse, checked for cash, and phoned her doorman to get a cab. Minutes later, she was standing in front of a Tribeca building where her sister owned the top floor loft.

She went up in the freight elevator that had been retained for its earthy chic, and fitted the key that Jennifer had given her into the lock.

"Jennifer," she called into the vast, high-ceilinged space. There was no answer. She called again, got no response, and closed the door behind her. It took only a few seconds to discover that her sister wasn't home, and then a few more to realize that Jennifer had taken a few essentials from her closet and her medicine cabinet before leaving. Scattered luggage confirmed her worst fears. Jennifer had left on an unannounced trip. Catherine guessed she had gone to California to be with Padraig.

She turned on the answering machine. One message was from O'Connell, with a witty remark about how much he missed her assets. Then there were two hang-ups, probably her own calls that had gone unanswered. She was about to leave when she noticed a photograph in a cheap paper frame open on Jennifer's desk. It showed her sister in a simple summer dress, holding a single flower in her hand. Padraig was next to her, a dark blazer over an open collar, with a floppy white flower in his lapel. Behind them, barely in focus, was a clergyman in a white surplice. She stared and was able to make out the stone facade of a church of Ireland in the background. She dropped the photo as if it had a lighted fuse, realizing what it was telling her. Jennifer and Padraig had gotten married in Ireland.

"We can still get an agreement," Catherine told Peter the next day. "Can't they agree on the ownership of their property? A memo of understanding on who gets what if they should ever decide to end the marriage."

"We can try," Peter answered. "But I wouldn't bet on his signing. Why should he?"

"Your worst fears," Catherine said idly.

"No," Peter said after a pause. "My worst fear was that they'd get married in a common-property state. In Ireland there's no hard division. If they divorce, a court would get to decide who keeps what. But that could be a legal nightmare. I'd love to have it all down in writing."

"So, it could be worse," Catherine mused.

"If Jennifer dies," Peter said. "Then, unless she has a will to the contrary, Padraig would own as much of the company as you do."

SIX

JENNIFER WAS buoyant when she returned to the office from her visit to Hollywood. The secret of her marriage had leaked under the doors of the boardroom and then out into the corridors. Now everyone at Pegasus knew, and she gathered good wishes and high fives at every desk. She found a huge paper wedding bell suspended in the engineering conference room and a magnum of champagne waiting in her office. She immediately popped the cork and invited her entire staff for a drink.

Catherine heard she was in the building and rushed to find her. She and Jennifer hugged, danced in a circle, and sipped champagne. And then Peter came to wish her well, apologizing for the pain he must have caused her.

When Jennifer was alone with her sister, she bubbled with the happiness she had found in her new husband. "I'm doing stupid, frivolous things that I never would have done before," she reported, and then asked, "Have you ever slept a whole night on a beach?" Catherine had, but she didn't let on.

Jennifer bounced into Peter's office to say that she really did understand his responsibilities for the business, that as usual he was right, and that she would be happy to put all his concerns to rest. "I told Padraig about the prenuptial agreement, and he said he'd be happy to sign anything you have drawn up, unless it's a temperance pledge." Peter laughed and promised that the document would avoid any mention of her husband's habits. By the end of the day, she was hard at work with her usual energy and even more than her typical enthusiasm.

"Do you believe him?" Catherine asked Peter, referring to O'Connell's willingness to sign away his financial claims on Jennifer and her stock.

"She believes him. And Jennifer is nobody's fool."

"But in matters of the heart, maybe just a bit out of her league?"

"I hope she's right," he answered. "I care a great deal about Jennifer, and I wouldn't want to see her hurt."

There was a note of uncertainty in Peter's voice. "But?" Catherine asked, telling him to hold nothing back.

"But . . . I don't think he's told her everything. O'Connell is trying to put together a production company. He needs money— a great deal of it. So far there are no takers."

"You think he'll ask Jennifer?"

"Why not? She's his wife."

"Oh good God, is that what this whirlwind romance is all about?"

"I sure as hell hope not. And if it is, I could easily be persuaded to break his neck."

They sat together quietly. Catherine gathered up the courage to say what it was that had been bothering both of them. "There must have been a thousand interesting, exciting, vivacious, stunning women at Cannes, most of whom would have hopped into Padraig O'Connell's Ferrari in an instant."

"Just the Ferrari?" Barnes asked facetiously.

"Well, bounced through the Ferrari on their way into his bed."

"And you're wondering why, out of that whole ocean of silicone and pulchritude, the world's most rakish actor decided on Jennifer."

"Is it awful for me to think that way? I mean, Jennifer is wonderful. She has qualities that—"

"That don't pop out of the top of her dress. If Padraig O'Connell were a saint or a scholar, then Jennifer might well be his first choice. But it's not awful for you to wonder why he made such a strong and successful play for your sister. It's just common sense. I mean no disrespect to either you or Jennifer when I say that I believe you would have been a far more credible target."

"I was available," Catherine said. "I saw him decide on the gangplank with Jennifer at the top."

"Don't you think he's smart enough to know that you wouldn't be impressed with his leprechaun's wit? You handle lines like his all the time. He'd never get out of the batter's box. O'Connell is an artist, so he knows the first rule of seduction: Always take someone who wants to be taken."

"Jennifer is not that foolish," Catherine said.

"Not foolish. But she is that vulnerable."

There was another long pause, again interrupted by Catherine. "If he signs an agreement, then it's just Jennifer's personal money that's at risk. And I'd bet every penny of it in hope that he keeps making her happy."

"If he signs," Peter said, reminding her that despite what O'Connell had told Jennifer, there was no reason for him to sign anything.

Padraig showed up in New York a few days later, appeared on the network morning shows to plug the movie he had made a year ago that was just being released, and took Jennifer to one of the Manhattan openings. They dined for the photographers at two French restaurants that vied year after year for the most ridiculously expensive menu, and then privately in Jennifer's loft, where he poured a two-hundred-dollar bottle of brandy into a flaming skillet. He visited Pegasus's offices, dazzled the secretaries, and let Jennifer introduce him to Catherine and Peter.

"Did I really say that your nipples were giving me an erection?" he asked Catherine.

"I thought it was you," she said, smiling, "but so many men claim to have the same problem."

"Touché," he surrendered, without his usual comeback.

He explained to Peter and the two sisters his plans for the new production company. "No need for the studios," he boasted. "We'll use your satellites for distribution. And once we do it, everyone will do it." Then he mentioned casually that he was shooting a few European commercials in Italy. Almost as an afterthought, he invited his wife to come along with him.

"We've had no proper honeymoon," he complained to Peter and Catherine. "You two keep Jennifer far too busy. Tell her right now that you don't want to see her for at least two weeks." Then he turned to Jennifer and suggested, "We could ship the car ahead of us. I'll take a villa in Positano. There are roads on the Amalfi Coast that will keep you from breathing for a full ten minutes."

There was nothing else for Peter to do. "Jennifer," he said, "I don't want to see you for at least two weeks."

She laughed and threw herself into Padraig's lap.

As the newlyweds were leaving, Peter managed to pull Padraig aside and bring up the marital agreement on Jennifer's stock.

"Her stock, her silverware, even her goldfish, old boy. Whatever you need. Just have your scribes draw it up and send it to my attorneys. I'll have it back to you instantly."

And then they were gone, smiling and waving their way through the outer offices like royalty on their way to St. Paul's. Peter never did get the name of the attorneys.

Padraig was waiting at the gate when Jennifer landed at Leonardo da Vinci, and had the Ferrari poised in the VIP parking area. He insisted that she drive while he folded and refolded the road map. "A left here, I think. See if you can find a road sign for Foggia." And then, when she flashed by the turn, "That may have been it, but no problem. The next sign will be for Dubrovnik. You can turn there."

She ached from laughing. Was it possible that anyone could be this happy? Could it be true, as Padraig told her, that he had been searching for her all his life? Did she dare to believe that she had finally been rescued out of Catherine's shadow?

They drove south around Naples and were suddenly in the long tunnels that carved through the coastal cliffs toward the Gulf of Salerno. They passed the turnoff for Sorrento and were suddenly on a road cut into sheer rock, hundreds of feet above the water.

"Can I handle this?" she asked Padraig.

"I certainly hope so," he answered. "God knows I can't!"

So she turned serious, caressed the shift lever, and followed the torturous road into Positano. When she finally cut the engine, in the driveway of the San Pietro Hotel, her expression exploded in joy.

"That was fantastic," she said.

"No, that was a road. You're fantastic!"

Their room jutted out from the side of the cliff, with a balcony that was almost frightening to step on. He ordered up a bottle of Brunello that came with olives the size of apples and almonds big enough to break in their fingers. They decided against dinner, tossed their clothes haphazardly, and were in bed together just in time to see the sunset over the gulf. They made love acrobatically, then passionately, and finally gently.

"You're wonderful," she told him.

"You should have seen me in my prime," he answered.

"That would be frightening."

"Well, maybe alarming."

"Could I have accommodated you?"

"That would be a stretch."

"You were that big?"

"No, but my body double was enormous."

Jennifer jumped up and hit him with the pillow. Padraig responded by taking up a pillow of his own. They battled furiously, over the bed, around the coffee table, and out onto the balcony. When the couple next door noticed them, Padraig held the pillow strategically in position. "Call the front desk," he begged the startled woman. "I have no idea who this woman is."

Seconds later they were back in bed with Jennifer sitting astride him.

"Well, aren't you the optimist?" he said.

"Isn't this what you do in your movies?"

"It's all special effects," he pleaded.

"Well, I'm waiting for a special effect."

In the morning they had breakfast on their balcony and took the elevator down to the small, rocky beach. Seeing all the women topless, Jennifer threw a towel over Padraig's face. "Don't dare move that until I get back," she said. Then she went back up to the hotel shop, selected the skimpiest bikini they had in her size, and settled into the chaise next to his. She took off her top, lounged back, and then told him he could lift the towel.

"Oh for heaven's sake," he said in mock anger. "I've seen those before."

They spent a full week without leaving the hotel, taking their meals on the beach, in their apartment, and by the side of the pool. Jennifer occasionally used her laptop to connect to her office files and stayed on just long enough to make sure that her satellites were still functioning. Padraig took the twice-a-day deliveries of air-express packages and tossed them into a heap in the corner.

"You should open them," Jennifer told him.

"Do you suppose there's someone more beautiful than you inside one of them?" he asked.

"I certainly hope not."

"Then why should I stop looking at you?"

But by the end of the week, economic instincts prevailed. He opened the packages, ranted and raved over their contents, and was immediately on the phone with his agents, his bankers, his brokers, and representatives of one of his ex-wives. "Just another minute, darlin'," he kept saying to Jennifer, but each minute seemed to require another call. So, as the second week of her honeymoon began, she accustomed herself to kissing his cheek while he talked on the phone, and finding distractions of her own.

"I'm going shopping," she announced. "Maybe a new dress will get you to pull your nose out of your paperwork."

"If it were new underwear, I'd leave with you immediately," he answered. "But some of these contracts have deadlines, so if it's just a dress, you're on your own."

"I thought I'd take the car down into town, so if there's nothing I like, I could run over to Sorrento."

"Oooh!" He seemed pained. "I need it this afternoon." He held up the pages he was looking at. "Lunch with one of these bastard lawyers. I already told the garage attendant to gas it up and have it washed."

"Well, then I won't go to Sorrento. I'll stay in town and have it back up to you long before lunch."

She kissed the top of his head and tried for a quick getaway, but Padraig pulled her down on the desk across the top of his papers. He kissed her passionately, then stood her up and patted her rump. "Be out of here, before I lose control and tear your clothes to shreds."

"Promises, promises," Jennifer sang as she walked to the door.

She was still smiling when she started the engine and spun out of the hotel's underground garage. Almost immediately, she cut a sharp right turn and powered into the steep switchback road that dropped from the top of the cliff down to the town of Positano. She sensed the quickening speed and swung her toe to the brake. It went to the floor.

The next five seconds came at her too quickly for her to save herself. She came off the accelerator and felt the engine try to brake the car, but the road was so steep that she was still gaining speed. She wasted two seconds pumping the brake, hoping it would catch. There was no sense of resistance. Then she pushed the clutch and tried to drop the gearshift into low. But with the speed of the wheels, the gears ground and the shift lever tore out of her grasp.

In the fraction of a second she had left, she popped the catch of the seat belt and grabbed the door handle. With her other hand, she threw the wheel into the turn, even though she knew she had no chance of making it at the speed she was traveling. It was a good choice; had she hit the wall head-on, the car would have blasted right through it. A better move would have been to turn the car into the stone wall that was flashing by next to her. Sideswiping the wall might have killed some of the speed and prevented the car from going over. But Jennifer had no time to think of alternatives.

The car lost traction. The passenger side hit the retaining wall. The Ferrari rolled onto its side, slid along the top of the wall, then flipped over into space. It still carried enough forward speed so that it didn't begin to fall immediately. Instead, it arched out away from the cliff, nose forward, rolling gracefully around its front-to-rear axis like an artillery shell. Its trajectory gradually began to fall into a sickening plunge. It bounced once off the sheer slope of the mountain. Its gas tank ignited. Then, as a fireball trailing a line of black smoke, it plunged into the continuation of the downhill road that it had just left. Instantly, a puddle of fire shot out in all directions.

By some mercy, it landed in a gap of what was normally bumper-to-bumper traffic. Cars collided with one another as they screeched to a stop at the edge of the flames. A motorbike managed to dodge the devastation. The firemen who put out the flames could be thankful that no one had been hurt or killed.

Except for the driver, who was not on the scene. Apparently, he or she had been thrown out of the car somewhere in its flight path. The rescuers went back up to the first hairpin turn, where the barricade was smashed and streaked with bright red paint. They stepped through the debris of broken glass and twisted trim that had peeled off the car before it went over the wall. Ten feet below, stretched out in a grassy tuft that was one of the few breaks in the cliff face, they saw Jennifer. From where they were, they could see that she was unmarked but most likely dead. But when they went over the top with ropes and a litter, they found her alive. She was unconscious, and her eyes didn't respond to light, but there was a pulse in her neck and a breathy froth on her lips. The medics ministered to her on the spot, then hauled her motionless form up into a waiting ambulance and rushed her off to the hospital. Within minutes, she was strapped into the litter of a helicopter and on her way to a trauma unit in Naples.

Padraig, whom she had left less than two hours earlier, was on the phone arguing with one of his agents when the policeman knocked on his door.

"She could handle those turns," he told the officers in the police car. "She's a great driver."

"Perhaps too much car," an officer suggested.

"Horse shit," Padraig snapped.

The officer shrugged.

They had no idea why she lost control, but it was clear that the car had entered the turn with far too much speed. The Positano switchbacks demanded nearly a full stop. The Ferrari must have been doing eighty kilometers an hour. What they did know was that she wasn't wearing her seat belt, because otherwise she never could have left the car. They assumed that she was thrown out as the car flipped from the top of the wall, probably after the drag of the collision had reduced the speed. A clump of bushes had broken her fall, and the bit of turf had cushioned her landing. She was lucky, if you could say that about someone in a coma.

While being flown up to Naples, Padraig learned the seriousness of her injuries. A concussion, but much too soon to tell how severe. "These things," the Italian doctor tried to explain in an unfamiliar language, "are hard to guess. Sometimes . . . nothing. The next day like nothing happened at all. But sometimes . . . not so good, no! The X rays will show us something."

She had broken a shoulder, a collarbone, and two ribs, all on her right side, probably from the impact of landing. Her left leg was fractured in several places, most likely breaking as it dragged out of the car. There was a bump and a contusion on the right side of her face. "All not important," the doctor said. "Time, of course, but all will mend. The danger is the head," he went on, pointing to his own. "And here," as he ran his hand up and down Padraig's spine.

"Her spine? Is she paralyzed?"

The doctor waved away the suggestion. "No . . . no. We know nothing yet. First she wakes up. Then we see about the rest."

Padraig couldn't believe the sight at the hospital. She was on a canvas rack instead of a bed. A ribbed plastic tube was stuffed into her mouth and flexed in rhythm with the rise and fall of her chest. A bottle of fluid dripped into her arm. The wall above this apparatus looked like the control room of a television station. There were half a dozen monitors beeping, blinking, and drawing bumpy traces.

"Sweet Jesus" was his only comment.

Doctors and nurses were rushing in and out, all happy to talk with the great film star and offer him reassurances. "She's doing as well as can be expected" was the common English phrase that told him absolutely nothing.

In the early evening, Jennifer and all her life-support hardware were unplugged from the wall and rolled into a nearby room. Padraig could recognize the doughnut shapes of CAT scans and MRI equipment. But he saw no signs of life from Jennifer as she was passed from one technician to another.

It was nearly midnight when he got his first informed assessment of her situation. A concussion, and a sizable clot pressing against her brain. "The clot seems to be dissipating," a very young doctor told him in flawless English. "And there is no indication of brain swelling. So, for the moment, there is no reason to open her skull."

The shock effects of the trauma were abating, another very good sign. No spinal or neck injury had been detected, and nervous response was "appropriate, considering her condition." The next day or so would be critical, but the doctor personally judged that, barring a setback, Jennifer would survive.

There would certainly be residual damage. Memory, speech, perhaps balance and movement. It could be permanent in some areas, but far more likely temporary. "We'll bring her back, let her bones heal, and then get her into therapy."

As soon as O'Connell left the trauma unit, he ran into a wall of reporters pushing cameras and microphones into his face. "I've just had a reassuring report from the doctors," he said into one of the mikes, "but you're much better off hearing it from them." He ignored the shouted questions about whether his marriage was failing, had she been rushing to meet another man, or had they had an argument. The tabloid bastards had no taste at all.

The hospital officials had set him up in a hotel across from the hospital in a decent suite that smelled of disinfectant and came up short on the air-conditioning. The light on the telephone was blinking urgently as he closed the door behind him. It was Catherine calling from New York, where an evening news reporter had just informed her.

"Oh, good Lord, you'll have to forgive me, Catherine. I should have called you. But it's been hectic, and I didn't have any information to pass on to you."

"She's alive?" Catherine asked hopefully.

"Yes, thank God. And according to the doctor I just spoke with, nearly out of serious danger." He repeated the prognosis, not pulling any punches on the need for a long recovery and the possibility of lasting damage.

"I'm on the nine o'clock flight to Rome," Catherine said.

They were together at the hospital in Naples from the moment Catherine was delivered onto the roof by helicopter. Jennifer regained consciousness that night, completely bewildered to find herself in a trauma suite, and at a loss for any explanation of how she might have gotten there.

"Perfectly normal," the doctor told them. "Short-term memory always takes a while. Frankly, I'm very encouraged that she even recognized you."

By morning she was remembering. "Oh God, Padraig, did I damage the car? Can it be fixed?"

"I'll buy you another," he assured her.

By noon everything had returned. "Who's filling my job?" she asked her sister. Catherine cried at the absurdity of the question.

The next day Jennifer was cut free from all the monitors and moved to a penthouse room with its own nursing staff. The day after, she was brought to surgery for several hours of procedures that pinned her collarbone and shoulder back together and used screws and plates to reassemble her leg. When she returned to her room, her leg was suspended and encased in plaster, and her right arm was cantilevered straight out from her body.

Padraig walked around her bed, taking her in from every angle. "I'm trying to figure out how we might make love," he explained, bringing tears of laughter to her eyes.

But then she became serious. "Padraig, I remember everything. Well, almost everything. It was the brakes. They didn't work at all. They went to the floor, and when I tried to pump them, they hardly came back."

"I knew it was nothing that you did," he said.

"But why would they just . . . fail. We never noticed a problem, and the car wasn't even being used."

"Could be any number of reasons, but you can rest assured that the people at Ferrari are going to get a good piece of my mind."

That night, while they were having dinner in the back corner of a restaurant, Catherine brought up the difficult subject of Jennifer's recovery. "I know it's your call, Padraig, but I think it might be best if we brought her back to New York."

He set down his fork and folded his hands.

She went on, "I'd like to get her to the New York doctors. There are special hospitals for orthopedic surgery, and I'd like her to be looked at by the best before everything heals. We shouldn't wait until it's all over before we find out that she can't move an arm or that her knee doesn't work. And then some of the best physical therapy centers are in the New York area."

He nodded but still said nothing.

"Then there's her job. I'm sure the faster she gets back to work, the better." A pause, and then she asked, "I hope you agree?"

"I'd see more of her in California. Hell, I'd see more of her here in Italy if this commercial thing turns into a campaign."

"Do you really know where you'll be working?" Catherine challenged.

He bowed his head. "No, I suppose not. The movie is hanging fire, and even when it gets the green light, who knows where we'll go for locations. But I am toying with this production company, and that means I'll be in California, at least for the near term."

She played her ace. "I'd be very interested in hearing more about your production company. It might be the perfect application of our satellites. But, of course, I'm in New York."

He smiled and tipped his head in a gesture of congratulations. "My, but you do play hardball."

"It's not hardball when it's good for everyone," Catherine answered. "Jennifer gets the best doctors, I get an education in movie production, and you may even end up with a backer."

"Then I guess it's New York . . . for Jennifer's sake, of course."

Catherine nodded to the waiter. She thought she might enjoy another glass of wine.

SEVEN

PETER HADN'T been sure of his motives when he had hired security agents to keep tabs on the honeymooners in Italy. He had told himself that it was a simple business precaution. You didn't let a major shareholder in an important company wander around Europe without protection. Too frequently, they became targets for kidnap and extortion schemes. But, if pressed, he would have admitted that it was more than that.

It was Padraig O'Connell. His sudden interest in Jennifer simply didn't ring true, and their whirlwind romance was almost adolescent in character, nothing like O'Connell's typical romances. In past times, an out-of-work prince who found himself short of spending money was expected to hook up with an heiress in need of a title. So why, in today's market, wouldn't an out-of-work actor go after a woman with a space-industry fortune who happened to be in need of love? Peter simply didn't trust the man and, probably for that reason, disliked him intensely.

There was another reason, and this was something that he didn't allow himself to think, much less admit. He had long been in love with Jennifer. Why, he couldn't say. Her low profile matched his preference for anonymity, so there was a level of compatibility. Her scientific interests were like his. Her athleticism made her a good fit for his recreational preferences. But, of course, none of those things explained his feelings. At best, they explained why he would have asked her to join him at road rallies or invited her to join his crew in a blue-water yacht race.

He had first suspected his feelings when she had fought him tooth and nail over personnel cuts in her department. As she argued, he realized that she didn't give a damn about the loss of status entailed in having her responsibilities trimmed. Nor was she trying to save her budget. It was the people who worked with her that she was defending. She had needed them once, and she would need them again. She wouldn't allow them to be mothballed just because the focus of her work had shifted.

Then, in the yacht race, he had watched her pitch in with all her might, not embarrassed to ask the dumb questions and with no fear of appearing foolish. He had decided that she was unusual in his business-mogul fraternity; unpretentious and basically honest. He knew that he wanted to know her better than their office relationship would allow.

His feelings were tentative and impossible to explain. By all odds, he should have gravitated toward Catherine, who was the perfect complement to his own weaknesses. She was daring where he was conservative, outgoing where he was introverted, forceful where he was reserved. He was dazzled by her energy and enthralled with her beauty. Her judgment at times was uncanny, almost as if she had foreknowledge of future events. And her vision, like her father's, was enormous. It was Catherine who had taken a high-technology venture in the old and tired telephone business and turned it into a new era of communications. It was Catherine who had taken an invisible business and made it into the showstopper at Cannes. But, irrationally, he felt no magnetic attraction to Catherine. If what he was experiencing was love, then he was in love with Jennifer.

But as quickly as he had recognized the feelings, he had purged them. He was, as he had always realized, the pivot on which the two sisters balanced. They were very different people, not entirely compatible. If he moved toward either one of them, he would upset the delicate scale that was the soul of the company.

Maybe that was why he despised Padraig. The man had stepped into Jennifer's life and waltzed off with her, winning in a week what Peter knew he could never win, shattering his secret hopes. And perhaps it was this dislike that made him fear for Jennifer's safety: The man had everything to gain from Jennifer's death. Or maybe it had been simply a prudent business decision. But regardless, he had hired security people to shadow the couple in Italy, with the instruction that if anything happened to either one, it better happen to Padraig. They had failed in their assignment.

He vanished from the office on a Friday, and without sharing his plans with anyone, he caught an evening flight to Naples. The next day he was with his Italian detectives, walking downhill to the switchback where Jennifer's car had launched itself into space.

They leaned forward across the temporary barrier and looked down the vertical face of the cliff. The fall took Peter's breath away. To his right, clinging to the stone wall, was the Hotel San Pietro where they had stayed. To his left, he saw the rooftops of Positano, tiny squares of clay tiles hundreds of feet below. The people in the streets seemed like ants. Directly below, the sea was lapping up on a minute stone beach.

The road wound like a snake, cut into the cliff for its short, straight runs, with the tight switchback turns built out from the mountain. From the top, it seemed like a meandering ledge. The odds of Jennifer's car landing precisely on the road were small.

Directly below them was the short, grassy ledge where Jennifer had landed. It was no more than twenty feet long, perhaps ten feet wide, and an infinitesimal target even for someone intentionally jumping from the barrier. There were lengths of the police's crime-scene tape still wrapped around one of the bushes.

They went to the garage where the car had been parked. A parking attendant rushed over and challenged them. "Pretty good," Peter observed. "It doesn't look as if some kook could have just wandered in."

The security officer suddenly realized that Peter's interest was more than academic. "You think someone was out to get her."

"You're the detective. You were on the scene. What do you

suspect?" Then he barked off a series of orders in drill-sergeant phrases. He wanted to know the complete history of the car from the time it started down the factory production line. He wanted a minute-by-minute account of the week it had spent parked in the San Pietro garage. He wanted things that might have affected the braking system listed in order of priority, with the factory's experience for each possibility. He wanted anyone who had ever touched the car interviewed. And he wanted the duty logs of all the officers who had been maintaining watch over Padraig and Jennifer.

Most of all, he wanted to know why Jennifer had been in the car instead of Padraig O'Connell. "It was supposed to be Padraig," the security officer apologized.

"Then how did it end up being Jennifer?" he demanded.

Jennifer was still in her casts when Peter wandered into Catherine's office. He dropped a file folder on the coffee table and walked past her desk to the wine closet.

"So early," she said, glancing at her watch.

"You're going to want a drink, too," he answered. He crossed back past her desk, a bottle of Chablis in one hand and two glasses in the other. He set the glasses down next to his papers and began working with the corkscrew.

Catherine sensed a crisis. "Hold my calls," she said into her intercom, then came out from behind her desk to join him. She waited patiently while he twisted and pulled and poured for the two of them.

"Here's to Jennifer," he said. "May her recovery be swift and complete."

They drank. Catherine waited.

"And here's to Padraig Aloysius O'Connell, who came to within a hair's breadth of being your partner and my boss."

He drank again, but Catherine still waited.

"Do you know how close he came?" Peter said, settling down into the sofa.

She nodded. "I think about it every day."

"What were the odds of her unbuckling the seat belt? I know I never would have thought of that. And the chances of her tumbling out of the car just as it crossed the wall, and then landing in the one flat grassy spot on the whole godforsaken Amalfi Coast."

"Don't remind me," she answered.

"But here's the real long shot. What are the chances that the first guy on the scene happened to be an expert in emergency medicine? Do you know how many guys there are like that in Italy? And then the odds of getting to a hospital where the doctor was humble enough to know that he was in over his head, and rushed her to a real trauma center? By the way, there are only a half dozen of them in the south half of the country. And then, in Naples, a young genius who's just finished a residency in head injuries was on hand. Bet you won't find guys like him falling out of closets all over Italy."

Peter finished his drink and poured himself a refill. "I'm probably not too far wrong when I guess that there was only one chance in a hundred of Jennifer living once those brakes failed."

"I suppose you're right," she said, still not knowing where his monologue was heading.

"But you know what has even longer odds?"

She gave no indication of trying to guess.

"The chances of the brakes on a Ferrari failing. The odds against that are astronomical. You see, they put in redundant braking systems, right down to double pads hovering around the disks. A drop of pressure in one system and the other takes over. So, even if, by some freak accident, a stone had cut a brake line or punctured a master cylinder, the brakes still should have worked. All Jennifer would have noticed was a dummy light on the dash, telling her to bring the car in for service at her earliest convenience. Oh, and the brakes are holed out and vented. They routinely run twenty or thirty hours on the racing circuits without overheating. They never could have overheated in the half mile between her hotel and the spot where she went over the wall."

"Where did you get all this?"

"Right from the horse's mouth. The Ferrari people. Until now they have never had a total brake failure on that particular model. And then I checked it with their competitors at Porsche. They figure it's about the same as the odds of all the engines on a jetliner conking out at the same time."

"Exactly what are you saying?"

"I'm saying that Jennifer's accident wasn't an accident. Somebody fucked up the brakes intentionally." He tossed down the second glass.

"So," he went on, "I put a few of our security people on to the case. I've been getting their reports in dribs and drabs, but today they sent it to me all together in one report." He opened the file folder. "I think you ought to read this and then lock it away. This isn't the kind of thing we'd want getting out."

"What does it say?" Catherine demanded without reaching for the document.

Peter leaned back. "The car was inspected by a Ferrari dealer in Italy as soon as it was shipped in from Ireland. There was nothing wrong with it, so they gave it a tune-up, changed the fluids, and rebalanced the tires. That was the condition it was in when O'Connell picked it up and drove to the airport to fetch Jennifer.

"They drove from Rome to Positano, and as far as Jennifer remembers, the car performed flawlessly. She said there were dozens of occasions when she braked down from better than a hundred miles an hour without any hint of trouble. And then it went into the garage at the Hotel San Pietro. It's a limited-access garage, patrolled by private security people.

"Now here's the kicker. First thing the morning of the accident, Padraig O'Connell calls down to the garage attendant and says that someone is coming in to work on his car. A few minutes later a man in a white uniform with the Ferrari emblem on his back comes in, goes to the car, and lifts off the engine cover. One of the security men wanders over, hoping to get a glimpse at a Ferrari engine. But the mechanic isn't at all gracious. He doesn't want to talk about the car and says he has only a few minutes to make a few simple adjustments. He works for a short while, then closes everything up, packs up his tool kit, and leaves. Less than an hour later, Jennifer comes down from her apartment, gets in the car, and drives away. The first time she needs the brakes, there aren't any."

"Your detectives checked with Ferrari," Catherine assumed.

"Of course. Ferrari mechanics don't make house calls unless the car isn't working. They never dispatched anyone to the Hotel San Pietro."

"They're absolutely sure it was Padraig who phoned the garage?"

"They're sure they recognized his voice. You don't get to hear many Irish brogues in Positano."

"Had he signed the nuptial agreement you drafted?"

"His lawyers told me they had advised him against it. They're still waiting for his reply."

Catherine was quiet for a moment. "I can't believe this," she finally said. "I was with him at the hospital while Jennifer was still critical. His fear and concern were obvious."

"He's a paid actor," Peter said.

Now it was Catherine who poured herself another drink. "Can I ask what you plan to do with this?" She touched her fingertip to the detectives' report.

"As president of the company, I should share this information immediately with you, Jennifer, and the board. But I'm not sure that I can go to Jennifer at the hospital and just drop this on her."

"No, please don't do that."

"Then I thought that maybe the best approach was to go to O'Connell. I could have the detectives call on him and lay out their case. Once he saw the evidence, he might agree to a quiet divorce in exchange for our dropping the matter."

"And what would he say to Jennifer? That he never loved her? That all he ever wanted was her money?"

"We'd have to work on that. I was thinking of funding a new romance for him with some glamour girl. So he could tell Jennifer that it was fun while it lasted."

"You think that would be easier on Jennifer?"

Peter took off his glasses and pinched some blood back into the bridge of his nose. "No, I'm sure it wouldn't be. I was really hoping that you might know a better way to handle it. Woman to woman? Sister to sister?"

Afterward, Catherine couldn't get back to work. All she could think about was the high probability that her sister's first adult lover had tried to murder her and come within inches of succeeding. Her head filled with images of how happy Jennifer was in her new marriage, and how she looked forward to O'Connell's calls and visits. Catherine wondered if there were any words to convince her sister that the joy the actor had brought her might have been part of his scheme.

Jennifer's recovery moved quickly. Within a month of her arrival in New York, she was out of her neck and shoulder casts and wearing only a light strap-on leg cast. She was then moved to a rehabilitation center in western New Jersey, where she set about regaining strength and her full range of motion. She was in the swimming pool immediately, at first with a flotilla of concerned attendants. But within a few days she was exercising her upper-body injuries with countless laps, and the staff had decided she needed no help in the water. The leg injury proved more difficult, but her determination was boundless. Jennifer hobbled on treadmills by the hour and had to be put out of the weight room at nights. Catherine, who visited almost daily, was amazed by her sister's progress, knew that she would soon release herself from the facility, and realized that she had to face up to telling Jennifer about the investigators' case against her husband.

That prospect seemed easier because of O'Connell's long absences. At first he had called nightly, complaining of the ongoing negotiations and wheeling and dealing that kept him in Hollywood. Then there were fewer calls, each apologizing for the phone calls that were missed. During the last week there had been one bouquet of flowers delivered with a simple "Love, Padraig," and one phone call squeezed in, as he claimed, between "horse-shit meetings."

"He's in some sort of crisis," Jennifer told Catherine, "and I should be there with him. I'm ready to travel, and everything I do here, I can do in a gym out there."

Catherine and Peter had been keeping close watch on O'Connell's affairs through their banking connections, and through a few of the top film executives they had met in Cannes. There was no interest in another picture in his adventure series, particularly with him in a starring role. There was no financial backing for his production scheme. Two scripts he had gone after had been lost to higher bidders. He was keeping up pretenses by dipping into a joint account Jennifer had set up with her own money, and if he was planning to keep up his efforts, he would soon have to ask her for a sizable deposit. Catherine knew she had to talk to her sister before she rushed out to California or poured more of her money into Padraig's pocket.

She took the cowardly approach of letting the detectives' report speak for her. "You have to read this," she told Jennifer, producing the papers at the end of a visit.

"What is it?" Jennifer demanded suspiciously.

"Something you don't want to hear and you won't want to believe. But you have to know about it, and you have to decide what you're going to do about it."

Jennifer never considered that it might be a company affair. "It's about Padraig, isn't it?"

There was a pause before Catherine answered, "Yes, it is."

"Then take it with you. I don't want to see it."

Catherine dropped it on her dresser. "Get mad at me. Hate me if you want to. I wish I didn't have to show you this, but I do."

"I won't look at it."

"That would be foolish, Jennifer, and you're nobody's fool." Catherine turned and left her sister's room.

Jennifer stared at the document. Then, with a grunt of contempt, she picked it up and carried it to her bed. She left it resting across her legs for a full minute before she sighed, picked it up, and began reading.

Catherine brought Peter with her the next day and found Jennifer sitting quietly in the garden between two of the buildings. She didn't greet them or even speak when they sat down next to her. It fell to Peter to break the silence.

"I'm sorry" was the best he could muster.

Jennifer ignored him, turning to her sister. "I am mad, and I do hate you!" she said. "You know, every time in our lives when I thought I was happy, you were always there to destroy my happiness. Every time! Why won't you let me have a life?"

"Jennifer, I never wanted to see you unhappy. I wanted Padraig to be real—"

"Then why detectives? Why bankers snooping into our affairs?"

Peter spoke. "I'm to blame for that."

"I'll get to you," Jennifer snapped with a viciousness he had never seen before. Then she jammed a finger into Catherine's face. "You just stay out of my life. And that's not a request. That's a warning. Padraig and I are in love, and I hope to God that we stay in love. I'm checking out of here today, and I'm already booked on a flight to Los Angeles. You've stopped me before, but I swear that if you try to stop me now . . ." She began to shake in her rage.

Catherine held out a hand. Jennifer slapped it away. She jumped up and broke for the door, hobbling slightly on her bad leg. Before she closed the door on the garden, she called back, "If you want your damn report back, you'll find it in the trash can. That's where it belongs."

———

Jennifer had the facility's limo drive her to Newark Airport, and then she settled into her first-class seat. She seethed during the first hour, waving away the flight attendant's attempts to deliver cocktails. The bastards, she said over and over again to herself. How could they possibly have turned their detectives loose on her husband? But somewhere over the Midwest, she began thinking more rationally. Of course Peter had to protect the interests of the company, and that had to involve her sister. And they had to find some way to tell her about the reports. Catherine certainly wouldn't have wanted a confrontation.

They were crossing the Rockies when she began analyzing the information she had read. Why had Padraig wanted the car checked over, and why hadn't he mentioned it to her? Was it just a coincidence that minutes later the brakes had failed? There was no disputing the evidence that he was in desperate financial shape. Why hadn't he mentioned that to her? She had no objection to his dipping into their joint account, but certainly he should have told her.

By the time she landed in Los Angeles, Jennifer had come to grips with the fact that her death would have solved all her husband's financial concerns and that, armed with Pegasus stock, he could have bought any studio he wanted. So he definitely had a motive for her accident and was probably the only one who had an opportunity.

She taxied from Los Angeles to Padraig's beach house in Malibu. He was waiting on the steps to gather her into his arms, smother her with kisses, and then joke that she must have been drinking on the plane because she walked crooked. Her doubts about him didn't stand a chance. They picked at a frozen dinner, drank a bottle of wine, made love, and then fell asleep in each other's arms, where she felt absolutely secure. How could I feel this way, she wondered, if he wanted me dead?

But in the fresh light of morning, she felt troubled again. Troubled enough to ask him, "Why did you have the car checked that morning?"

He seemed surprised. "Checked? There was nothing to check. All I did was ask them to wash it."

"But you phoned down to the garage," Jennifer reminded him, and when he denied it, she mentioned the testimony in the report.

"Ahh," Padraig said. "So I'm being investigated."

"Not by me."

"No, but by your sister and her hirelings."

She looked away in embarrassment.

"You know, darlin', when I went into your display at Cannes, I heard your voice before I even saw you. Smart and sexy, that's how it hit me. I had to get a look at you. And when I saw you, I thought, Smart, sexy, and honest. The streets of the festival were littered with phonies, so 'honest' had a certain appeal to me. My lust simply boiled over, I admit, and I thought that I simply had to have you. At least for an hour, maybe even a whole day. But the fact is that I had no idea who you were, and I certainly wasn't planning on marrying you for your money."

"I know that," Jennifer assured him, trying to close the issues she had raised.

But he put a finger to her lips and went on. "I found out who you were when I saw your picture in the handouts. Oh, I read all your propaganda, but I couldn't stop thinking of you. As you know, I went back for another look, and when we sat together, I listened carefully to all your damn explanations about footprints and frequencies. But all the time I was thinking about this lovely woman who seemed to be exactly what I needed at this stage of my miserable career. So you see, darlin', when I went aboard your yacht, I had no intention of robbing you. I went there hoping to seduce you. Just for a day, mind you. I still fancied my freedom.

"It was in the car that I fell in love. Maybe a deathbed panic, because there were a few moments when I thought you were going to get us killed. But from that day on, you've been my life. Nothing frightens me more than the thought of losing you."

"You're so dear," Jennifer whispered.

"No I'm not. At this moment I'm a terrible bastard. I'm going to share with you my darkest thoughts on who might have sent the mechanic to tamper with our brakes. The first one to come to mind is your dear sister, who's having a devil of a time playing second fiddle to your newfound celebrity."

"Catherine—"

"Hear me out, darlin', because now that I'm started, I don't want to stop. You've told me more than once that you and your sister were always rivals. And I think she was pretty sure that she had won the contest hands down with her playing in Cannes while you were lighting rockets in some South American jungle. But now you're in the limelight, and I don't think she can stand it."

"Please, Padraig—"

Again his finger was on her lips. "My second candidate is that stuffed-shirt baron of finance, your dear friend Peter. The prig enjoys playing puppeteer with Catherine and you, and you can just imagine how he feels about being replaced by an aging actor. The thought of another man in his personal financial harem would be cause for jihad. And if you don't think he's capable of things like murder, I'd suggest that you and your sister take a good look into his background. There's a skeleton in his closet just screaming to get out."

"Peter?" It was a breathless question.

"Good old reliable Peter. I've looked into a few things myself, and you may be surprised to know that Peter wasn't always a loner. He used to have a partner who was really the technical genius of the two."

"But try to murder me? Peter? Catherine?"

"You? Oh, for God's sake, woman, have a bit of sense. No one wanted to kill you. You weren't the threat to Catherine's self-importance or Peter's mastery of outer space. I'm the threat. I was the one they wanted dead. Don't you remember? I was the one with the lunch date. I was the one who was supposed to be taking the car. And with everything else their damn detectives have come up with, finding out that I'd be the one to start down the hill was probably child's play."

"Oh my God," Jennifer managed.

"My God, indeed. And lucky for me that you decided to go shopping, darlin', because the one thing you did that I never would have done was unbuckle that seat belt. If I'd been in that car, I would have ridden it all the way to the bottom, with no stuntman and no Hollywood escape."

She pushed out of her chair and fell into his arms. "Oh, Padraig . . ."

He let her kiss him, and then he said, "You know, now that we're friends, you could really call me Patty!"

PART TWO

EIGHT

Did I want her dead? I suppose that's the bottom-line question, isn't it? But I'm not sure I know how to answer it.

I know I never could have killed her. Held a gun to her head and pulled the trigger or tied a noose around her neck. I couldn't do that to anyone. Not even an animal.

When we were still in high school, we had this dog. "Inky," we called him, because he was jet-black. He wasn't pedigreed. Just a mutt. My sister used to hug him and nuzzle him and let him lick her face. He even slept in her bed. I liked the dog, of course, but I'd never let him that close to me. I didn't want dog hair on my clothes, and certainly not in my bed, so whenever Inky came close, I'd push him away. I suppose he really was her dog.

But when Inky got old and sick and it was obvious that it was time to put him to sleep, she couldn't do it. The dog was good for nothing and probably in pain, but my sister wouldn't face up to it. So when I came home from college on a weekend, my father gave me the job of taking Inky to the vet. "Your sister can't," my father told me, "and it has to be done." See what I mean. He just assumed that I had nothing better to do than pick up after her. So I took the dog to the vet. But I couldn't be part of it. I couldn't even wait around while the vet was doing it. I didn't even like the damn dog, but I couldn't have killed it.

No, I don't think I ever wanted my sister dead. I just wanted her out of my life. Whenever the two of us were together, she always got the attention, so it was better if we went our separate ways. Like when we went to two different colleges. For the first time in my life,

I had room to breathe. I was the one pledged into the sorority. I was the one elected sophomore homecoming queen. There was another girl who tried to beat me out, but she was caught with crib notes in an exam. She tried to blame it on me, but the notes were in the pocket of her blazer. Now, if that had been my sister, you just know that everyone would have believed her. So I was really better off without her.

Of course we still chafed when we were home on vacations. We had moved by then to Hilltop, which was some railroad baron's old estate, so we should have had plenty of room to avoid each other. But she kept the household staff so busy with her stupid errands that I couldn't even get a blouse ironed. She used to eat her breakfast in the kitchen so the maid didn't have to set up a decent breakfast in the dining room. It was as if she owned the place and I was only a guest.

Then there was the country club. Wherever I went, around the pool or down at the tennis courts, she would show up. Sometimes she would even find out where I was going so that she could be there first. She'd say, "What do you mean, following you? I've been here all morning." But you don't have to be behind someone to follow them, if you know what I mean. If you know where they're going, all you have to do is hang around until they get there.

It was just like when we were kids. If I was in the pool, she'd bring all our friends up to the sundeck. If I was up sunning, she'd organize some sort of water game. Anything to be the center of attention.

The club had a members' tennis tournament that I entered, and of course, my sister signed up an hour later. Neither of us was really a good player. We were okay, but not club champions. So we both wound up in the second flight. We each had a good run and ended up meeting in one of the semifinals. I beat her in straight sets, and she came jumping over the net like a wonderful sportsman and shook my hand. But then, behind my back, she joined the mixed-doubles matches with a guy who later turned pro. So while I was losing the singles final to a girl who got all the breaks, there was my sister hugging the doubles trophy with this stud's cheek pressed

*to the other side of the loving cup. You can see what I mean. I beat
her easily, and yet she ended up getting all the attention. For the
whole month of August, I had to look at her photo on the clubhouse
wall.*

*Then, after our junior year, we went to Europe for the summer.
I really wanted each of us to go our separate ways. I mean, why
couldn't I have gone to France while she went to Italy? It's a big
continent. We could have spent the summer without ever coming
across each other. But we must have hidden our feelings pretty well.
We never argued in public, and we were always smiling and being
very solicitous. I don't think anyone ever guessed how jealous she
was of me.*

*It should have been a great summer. Daddy arranged one of those
tours where we flew over on British Airways and then came back
on the QEII. We went from England to Holland, to Germany and
Austria, and finally to Greece. Then we came back through Italy,
Spain, and France. We saw everything worth seeing and were in
and out of a hundred museums. For the most part we got along fine.
After all, we're sisters. It's not as if we're always fighting.*

*But there were still times when she pushed me aside so she could
be the center of attraction. There was something about her. She
simply had to do me one better no matter what the occasion. Right
off the bat, she started after the English tour guide, an Oxford stu-
dent who did tours of London as a part-time job. He was quite
handsome, and I made it pretty obvious that I was interested in
him. But she moved right in. All of a sudden she developed a passion for history. You should have seen her pretending to be breathless over the crown jewels, dropping names and dates as if she'd
been living in England since William the Conqueror. Before you
knew it, my sister was getting a personal tour of the country. The
rest of us were only tagging along. Someone must have complained
to the tour company, because the guide was replaced by a woman
in a wool suit and tennis shoes. As it turned out, she was a better
guide anyway.*

*In Germany, my sister suddenly developed a taste for classical
music. We had both taken piano lessons and played flute in the*

school orchestra. She was no more into music than I was. But she put a move on one of the German teachers who was lecturing us on Bach, Beethoven, and Mozart—the big three, he called them. Our last night in Munich, they sat together at a chamber-music recital, her head on his shoulder, completely ignoring the rest of the group. She didn't come home until early in the morning, then had a fit when I told her she was an embarrassment.

In the Greek Isles, the whole tour group went to a topless beach. I found a spot with a bit of privacy, but not her. She was topless in a second right in front of the others, and then all the other women joined in. And then she acted as if there was something wrong with me because I didn't want to be part of their tasteless display. "It's just for laughs," she said, but I knew she was doing it to embarrass me. It was her way of getting back at me for the things I said to her in Germany.

There was no stopping her. In Italy she was an opera lover; she even sang with one of the gondoliers in Venice. In Spain she used her high school Spanish to flirt with the men. I know as much Spanish as she does. I think I even got better grades. But I wouldn't stumble through someone else's language simply to try and make an impression. And in France it was impressionist painting. She actually missed two days of touring to spend the time with some French sidewalk painter at the d'Orsey. I didn't mind, because at least she wasn't bothering me on the bus. But it was hard to explain to the others where she was without making her look cheap.

I finally got rid of her on the way home. The night before we were supposed to board the QEII, I dumped her passport down the hotel incinerator chute. There was a big row at the pier in Southampton, but no matter how we pleaded, they wouldn't let her board. She missed the ship while she went back to the American embassy, so I enjoyed the cruise without having to put up with her little tricks. She ended up flying home.

So, yes, to answer your question, I did think I was better off without her. She was always spoiling things for me. Maybe she didn't mean to all of the time. Like when she entered the tennis tournament, I'm sure that wasn't just to ruin things for me. She

*enjoyed tennis, too. But there were times when she very intention-
ally rained on my parade.*

*I brought a boyfriend home from college for one of the vacation
weekends. There was nothing serious between us, but we had gone
out together a few times. Then he invited me to a fraternity party,
which was exciting because this particular frat had great affairs and
it wasn't easy to get invited. When a three-day holiday came up, a
lot of people were going home, but he lived too far, down in Texas
or someplace. So I felt sort of obligated to invite him home with
me, and he jumped at the opportunity. I don't know how my sister
found out, but when we walked in the door, there she was, waiting
to be introduced.*

*For the whole weekend we couldn't get away from her. If we put
on the television, she would sit down to watch. When I had lunch
brought out, she came right out and joined us. Of course we invited
her. We had to be polite. But she certainly knew that she was barg-
ing in. And then, when we came back home from our evening out,
she and her date were already in the family room, curled up on the
sofa. "Oh," she said, like the most gracious person in the world,
"come in and join us. We're just watching an old horror flick."
"Come in and join us," like she owned the place. You see what I
mean. She knew it was my weekend home.*

*I could go on and on with one story after another. But that
wouldn't answer the question. It's obvious that I wanted room to
breathe. I have no doubt that I wished she weren't in the picture.
But that doesn't make me some sort of a homicidal maniac. There
was nothing unreasonable about wanting her out of my life.*

*But wanting her dead? I think that's pushing things too far. I
would have wished her a long and happy life if I'd just known that
she would lead it someplace else. In a different family, with a different house. Or maybe the same family but during alternating
months. I was fed up with the rivalry. I was sick and tired of being
second chair. I was entitled to my own space and my own successes.
It wasn't right that I had to share everything with her, and it certainly wasn't right that she could take from me whenever she
wanted to.*

As for actually killing her, I certainly couldn't have done that. I know I couldn't, because I often had the opportunity. If I had wanted to kill her, I would have done it in a way that no one ever would have suspected. For instance, we used to dive together. While we were in college, we took a family vacation to the Caribbean, and my father had arranged for us to take scuba lessons. We both got certified, and then every winter we would go off to Tortola or Belize or some other diving mecca. You always dive with a buddy, so she and I would often go together. There would be just the two of us, all alone in this underwater world that was filled with all kinds of dangers. I mean, a shark or a moray could attack you. Or you might slice your leg open on a sharp piece of coral. Maybe your breathing system would fail and you'd suffocate before you could get back to the surface. It wasn't something that you worried about. Diving is pretty safe if you know what you're doing. But there were always dangers.

Once, I think it was in Belize, I thought of a way to get her. She had charmed our boat captain, a big lanky guy who was kind of a dropout. I certainly had no real interest in him, except maybe as a one-night drinking partner. I don't think I would have risked bringing him back to the hotel. But before I could even get close to him, she had him up and dancing to reggae music. And she wouldn't leave even when I wanted to leave. I was really furious. I had just about had enough of my dear sister.

I was still burning the next day when we were down about sixty feet, only the two of us. She was swimming ahead of me, swinging her ass the same way she had been swinging it on the dance floor. I should have been concentrating on the dive, but all I could think of was what a sneaky little bitch she was and how glad I'd be to be rid of her. And I saw how easy it would be. Just pull off her air hose so that she got a faceful of water instead of air, then sit on her shoulders so she wouldn't shoot back up to the top. Once she was out of air, with her weighted belt, she'd sink to the bottom, and then I could go up and act as if I expected her to be up there waiting for me.

What would they find? A diver who had drowned because her

air line had separated from the tank. Tragic, but certainly not sus-picious. We were both pretty much novices. All they would think was that she had breathed in water, panicked, and kept trying to suck in air when there wasn't any. All I had to say was that she was behind me, and when I turned around I couldn't find her. Naturally, I had come right up to investigate.

I swam right up to her. I was inches above her, and I actually had my hand on her air line. But she must have felt me, because she turned her head to look up. I got a glimpse of her face. And then I couldn't do it. Maybe if she hadn't looked at me, if she had been just a diver in a wetsuit, I could have done it. But when I saw her face, I couldn't. I smiled and pretended to be pointing out something I had seen. We both looked around for a few seconds, and I sort of signaled that it must have gone away, so we got back to our diving. I didn't think about it again.

But my point is that I couldn't kill her, any more than I could have killed Inky. I'm not that kind of person.

So, what am I saying? That I wanted to be rid of her, and with very good reason. But I didn't really want her dead, just gone. And that I don't think I ever could have actually killed her, although it might not have bothered me if someone else had.

There must be a million people who feel that way about some other person. A sister or brother, a parent, maybe even an acquain-tance. I know people who feel exactly that way about a business partner or a boss.

Are they all crazy? Is anyone who feels that way a psychopath? You see what I mean, don't you?

NINE

"WHY?" PETER Barnes asked Catherine.

"Because we should be making an investment in a production company. It will give us a way to develop and test services."

He cocked his head skeptically. "And why O'Connell's company, which as far as we know doesn't even exist?"

"Because it won't take a very big investment. We can own the lion's share for just a bit of seed money."

"You're suggesting that we go into business with a man who may have tried to murder your sister."

"So he won't need any of Jennifer's money. Or her stock."

"Hoping that if he doesn't need her, he'll leave her alone?"

Catherine sagged into a chair in Peter's office. "It's one way to protect her. We have to do something. She won't face the facts. She won't even look at the evidence. And the more desperate O'Connell gets, the more dangerous he'll become."

"You think he's going to try again?" Peter questioned. It was his way of working to question every suggestion and expose it from every angle.

"If he tried once, why wouldn't he?"

"Because he knows that there's a pretty good case against him. He can guess that we're watching him and that another 'accident' would get thoroughly investigated."

"But he could romance her into putting up her money. He might even get her to put up some of her stock."

Peter nodded. "That makes sense. We put up a little money

so that he isn't scheming for a lot of money. But that won't buy him off. That will only buy us a little time."

"And with a little time, Jennifer might begin to see the light. At a minimum, she might press him to sign the agreement. By now she should have figured out that he was bluffing when he promised he'd sign anything."

"And when will we get your sister back in her office?"

Catherine shook her head. "Not while that Irish con man has his arms around her. Maybe if she sees him snatch up the money, she'll come to her senses and realize what he's after."

"You want me to call him?" Peter asked.

"First call Jennifer and tell her you need her back here. I'll get to O'Connell and tell him we have a proposition to discuss. I bet he'll bring her back on the first flight."

It worked the way Catherine had envisioned. Within hours Jennifer called to say that she was returning and that her husband would accompany her back to New York. Peter met privately with Padraig, handing him a check for $2 million and promising him a call on $10 million more.

"A fifty-one-percent share of the production company you open," Peter said of the contract that had been under the check. "You run it any way you want. The only stipulation is that you distribute electronically through Pegasus Satellite Services."

"The only stipulation?" Padraig asked with narrowed eyes. "Nothing about the peace and order of my household?"

"What you and Jennifer decide is entirely up to you. Personally, I think you're a conniving snake, maybe even a cold-blooded murderer. But I think we need an early stake in a business like yours. And I think having a chain around your finances may prove good for Jennifer's health."

O'Connell took the contract and the pen that went with it. "I'd think, with your past, you'd be a little slow to make charges of cold-blooded murder." He looked up in time to see Peter stiffen. He smiled. "Oh, I see you haven't told the good sisters all the grizzly details of your youth." He signed with a flourish.

"Probably smart," he allowed. "Wouldn't want them wondering exactly what befell your partner. Especially if there might be a killer in our midst."

Peter never glanced at the contract that was pushed back to him. His eyes stayed locked on Padraig O'Connell until the actor left the room. He rose and paced around his desk for just a minute. Then he picked up his phone, keyed in to his private line, and dialed the number of his detective agency. He arranged for an off-site meeting later that day with the firm's owner, a National Security Agency investigator who had gone into business for himself.

O'Connell stayed at Jennifer's loft apartment for the next few days, spending most of his time on the telephone. Even when she arrived home in the evening, he waved away her attempts at conversation as he continued his deal-making well into the Hollywood evening. Jennifer noticed a change in his attitude. Padraig was strident and at times even arrogant. Before he had been asking. Now he was telling. Instead of trying to talk his way in, he now sounded as if he were in charge.

"Get it for me, dammit," she heard him shout angrily during one call. "I don't care how high you have to go." And, during another call, "No, not him. I don't want to work with that little prick!"

"Is everything all right?" she asked after listening to his side of the conversations for three straight evenings.

"Splendid, darlin'. Couldn't be better. People are finally coming to their senses. But I will have to get back out there next week. At least for a few days. Some of these things can't be done over a telephone."

They spent a pleasant weekend together, with Padraig joining her on the walks that were part of her therapy and waiting in the gym where she was swimming. Jennifer teased him about the attention he was getting from all the women going in and out of the gym. "I've never seen such raw lust in women's eyes," she told him.

"A burden I've been living with for years, darlin'," he answered. "And if I may say so, some of the young men seemed to be taking a shine to me as well."

He kissed her goodbye on Sunday afternoon and taxied out to La Guardia Airport in order to be in Hollywood Monday morning. In his film roles as a spy, O'Connell was always aware of the things happening around him. But he never noticed the man in a casual windbreaker who had followed him from the loft and was seated on the plane two rows behind him.

Catherine called Padraig at his Malibu apartment on Monday and left word that she was arriving on Tuesday. "I could help you," she said, "deal with any problems about the source and reliability of your financing. Besides," Catherine added, "I want to keep track of my investment."

Padraig had thought of Catherine as a society-page poster girl who served her company best by mingling with celebrities, garnering publicity, and bringing in well-heeled customers. He assumed that the inner workings of Pegasus were as foreign to her as they were to the original winged horse. So he began with a condescending greeting when he met her in the lobby of her hotel.

"Come to mix with the glamorous folks, have you?" he said.

She steered him to a corner table, ordered his single malt and her dry martini, and said little until the drinks had been delivered and the toast exchanged.

"Your eyes have a color similar to your sister's," he said, "which makes them particularly lovely."

"It's the *same* color," she answered, "only mine are a bit nearsighted. Now, can we dispense with the happy horse shit and get down to business. You bought two scripts today, one at an outlandish price. I'd like you to tell me about them."

He leaned back from the table. "I thought there was to be no interference."

"None at all," Catherine said, "but as our money flows out, we'd like some information coming in. Like why we're buying a script that has been passed on by all the majors. And who in hell is this Tommy Devlin you're promoting for one of the leading roles?"

"The majors," he responded slowly, "would pass over the story of Jesus Christ because it doesn't have enough helicopters in it. And they'd want him to die in a slow-motion fall from the top of the Empire State Building rather than on a cross.

"As for Tommy Devlin, he's an eighty-year-old gentleman with yellow teeth and a twitch in his eye who just happens to be the best character actor since Olivier. The man can make you laugh and cry your heart out at the same time. And that, dear lady, is the end of my report to management."

Catherine sipped her martini. Then she said, "Your artistic preferences are noted. But I really wanted to talk about money. The studios loved one script that you bought. They just said it couldn't make any money. Expensive to produce with very limited audience appeal. And Tommy Devlin hasn't made a movie in six years. His last picture was about an Irish sheepherder, and according to the critics, the sheep stole the show."

"My, but we've been doing our homework, haven't we," he said.

"That's only the first page of my information. There are twelve more pages that I'd like to review."

He stood up and stayed standing as he finished his drink. "I have taken a small office in West Hollywood," he said. "I'll phone the desk and leave you the address. Be there at nine. We'll go over the rest of your pages, and then a few pages of mine." He stormed out, leaving her to finish her martini.

The next day was all business. O'Connell began with a spirited defense of his decisions and let Catherine listen in as he began pulling together the pieces of his company. "A production company isn't a fixture, like the gas company. It doesn't come into existence until it has something to produce and talent to do the producing. For the past year, the only place that your company existed was right here." He pointed at the side of his head. "It was born when we acquired a promising script, but it will die if we don't attach talent."

"It will die if it doesn't make money," Catherine countered.

"It will make money," he fired back, "because with your satellites, we won't be paying a studio its usual obscene cut from the top, nor will we be paying millions for prints. That's when you'll get rich, when the industry catches on to how easy it will be to get from an idea to a theater."

She noticed that Padraig's signature lilting brogue had vanished. He was talking the West Coast version of English. And he wasn't sprinkling his conversation with references to fairies and leprechauns. He was talking dollars and cents like an accountant.

"I think we've stumbled into a very promising investment," she reported to Peter Barnes at the end of her first day with O'Connell. "This guy is anything but the lyric poet he pretends to be. He has a very calculating side."

"I know," Peter said, thinking of Jennifer's accident and the blackmail insinuated against himself. "A darlin' fellow."

O'Connell told Jennifer only that he had "run into Catherine out here on the coast."

Jennifer's surprise sounded genuine. "What's she doing out there?"

"Oh, lining up movie business for your satellites, I suppose."

"Did you get along?"

"If you mean did she scratch my eyes out, she did no such thing. Very polite. Even took an interest in what I'm up to. Just her charming self, she was."

"Oh, Padraig, I want so much for everything to work out." Somehow, she hoped, the suspicions against her husband could be dismissed, and his charges against Peter and her sister put to rest. "It was only an accident. All these accusations and insinuations are ridiculous."

That night, when Catherine and Padraig settled down for their drinks, there was a newfound respect between them. He knew that she was much more than a glamorous front for the company, and she no longer considered him a rogue and a braggart. Their dinner conversation was about the business and the prospects that were looking much brighter than they had only hours earlier.

The next day Catherine traveled with him on his rounds of talent agencies, where doors were flung open now that he was funded. She followed with great interest the conversations about matching talent to story lines, and enjoyed the inside gossip about who had proven to be too difficult on the set of a recent picture, who was dangerously involved with drugs, and whose talents fell short of the demands of the script.

For his part, O'Connell was delighted to have Catherine on his arm. She was, as always, dazzling, instantly recognized, and at ease with the fawning that her wealth provoked. People who might not have considered working with Padraig found ways to get into the meetings so they could spend a few moments with Catherine. People who wouldn't have crossed the street to meet Jennifer broke appointments to be with Catherine.

"I thought I was the celebrity," Padraig said after one meeting.

"No, you're the actor," Catherine answered. "I'm the real thing."

The talent and the agents were also impressed with her savvy. There were legions of beautiful women in Hollywood, on the arms of executives in public places and on the peripheries of meetings. But no one expected them to intrude into conversations. As one producer had said of a starlet's lips, "They're for pouting, not for talking." But it was obvious to all, and increasingly so to Padraig, that Catherine had done her homework. She knew their concerns and spoke directly to them. They appreciated that she advanced no opinions into film arts but had focused strictly on the return on investment.

At the end of the day, when she kicked off her heels in the sitting room of her suite, she knew she had done a good day's work. Padraig was simply in awe.

"If you're not careful, you might end up owning this town," he told her. "That would make you responsible for all its sewage problems."

"We're going to make money on the films," she predicted, "and then more money on the satellite services. A year from now you'll be the toast of Tinseltown." She accepted the glass of bottled water he brought from the bar, then gave a sigh. "Let's not do dinner tonight, Padraig. I've got an early flight in the morning."

He recognized his dismissal but stayed in his chair. "Do you still think I had anything to do with your sister's accident?"

"That's in the past," she answered. "Just so long as there are no more accidents in the future. I think you can see that there are many ways I can help you. I have a lot more to offer than Jennifer's money."

He whistled softly. "Jay-sus. You're as hard as a diamond and just as cold."

"As attractive as a diamond, too. I'm very good currency. Better than paper, and maybe even better than gold. And Padraig, be very straight with me. Don't ever give me reason to turn against you."

When she returned to New York, Catherine made a point of telling Jennifer that she had struck up a business relationship with Padraig. But her explanation was not entirely honest. "We need a stake in a business like his, and I suppose we might as well keep it in the family."

Jennifer showed suspicion, so Catherine elaborated. "Not that I'd trust him for a minute, if I were you. But with Pegasus money, he won't have to dip into yours."

When Padraig called, he told Jennifer that he had persuaded Catherine and Peter to lend their full backing. He made it sound as though it was their apology for having suspected him. "It's all working out fine, darlin' girl." And then he promised that within a week or so, he'd be able to handle most of his business out of New York. Jennifer was overjoyed. But she had to swallow hard to take in her sister's repeated trips to Hollywood, and the gossip speculations that Padraig was wooing the more glamorous sister.

"They're all liars," he told her when she flew out to spend a weekend with him. "Catherine and I are doing business deals and nothing more. But here in Gomorrah, everyone kisses everyone. At least before they plunge the knife into the back. And the journalists are like whores making up stories. They'll have me sleeping with her next, and then with both of you at the same time."

"I couldn't stand that," Jennifer said.

Padraig rubbed his neck. "I've heard good things about a ménage à trois."

"I mean you sleeping with her. If that ever happened, your brakes would fail with her in the passenger seat."

"Not to fear, darlin'. She's not my type. Too busty. And I don't care for her tattoos."

"Tattoos?" Jennifer screamed.

He covered his mouth. "Did I let the cat out of the bag?"

She began pounding him with a pillow. "You're just damn lucky I know she doesn't have any tattoos."

En route to New York, her flight path crossed Catherine's, headed for Los Angeles.

"Am I never to be rid of the Pegan sisters," O'Connell complained in mock grief when Catherine appeared at his office.

"I can't speak for Jennifer," Catherine answered, "but I'm going to stick to you like your hairpiece. We're in business together, and I try to stay close to my money. Even more so now."

"Now? Has something changed?"

"For the better," Catherine answered. "Peter wants to raise the stakes. We want to put up more money, and we want to set this company up on its own, as an independent corporation. Peter, you, and I are the directors. We each own a third of the stock. I'm chairman and you're CEO."

Padraig smiled suspiciously. "And you've come to ask my opinion."

"No, I've come to get your signature. This is the way we want to invest our money. And we thought you wouldn't mind owning a smaller piece of a bigger operation, particularly with all the perks."

"What perks?"

Catherine tipped her head and studied him carefully. "I thought you would have figured it out by now, Padraig. I'm the star in this family. I'm the one who belongs in Hollywood. You're married to the wrong sister."

They finished the day dining with agents who brought new projects for their consideration and suggested casts and directors. "This is *Private Ryan* meets the army air force," a reptilian promoter whispered as he pushed a paper-bound screenplay around the wineglasses. He turned his head to check the room, implying that it would be dangerous if word got out that such a treasure existed. "George Clooney is dying to do the colonel, and we're thinking of Russell Crowe for the squadron commander."

"Is there a part for me?" Padraig asked with feigned seriousness.

"Fantastic," the promoter said as if God's hand had just reached down to touch his finger. He consulted with his young associate. "Why not? Maybe an RAF general who pulls their asses out of the fire." His eyes flicked from Padraig to Catherine. "And we could give the guy a back story. Like he turned back from a mission once, so no one takes him seriously. But in the end he's aboard one of the bombers and has to take over."

"From Russell Crowe?" Catherine asked innocently.

"No, no, from one of the other pilots. But can't you see it? Their planes come together, and Crowe tips his cap in recognition. Sort of redeeming Padraig's character."

They bid their hosts good night at the door to the restaurant and watched them walk to a big Mercedes. "How does such a pathetic fool get a car like that?" Catherine asked.

"Out here you rent them by the hour," Padraig said. "It shows that you're to be taken seriously. He probably has to have it back by midnight. And then he'll call Visa and claim that the card he used to pay for dinner was stolen this afternoon."

The attendant drove up in Padraig's roadster and ran around to open the door for Catherine. "Do we have to drop this off someplace?" she asked about the car.

"Not until after I drop you off," he deadpanned. He started the engine and reached for the shift lever. Catherine's hand settled on his.

"I'm not in a hotel mood," she said. "I'm leaning more toward skinny-dipping in the Pacific. Do you know anyone who has a beach house?"

He slipped his hand from under hers and then moved his on top. "Would it be my place you're thinking of?"

"I was thinking of *The Quiet Man* meets *From Here to Eternity*."

"And would there be a part for me?"

"Oh, you'd have the lead."

He shifted and peeled out of the parking lot, his head thrown back in his theater-poster smile. Once again the great secret agent failed to notice that he was being followed. A Ford Taurus had to run a light to keep up with him.

They kept up a light banter as they drove out to the beach house, Catherine reading lines from the script they had been given and Padraig improvising the responses. "But what will I do if something happens to you?" she read, the line of a young woman whose lover was about to take off on a dangerous mission. "Frankly, my dear, I don't give a damn," he answered in his best Clark Gable drawl. They were giggling like children when they left the car by the road and walked down the steps to his house.

But the mood changed once they were inside. Catherine waited out on the deck while Padraig fixed each of them a dash of his favorite Scotch. Then she moved easily against him while they listened to the surf that was barely visible in the darkness. In a second, she was in his arms and their lips were just touching, and then they were rocking in passionate embrace.

"We don't really have to do this in the surf like *From Here to Eternity*," he told her. "I have a very comfortable bed inside."

"I hate it when sand sticks to me," she answered.

They shed clothes on the way to the bedroom, somehow managing to keep their faces pressed together in the process. As he was easing her onto the bed, he asked, "Have you given any thought to what I should tell your sister?"

"Tell her you're a heel. She'll believe that."

They made love, sipped their Scotch, and then started over again, this time lying across the bed. They ended locked in each other's arms, breathing heavily, their feet hanging over the side. There was light in the sky and birds singing when Catherine heard soft snoring deep in his throat.

She was surprised to find him sitting out on a deck chair when she awoke. "Either you're in fantastic shape or I'm slipping," she said as she walked up behind him. She tousled his hair. "Wow, you really could use a hairpiece."

"Fix us some coffee," he told her, "and then come out and sit with me. I think we have to talk."

She returned a few minutes later, a steaming mug in each hand. "This will test your courage. I haven't made coffee since college."

He tasted. "Dreadful," he decided. "Worse than your sister's. Hasn't either of you ever kept house? I had hoped that at least one of you could do windows."

"If that's what you want, then Jennifer would be your best bet. She has high-tech experience." She settled into the chair next to him, and they spent the next few minutes staring out at the surf. Padraig finally raised the obvious issue.

"Have you given any thought to how I stay married to your sister and in business partnership with you? The reason I ask is that I'm not sure I'm up to flying cross-country from bed to bed with any regularity."

"It didn't seem to be a problem last night."

"No, and it wasn't a problem over the weekend when your

sister—my wife, as you may remember—was out here for a visit. An occasional indiscretion is important to my fans. But now I have long-term agreements with both of you. And while you and I seem comfortable with the arrangement, I'm not sure what Jennifer's reaction will be."

"She'll put out a contract on the two of us."

"That would be my guess as well. So perhaps you and I should limit our relationship to just business."

Catherine looked mock-aghast. "You mean I do all the work and she has all the fun?"

He stood and dumped the dregs of his coffee over the side. "Do you have another suggestion?"

"I'll have to tell her."

He was too stunned to think of a glib remark.

"Padraig, you and I are going to be a great team. This business venture is going to succeed wildly because both of us are at home in the limelight. We've got these people falling at our feet. As for our personal relationship, last night was only the beginning. I don't want to feed your ego, but you're better than your press notices. And you seemed to find me interesting as well."

"Indeed I did," he allowed. "But from a long-term perspective—"

She cut him off. "I am looking long-term. I set up our company independently so that no one could ever cut it off except you and me. And I don't plan to cheat on my sister for the rest of my life, either. I see the future very clearly, Padraig, and I'm not going to lose it just because Jennifer saw you first."

"But she's my wife—"

"You've had others. And you've dropped them for a lot less than you'll be dropping her for."

He whistled softly. "It's the devil I'm hearing."

"Cut the blarney, Padraig. You know your choices. You can have Jennifer or you can have everything. Since you married her in order to get everything, I don't see why it should be such a difficult choice."

TEN

WHEN SHE entered Peter's office, Catherine found Jennifer waiting.

"Did you read it?" Jennifer asked without a word of greeting. She held up the document that had been resting on the conference table in front of her.

Catherine nodded as she took a seat across from her sister.

"Kind of shocking," Jennifer offered.

"Surprising. But no big deal."

The door from Peter's washroom opened and he came out, trying to button down one of his collar tabs.

"Hi, Peter," Jennifer tried in greeting. Her voice trailed off. This wasn't going to be business as usual. Catherine looked up but broke eye contact instantly.

He sat at the head of the table and reached down for the document that Jennifer had brought to the meeting. "I had this prepared by our investigators because I wanted it to be completely objective. I've read it, and it seems to cover everything, at least as far as I remember. It was over twenty years ago."

"Why?" Catherine asked, and when Peter seemed puzzled, she added, "Why did you have them dig all this stuff up?"

He nodded. "Because someone else seemed to know about it, and I detected an implied threat of blackmail. The only way I could make the information useless was to bring it out into the open."

"Blackmail?" Jennifer was horrified.

"Not specifically," Peter answered. "Just the implication that

111

if I didn't try to be more . . . cooperative, you two might get to hear the whole lurid story. So, I thought it was best if you heard it from me."

"Is it true?" Catherine asked.

"It's factually accurate."

"That wasn't my question. There's an implication here that Dan Holland's death was very convenient for you—"

"It was. It launched my career."

Catherine stared at him, waiting for the rest of the answer. Peter didn't seem anxious to elaborate.

Jennifer finally took up the issue. "Peter," she asked, "were you in any way involved with your partner's death?"

He looked at her directly. "That's the question I've been asking myself all my adult life. You've read what the investigators have to say. What do you think?"

Jennifer's eyes lowered. She didn't want to say what she thought. The report pulled no punches. There was motive and there was opportunity. If she looked at the scenario dispassionately, she saw Peter as a prime suspect in his partner's death. But she had known Peter for ten years, and the person she knew simply didn't fit the crime.

Catherine spoke up. "You can't do that now, Peter. You always turn our questions back on us, but not this time. I think we're entitled to an answer."

He dropped his chin and pursed his lips. "Of course you're entitled to an answer. But there just isn't one. I didn't start the fire. But then again, I didn't put it out."

"Did you want him to die?" Jennifer asked after a long silence.

"No, but I wanted to get away from him. And the fire made it easy."

Neither sister seemed to understand, so Peter Barnes went back to the beginning and tried to put some soul into the body of the investigators' report.

In the seventies, some of the teenagers in California had stopped hopping up their automobiles in favor of building computers. The internal combustion engine was reaching its physical limitations no matter how they bored the chambers or tricked the valves. The computer, on the other hand, had just reached day one. The integrated circuit had arrived, and solid-state memory was replacing wire and iron cores. String a few components together and find an old television set and you could play Ping-Pong on the screen. Or, if you could write a few lines of code, you might be able to create a database for your baseball cards.

Within a few months, high school kids could do more with a circuit board than the engineers at IBM. They were meeting at clubs, swapping ideas, and then building crude computers with names like Apple, and Apricot, and Acorn in their garages. Soon Wall Street investment bankers were standing around the garages trying to buy in on some of the better ideas.

"Dan Holland and I had a desktop computer with a built-in tape drive that took tiny tape cartridges," Peter told them, smiling at the memory of their impractical idea. "The programming language was impossible, and the hardware clinked and clunked like a record changer. But still, we got seed money. The bankers were covering the table."

Peter had tried to make the machine work, but his partner had found a new love even more exotic than the computer. The laser had been invented, and Dan Holland had immersed himself in the wonders of coded light. Peter had argued with him, pleading for him to throw his efforts into saving their computer. Instead, Holland had built a system to bounce light beams around inside the garage. "Cool, huh?" he had said to Peter, smiling. Peter had screamed in frustration.

"He was right, of course. We were hopelessly behind any number of people with our computer. There was no sense in killing ourselves over a second-rate concept. But still, it galled me to see him putting on light shows while I was busting my butt. I knew I needed to find another partner, but Dan and I had been friends since grade school. I couldn't just cut him out."

Then, one day, Dan had wrapped the entire garage in pencil-thin beams of blue light. "How many damned lasers did you buy?" Peter had demanded, and had been stunned when his friend explained that it was all the same laser. What he had done was dope a few filters so that when one laser beam went in, two came out.

"I couldn't believe what I was seeing," Peter told the sisters. "The color of the light wasn't changed, and as far as we could tell, there was no dropoff in energy. You could split one beam into two, and then two into four, and four into eight. It was like the loaves and the fishes. We could take one optical signal and send it to eight users."

Peter had put the computer aside to work with Dan on the light-wave splitters. In less than a month they had made a dozen eight-to-one multipliers and figured out exactly how to make them in quantity. Peter had filed for the patent in their company's name. They had shown the concept to investment bankers who were positively salivating.

"Then," Peter went on, "Dan came up with another brainstorm. 'Who wants to do business with telephone companies? We can take our equipment and do light shows for rock groups. We can go on tour. Know the stars. Have our picks of the groupies.' We had a billion-dollar business right in our hands, and Dan wanted to drive around the country in an old Volks bus setting up light shows! I needed technical proposals for bankers, and Dan wanted to light the stages for rock bands."

They had come to a parting and pretty much decided to break up their company. But there was one problem. Bankers wouldn't invest in a technology unless they controlled the patents, and Peter couldn't deliver on Dan's rights. They couldn't buy him out because Dan didn't care about the money. He wanted patent protection to keep someone else from doing the lighting for tour groups.

"That's where we were at the time of the fire," Peter continued. "At an impasse. I was dealing with investors who had cash in their hands, and Dan was wiring the garage for 'the most spectacular laser demonstration of all time.' He dragged me over to the garage to see it. 'Sit right here,' he told me, and he set up a beach chair in the middle of the doorway. Then he went into the back of the garage behind a black curtain he had hung floor to ceiling. Here we were on the verge of owning the market for an important technology, and Dan was all excited about a light show in a garage."

He shook his head at the absurdity. How could you explain such things? The bonds of a lifelong friendship had tied him to a boy who refused to grow up.

" 'Are you ready?' he called from behind the curtain. 'Yeah, I'm ready,' I answered, determined not to show any enthusiasm. I heard a click. A second later, the curtain turned into a wall of fire. I jumped up and started into the garage. 'Dan, what happened? Are you all right?' He never answered, and I never got any further. All of a sudden the rat's nest of wires that he had tacked along the walls and the rafters began hissing and burst into flames. Smoke was billowing, and the temperature shot up until it felt like an oven. I turned and ran, tripping over the beach chair on my way out. And then I just sat there on the ground, watching the place burn until the heat drove me back. It took only a few minutes—ten at the most—for the garage to collapse and the roaring fire to settle down into tiny flames flaring up out of the ashes. There was no sign of Dan, or of the equipment. They couldn't even identify the body. They had to take my word that Dan was the only one inside."

Barnes looked up sadly at his riveted audience.

"It was an accident," Jennifer said, conviction obvious in her voice.

"The fire? Absolutely! Probably one of the transformers he used to raise the voltage exploded. My guess is that he threw the power switch and was instantly engulfed in the flames. Or maybe he was electrocuted before the fire hit him. That might explain why I didn't hear him scream. Why he never made a sound. It was an accident, pure and simple, at least as far as it goes."

"What more is there?" Catherine asked him.

He slipped off his glasses and, in a familiar gesture, pinched the bridge of his nose. They had seen him do it many times before, always when he was about to announce a decision in some matter.

"What more is there? Well, there's the question of whether or not I could have saved him. I was less than twenty feet away from him when the fire started. So you could make a case that I might have gotten burned but I certainly could have gotten him out the door. Even if he had been on fire, I might have been able to roll him on the ground, smother the flames, and save his life."

"And you might have been trapped inside with him," Jennifer pointed out. "No one can blame you for not running into a roaring fire."

"No one has blamed me. At least not officially. But there's another question that's even harder to answer: Did I *want* to rescue my best friend? Because, you see, in less than a week I had all the capital I needed. And within a year I was on the cover of *Information Week*. But if Dan had survived, who knows. I might be doing laser shows for the Rolling Stones."

"Did you want to rescue him?" Catherine asked.

He held up his hands helplessly. "A hundred things may have gone through my mind in the ten minutes it took the garage to burn to the ground. One of them was certainly the realization that I now had complete control over the most valuable patent in telecommunications. But the fact speaks for itself. I made no effort to get back inside the garage."

He stood slowly, as if exhausted by the tale he had just told. The weight of his guilt was visible. "So, that's it. Don't rush to judgment. I like working with you and I very much like what we've built together. I'm not anxious to leave. But if you're uncomfortable trusting your future to someone with a track record of failing his friends, I'll understand. There are times when I find it hard to trust myself."

"Don't be ridiculous," Catherine snapped. "Our father trusted you completely, and Jennifer and I owe you more than we could ever repay."

He gave a brief nod of gratitude and glanced at Jennifer.

"This changes nothing, as far as I'm concerned. I agree completely with Catherine."

They heard him sigh, a gasp of weakness that they had never seen in Peter before. "I think," he said, "that we each get one chance at greatness: one clear-cut opportunity to show someone that we care more about him than we do about ourselves. That fire was my opportunity, and I have to live with the knowledge that I fucked up. I keep hoping that I'll have another chance."

He was standing by his window while Catherine and Jennifer moved quietly out of his office. It was Catherine who turned at the last minute.

"Peter, who was it that was trying to blackmail you?"

He met her eyes from across his office. "I'd rather not say."

"It was Padraig, wasn't it?" Jennifer followed.

He thought for an instant and then decided, "I'd rather not say."

Jennifer couldn't find peace with the idea that her husband may have been trying to blackmail her mentor. For years Peter had been the man in her life, the big brother who had guided her into adulthood and launched her career.

But then he had become something more. She had gone through romantic fascination, and then into a full-scale crush. He was older than she, of course, and it seemed nearly obscene to be fantasizing about someone who had only recently been her teacher and protector. She should have come straight out and told him her feelings. But the bottom line was that she was his boss, and she didn't want to put him in the awkward situation of explaining why he wasn't interested. So she had taken a much more subtle approach, hinting that she might welcome his advances.

She had edged into his road-rallying, learning the right-seat navigator's role. They had scored well in two or three events and he had seemed delighted with her company. Or was he just paying deference to a major stockholder? He had invited her aboard his boat for the racing season, and if she hadn't become a competent yachtsman, she had at least served as a decent deckhand. While riding at the mooring one night, after a twilight race, she had given him his opportunity. "Do you ever sleep aboard?" she had asked.

"Sure. In the summer months it beats an air-conditioned apartment. Open a hatch and let the wind rush through. The rocking motion. And then the tinkling of the rigging. It's a great night's sleep."

Was he going to invite her to stay aboard? She had actually thought she could see him framing the invitation. But he had decided that he needed to get work done for a morning meeting and had picked up the radio to call for the yacht-club launch.

On another occasion he had driven her home after a regatta on the New Jersey shore. "Come up. I'll make you a cup of coffee," Jennifer had offered. He had gone as far as her doorway but then had turned back. Reluctantly, she had finally admitted that he didn't share her interest. Or, if he did, his concern for the company was much stronger than his passion for her. She had given up trying, although she still wondered if he ever thought about her.

But she had been enraged when he had tried to implicate Padraig in her accident. And now she was equally enraged by the thought that her husband had threatened to destroy Peter.

She challenged Padraig when he came east for a weekend. They were having breakfast at her loft, each involved with a cup of black coffee at the butcher-block kitchen table. "Padraig, did you threaten Peter with things from his past?"

He looked up uncertainly. "Did I what?"

"Did you threaten to tell Catherine and me about the death of his partner in a fire?"

"Certainly not!" He seemed hurt by the suggestion.

"Well, did you know about his partner? And about the fire?"

He paused uneasily. Then, "Yes, I knew about it. It's no great secret."

Jennifer answered, "It's been a secret as far as I'm concerned.

I've known Peter for ten years and I never heard about it."

"His partner had a lot of friends in the entertainment business," Padraig explained. "I suppose that's why the story made the rounds out on the Coast."

"When did you first hear it?" Jennifer persisted.

"Oh, I don't know. I think I remember it from way back. And then someone brought it up when I first began mentioning your name and praising your virtues." He had recovered from his initial shock. The brogue was creeping back into his voice.

"But you never told Peter that you knew?"

"Not in so many words. But I must admit that I was dearly pissed off when I found that he had put his detectives on me. And I may have said something about people in glass houses. Intemperate, perhaps, but certainly not threatening. I'm really not one to dredge up someone's past, what with all the skeletons trying to kick their way out of my closets."

He seemed not to give the issue another thought during the day. They went down to the seaport and joined lines of tourists, lunched on clam chowder and crackers, and then took a cab to a showing of an artist Jennifer liked. They dined in the backyard garden of a small Italian restaurant while the owner's wife paraded the neighbors by so they could sigh over the movie star. And finally, they went back to her apartment, where they sipped wine in the bathtub and made love while their bodies were still wet.

But on Sunday, while he was packing for his trip back to California, he returned to the charges of blackmail. "Now remember, darlin', don't believe everything that your dear friend Peter says about me. And I'll give no mind to the rumors about you luring Boy Scouts into your bedroom."

"What would Peter say about you?"

"Well, so far only that I'm a murderer and a blackmailer. There are any number of felonies left that he can choose from."

"Peter didn't say that you tried to kill me. That's what the company's security people implied. And he didn't call you a blackmailer. He said someone was blackmailing him about his past, and I wanted to be sure that it wasn't you."

He closed the suitcase and snapped the latches ceremoni-ously. "I suppose he doesn't hate me. After all, he's given me a very generous business deal, even though I'm a bargain at any price. But he sees me as unworthy of your affections. And that, I think, is because he'd like to have you for himself."

"Peter?" She hadn't entertained the notion of Peter wanting her for quite some time. "He's never even shown an interest in Catherine, much less me. He's never been interested in any woman for more than a few months."

She put him in a cab at her front door, then walked to the sub-way for her trip to the Upper East Side, where she was joining Catherine for dinner. Catherine had set the café table on her balcony with a view of the East River.

"The good silver," Jennifer teased, "and on the maid's night out."

"I see you dressed for sandwiches in the kitchen," Catherine countered. They both laughed at the contrast, Jennifer in jeans and a sweater while Catherine was in her basic black with a knotted string of pearls. They worked together in the kitchen, Jennifer tossing the salad while Catherine sautéed the fish, then they carried their plates to the balcony.

"Padraig was the one who threatened Peter," Jennifer said as soon as they had begun eating. Catherine looked up abruptly but said nothing.

"He didn't make a big deal out of it. Just tit for tat because Peter was making insinuations about him. But I think Padraig was lying when he said he just happened to come across the information. I think he's been digging."

Catherine's fork dangled in midair. Jennifer gave up all pre-tense of eating. "I suppose I knew that he was a braggart and a philanderer. In a crazy way, that's part of his appeal. But I never guessed how much it would hurt. I know he's lying about the blackmail. And I'm tired of his explaining everything away with his damn phony blarney. I'm not casting a movie. I'm trying to put together a life."

Now Catherine set down her fork. "There was something I was going to get into later. But we're talking about it now, and I don't think either of us is very hungry."

"Oh God, is it bad?"

"It's about your husband, and it isn't good. I'm afraid you're going to hate me."

"You? You're involved?"

"We've both been taken in," Catherine said, "by the same damn phony blarney."

They left the balcony and went inside to the den that was a cross between an art gallery and a library.

"I'll fix a drink," Catherine offered as they passed the bar.

Jennifer shook her head. "No thanks."

"You're going to need it."

"Scotch, then," Jennifer decided.

Catherine laughed. "We've both picked up your husband's lousy habits."

She began by explaining her plan. She had become convinced that O'Connell was a schemer, desperate for money, and that he had married Jennifer with money in mind. Jennifer bristled but continued to listen while her sister once again linked Padraig to the auto accident. "It was inescapable to Peter and obvious to me. We both felt you were in real danger. That's why we stopped pressing for the marital agreement, and why we decided to give Padraig another source of revenue. We put up the money he needed so he wouldn't have to get it from you."

"Did it ever cross your mind that I might want to share my money with my husband?" Jennifer interrupted.

"It crossed my mind every day. And I kept telling myself that it wasn't my business. But we weren't going to let him break the company, and we didn't want him to end up breaking your heart. It seemed like something we had to do."

"You and Peter?"

"No. It was my plan. Peter didn't agree with it. He didn't want you hurt, but he thought our butting in might hurt you even more."

Catherine went on, explaining how she had gone out to Hollywood to help launch the new partnership. She spent the best part of an hour detailing how they had worked together to pick the half-dozen projects they would work on, and to sign up the support they would need. "It's an exciting business, and Padraig's name is prime capital. It could be a great success."

Jennifer was nodding. Padraig had told her all that. She was thrilled that he could be a help to Pegasus and still do his own thing. She didn't see any bad news.

Catherine gathered up their glasses for a refill. "There's more. A lot more, I'm afraid."

She told her sister how eagerly Padraig had agreed to a reorganization that put more money in his hands. "Leprechaun, he wants to call it. Leprechaun Productions." And how happy he had been to parade his wife's sister before potential backers and associates. It was obvious that his only interest in the Pegan sisters was as an almost boundless source of funding. He had even implied that two bed partners might bring in more money than one.

"So, I decided to have him followed," Catherine said. "Was he the loving husband you deserve or the self-centered bastard I was seeing?"

"I don't think I like where this is going," Jennifer interrupted.

Catherine agreed. "I could stop right here with just a word of advice."

"No, you can't. Not when you've gone this far."

"He went straight to some movie-star wannabe. I have full reports on the whole lurid scene."

Jennifer caught her breath. "You bitch!" she finally managed. "You have no right."

"I have a right to find out whether the person I'm funding can be trusted, or whether he's a lying cheat. And I have a duty to make someone I care for see what she doesn't want to see."

Jennifer was breaking into tears.

"There were pictures. They turned my stomach. All I could do was burn them."

Jennifer rushed at Catherine and began swinging and clawing wildly. "You took my husband from me. You ruined my marriage. . . ."

Catherine fended off the attack and then grabbed Jennifer's hands. "I didn't take your husband. I showed you that you have no husband. Padraig O'Connell doesn't love anyone except Padraig O'Connell."

Jennifer stopped flailing, letting her hands and arms be captured. Then she fell against Catherine's shoulder, sobbing uncontrollably. The two sisters hugged and rocked in each other's arms, Catherine's makeup running in dark streaks down her cheeks. "I'm so sorry," she kept repeating, an apology that Jennifer finally acknowledged with a nod.

"I'd like to leave now," she said when she was able to pull out of the embrace.

"Stay for the night. You're too upset to be home alone."

"I'll get more upset if I stay here and keep looking at you."

"I know . . . I did something terrible. But I had to find some way to make you see him for what he was. Please don't hate me so."

"Not you, him! I want to tell him I know and see what kind of funny Irish explanation he'll come up with. See if he has the balls to call me 'darlin' ' with his mischievous little smile."

"Just get a lawyer and be rid of him," Catherine advised. "I'll get even for you. I'll put that bastard through so much hell—"

"No! He's my problem, and I'll take care of him," Jennifer said in a tone that invited no discussion. "What I'm wondering is how I'm going to take care of you."

"Jennifer, if there had been any other way, I never would have done this to you."

Jennifer sneered. "Oh, I'm sure of that. But why is it, Catherine, that every time I find happiness, you're the one who takes it away? Why are you always the cloud that appears just in time to rain on my parades?"

ELEVEN

THE ENVELOPE was postmarked from the New York City main post office on Thirty-third Street. Plain brown, nine by twelve, fastened with a metal clasp, glued, and then taped over with cellophane tape. The address had been hand-printed with a felt-tip marker.

Jennifer fingered it before tearing it open. Inside, there were two cardboard stiffeners protecting half a dozen black-and-white prints. She pulled back in shock. Padraig, buff naked, was stretched on top of a dark-haired woman with a voluptuous figure. Jennifer couldn't believe her eyes, but then again, there was nothing here that Catherine hadn't told her about. It was just that the graphic evidence was much more jarring.

Cautiously, she pushed the picture away and saw the second photo. This time it was the back of the woman, who was now sitting atop a man. Jennifer couldn't see either face, but there was no mistaking Padraig's elaborate headboard.

Then a repeat of the second photo, only this time with Padraig's face visible. His eyes were open and he was smiling broadly. She could almost hear him making one of his outrageous jokes. He liked to talk during sex.

The next two photos had the lovers in various poses that might have been cut from a porno magazine. Padraig's face appeared in one, and the other showed the telltale headboard. The woman's face couldn't be seen, but Jennifer didn't really care who she was. In fact, she didn't want to know.

But then came the final picture, the one she knew she was

really meant to see. The woman had turned in the bed as if about to get up and had been caught naked, staring full-face into the hidden lens.

It was Catherine.

Jennifer let the photos fall onto her desk and sat staring into space, the final image still burned into her eyes. She glanced down and scanned the evidence. Now she could recognize her sister in each of the pictures: her hair, the taper of her shoulders, the wasp-thin waist. Her sister romping with her husband, to the obvious delight of both. Her husband bathed in pleasure beyond what he had shared with her. They went well together, two celebrities in love with their status and sharing it in the public eye. Two stars high above the world, making love in a way that normal earthbound people could only imagine. Jennifer felt like an outsider gawking into a magazine that embraced the lives of the rich and famous. She felt rage but with an aftertaste of envy. She felt betrayed but also cut out, as if she had been dismissed and sent back to her less glamorous surroundings.

Carefully, she reordered the prints, slipped them between the cardboards, then closed the clasp. She walked as steadily as her shaking legs allowed down the hallway to Catherine's office.

Catherine was at her desk, editing a document, while a secretary bent over her shoulder. She glanced up at the interruption, caught her sister's cold glance, and dismissed the secretary. Neither of them moved until the girl had closed the door behind her.

Catherine started to get up, but Jennifer bounded toward her and tossed the envelope on her desk. "This morning's mail," she said, then stood and waited while her sister glanced up from the envelope to Jennifer, then back to the envelope. She opened it carefully and slid the photos out.

She recognized herself even in the first photo where her face was hidden. "Oh my God" was the best she could manage. She looked up at her sister with fear in her eyes. Then she started, "Jennifer—"

"Look at the others," Jennifer ordered. "They all do you justice."

Catherine fingered her way through the prints. When she got to the final picture, she let her face fall into her palm.

"No wonder you burned the pictures. You certainly didn't want me to know just which Hollywood wannabe Padraig was with. Or were you just shy about posing in the raw?"

"Jennifer, there were no pictures. I just made that up. I had no idea someone was actually taking pictures. But it proves what I said last night. He wanted the money and then he wanted me." She gestured to the prints in front of her. "I don't know, but maybe he hired the photographer so he'd be able to keep me paying. Blackmail, in case I ever wanted to cut off his funds and get out of his business."

"What are you saying, that he drugged you and dragged you into bed for a photo session?"

"Of course not."

"Good, because I wouldn't believe you. You seemed to be having too much fun."

Catherine nodded. "No, I wasn't drugged. I wasn't even dragged. I just wanted to know whether he would betray you for money, and I learned that he would. Maybe it's good that you've seen these, because now you know the truth. He's a bastard, Jennifer. What he saw in you are the same things he saw in me. Dollar signs!"

"I don't believe that!" Jennifer screamed in a voice loud enough to earn glances from the secretaries outside the glass door.

Catherine simply gestured to the pictures. "Isn't this enough proof?"

"It's more than enough proof of how much you hate me. How in God's name could one sister climb into bed with the other sister's husband? Were you jealous that the movie star picked me instead of you? Or is it that you just can't stand to see me happy?"

"What are you going to do?" Catherine asked.

Jennifer couldn't wait to answer. "Send these to Padraig. I want to hear whatever ancient Celtic spell he uses to get out of this."

Catherine's eyes lowered. She wasn't sure there was anything more to say. But Jennifer kept talking, her voice becoming more ominous with each word. "And then I'm going to get back at you, sister dear. I'm not sure exactly how, but it will be your worst nightmare. This time you've gone much too far."

"Sweet Jesus, you're merciless," Padraig said as soon as Catherine came on the line. "Private detectives and lurid photographs? Did you have to grind the poor girl down into the dirt?"

He had just received the photograph in the mail, along with a terse note from Jennifer.

> If this is really you, could you autograph it for my photo album.
> Your fan, Jennifer.

He had cringed at the image, which made him look heavier and older, and then tried to figure out how it had been taken. The view was through the sliding glass door at the side of his bedroom. He was on his back in perfect profile. She had been caught looking into the camera.

The photographer, he reasoned, had somehow climbed up onto the deck from the beach side, then gone around to the bedroom window. It was embarrassing to think of what else might have been photographed, and to see how ordinary he looked making love. The movie scenes of him slipping under the sheets with a naked nymph implied an ecstasy that he found lacking in the photo.

"I didn't bring the photographer. I thought that was your idea," Catherine said.

"Mine? Now, why in hell would I want pictures of one of my more shameful moments?" he countered.

"Maybe to blackmail me. You could threaten to show them to Jennifer."

He groaned in exasperation. "Then why would I send the pictures to her? Wouldn't showing them to Jennifer make them rather useless?"

Catherine was suddenly speechless. Then she asked, "Well, who then?"

"I don't know," he answered. "I'll have to figure that one out. But in the meantime, exactly what am I supposed to say to my wife?"

"As little as possible. Just agree to a quiet divorce and don't quibble about the property settlement. I'll be bringing more than enough to the partnership."

"But I have to explain to her," he protested.

"The picture explains everything," Catherine answered. "And if you get into one of your witty Celtic moods, she may take a pistol to you. Be particularly careful not to call her 'darlin'.' She told me that would really enrage her."

Catherine set up a schedule of weekly trips out to California, where she spent long days touring the industry. She sat through the casting meeting for a movie about a boy and his dog, a wholesome family picture that would get maximum satellite distribution. "How in hell do you interview a dog?" she demanded during the lunch break. She looked at the camera work of cinematographers who might shoot a moody story about an older man obsessed with a much younger girl. She was introduced to new faces who might be ready to make the jump to stardom. She dined with agents until she could almost predict their pitches. On each trip, she stuffed her bag with scripts that Padraig thought were worth considering.

On most trips she slept with Padraig, who seemed fully recovered from his disastrous breakup with Jennifer. "Am I on *Candid Camera*?" he asked one night as he was slipping out of his briefs. He made a great show of pulling the shades and drawing the blinds. "Is this thing bugged?" he wondered on another occasion before using his bedside telephone.

"This is really a wonderful arrangement," he admitted one morning while Catherine and he were sharing coffee on the deck. "Money, power, and sex, neatly served in a spectacular chafing dish. Brought from New York to my bedside every week."

"Just don't do anything to spoil it," Catherine warned him.

Padraig knew that the warning was to be taken seriously. That was the bitter herb that came with the chafing dish. Catherine had taken control of the venture, reserving the more important decisions for herself. At times it seemed that she was purposely humiliating him. She had forced him to back away from a commitment to an industry mogul known for his vast ego. The man could make stars fade very quickly for less brazen insults to his power. She frequently overruled him at meetings with his associates, leaving little doubt as to who was in charge. At first she had been the surprisingly knowledgeable ornament on his arm. Now he was becoming a decorative scalp hanging from her belt. He had protested several times, but she had dismissed his complaints as silly pouting. And she had reminded him of the facts. They were further along than he ever would have been on his own. The profits would soon be pouring into Leprechaun Productions.

Jennifer's recovery wasn't nearly as quick or as painless. She decided to leave Padraig and began divorce proceedings. She plunged back into her work with an energy that bordered on insanity, arriving early, leaving late, and eating a packaged lunch at her desk. She cut off social contacts with her staff, appearing at meetings through a private door and disappearing the moment that the business was completed. Her secretary generally returned calls from Catherine and Peter, acknowledging that Jennifer had seen the memo, studied the proposal or whatever was involved, and that her comments would be forthcoming.

Peter, who had only suspicions about the relationship between Catherine and O'Connell and no knowledge of the damning photographs, was clearly worried. He had tried several approaches to forcing meetings with Jennifer and had always been put off. He had tried to talk to her during the legal exchanges of her divorce when her stock ownership was at issue. Again there were only notes, and most of these from her lawyers.

"How much of this was my fault?" he asked Catherine while they were having lunch together.

"How could it be your fault?" she responded.

"I'm the one who had the security people investigate the accident. I guess you could say that I was the one who tried to implicate O'Connell. And then I told her that her husband had tried to blackmail me."

"You never accused him."

"No, but I didn't deny that it had been him. So it was pretty obvious whom I was talking about."

He suggested that it might be best for Jennifer if they pulled out of their corporate partnership with O'Connell. Catherine reminded him they had a great deal invested.

"I'd just as soon write it off as a loss and get Padraig O'Connell out of our lives. It can't be easy on your sister to have us arm in arm with a man who treated her badly."

"A loss?" Catherine seemed shocked. "Do you have any idea how much effort I've put into this? We're going to be very successful as producers. And we're going to bring the whole damn industry onto our satellites. I'm not writing it all off as a loss."

When he finally succeeded in cornering Jennifer in her office, he faced the issues head-on, first with an apology for his part in the strain on her marriage.

"As it turns out, you were probably right," she answered with little fanfare. He was surprised to see that she seemed to have accepted that Padraig was behind her accident.

Next he had attorneys study the deal between Pegasus and Leprechaun. He wanted to find a way for Jennifer to participate without having to deal with her soon-to-be ex-husband.

"Just get us out of it, Peter," she said. "I can't work on a project where his name is going to keep coming up."

That, he agreed, was his thought as well. But, as he explained, the organization put Padraig and Catherine in control. Peter could take back his interest, but they could go on and hold Pegasus to all its financial commitments. "We need the business, or something like it, so I'd rather get Padraig out than take ourselves out."

"But Catherine won't go along with you?" she asked, suggesting that the cause of his dilemma was her sister.

"Not yet. He's the only industry insider in the company. She feels that we still need him."

Jennifer leaned back, smiled for a moment, and then fell into a sadistic laugh. "First she takes my husband," Jennifer said, shaking her head in disbelief, "and then she flaunts him in front of me."

Peter defended Catherine. Her ties with Padraig, he explained, had started because he would have gone on taking Jennifer's money. "It was all to protect you. That was her concern—"

"She has some photos she might let you see, Peter. They'll clear up your delusions. This isn't about business opportunities or saving me from myself. This is about the war between my sister and me."

Peter had long been aware of the rivalry between the two. In their personal lives, it kept them from being best of friends, but then sisters seldom were. In their business commitments, it was healthy, as each tried to score the important contributions. His contribution had been to remain scrupulously neutral between them.

But now he saw something deeper. The rivalry had spilled over into hostility. He remembered when Catherine had first suggested her own involvement in Padraig's production company. Had he been naïve to think that she was concerned for Jennifer's well-being? Had he overlooked that she might be trying to reclaim her star billing and her place in the spotlight?

Was he now making too little of Jennifer's lonely brooding? There was no doubt that she hated O'Connell. And, to Peter's mind, with good reason. He had tried to kill her, and once his money was secured from other sources, he had basically abandoned her. Just as Catherine had predicted, he had bitten hard for the money. But he was also sensing a burning jealousy of Catherine's glamour and success as Jennifer fantasized the worst possible motives for her sister's actions. The breakup of her marriage had been a tremendous shock. Had it pushed her beyond reason?

He had a quiet meeting with Catherine just as she was leaving for a West Coast flight. "I want you to reconsider my suggestion that we sever our relationship with O'Connell."

She started to respond, but he held up his hand. "I know you have good business reasons for keeping him aboard. And I appreciate that you've put a great deal of work into it. But I think we have to consider what it's doing to Jennifer. I'm alarmed at how much she blames you for the breakup. She thinks you stole her husband and that you're flaunting him in front of her."

"That's ridiculous," Catherine snapped. "You know why I had to get involved in Hollywood."

Peter nodded. "I know, but I have to give priority to what Jennifer *thinks* your motives were. She's been knocked down, and she's not making any effort to pick herself up."

Catherine glanced at her watch. "This isn't a good time, Peter. I'll be back on Sunday. We can talk on Monday." She started away from him toward the elevators.

"Catherine!"

She stopped and waited until Peter had caught up with her.

"Jennifer mentioned some pictures you have. Are they important?"

She answered instantly. "They're pictures that show just what a philandering prick Padraig O'Connell is, and why I'm going to take such delight in nailing his skin to a wall."

In California, Catherine went straight to O'Connell's office, stopping to admire the new furnishings in the lobby and the new receptionist behind the curved glass desk. He was on the phone when she reached his private office, well into the lyric cadence of an Irish poet. He gestured her into a simulated director's chair made of chrome bars and black cushions, and swiveled his back to her. Then he went on chatting while she cooled her heels.

After a few minutes, Catherine stood, walked to the bar, and poured herself some of Padraig's favorite Scotch. He gestured wildly, indicating that she should fix one for him, and she took down a second glass, scooped in the ice cubes, and topped them generously. She walked up behind him, listened for a few seconds to his half of the conversation, and then poured the drink over his head.

"Jay-sus!" He flew up out of the chair, wiping furiously at the alcohol and ice cubes sliding down his shirt. "Jay-sus Kay-ryst," he screamed, forgetting he was on the telephone. And when he remembered, he made an excuse about spilling water all over everything and slammed down the handset.

"Have you gone crazy," he screamed at Catherine.

She walked casually back to her chair. "Don't ever turn your back on me, Padraig. And don't ever keep me waiting as if I came in to take dictation."

"That was Irving Simmler I was talking to."

"I don't care if it was Moses himself. And you can drop the brogue. We're alone."

He pulled off the tie and began unbuttoning the drenched shirt. "I think you've gone stark raving mad."

"Who did the remodeling?" she demanded, ignoring his charge.

"Rooks. Rooks, Limited."

"From Rodeo Drive?"

"Yes, from Rodeo Drive."

"And the furniture?" Catherine persisted.

"Why in God's name do you care? Are you planning on redecorating your hotel room?"

Catherine laughed. "Let me guess. Harry Chaplin?"

"It just happens it was. How did you know? More detectives, I suppose."

"I just guessed because he's the most expensive. And because all the other tycoons are using him. How much of our money did all this set us back?"

"A pittance, next to what you spent decorating that cathedral you work in back in New York."

"We should have talked about it." Catherine paused to sip her drink. "We want our investment going into material and talent, not into your delusions of grandeur.

"People don't invest serious money in a hovel," he argued.

"I did," she countered as she reached into her briefcase and drew out the scripts she had been reading. She moved smoothly into the business at hand, carelessly tossing the scripts she didn't like onto the floor and stacking those she had judged worthy of discussion on the desk.

They spent Saturday aboard a studio head's yacht, sailing out to the islands. Catherine held court in the shaded cockpit under the blue canvas dodger. She was striking in a white bikini under a white denim jacket, and witty as she quoted the worst lines from the scripts she had read. She turned her attention to Padraig only when she needed her drink refreshed.

"I'm not your houseboy," he protested when they were back on dry land.

"Don't be so sensitive," she teased. "You'll get your reward back at your house."

He was in a better mood in the morning when he roused himself and joined her out on his deck. "You were extraordinary," he said, kissing the top of her head as he passed.

"The best you've ever had," she answered.

He looked thoughtful as he poured his coffee. "Well, there was this fifteen-year-old girl on Capri who was really the best, but still, considering your age . . ." They both enjoyed a laugh.

But tempers flared as soon as they got back to business. She pointed out that he was overbudget, and he answered that he couldn't care less. Then he raved about the potential of one of the screenplays only to have Catherine veto it out of hand. He reminded her that he was supposed to have full artistic discretion, and she reminded him where the money came from.

Her parting shot was an order that he get rid of his new receptionist.

"Like hell I will. She does a fine job."

"Better than the fifteen-year-old on Capri?"

"Damn you," he shouted.

"Take her sailing. Or bring her here, for all I care. But get her out of our office."

"It's not *our* office. It's *my* office."

"Check the rent receipt," she said. "And be thankful that I let you keep the furniture."

It was after midnight when Catherine reached her apartment building. She smiled wearily at the doorman who helped her out of the limo, and checked with the concierge for messages. The elevator up to her penthouse seemed to take forever. She fumbled with her key and let herself in. The security-system switch was in her foyer and she went directly to it.

"Damn!" It wasn't set. Her housekeeper must have forgotten when she left for the weekend. Catherine set it carefully, promising herself to leave a scathing note for Inga. She went upstairs to her bedroom, discarding her jacket across the back of a chair and stepping out of her skirt. She reached for the light switch but was stopped by a sound behind her—a stir in the air, a footfall on the soft carpet. She didn't have time to turn before an arm locked around her neck.

The powerful hook snapped her backward, lifting her feet off the floor. She started to scream, but a rubbery hand clamped across her mouth. She twisted violently but couldn't break free. She was being carried, her spike heels dragging, across the bedroom toward the French doors that led to her balcony.

The hand left her mouth, and she gulped down air. But before she could scream, the arm tightened around her neck. She heard her own gasping and the gurgle of air in her throat. Then she heard the click of the latch and felt the blast of air as one of the

French doors was opened. As she struggled, she caught glimpses of a few stray lights in the skyline and, through the bars of the railing, the dark path of the river forty stories below.

She raised an arm and fired her elbow. A man's voice winced, but his grip only tightened. A second stab with her elbow brought an angry groan. But she was already out on the balcony and could feel herself being twisted toward the rail.

She got a foothold on the brick deck, raised a knee, and stamped down with the spike heel that she was still wearing. She felt it crunch through her attacker's foot. He struggled to swallow his scream. His grip slackened. Catherine aimed another elbow and spun out of the grasp.

She caught a quick look at him. A black ski mask with two eyes squeezed shut in pain. A black shirt. Incongruous white Latex gloves. Tall, half a head higher than she in her heels. Fit. He seemed to be all shoulders and arms. Catherine ran through the open door and tried to slam it shut behind her. But he had recovered enough to block it with his hand and was pushing through after her. He snatched the collar of her blouse, jerking her back. She twisted out of the blouse and flailed at his eyes with her nails. He stopped, giving her the half-step she needed to bolt out of the bedroom.

She started down the stairs, but she was still in her heels. Two steps and she was falling, grasping at the banister and then rolling down the steps. As soon as she tumbled onto the floor, she scampered back to her feet and ran for the door. One of the heels had broken off in her fall, and she staggered. This time the hand clutched into her hair.

Catherine wheeled and swiped again with her nails. He let out a shrill scream. For an instant, the man was on the defensive and that was when she drove her knee into his groin. He toppled backward, immobilized. Catherine broke for the door.

She was working the lock when he caught up to her again. He grabbed her arm and spun her away from the door and back into the living room. She saw the windows ahead, with the glass doors out to the lower balcony, and knew she couldn't flee in that direction. Then she remembered the service door.

She ran into the kitchen, managing to scream, hoping that someone in the two apartments below would be awake. He was right behind her, his hand touching her back as she hobbled on the broken shoe. Catherine reached for the door but he had her again, this time with a hand on each of her shoulders. Again she stabbed down with the spike heel but this time she missed her mark. She was spun around and flung back against the door. The hands left her shoulders and locked around her throat. With grunts of rage, her attacker began slamming the back of her head against the door frame.

She punched and kicked, hitting and missing, but the hands at her throat grew stronger. She was choking for air and stunned by the blows to her head. Her screams had been cut off and her only sound was a rattling deep in her throat. She got one hand up between his arms and scratched at his eyes. He jerked his head back, but not far enough. Her beautifully manicured thumbnail stabbed into his eye. The man screamed and fell back away from her.

Catherine turned to the door and snapped open the deadbolt. She was fumbling with the chain when his gloved fist exploded against the side of her face. Her knees buckled, and nausea filled her stomach. She felt herself sliding down the wall and fell dizzily into a heap.

His arms were under hers, and she realized she was being dragged across the tile floor. She told herself to fight, but her limbs were paralyzed. She tried to scream, but her mouth wouldn't respond. They had reached the kitchen doorway and he was lifting her to her feet when the telephone rang.

He stopped, frozen momentarily by the sound, uncertain whether it was a doorbell or maybe even an alarm. Desperately, Catherine made a last stab with the stiletto heel and felt it cut into his shoe. She pulled away and staggered back into the kitchen, where she nearly fell into the knife handles protruding from a chopping block. She seized a handle and rolled around against the counter. She held a foot-long carving knife.

The man was still in the doorway, one foot held painfully off the floor, balancing against the doorjamb. There were streaks of blood in the window of his mask. The telephone was still ringing, its urgency driving him to act quickly. He planted the wounded foot, steadied himself, then rushed forward, disregarding the knife that Catherine could barely keep raised. But as he lunged for her hand, she managed a feeble thrust toward him. Just enough to elude his grasp. Just enough to send the point of the knife through his shirt and into his flesh.

He stopped dead, as much from shock as from the impact of the wound, and stood with his one clear eye wide in amazement. In that instant, Catherine hurled herself against him. His muscles resisted, but once the point of the knife broke through, the blade slid in easily, all the way to the hilt. They stood chest to chest, almost in an embrace, a river of warm blood running down between them. Catherine didn't let go of the handle until her attacker was slumping to the floor.

She stood over him, her bloody slip plastered against her body, suddenly disinterested in the man who was dying at her feet. It was several seconds before she heard that the telephone was still ringing. She stepped over the body and took the handset from the kitchen wall phone.

"Yes . . ." She breathed.

"Miss Pegan?

"Yes . . ."

"This is security, ma'am. We have a signal that someone opened one of your locks. Is everything all right there?"

She felt the blood running down her arm from the handset to her elbow. She saw her own handprint in bright crimson. And then her violent world went peacefully blank.

Catherine awoke in her bedroom, staring up at faces she didn't recognize. She jumped with a start.

"Easy . . . easy . . ." a black man's voice soothed. "You're doing fine. Just fine."

She sat up. The man speaking to her was one of three white

coats. There was also a policeman wearing a uniform cap. Two men in suits were conversing in her doorway.

"Take it easy, now," the black man said in a singsong cadence. "We're going to take good care of you."

Catherine liked him. She lay back and closed her eyes.

"Thatta girl! It's just routine. Everything's fine."

She trusted him completely.

Her hospital room was chaotic. Jennifer and Peter were at the bedside, both trying to assure her comfort. Jennifer held a cup of ginger ale, slipping the straw into Catherine's mouth at every opportunity. Peter had the bed control and kept raising the head and adjusting the knee level. There were two detectives at the foot of the bed, waiting for permission to pounce with questions. Next to them were two doctors who were debating the entries in her chart. A nurse on her left was pumping air into a cuff that was squeezing her arm. In the background, uniformed policemen were milling about. They were checking everyone coming in and out of the room, even the candy stripers who were trying to deliver magazines.

Catherine was badly battered. Her right eye was black and squeezed shut. Her cheekbone was swollen so that one side of her face was twice as big as the other. There were contusions at the back of her head, wrapped in a bandage that wound around her forehead. But the injuries were superficial, at least as far as the X rays showed. What she badly needed was a sedative to help her recover from the shock of the ordeal, and ice packs to stop the swelling in her face.

Her vague recollection was that she had surprised a burglar. She remembered that the security alarm inside the front door had been tripped. She guessed the intruder had fled upstairs to the bedroom when he heard her opening the door. She had gone upstairs immediately, probably following him into her bedroom so that he had no choice but to try to eliminate her.

"You never saw the guy before?" one of the detectives asked.

"I never saw him at all," Catherine answered. "Just his eyes looking out through the ski mask."

Peter objected that she was in no condition to answer questions. Then the doctor stepped in with a hypodermic, promising it would help her relax. She fell asleep within a few seconds.

The next day was more orderly. She awoke at noon to find her sister still sitting by her bedside. There was a nurse at the foot of her bed, and through the glass door she could see a policeman outside in the corridor.

"Am I going to be all right?" she asked.

Jennifer bolted up from her chair, startled by the question. "You're fine. Nothing is broken. No internal injuries. They just want to keep an eye on you for a few days, and then they'll be sending you home."

"Where's Peter?"

"At the office. He wants to be called as soon as you're awake."

Jennifer picked up the phone. The nurse came around the bed with a thermometer in her hand. The two detectives opened the door slowly and stepped in quietly.

The first shock to Catherine was that the intruder hadn't been a burglar, at least not according to the police investigation.

"He came through the front door and turned off the alarm fifty minutes before you arrived," one of the detectives told her. "But he never opened a drawer or looked for a safe. Burglars with enough experience to get through your lock and disarm the security system are usually in and out in five minutes."

"So?" Jennifer asked on behalf of her sister.

"So, it's most likely that this guy was waiting for you."

"Why?" Catherine asked.

The detectives looked to each other and then one of them volunteered an answer. "We think he came to kill you. The physical evidence shows he was waiting in your room. And you told us he dragged you out onto the balcony. If he was just trying to escape, all he had to do was hit you over the head."

Catherine was bewildered and looked to her sister for support.

"Have you ever seen this man?" When Catherine turned back to the detectives, one of them was holding a copy of a photograph. The man, leaning into the camera like an actor's photo in a theater lobby, was strikingly good-looking. Blond hair brushed softly back from his forehead. Piercing, animated eyes. A smile that was both serious and frivolous. Perfect teeth, each one precisely capped by a master.

"Not that I remember," Catherine said.

One detective scribbled notes. The other went on with the questioning. "Will Ferris is his name. Does that ring any bells?"

Catherine was still examining the photo. She shook her head.

"He's an actor. Song-and-dance man. You're involved with the theater, aren't you, Miss Pegan?"

"Yes. Legitimate theater and movies."

"And you never came across him in casting calls?"

She refocused on the photo and again shook her head.

The detective turned to Jennifer. "Does he look familiar to you, ma'am?"

Jennifer shrugged. "Well, vaguely familiar. But I don't know where I would have seen him."

"How about the downtown rehab center?" the policeman went on.

Jennifer recoiled. "The rehab center? I went there after my accident. To swim and exercise my leg."

He handed her the picture. "Take your time. Did you know him?"

Jennifer studied the picture. The detectives studied Jennifer. Catherine looked from one side to the other.

Jennifer shook her head. "Maybe, but I can't be sure. There are a lot of temps down there. He certainly wasn't one of my trainers."

"How about the Peachtree Restaurant?" the detective pressed. "It's near the rehab center. He was a waiter there." He centered the picture directly in front of her.

"I had coffee there in the mornings. But I don't think I ever saw him there. As I said, he's familiar, but I can't place him. I'm positive I never spoke to him."

The detective leaned in closer. "Not even in your elevator?"

Jennifer was startled.

"He lived in your building. He had an apartment on the second floor."

Her hand went to her mouth. She looked from the detective back to the picture and then turned her eyes to her sister. "I can't believe it. Honestly, I don't know this person."

The detective kept his eyes riveted on Jennifer. Then he nodded and put the picture back into the envelope. "Look, there were a lot of places where you could have seen this guy. If you remember anything specific, give me a call, okay?"

She nodded.

He turned back to Catherine. "We're pretty well convinced he was hired. He put ten thousand dollars into his checking account two weeks ago. He had no acting jobs, and he was working for tips at the restaurant and at the rehab center. So he came into some quick money."

"Ten thousand dollars? He would have killed me for ten thousand dollars?" Catherine was insulted that her life could be bought for such a paltry sum.

"His balance had been bouncing around between a hundred dollars and one-fifty. Ten thousand dollars would have looked like a fortune."

Peter arrived shortly after the detectives left, expecting to find Catherine in a fog from her sedatives. Instead, he found her angry that someone had hired an amateur to kill her. She and Jennifer explained the evidence pointing to a hired killer. Jennifer was still flabbergasted by the fact that the assassin had lived in her building. As he listened, Peter's mood grew darker. He was snarling by the time the women ran out of information.

"Have they figured out who's responsible?" His tone indicated that it was no mystery to him.

Catherine shook her head and shrugged. Jennifer said, "Right now I think I'm the prime suspect."

"No one has mentioned Padraig O'Connell?" There was disgust in his voice.

"Padraig? He's in California," Catherine said.

Jennifer's eyes narrowed. "Peter, what is it with you and

O'Connell? He's a bastard, but he doesn't have the courage to kill anyone."

Peter walked around the bed, spent a moment at the window, and then turned back to the sisters. "Doesn't it seem odd that whenever one of you gets involved with him, something dangerous happens? Jennifer has a one-in-a-million accident, and then an amateur hit man turns up in Catherine's apartment." He looked at Jennifer. "He wanted your money." He shifted to Catherine. "And he wants you out of his production company. O'Connell would have been the beneficiary in each case."

The sisters glanced at each other and then back to Peter. "I don't buy it," Jennifer said. "I think"—she looked at Catherine—"I hope that I know him better than either of you. He never walks on the lawn, because he's afraid to kill the grass."

"And the man has style," Catherine joined in. "If he were hiring a hit man, he'd hire the best."

"So this is just coincidence," Peter said sarcastically. "Two sisters. Two near tragedies." They both looked back at him blankly.

"Okay, I'll see you back at our office. But do me a favor, Jennie, and get your divorce finalized. Every day that he's your heir is frightening. And as for you, Catherine, my original idea stands. Let's buy him out and be rid of him." Peter left and closed the door carefully behind him.

He was surprised when he reached his apartment late that night and found an urgent call from Catherine. He called her back at the hospital and heard her whispering into the telephone.

"Can you hear me, Peter?"

"I'll hear better if you speak louder."

"I don't want the nurses to hear me. I'm under the covers. Try to listen."

Catherine told him all the details of the interview with the detectives. She emphasized how evasive Jennifer had been when viewing pictures of her assailant. And then she laid out the improbable coincidences of the man having worked at Jennifer's gym, waited tables at her coffee shop, and lived in her building.

"How could she not have recognized the picture?"

"What are you suggesting?"

"You know damn well what I'm suggesting. Didn't you tell me that she said I had stolen her husband? Didn't she think I was rubbing her nose in it? And she told me she'd get back at me. She said I had gone too far."

"Catherine, your sister doesn't hate you."

"Damn it, Peter, we go back a long way before you were part of the family. She's always been jealous. Always hateful. I could tell you some of the truly terrible things that she's done to me. Remind me to tell you about field hockey."

Peter sighed. "I don't want to hear about field hockey. And I don't want to hear any more accusations against Jennifer."

"You asked me about those pictures. The ones Jennifer mentioned. She kept the most revealing one to send to Padraig, but I have the others. They're in my desk file drawer. The key is in the wine chiller. Peter, you have to look at them. They show me in bed with Padraig. I think they might have made her mad enough to have me killed."

"Jesus." Peter's voice sagged. "You and Padraig?"

"Someone sent them to her. I didn't know they existed until she showed them to me."

"Catherine, I don't want to see the pictures, and I think it was a terrible mistake for you to let yourself get involved with her husband."

"Maybe it was. But that's not the point. If she tried to kill me once, what's to stop her from trying again?"

Peter's patience was breaking. "I'm going to hang up now, Catherine. I don't want to hear any more nonsense about Jennifer trying to kill you." He hung up, leaving Catherine to reach out from under the covers and tap the hook switch.

Peter visited Catherine early the next morning and again refused her request to look at the photos. "I'll take your word for it," he said. "They're inflammatory. But they wouldn't change my mind. Jennifer never hired the man in your apartment."

"Then who did?" she demanded. "For God's sake, Peter, the guy lived in her building. He managed her gym."

"I'm not saying that he didn't learn about you from Jennifer, or that he might not have picked your key off Jennifer's key ring. I'm just saying that he acted on his own. I won't believe that she hired him."

"And where did he get the ten thousand dollars, out of her wallet? It's obvious, Peter. Someone paid him to kill me, and Jennifer was the only one who knew him."

When he reached Pegasus, Peter went straight to Catherine's office, retrieved the key from the wine chiller, and opened her file drawer. He took the photos back to his desk. He had a prurient moment when he saw Catherine naked and followed her through the sequence of sex. But his real focus was on how the pictures would have struck Jennifer. He remembered that at the time Jennifer had been deeply committed to Padraig still, and that she had been spending weekends with her husband. Realistically she might have wondered about his fidelity, but romantically she probably visualized him ignoring the advances of ambitious women and working late hours to get his struggling business off the ground. She knew that he had "run into" Catherine out on the Coast, and knew that Catherine had decided to invest in his business. Nothing in that scenario would have prepared her for the photos. An ambitious tart she might have gotten over. Her own sister straddling her husband was certainly cause for murder.

Most women probably would have turned their gun on the husband. But Jennifer knew Padraig's vulnerabilities and certainly understood Catherine's domineering personality. It was far more likely that her sister had offered the apple than that her husband had come up with the idea. Certainly she had gone into near shock, as evidenced by her withdrawal from her friends and her career. Was it unthinkable, then, that in her rage and humiliation, Jennifer might have thought of the fledgling actor who was desperate for a payday?

Peter could visualize the meeting. The key. The layout of the penthouse. Catherine's schedule. The housekeeper's night off. The money in untraceable cash. Perhaps even the promise of a screen test with Padraig O'Connell. Padraig wouldn't refuse, with two thirds of his company in the hands of Pegasus Satellite Services. For a rejected actor, the price was probably more than generous.

He checked the backs of the photos. As he suspected, there were no print numbers or studio identification that might lead to the photographer. Even the paper manufacturer's logo was missing. Just cheap prints that could have been processed in a closet.

Certainly they had been taken in Hollywood, where Catherine and Padraig were alone together. But the envelope had been mailed from New York's largest and most anonymous post office. Either the photographer was from New York or the person who ordered the photos had a contact in New York. There certainly wasn't much to go on.

And yet this was a career-making assignment. This wasn't just some bored husband having an affair with his secretary or a housewife cheating on a traveling husband. This was a Hollywood leading man whose physical prowess had been vastly enlarged by special effects. Everything the man did was industry gossip and a news feature on the television tabloid shows. A photographer or a detective hired to photograph Padraig O'Connell in sexual ecstasy probably would have made a few extra prints for bragging rights. He might not be able to let such a special assignment go unnoticed.

Peter would get his security people working on it. They had failed Jennifer and had fallen down on the job of protecting Catherine. But they had contacts and could quickly cover the less artistic photographers on both coasts. If he could find out who had ordered the pictures, then he could either prove his case against Padraig or learn who was really destroying the Pegasus heiresses.

Padraig phoned Catherine with expressions of concern. He pleaded the press of critical negotiations as the reason for not rushing to her bedside. But in fact he was afraid of coming face-to-face with Jennifer. He had crushed her, he knew, beyond forgiveness. The only caring gesture he could offer would be to vanish from her sight.

"I can't understand how it could happen," he said. "A penthouse with more security than Fort Knox. How did the bastard even get into the building, much less into your apartment?"

"It was someone who knew me. The police think he was hired to kill me."

"What?" he screamed, forcing Catherine to pull back from the handset. "That's deplorable. Much as I'd enjoy boiling you in oil, I can't imagine anyone hiring a killer. Do you have any enemies who happen to be Italian?"

"This isn't a joke, Padraig. Someone paid him ten thousand dollars to throw me off my balcony."

A pause, and then O'Connell burst out laughing. "Only ten thousand dollars? Your pride must be hurting more than your head."

"Padraig . . ."

He was laughing uncontrollably. "Jesus, but I never knew that hit men held sales. What do you think, darlin'? Weekend rates?"

She slammed down the phone.

Catherine left the hospital that evening. She couldn't return to her penthouse because the police still had rooms cordoned off with orange tape, and the painted outline of Will Ferris's crumpled body still decorated the kitchen floor. Jennifer volunteered her loft, offering to move out so that her sister could bring in her housekeeper and nurse. But Catherine refused, claiming she didn't want to be a bother. She knew she could never fall asleep in a place where Jennifer had the key to the front door. Instead, she took a suite at a Trump hotel and had Peter hire a security officer who sat outside in the hallway.

She kept the nurse nearby when Jennifer came to visit and

received her in the living room, where there would be a constant flow of traffic.

"You're looking better," Jennifer told her. Catherine's hand went up to her face. "I mean, it's still discolored and swollen, but your eye is open. At the hospital I could hardly recognize you."

"I look like a *Star Trek* alien," Catherine answered. "That bastard friend of yours nearly beat me to death."

Jennifer smiled and shook her head. "He wasn't a friend of mine. I may have seen him a couple of times, but I don't think we ever exchanged a word."

There was a long, awkward pause. Catherine finally spoke. "Have you forgiven me for . . . Padraig?"

"No. In all our years, that was the hardest you ever hit me. But now I'm just as mad at him. So maybe you opened my eyes. Maybe you showed me that I don't really have a husband."

"I swear, that's what I wanted to do. I just couldn't let you throw your life at a man who was using you."

Jennifer turned away. "That doesn't make me feel any better, Catherine. I enjoy pretending that he cared for me at least a little, even if it's obvious that he didn't."

"My God, you aren't still in love with him."

Jennifer smiled ironically. "No, not in love. Not after what he did to us."

"Us?" Catherine was stunned by the thought that Padraig O'Connell had done something to her.

"Who do you think hired the man who attacked you?"

"Padraig? You think Padraig hired him?"

"Well, he tried to kill me, didn't he?" Jennifer reasoned. "Isn't that what the investigators said? I keep thinking of Peter's comment. Each of us almost got killed as soon as we got involved with him. It's too much of a coincidence."

"Padraig?" Catherine asked again. The thought seemed too difficult to comprehend. Then she said, as if to dismiss the notion, "He wasn't using me. I was using him."

"Maybe that's what you *thought*. Maybe the great screen hero is smarter than either of us gave him credit for being. He used both of us. If Peter is right, he tried to kill me for the money, and when that didn't work, he got you to put up the money. And when you moved into his limelight, he decided to get rid of you."

"That's asinine!" But even as she said it, Catherine realized that it might be true. Padraig O'Connell had an expansive self-image, and she had been less than genteel in walking on his turf. He needed her, and he had clearly paid deference to her. But had she come on too fast in trying to establish her own credentials in Hollywood? Still, it didn't make sense. Why would he try to destroy his best source of funding? Certainly he wouldn't want Peter taking over her role in his production company.

When her sister left, Catherine felt exhausted and returned to her bed. But she tossed and turned sleeplessly. She had been so sure that Jennifer had finally come unstrung. Their rivalry was lifelong, always spiteful, at times fierce. She had always sensed her sister's jealousy and been careful never to push it too far. But this time she might have erred. Exposing Jennifer's husband was one thing, but injecting herself into their marriage had been a dangerous way to prove Padraig's infidelity. Until an hour before, she had been nearly convinced that Jennifer had tried to kill her.

But now she had to consider the possibility that it might have been Padraig. Peter, whose judgment she had always trusted, had no doubts. Two near deaths of the women O'Connell was involved with only confirmed the implications of the investigators' report on the auto accident. Now Jennifer had advanced the same conclusion, for different reasons. She had based her judgment on O'Connell's fierce pride. Catherine knew that she had abused that pride.

The difference, Catherine thought, was that the assailant had ties to her sister. Padraig, she reasoned, had no way of knowing a part-time actor, waiter, and gym rat who lived on the other side of the continent. How could he have hired Will Ferris? But then she remembered that O'Connell had, for a time, lived in Jennifer's apartment. Maybe he was the one who had met Ferris in the elevator. Or chatted with him in the lobby while Jennifer was busy swimming laps.

TWELVE

PADRAIG CAME east the following week when the police lines were down and Catherine was able to get back into her apartment.

"Jay-sus," he announced when he saw her face. "You look as if you're made up to play one of Macbeth's witches. Was it a baseball bat he took to you?"

She wasn't entertained. "I thought I was looking better," she said. And she was. She had the remnants of a black eye and a purple cast to her cheekbone. But the swelling was gone, and the awful green bruises had vanished completely.

He took her in his arms, hugged her, and rocked her gently. "You're a bossy lady," he whispered, "but I must say I've grown fond of you. Like a man who loves his dog even though it pees on the rug."

Catherine pushed him away, but when she saw the wide grin of his perfect teeth, she had to laugh. "I have been awful, haven't I."

"Oh, no! Don't be talking that way, lass. You're like butter melting in my mouth."

"I've been a perfect bitch!"

"That's the word I was looking for."

She pushed him into a chair, kissed his forehead, and then sat next to him. "Padraig, who could have done such a thing? It's so cold-blooded. So ghastly."

"Oh, darlin', from what I understand, all the hit men were

getting offers. Everyone wanted to see you go over the balcony rail."

"Damn it," she snapped. "Stop playing the fool. I'm frightened. Someone is trying to kill me."

He took her hand. "Sorry, love. I was just trying to cheer you up. But I'm frightened myself. All I've been thinking about is who might be behind it. And I haven't any answers. Lots of people have made my bile boil, but I never could kill anyone. I have no idea what it takes to pull a trigger."

"Or to cut a brake line?" she asked directly.

He was stunned into a rare moment of silence. Then, in a very soft voice with no trace of his brogue, "Is that what you think? That I tried for your sister and then settled for you?"

She looked away.

Padraig reached out and turned her chin roughly until she was facing him. "Don't turn away from me, Catherine, not after accusing me of murder. Put it straight. Do you really think I tried to kill Jennifer? Do you think I could ever have hired some loser to throw you off your balcony? Because, by God, if that's what you think, then there isn't enough money in the whole damn family to keep us together."

Catherine pulled her face out of his grasp. "I just don't know—"

"That's not good enough," he said, his voice hard as stone. "I've put up with your love of the limelight, and I've taken insults that I have never taken from any living person. Money, to be sure! Your damn money has made it all possible. But I've never sold out for money. The fact is that in my own perverse way, I love you. I love your talent, and I love your daring. And that buys a lot of patience, dear girl."

"Padraig . . ." She was unsure what she should say.

"Don't talk!" he ordered. "Just listen. Whatever it is that I feel for you, I know it isn't murder. So if you have any doubts, let's hear them. I'll catch the first plane out of here and the ripped-up pieces of our agreement will come to you in the next mail."

Catherine's eyes were filling, a sight Padraig had never witnessed. "Padraig, it's been awful . . . so confusing. Peter said that something terrible happened to each of us when we were involved with you. Jennifer said—"

"Peter!" He cut her off abruptly, nearly screaming the name. "That sycophant son of a bitch. What kind of spell does he hold over you and your sister?"

"He's been our friend for as long as—"

"Your friend? He's been living fat off the two of you since you were children, and you still haven't figured him out!"

"We trust him. He's looking after our interests."

"Catherine, my love, can you imagine a cozier deal than dear Peter has made for himself? He runs your company like a private fiefdom. He pays himself handsomely, and he never has to answer to the shareholders. He got his start stealing his partner's patent and made himself a big man by using your father's ideas and your money. You don't really think he wants to share all that with a scoundrel like me, do you?"

"Peter couldn't do this to me . . ."

"He could if it meant getting rid of me. Don't you see? I've become a rival to a man who allows no rivals. When Jennifer brought me into the family, her car went over a cliff. And when you bring me into the business, you nearly go over the balcony railing."

"I can't believe it."

He pointed his finger at her forehead. "Think, for God's sake. What could I possibly gain by killing you? With Jennifer, it was easy to show that I had a motive. But you're the one who's been financing me and bringing in the material and the talent. If something happens to you, then I'm partners with a man who hates me. And he and a woman I wronged are holding the purse strings. The fact is that it's in my best interests to take a bullet for you, not to drop you into the East River."

She took his hand. "Padraig, I really didn't think it was you. I thought that maybe Jennifer hated me so much . . ."

"Jennifer? Catherine, how can you think that? The woman is afraid of the sound of her own voice."

"You don't really know her. All our lives she's been jealous of me. She's done terrible things without ever losing her angelic smile."

"You're daft. If she hates anyone, it's me, and with good reason. I'm the one Jennifer would love to see come to a ghastly end, not you."

"But—"

Padraig put his finger to her lips. "Just let me finish. You and Jennifer are big girls now. You're both well educated, very experienced, and bright as hell. Neither of you needs a full-time baby-sitter, which is the only service that Peter Barnes provides. You'd both be a lot safer if you gave him a nice retirement package and sent him packing. Let Jennifer run the satellite business. And you keep finding new customers that need satellite service. Maybe then you and your sister will be able to find a way to get back together."

He stayed the night with her, and Catherine enjoyed both the security and the affection. In the morning she found him standing in the kitchen, staring down at the floor. "Can you get someone in here to scrub this place down?" he asked her. "There's still blood between the tiles." He crossed to the service door and scratched the paint adjacent to the doorjamb. "Here, too," he said. Then he turned to her. "God, but it must have been awful." He made some calls to New York agents and spoke at length with a writer that he hoped to attach to one of his projects. Then he left for the airport and caught the late flight back to Los Angeles.

Jennifer's recovery ran parallel to Catherine's. Gradually she emerged from her dark shell of silence, began spending more time with her staff, and returned Peter's phone calls. When Catherine came back to the office, wearing a scarf over her hair and dark sunglasses to hide her nearly invisible wounds, Jennifer joined her in meetings. At the regular meetings in Peter's office, she chatted over a late-day glass of wine.

Catherine brought studies that showed the increases in traffic on Pegasus III and, as a result of wider coverage, on all the company's satellites. Just handling movie reruns for cable service was filling the available channels. "If we're going to handle new film distribution," she told her sister, "we better begin planning another satellite."

She had not yet ventured back to Hollywood. She had no intention of showing her face until the last traces of her beating had vanished. But she had been in daily contact with Padraig and his staff. "We've greenlighted two films," she reported, "without any distribution agreements. We're talking to screen owners about picking them off our satellites at about half the cost they usually front to the studios."

The two sisters talked about production schedules, and when channels would have to be cleared to handle the broadcasts. Peter sat back, listened, and raised a few questions. But it was clear that Catherine and Jennifer had matters firmly in hand.

When they finished, he shrugged, indicating that he had no questions. "That's it, then." He smiled. "You have everything covered. Maybe it's time for me to take a vacation. A long vacation." Catherine remembered Padraig's diatribe against the man who had shown them how to build their business. Maybe they didn't really need him anymore. Was that what Peter was telling them?

Padraig plunged into production of the two films, laboring over the locations, set designs, costumes, and special effects, assigning the myriad of production details to his underlings. As the location for the dark drama of the man obsessed with the young girl, they chose a struggling private college in Pennsylvania, and the small backwater town that served it. The budget was minimal and the shooting schedule rushed. It wouldn't make much money, but Padraig promised that it would earn critical acclaim.

"We'll be able to sell it for a song," he told Catherine. "I think we'll bring some of the independent screens and art theaters into the fold."

The boy and his dog, on the other hand, had grown wildly from the first concept. It was to be shot in Ireland against the background of the Irish civil war. Padraig had taken over an entire village in the rolling green country of Kilkenny and was in the process of returning it to its original 1920s character. He had also leased a landmark castle to serve as the decaying manor house of the former English landowner, and bought a herd of sheep to wander over the pastures. His budget was out of control from the first moment.

Then the director had decided that any tale of Ireland had to include the land and the Church. For the land he planned overhead shots, following the hunt through valleys and across streams. "Three helicopters?" Catherine had howled when she saw the costs. "I didn't know they had helicopters in the Irish civil war." The shots of the Church had to show its intimacy with the life of the tenants, which meant that a church far removed from the village wouldn't do. "You want to move a church?" Catherine had demanded. "Don't we need some sort of permission from Rome?"

"A small stipend," Padraig had answered. "My God, woman, we can't have a proper Irish village without the goddamned church!"

As the principal photography began, a new list of expenses arrived. The stream that the horses jumped had run dry. They had to bring in water and a pump. Sheep were hard to see from the air, so cattle had to be substituted. And the dog had turned out to be less heroic than the script called for. He wouldn't run into the burning barn, so they were investigating the use of a mechanical dog, which involved engineering and programming costs.

"Jesus, Padraig, this is going to cost more than the real Irish civil war," Catherine complained. She summoned him from California to New York and suggested that he pack his bags for Ireland.

"Do we need to bring Peter back from his vacation?" Jennifer asked.

Catherine bristled at the suggestion. "Padraig and I can handle this part of the business. What's Peter going to do? Double for the dog?"

Padraig arrived in Kilkenny with a new budget and the threat of a new director if the budget was overspent. He threw himself into every detail of the shooting, amending schedules, suggesting alternatives, and trying to get the production back on track. Catherine flew over frequently for business meetings that turned into shouting matches. Sometimes she won the point, dashing one of the director's dreams. But more often Padraig was able to hold his own. "It's a moment of beauty," he said of one terribly complex landscape. "It will pay for itself in promotion stills."

When all else failed, he took Catherine to the castle and to a bedroom where he told her Edward and Mrs. Simpson had slept. "You told me it was Oliver Cromwell," she reminded him. "I never said that," he answered. "How could Oliver Cromwell have slept with Mrs. Simpson?" In the stone turret, furnished with a four-poster bed and tapestries and lighted by enormous candles, it was hard for Catherine not to believe that she was truly a princess. Padraig squeezed a few million dollars out of her by pressing her into the goosedown mattress.

Jennifer, alarmed at the overruns, found Peter sailing in the Mediterranean. "We're in trouble with the boy and his dog," she said. "It's beginning to look like the biggest overrun since *Apocalypse Now*."

"What does Catherine say?" he asked over the satellite telephone circuit.

"That epics tend to be expensive. I think she knows they're in trouble, but she hasn't figured out how to reign in Padraig."

"I can't stop them. They have two votes to my one."

"You and I can close the pipeline from the satellite company to the production company."

He hesitated. "Give me a few days to get back to you. I think I should meet with Catherine before we do anything."

After a night in the castle with Catherine, Padraig returned to the site and gave the go-ahead for a three-helicopter panorama shot. The boy would be carrying a message from one rebel leader to another and would race across a field that was to become the no-man's-land between two banks of artillery. The concept was awesome, with Great War artillery pieces belching flame and smoke while preset explosive charges tore up the meadow. There would be many cuts to the boy's face and to the barking dog, which could be staged with simulated blasts throwing mud in their faces. But for the aerial panorama, a stuntman double and a stand-in dog would run a precise path amid real explosions while the helicopters would capture the scene from different angles and altitudes.

Padraig and Catherine spent the morning in walk-through rehearsals, making certain that the stuntman hit each of his marks and that the cameras were able to follow him. They were getting ready for their airborne run-through when a rental car rolled up to the site and Peter Barnes stepped out.

Padraig nearly went into shock. "What's that bastard doing here?" he demanded of Catherine.

"He's our partner," she answered. "Don't get excited. I'll take care of him." She rushed from the rehearsal conference down to the parking area and threw her arms around Peter. "What a surprise. I thought you were in a sailboat, out of touch with the world."

"I had enough sailing," he lied. "I couldn't figure what to do, and then I heard we were making a movie."

Catherine forced a smile. "From Jennifer, I suppose."

He nodded.

"And I suppose she told you that we were overbudget?"

"She did. But she didn't seem concerned. Why do you ask? Have you spent everything we own?"

They laughed as if the money were insignificant. Catherine took his arm and led him up the slope to where the helicopters were waiting. "You're just in time," she said. "We were about to take off for a run-through on a spectacular scene." She filled him in on the details of the shot.

"Live explosives?" he asked with a hint of apprehension.

"Not now. We have to simulate the shot and see if we run into any problems. It's a final rehearsal. But you can ride in one of the helicopters. It should be exciting." They reached the gathering where Padraig was presiding. "Padraig, look who's come to join us!"

Only years of training enabled Padraig to form a genuine-looking smile. "Peter, what brings you here? Have your detectives turned up some new dirt?"

"Just looking after my money," Peter said, offering a handshake that lacked enthusiasm.

Catherine jumped in. "I told him he was about to get an aerial view of what we were doing. Can he ride in one of the helicopters?"

"Sure," Padraig allowed. There was an empty seat next to the pilot in each of the choppers. Certainly there was room for the biggest backer.

They gave Peter a windbreaker and strapped him into one of the photo helicopters. Padraig gave him a quick rundown on the setting, and what it was that they hoped to accomplish in the shot. Peter seemed more concerned with the latch on the seat belt. Then the photo crew took to their helicopters.

Padraig lifted off first, sitting right behind the director. The helicopters took their positions on each side of the long meadow. "Action," the director called into his microphone, and the stuntman broke out of a small thatched cottage and began running, pumping furiously to imitate the untrained gait of a young boy. Trailing behind him, fastened by a thin wire to his belt, came the dog.

They ran in a zigzag pattern, avoiding the lights that flared up as they approached. "Those will be explosive charges tomorrow," the cameraman explained without lifting his face from the viewer. "Wow!" Peter said in acknowledgment.

"They'll look like artillery blasts," the cameraman went on. "You see those cannons in the woods right under us. Tomorrow they'll be firing. Blanks, of course, but what you've got are the cannons firing and then the shells exploding. All hell will be breaking loose."

Peter could see the cannons, outdated artillery pieces with oversize wheels. He could imagine the close-ups that would be cut into the sequence. Men ramming in shells, then turning away as the cannon fired and recoiled. The gritty details would complement the explosive puffs and the floating smoke rings from the helicopter shots.

The running boy was exciting even in rehearsal. He had to move quickly to keep up with the pattern of the lights. When he was close to a light, he hurled himself sideways, sprawling out on the ground. The dog pulled up next to him and raced to the figure, struggling to his feet in a show of concern. It all seemed very realistic. It was easy to fill in the violent explosions that would replace the lights, and the hundreds of tight shots that would show the terror on the boy's face. Peter's only problem was imagining how they were going to get close-ups of the dog.

He also wondered about the obvious dangers. The stuntman would be running within a few feet of the explosions. A false step and he might be blown to pieces. Then there were the blank artillery rounds. His understanding was that even blank rounds fired pieces of the wax plug and hot chars from the burning powder. Was it safe to fly helicopters through a cloud of this kind of debris? And there were the maneuvers of the choppers. At the director's orders, they were dropping suddenly to ground level and then climbing rapidly. They were touching the treetops and turning sharply to soar out over the field. The possibilities of a miscalculation seemed obvious, and he could imagine what would happen to a helicopter if it lost a rotor against the top of a tree.

"Spectacular," he said to Catherine as she was helping him out of his seat belt. "This is going to be fantastic." He went directly to Padraig. "It's marvelous! I can really picture it. How can you see all this in your imagination?"

Padraig was flattered. "That's what I do, boy. It's magic."

Peter joined Catherine, Padraig, and some of the crew in an evening trip to the pub where Padraig took particular delight in holding court. "Drink up, my boy," he ordered each time he carried a bottle to Peter's table.

"I hope none of your helicopter pilots is here," Peter told Catherine, indicating the crowd of loose tongues at the bar.

"Do you want to go up again for the real shooting?" she asked.

"Not on your life. This business is a lot more dangerous than launching satellites."

"Peter?" she had to ask. "You don't still suspect Padraig of . . . hiring that thug?"

He answered as if he had been expecting the question. "Doesn't matter what I think. It's what you think. And you seem to feel that you're perfectly safe."

"I am. I know I am."

Peter took her hand. "Good! Then the only thing I have to worry about is the budget. How badly are we over?"

She began itemizing expenses. They were way over on props and special effects. Lots of the shots required dollies and cranes, and of course there were several that would use helicopters. But, on the other hand, they were a day ahead of schedule, and if they could hold to that . . .

Peter cut her off with a gesture. "A figure?" he asked. "Or a percentage?"

She pursed her lips. "Peter, this is a totally new kind of business for us. It's not as precise as the cost of building a satellite or outfitting an earth station."

"And never in your life have you not known how much you were spending," he answered. "So where are we?"

"Twenty million over. Maybe twenty-five. I really don't have the exact figures."

"Maybe thirty-three?" he asked, quoting Jennifer's best estimation.

Catherine slammed down her drink. "Okay, maybe thirty-three. As I said, I'm not a bean counter. And if that's more than you can handle, then Padraig and I will buy you out. You can stick with a business you understand and leave the more adventurous stuff to me."

He nodded slowly. "Okay. If that's your best answer. But I don't think Jennifer is in any mood to finance a Padraig-and-Catherine production. So your funding will be cut off."

Catherine swallowed hard. Her eyes blinked as she calculated the equations. So that was it. Jennifer and Peter were going to put Padraig out of business.

They started early in the morning, before the usual mammoth clouds could blow in from the sea. The morning also gave them a low sun, so the shadows of the helicopters would fall well away from the action.

"We're only going to do this once," Padraig warned his team. "What we get is what we'll have to go with. There's no money for reshoots."

Catherine looked around for Peter, hoping that he would hear evidence of her concern for the budget. But he wasn't in the gathering. True to his word, he had no intention of flying through a war zone—even a simulated one—in a helicopter.

They made a final check. Cameras loaded and powered. Buried charges connected to the sequencer that would fire them in a precise pattern. Blank rounds ready at all the cannons. Communications systems working. Padraig was satisfied. He gave the signal for takeoff.

The copters lifted, circled briefly, and then formed up. At the director's command, the artillery pieces began firing. Then the stuntman raced out of the house and started across the field. The helicopters swooped in around him.

The stuntman ran up a slope. Ahead, a charge exploded, simulating the hit of a cannon round. He darted right, leaping over the edge of the still smoldering crater, the dog yapping at his heels. Another simulated shell hit, this time closer to his right. The stuntman, who really did look like the boy he was standing in for, launched himself into the air, landed on his side, and rolled down the hill. Instantly, he scampered to his feet, looked around quickly, and then ran back onto his heading.

There were random-looking explosions in the distance, each supposedly a stray shell from the cannons that were firing and belching smoke. Then another landed in front of the boy, knocking him backward. Again he picked himself up and darted ahead, mud and turf raining down on top of him.

In the helicopters, all the cameras were rolling, one panning the landscape, another flying above the action and shooting down. The director's chopper, with Padraig aboard, was down at treetop level, ahead of the stuntman and shooting back into the action. It paused, hovering, to get the sense of the boy running toward the lens, then darted in from behind to see the dog pull up next to its fallen master. It peeled away from the action and flew to the edge of the meadow, going for a rising shot that would start close on the boy, spin around, and gradually envelop the whole countryside. When it reached height, the running boy would be simply a dot, insignificant in a landscape of devastation.

Suddenly, the helicopter shuddered. A puff of dark smoke billowed out from its turbine exhaust. The rhythmic popping of its rotors against the air turned into a steely whine. The body of the helicopter began to spin, then the craft spiraled down toward the ground.

Aboard, the pilot battled the controls, trying to get the aircraft to respond. The cameraman let go of the camera and grabbed the open door frame to keep from being thrown out. The ashen director screamed into the microphone. Padraig, pinned into the corner of the backseat, rushed into the recitation of a Hail Mary.

Catherine, watching from the ground, wasn't aware of what was happening. There were clouds of smoke puffing out from the cannons, detonations across the field, and the hellish crack of shellfire. She couldn't separate the smoke and whine of the sinking chopper from the planned catastrophe it was filming. Nor did the fact that it was falling register. It had been in the process of swooping all over the sky. All she knew was that the director was screaming into her earphones. Something terrible was happening. Maybe a camera had lost power and was missing the shot. Worse, maybe the stuntman had run too close to one of the charges. Was someone hurt? Why was the director suddenly out of control? She put her full attention to the babble of voices ringing in her ears. She didn't notice Padraig's helicopter crash into the trees.

The crews manning the cannons were closest. Most were too involved in the firing to register that the aircraft was in trouble. The few who did see it stayed frozen at their positions, too stunned to act. They watched the fuselage smash into the trees, followed by the rotors, which cut through the branches like a giant lawn mower. Then the rotors splintered and threw down a shower of shattered metal.

On the headsets a voice was screaming to stop the filming. Within seconds, a ghostly peace settled over the battlefield. The shell bursts stopped and the cannons were suddenly quiet. The two helicopters still in the air veered away. The gun crews broke from their positions and rushed to the broken body of the chopper resting gently in the trees. Catherine heard scraps of the commotion. "It's down in the trees!" Another voice, "What happened? What hit it?" Still another, "I'm at the crash site. I see the plane. I don't see anyone." Then a voice with more authority ordered, "Get a cherry picker over there. Some ladders. And someone call the hospital."

Padraig was still praying when he opened his eyes. He found himself in a tree house, with branches broken against his window. One branch had cut through the floor and looked like a houseplant standing just inches from his face. The cameraman had fallen into his lap. There was a deep scratch on his forehead and a tuft of leaves growing out of his shirt collar. Behind the houseplant, he got a glimpse of the director, who was sobbing with his face buried in his hands. The pilot was sitting upright, rapidly throwing switches on the control console. It was as if he didn't know that his mount had crashed.

What had saved them, they reasoned when they were brought down from the tree, was the superb skill of the pilot. When he had seen that he couldn't recover from the spin and that his helicopter was doomed, he had switched instantly to crash-survival mode. He had killed the engine and shut down the fuel lines, which had kept the wreckage from bursting into flames. The trees had cushioned the fuselage and harmlessly dismantled the rotors. The impact had been abrupt and had broken the helicopter into pieces, but the cabin space had remained intact.

What no one could figure was what had caused the accident. "Something hit the engine," the pilot ventured. "At least that's the way it felt." But he had no idea what it was. No one had seen any birds, but there was still the chance that one had been sucked into the air intake. They hadn't felt that they were being hit by any of the debris from the explosions, but it was nevertheless possible that a rock, blasted into the air, had pierced the skin and gone into the engine compressor. Or perhaps the engine had destroyed itself. Gas turbines were known to throw compressor blades right through the side of the craft they were powering.

Padraig thought of another possibility when he saw Peter Barnes's car pull into the parking area. "Could a rifle shot have done it?" he asked.

The pilot looked confused. "No one was firing rifles, were they?"

"None of our people," Padraig said. "But could you bring down a helicopter with a rifle?"

"Sure! A shot into the rotor control mechanism might cut one of the linkages. Or a bullet into the compressor could cause all kinds of damage."

Catherine saw Padraig's eyes on Peter, who was walking up the hill, gradually showing awareness that something must have gone wrong. "Padraig, don't even think about it. Peter wouldn't know how to fire a rifle. I don't think he even owns one."

"There better be someone who knows where he's been all morning."

"How could he hit a moving target? He's not a marksman. He probably doesn't even know how to aim."

"Well, he could hire a marksman, damn it. He's already hired an auto mechanic and an intruder. The man is a psychopath."

Peter came close enough to understand the gist of what had happened. "Is everything all right?" he asked to no one in particular. Then he focused in on Catherine. "Was anyone hurt?"

"One of the cameramen," she answered. "But it's not serious."

"Padraig, are you all right?" Peter asked when he noticed O'Connell's torn and stained clothes.

"Peachy," the actor answered. "Couldn't be better. My heart is flooded with gratitude that no one was killed. I'm not even thinking of the millions lost in the shoot and the price of the helicopter."

Peter sat down next to Catherine, across from Padraig. "What caused it? Does anyone know?"

"Just what we were discussing," Padraig said.

"Something hit the engine," the pilot filled in. "The investigators will tear the wreck apart and put it back together again. They'll have some answers."

"Perhaps it was a bullet," Padraig interjected, "fired from over there on the hillside by one of my enemies. You haven't noticed anyone around here who isn't particularly fond of me, have you?"

Peter grinned. "No one besides me. And I couldn't hit that helicopter from twenty feet away, much less than from up there on the hill."

"And I suppose you spent the entire morning in the quiet of your room?"

"Not at all," Peter answered cheerfully, knowing exactly where Padraig was leading. "I drove down to New Ross to see about chartering a boat."

Padraig, too, was enjoying the game of cat and mouse. "And did you find a suitable craft?"

"Sadly, no. I looked around the harbor, but there was nothing that I would enjoy. So I think I'll just call it a vacation and get myself back to New York."

Padraig had to cancel the rest of the day's shooting schedule and thought that they might lose as much as a week. His director was still in shock, unable to speak, much less create, and there were police and government officials all over the place. The crash of any commercial aircraft required a scrupulous investigation. The cast of extras had been recruited by the authorities to walk shoulder to shoulder over the entire field, retrieving even the most minute pieces of the helicopter. The manufacturer had set up a large tent where the parts would be reassembled. Policemen were pulling members of Padraig's staff aside for questioning.

That night, in his and Catherine's tower bedroom, Padraig broke even more bad news. They hadn't gotten all the footage they needed of the boy running through the field. The panorama was fine, but all the angles shot from the downed helicopter had been lost when it hit the tree; the camera had fallen out and broken open on the ground.

"What are we going to do?" Catherine asked, stopped cold in the middle of dressing for bed.

"Restage it and reshoot it," he answered grimly. Then he went on with a litany of problems. It would take several days to get back to their shooting schedule, and they would lose more than $100,000 each day in fixed costs. Some of the cast members had deadlines before other commitments. He would pay dearly for the privilege of holding the actors and actresses over. "We're going to need at least another five million," he calculated, "maybe as much as ten."

Catherine's eyes widened and breath escaped from her lips. "My God, that much," was the best she could manage.

"We won't need it until the end of the month," he allowed,

"but you might want to prepare your associates for the shock."

"Padraig, they might not go along with this. What do you think Peter was doing here? He came to tell me in no uncertain terms that enough was enough."

"Dammit, girl, it's your company. Who the hell is Peter to tell you that enough is enough?"

Catherine sat down on the edge of the bed. "Peter is nothing. But Peter and Jennifer together are a voting majority. I can't fire him if Jennifer doesn't go along, and I can't get any more money from him if he and Jennifer don't agree."

He bounded out of the bed and stormed in circles around the medieval room like an ancient prince whose will had been thwarted. "So what does he want me to do? Shut down the production? They've got fifty million sunk into our company, and they won't get ten cents on the dollar unless we finish this picture. There's nothing to discuss. Either they put up more money or they lose everything. It's just good business."

Softly, Catherine reminded him that it might not be just a business decision. "Peter won't lift a finger to save you, and Jennifer has good reason to get even with the both of us."

"Damn them!" he shouted. "What do they want to do? Destroy us just because we hurt their feelings? This is a great film that they'll be throwing into the trash bin."

He vented his rage for another half hour, calling on all the saints in heaven to rescue him from his enemies. He compared Peter and Jennifer to religious fundamentalists who thought nothing of smashing works of art. Most chilling, he stoked up his case for charging Peter with attempted murder. "It was me he was after. Probably hired some sharpshooter to put a few rounds in the engine."

"Padraig, please," Catherine begged.

"Where do you think he was this morning? Looking for a boat, my arse! He had a boat. He was off hiring his assassins."

Even after calming a bit, Padraig insisted that Peter had brought him down. "He'd do anything to keep me from moving in on his turf. Arrange Jennifer's accident. Hire a second-story man to take care of you. And now this! A gunshot through the engine. Do you know that the pilot told me there are usually no survivors in a helicopter crash?"

Catherine reminded him that charging Peter with murder was hardly the way to win his support for a $10 million advance. "Peter wouldn't do that," she insisted. "You're blaming the wrong person. The crash was an accident and nothing more. Now, will you stop screaming bloody murder and help me figure out how to get the money."

It was then Padraig suggested offhandedly that she might tap in to her own funds. An added interest in this one picture, or perhaps a straight loan that would earn her a fast return at good interest.

"It's not that easy," she said.

"Catherine, darlin', with all the money you have in your mattress, we're talking about pocket change."

"My own money, right now, is paying for a huge exhibition at the Met, and an air-freight service that's flying food to East Africa. I also have a batch of loans out to dance companies and orchestras. I don't keep my spare millions in a bank."

"You're . . . broke?" His voice cracked at the absurdity of the idea.

"Of course not. But I don't have an idle five million to lend to a project that my sister might throttle. Without their go-ahead, I wouldn't even borrow the money."

He winced in pain.

"Face it, Padraig, either Jennifer agrees to back us or Peter can shut us down. We're past the point where we can just walk away and do the movie on our own."

He was ashen. In the yellow light of the torches, it seemed almost as if he were laid out at his funeral.

THIRTEEN

CATHERINE AND Peter flew back from Ireland together, with drinks between them. As the plane climbed to altitude, Catherine described the scope of the film and gushed over its artistic content. "Setbacks happen," she said of the helicopter crash, "and cost overruns are part of the business." Staying within a fixed budget might please the accountants and some of the inexperienced investors. But it robbed the director of his artistic insight. "You could shoot the whole thing on a soundstage," she said in a tone that dismissed the idea even as she offered it. "But it would die on a big screen."

She praised the realism of the work. "We show the daily rushes to the townspeople, and some of them have actually cried. They tell us they're seeing the countryside they knew in their childhood. The village we've created is so authentic, one woman remembered exactly what was in the bakery window when she was a little girl." And the story line! "These people had won. They got their country back. And then they took to fighting among themselves."

During the meal service, she told Peter how effective all this was when seen through the eyes of a boy. "All he lost, and then even his hopes were dashed."

It was during dessert that Peter raised the problem of money. None of the major screen owners were committed to fixed payments. Pegasus had planned to land the film right at theaters with a satellite dish. They would show it only as long as people came to see it, so the payback was completely uncertain.

"We were going to keep cost down to minimize the financial risk," he reminded her. "Now, with all that's been spent, we're awfully vulnerable."

The next day, in their afternoon meeting, the movie venture was the first item on the agenda. The accountants tallied the amount already plowed into the company and its two films, then added in the budgeted amounts still left till completion. The smaller film would pay for itself and recover about half of what had been invested in Leprechaun Productions. The Irish film didn't have a prayer.

The recommendation was brutal. Finish the movie quickly with no further investments in sets, costumes, or special effects, then sell it to normal distribution channels for whatever it would fetch. Adding in video and television revenues, a studio could make money, and Padraig's production company might escape with a $20 million loss. According to the accountants' best projections, completing the film risked a $50 million loss. Going on with the project would make sense only if the movie took in better than $180 million.

Catherine tore into the projections, arguing that the loss would be smaller and would really be an investment in developing the new satellite-distribution business. Jennifer countered that the smaller film would give them all the information they needed about satellite distribution of movies. Peter sat in judgment until all sides of the argument were exhausted. Then his glasses came off and his fingers squeezed into the bridge of his nose.

"Personally," he said, revealing his thinking, "I wouldn't invest another dollar with Padraig O'Connell. As to the choices we've been offered, it's really a case of making a very big bet on a long shot or a much more modest bet on a contender. The latter is a better idea."

"Meaning?" Catherine said.

"Meaning that we complete the picture at minimal cost and

try to sell it. But that we bring in a new line producer to replace Padraig. Otherwise, I have no confidence that he'll complete the picture at any cost."

Catherine raged. She and Padraig would never vote to replace him, so Peter might just as well forget that idea. And she wouldn't vote for bare-bones completion. They should invest in the best picture they could make and then bet that the public would come in droves.

"That's the long shot," Peter said.

"And that's the way Padraig and I are voting."

Peter nodded. "Then my vote is that Pegasus advance no more money to Leprechaun. Which will mean scrapping the picture and swallowing the loss."

Peter and Catherine were suddenly locked in a power play. Catherine could outvote Peter on Padraig's role. But Peter, along with Jennifer, could kill the entire project. Which did Catherine want? The truncated movie without Padraig, or no movie at all?

She snatched up her things and stormed out of the office. None of the heads at the meeting dared to turn and look after her.

Peter thanked the accounting group and saw them to the door. Then he turned back and dropped into the chair next to Jennifer.

"Why not let Padraig finish it up?" Jennifer asked.

"Because I think he'll go through whatever amount we give him and be back in three weeks for more."

They were silent for a few seconds. Then Jennifer asked, "Is that the only reason? Is it just profit and loss?"

"No," he answered without an instant's hesitation. "I'd be lying if I said it was only dollars and cents. I hate the man because he tried to kill you. And if that wasn't enough, he tried to have Catherine killed."

"I don't think he did," Jennifer said.

Peter turned to face her. "You're not still trying to convince yourself that your crash was an accident?"

"No, it wasn't an accident. Someone tampered with the brakes. And the Italian police caught the guy."

He couldn't believe what he was hearing. "The police? How do you know?"

"I had to know. Was it an accident or was someone trying to kill me? I called the police inspector in Positano every day for the first week, and then a few times a week for the next several months. He never had anything to report, so eventually I gave up. But, last week he called me. They had caught a burglar trying to blow his way into a vault. The man made a deal and turned in all his associates for a lighter sentence."

Peter's eyes were narrow. He didn't understand where Jennifer was leading.

"The crook mentioned that he had cut the brakes on a car at the San Pietro Hotel. The inspector remembered me and called back to tell me that it had been no accident."

"Which is what I've been saying all along," Peter reminded her.

"Yes, but you said Padraig had hired the guy while we were traveling on the Amalfi Coast. The safecracker said that the arrangements had been made from New York."

"So what?" Peter asked. "Padraig was here in New York with us when we raised the issue of the marital agreement. That's when he made the arrangements."

"Not likely," Jennifer said. "I've been giving this a lot of thought. He couldn't have told the man where the car would be while we were in New York because we didn't know where we would be staying in Italy. How do you a hire a person to do something when you can't tell him where or when?"

Peter thought. "Maybe you just tell him what to look for. Padraig O'Connell driving a red Ferrari shouldn't be too difficult to spot. Then all the guy would have to do was follow the car to see where you were staying."

"Could be, but that's not what the safecracker told the inspector in Positano. You see, the man is actually French. And his first instructions were to get to the car in Ireland. You remember Padraig and I were in Ireland. But then we left there suddenly to come back to the States. Then, when we decided to go to Amalfi, the man was told to get to the car in Italy."

"So what?" Peter asked. He still didn't understand.

"Well, it was Padraig's idea that we go to Ireland. So why would he tell someone to kill me in Ireland, then suddenly leave Ireland before the hit man got there? Isn't it pretty obvious that whoever hired the man didn't know about our travel plans? And, of course, the one person who certainly knew was Padraig. He was making the plans."

Peter was once again massaging his nose. "Then who?"

Jennifer shrugged. "I don't know. Maybe someone who works for me. Or one of our competitors. Or maybe Catherine, or maybe even you. I have to tell you, Peter, you moved up the list when Padraig had a near-fatal accident the day after you arrived."

He nodded. There was nothing wrong with Jennifer's analysis. "Do you really believe that I would try to kill you?"

"No," she answered instantly. "Otherwise I wouldn't be sitting here with you now. No, I think whoever cut the brakes on the Ferrari was after Padraig. He was supposed to be the one driving the car that afternoon. My shopping trip was just a spur-of-the-moment thing. In fact, he had called the garage to tell them precisely when he would need the car. He even wanted it washed. No one could have known that I would be the first to drive it."

"So then the attack on Catherine?"

"If there's a connection, you'd have to look for someone who wanted to get rid of Padraig, and once Catherine joined with him, decided to get rid of her."

"And that would be me?" Peter challenged.

"Maybe," Jennifer answered. "As I said, Padraig's helicopter crash makes you a prime suspect. But it could also be someone out in Hollywood who has it in for Padraig. His enemies are a cast of thousands. Or I could be the one who went after Catherine and then Padraig. No matter who cut the brakes on the Ferrari, I would certainly have reason to get back at my dear sister and my soon-to-be ex-husband."

"Well, you can put your mind at ease," Peter said. "I didn't try to kill anyone."

Jennifer laughed. "That's what you'd have to say. I didn't try to kill anyone, either, but of course that's what I would have to say. So it all gets pretty confusing. The one thing I'm sure of is that Padraig didn't cut the brakes on the car. He didn't try to kill me."

"I still don't trust him," Peter answered.

"I know," Jennifer said. "But in this decision I'm going to side with my sister. We'll go for the smaller budget and then try to sell the project. But I'm not going to kick Padraig out. Not when the only thing he might be guilty of is trying to make a great movie."

Padraig went to work immediately, not cutting his budget but trying to build a case for all the money he would need. He would cancel the reshoot of the helicopter scene immediately to show Peter and Jennifer that he had gotten the message. With more close cuts to the boy and the dog, he could make do with the footage from the other two helicopters.

But he had no intention of compromising anywhere else. Within a few days he had revised shooting schedules for the rest of his story. Then, with all the film in the can, he would go back to Peter and Jennifer with a simple choice. They could let it die or put up the additional costs for editing, sound, and the rest of the postproduction.

Catherine, who had returned to Ireland with the company's decision, balked at his plan. "They're not stupid," she reminded Padraig. "Peter will see exactly what you're doing and will cut you off at the knees. And this time Jennifer won't bail us out. She'll feel lied to and betrayed."

"I told you to fire the bastard. Without him, there wouldn't be any problem."

"Firing Peter would change nothing. It would still leave Jennifer and me equal partners. She'd still be able to vote us out of existence just by withholding funding."

"Well then, darlin'," he said, patting her backside, "I suggest you get back to New York and go to work on your sister. Because she's going to get a bill in less than thirty days, and she damn well better be ready to pay it."

"Padraig, nothing would give Jennifer greater pleasure than to have me beg her, except the joy of turning me down afterward. Jennifer hates me."

He rolled his eyes. "How could she hate you when you said yourself it was her vote that saved us?"

"She didn't save *us*, Padraig. She saved *you*. She agreed with Peter about getting out and cutting losses but wouldn't go along with firing you on the spot."

"Ah, then she still has a soft spot for me."

Now it was Catherine who rolled her eyes. "All she was doing was apologizing for having accused you of murder."

"True," he admitted. "But who does she suspect now? Our dear friend Peter?"

"Maybe, but it's much more likely that she suspects me. So if you're going to need more money, you're going to need another plan."

PART THREE

FOURTEEN

Nothing really changed as we got older. My sister and I were still bitter rivals. The only difference was that we covered it up better. We were arm in arm at openings and charity events. We leaned in close to smile at cameras. We were always pleasant in the office. Some people even commented how nice it was that sisters could be best friends. But the bottom line is that were still fighting tooth and nail. She pretended to be proud of my accomplishments, and that might have fooled a lot of people. But I knew her better.

I remember my first industry award, when Pegasus II went up. The trade magazines made me "Man of the Year." Actually, they had to change the title to "Person of the Year." No woman had ever won it before. It was no big deal. I was on the cover of the magazine, got interviewed on television, and then they awarded me a plaque at the annual banquet. Nice, but not like winning the Nobel Prize. I don't remember the name of the person who won it before me, and I have no idea who won it after me. You see what I mean. It was nice, but in the long run nobody really cared.

Except for her. It galled her that they had picked me instead of her. Oh, she didn't let on. She didn't come right out and say that her contribution was more important than mine. But you could see it in her eyes. She was sick with jealousy. So she came up with a fantastic scheme to ruin it for me.

The night before the award banquet, my dear sister collapsed at her desk. She buzzed her secretary, said she didn't feel well, then grabbed her stomach, let out a shriek, and did a swan dive right out of her chair. You can imagine the drama of it all. EMS people charged into the room with their equipment, gave her shots, put her on oxygen, and then wheeled her down the hallway while her whole staff stood watching. "She hasn't been looking well," her secretary said. Of course she hadn't. She was green with envy.

At the banquet, she was the only one they talked about. They made a big thing of playing down the award. "How small it seems when your sister is in grave danger," the MC said as he handed me the plaque. Then he went on to talk about what she meant to our industry. She ended up getting more praise than I did.

And do you know what it was? She had appendicitis! Everyday, run-of-the-mill appendicitis. A fifteen-minute operation. God, you don't even have to be a doctor to perform those things.

And then came the hypocrisy. She spent the next month telling anyone who would listen how terribly she felt for ruining my big day. And of course I had to gush with concern. How could she possibly think of my award when her very life was at issue? That's what I mean. The rivalry was as intense as ever. What was different was that we both had learned to cover it up.

Then there was the space-suit nonsense. It was a silly little thing, but it shows how vain she's always been. Even when the good of the company was involved, she couldn't stop thinking about herself.

The ad agency wanted to do something to make Pegasus really stand out, but how do you advertise a satellite service? You can't photograph the damn things. They're out in space. And you can't show the results. If you show a kid watching television, you don't know whether his show came from our satellite or a VCR. They were trying everything, even gluing wings on a horse. But nothing showed any promise.

Then they came up with the space sisters. They designed these space outfits made out of aluminum foil that we were supposed to wear. The sets were right out of Star Wars. A big air lock would open and the two of us would walk out. Or we'd both suddenly appear in a glass cylinder as if beamed down from space. Then we'd have this little dialogue about the wonders of space communications and assure the viewers that their traffic was safe and secure with *us. Sure, it was over the top. But the agency felt it was strong brand identification, like the Marlboro Man.*

Even though I felt a little embarrassed, I would have gone along with it. But not my sister. You'd have thought they wanted her to appear nude. The suit looked stupid, she said. It was too masculine. It would make her a laughingstock. No matter how many people they brought in to persuade her, she wouldn't budge. Then one of them suggested that they use a model to play her part. The agency was trying to save the idea, but I think they only made the situation worse. They should have known there was no way she'd let me be the company spokesman without her.

She came up with all sorts of business reasons. She claimed the ads would hurt our credibility if they substituted a phony sister. She knocked the whole idea as the worst kind of gimmickry. But everyone knew the real reason. She didn't want to look silly for even a second—that was her vanity—and she didn't want me going ahead without her; that was her jealousy. So the whole idea, with all the creative sketches and all the media plans, had to be scrapped. I can tell you that there were a lot of agency people who gladly would have thrown her out a window. But even then I defended her. After all, she owned half the business and was entitled to her vote. I was seething, but I never once let it show.

She covered up her feelings, too. Even when she wanted to kill me, she kept a sweet smile and a soft voice. It was like she was biding her time. I knew that her jealousy was pushing her beyond all reason. I knew that sooner or later she would explode. I should have tried to get her help, but how do you say things like that to someone?

The best example was probably the Venetian glass vase. It was a beautiful piece, about two feet tall, wide at the base and narrow at the neck, with handles on the sides like a Greek urn. While it was still being fired, the glassblower had twisted it so that it seemed to be swirling upward. The colors were extraordinary. Deep cobalt at the base spinning into purple, and then red, and the red fading into yellow. At the very top the glass was absolutely clear. You couldn't tell where the vase ended. It seemed to vanish into thin air.

Our father had seen it during one of his European business trips and brought it back as a gift for our mother. I think he paid $2,000 for it, which was the most he ever paid for a piece of art. It was pretty, and he liked it. The fact that it had been done by Antonio Serini meant nothing to him. Serini had just gotten started, and his glass was virtually unknown.

After Mother died, Dad kept it on a table in the corner of his study. It wasn't on display. No special lighting or anything. Only a vase on a table. I've already mentioned how my sister sucked up to our father. She visited him a few times a week when he was sick and kept telling him how much she liked the vase. I don't think she ever mentioned that Serini had become world-famous and that the vase was worth a small fortune. So, one evening he picked it up and handed it to her. "Here, take it," he told her. "You like it, so you ought to enjoy it." Like it was an old soda bottle or something. He just handed it to her.

It didn't become part of our father's estate and was never even mentioned in his will. He had given it to her, so it was hers. It was a beautiful piece that we both loved. In all fairness, I should have had an equal claim. And at the time, glass by Serini was going for up to a quarter million in the galleries. So it should have been part of the estate assets. I thought it was mean-spirited of her, to say the least, and downright theft if you wanted to get technical. But as I said, I had gotten very good at keeping up pretenses, so I never said a word.

Not even when she began flaunting it right in front of my face. She was giving a small dinner party for friends from the company, and there was the Serini glass on a delicate pedestal, lighted by small spots hidden in the ceiling. You couldn't take your eyes off it. It really dominated the room. Naturally, everyone asked about it, and she took great delight in showing it off and explaining how our father had come to buy it. I knew exactly what she was telling everyone: that it had been given to her because she would truly appreciate it. Her sister had nothing like it.

I should have stood up and exposed her whole dirty little fraud.

But I said nothing. Once I even had to get up and leave the room. I could feel my skin burning with anger that she would find such an innocent way to embarrass me in front of our friends. I knew people would notice and think that I was the jealous one. So I left the room to avoid an incident.

I guess I'm wandering. My point was that my sister did as good a job as I did of covering up true feelings. It must have been months after the dinner party. I had thought again and again of how she had used the vase to flaunt her superiority, but I had never mentioned my feelings; she really had no reason to be angry with me.

I was visiting her one evening and she left the room to take a private telephone call. While I was waiting, I was suddenly drawn to the vase. It was standing by itself, beautifully lighted, dominating the entire atmosphere of the room. I walked over to it, examined it, and then picked it up carefully. It was the first time I had ever touched it. I carried it across the room to hold it up to a brighter light. Just to see the full value of the color, the way you do when the sun hits a stained-glass window. I was turning it slowly, watching the color as it seemed to move upward and then disappear. I didn't realize that it was slipping through my fingers until it was falling.

I made a frantic effort to catch it. One of my hands hit it up at the top. The other almost caught one of the handles. But the net effect was that it tossed out in front of me, hit the bare floor, and shattered. It broke into half a dozen big pieces and hundreds of tiny shards.

The noise was like an explosion. My sister came flying into the room and pulled up abruptly when she saw what had happened. There were the two of us, standing on opposite sides of a pile of shattered glass, neither one of us able to speak a word. Finally, she got down on her hands and knees and began lifting the pieces, matching the broken edges as if she could put it back together again. I got down next to her and tried to help, but she pushed my hands away. And she looked at me with pure hatred in her eyes. She thought that I had smashed it on purpose.

It was an accident. A terrible accident, to be sure, but purely

and simply an accident. Naturally, I offered to pay for it. She re-
fused. Then I said I would take the pieces to a glassblower to see
if the vase could be put back together. She said it would never be
the same, which was probably true. But if it meant that much to
her, at least the basic form could be salvaged. I apologized profusely,
and she nodded but never came right out and said I was forgiven.
She never acknowledged that I hadn't broken it intentionally.

Yet she never once came right out and accused me. In fact, she
never mentioned the vase again, not to me and not to any of our
friends. She just brooded and nursed her hatred of me. Whenever
we were together, she feigned affection for me, smiled at me, and
complimented me. The way she acted, you would have thought there
was never a vase at all.

You see, she was good at it, too. She hated me. I know she
wanted to get back at me. But you never would have guessed.

It was a few months after that when she may have tried to kill
me. I can't be absolutely sure, because it may have been coinciden-
tal. Quite possibly, she had nothing to do with it. Maybe no one
planned it. But at the time it certainly was suspicious.

We were in Aspen for the Christmas festival. It was a business
trip rather than a vacation. A lot of our customers were there, and
one of the cable networks was sponsoring a big bash. Neither of us
are particularly good skiers, but we joined the evening ski run, fig-
uring on one pass down the mountain and then meeting at the lodge.
I thought we should go straight to the lodge, but she was particu-
larly insistent that we join the others on the slope. I didn't see why
it was so important, and that's one of the things that was suspicious.
She was dying to get me on that mountain.

There were at least a hundred of us who assembled at the top of
the lift, and we were all given lighted torches. It was supposed to
be breathtaking, all those flames weaving down the slope. We started
down, everyone carving wide, easy turns. My sister was somewhere
behind me. I was in my second traverse, coming to a turn at the
edge of the trail when, without any warning, the person in front of
me fell. But it wasn't a typical sprawling fall down the slope. It was
almost as if he lurched back, right across my path. His torch flew

up into my face. All of a sudden I was blinded and out of control. Instinctively, I edged, trying to stop, but someone coming down behind me slammed into me. It wasn't a mere bump. Whoever it was pushed me and sent me careening off the trail. I saw trees everywhere, and rocks sticking up through the snow. Fortunately, I had the presence of mind to fall. I hit the snow and lost speed as I slid. I plowed into a boulder feet-first, which is what saved me. Even at reduced speed, a headfirst crash probably would have killed me.

The skis were jammed tight. I couldn't pull them free, so I had to release the bindings and pull my boots out. When I stood, I felt a flash of pain in my right ankle. I had sprained it, but at the time I thought I might have broken it. I was well off the trail and down a slope. I couldn't see anything or hear anything except the wind. And then it struck me. How was I going to get down the mountain?

The person who fell in front of me must have seen me go off, and the person who hit me from behind as well. They had to know that I was in the woods. So I thought I'd wait until they came up with a snowmobile and then scream my head off. I probably waited an hour. Maybe more. No one came back up the mountain. It was night, the temperature dropping and the wind picking up. I got really frightened. If I stayed where I was, I might die of exposure. So I began climbing up the slope, trying to get back on the trail. I couldn't put any weight on my foot, and getting traction in the snow was almost impossible. I dragged myself halfway up and then slipped back down. I tried again, and again slipped back. I was beginning to get desperate. I wasn't sure I was going to make it. I probably struggled another hour, getting hysterical at times, until I got back to the trail. And still there was no sign of anyone searching for me.

I started sliding down. I was sitting on the snow, using my good foot and my hands to keep me in a straight line. But it was getting colder and colder, and my clothes were beginning to soak through. It was a slow, painful progress. To this day I don't know whether I could have made it all the way down on my own.

But then I saw the lights of snowmobiles. My sister had finally told someone that I was missing, and they were coming up looking for me. I screamed and waved, and that's how they found me. They brought me down, thawed me out, and put one of those plastic casts on my foot. No one was too concerned: Why didn't I get into some fresh clothes and catch the end of the party? I had to beg them to keep me in the hospital overnight.

You may wonder why I think my sister was responsible. There are lots of reasons. I knew she would try to get back at me for breaking the damn vase. I guess I thought she would find some way to break something of mine. But later I learned that she had been doing a lot of looking into my side of the business. So then I knew. She wasn't just out to avenge a vase. She was going to take over everything.

She was behind me, so she certainly could have been the one who pushed me. She might have paid the person who fell in front of me. And, of course, she would have had to report me missing. Otherwise she would have seemed completely indifferent. She might even have come under suspicion.

My guess is that she gave it a few hours, figuring that if I didn't make it down by then, I was probably smashed against a rock or impaled on a tree. Then she sent the ski patrol so she would look concerned and could play the distraught sister.

But, as I've been saying, we both got very good at hiding our feelings. She was at my bedside when I woke up, all worried and solicitous. She brought a couple of specialists in to make sure I wasn't badly hurt, and wanted to have me flown back to New York on a charter. You should have seen the show she put on when I finally made it back to the lodge. Her arm around me, supporting me. A pillow under my foot. Telling everyone what a narrow escape I'd had and how worried she had been. She fooled everyone, but not me. I knew that even if she hadn't planned it, she would have been overjoyed if they'd brought me down in a body bag.

We never got any closer. If anything, there was more distance between us. I knew she was dangerous, and I gave her plenty of space. The idea of two sisters who were best friends was good copy for the trade press. But it wasn't true.

FIFTEEN

JENNIFER'S DIVORCE was dragging on. The issues were simple and generally uncontested, but O'Connell's lawyer seemed to be in no hurry. He reworded drafts, insisted on meetings to review the new language, then forwarded pages to Padraig in Ireland. Padraig, pleading that he barely had enough time to finish the movie, much less read "legal mumbo jumbo," took days to respond. And then his response was generally a request for additional clarifications.

"What in God's name is the problem?" Jennifer finally demanded. "An imbecile could understand it. I keep what I brought to the marriage and he keeps what he brought. Neither of us has any future claim on the other."

"He's distracted," O'Connell's lawyer offered. He proposed waiting until the movie was completed. Then they would have Padraig at the table, and any remaining issues could be hammered out to everyone's satisfaction.

"He's shaking you down," her attorney responded, suggesting that O'Connell was dangling the divorce in case he needed Jennifer's vote for more money from Pegasus. Conceivably he could trade his signature on the divorce agreement for Jennifer's approval of further financing. Her lawyer threatened to seek a summary judgment that would impose the terms of the divorce whether Padraig liked them or not.

With the atmosphere deteriorating and the simple, no-contest divorce threatening to get ugly, Jennifer was startled to hear Padraig's voice on the telephone. "I'm in town and I can be down to your place in an hour," he said. "If you've got those damn divorce papers, I'll be happy to sign them."

"I'll arrange a meeting," she offered.

"Fook the meeting, and fook the lawyers," he said, turning on the brogue. "With all I've put you through, darlin', I'll sign any damn paper you put in front of me."

"No! I don't think—"

He cut her off. "I'll be getting into a cab right now. It won't take me a minute." The phone went dead.

"Damn it!" Jennifer snapped. She didn't have the papers. Her attorney had them. And the last thing she wanted was a useless visit from her cheating husband. She dialed the lawyer and got his secretary, who promised he would call back instantly. "Instantly" turned out to be twenty minutes.

"Can you get down here right away with the divorce agreement? Padraig is on his way and he seems to be in a mood to sign."

"An hour," he shot back. "There are still a few changes to be made, but I'll have them done right now and be there in an hour."

It seemed like only seconds before Padraig called up from the front door. Jennifer had no choice but to invite him up to her loft and hope she could keep him entertained until the lawyer arrived with the paperwork.

He seemed much smaller when she opened the door, and there was certainly less color in his face. His eyes were dead, like neglected windows, too opaque to look through. His mouth was tight, with no trace of the broad, mischievous smile. His shoulders were slumped, as if there wasn't enough spirit left in him to inflate his chest. Jennifer had never seen him look so insignificant or so crushed. She invited him in, watching him walk lifelessly into the room and settle into a place on the sofa without even acknowledging her greeting.

"There's still some of your single malt in the bar," she said, inviting him to help himself.

"Just a dash over an ice cube," he answered, expecting to be waited on.

She made his drink and then poured one for herself. She glanced at the clock. Somehow, she had to keep him involved for another forty-five minutes.

"Tell me about the picture," she said as she set the glass in front of him. "How's it going?"

He nodded. "Good. Better than you could expect, considering the hurry." He sniffed at the edge of the glass and then wet his lips. It was clear that he wasn't going to elaborate.

"And how are you?" she asked. "No more helicopter accidents. I hope?"

Padraig shook his head and sipped again. Jennifer didn't know where to take the conversation, so she joined him in his morose drink.

Finally, he looked up at her. There was a flicker of his old self in his expression. "And how are you, Jennifer? I know I nearly destroyed you, though God knows I never meant to."

Now she nodded. "Good. Pretty well recovered." This would never do. They seemed to have exhausted their conversation in just a few seconds. She needed to keep him here for her attorney.

"Padraig, for what it's worth, I know you didn't try to kill me in Positano. I heard from the Italian detective who was handling the case." She repeated the information she had received and explained how she had interpreted it.

" 'For what it's worth'?" he asked. "Don't you know that it's worth everything to me?" His eyes filled with the emotion that seemed to be suddenly exploding inside him. "What do you think it's been like, knowing that the woman I love thinks I tried to kill her? What do you think I feel doing business with the lying bastards who came between us?"

"Padraig, it wasn't Catherine and Peter who broke my heart—"

"It was the two of them that broke mine," he answered in an explosion of anger. "And now they've beaten me. All they ever wanted was to keep us apart." He shook his head in disgust. "So give me the damn divorce decree. Let me sign it and get out of your life."

"That wasn't what broke us apart, Padraig, and you know it. I never believed that you tried to kill me. Or if I did, I never admitted it to myself. It was those pictures. You and my sister. Of all the people you could have cheated with, my own sister."

"You think that was something different? You think blaming me for the car and dragging me into bed were two different sins. For Christ's sake, Jennie darlin', don't you see it was all one plan? 'Let's get rid of the stupid actor, and if that doesn't work, then let's drive him out of the family.' You think your sister couldn't find anyone else to screw her? Is it likely that with all the men fawning on her, she found me irresistible? Open your eyes, child! She didn't love me. What she wanted was to stop you from loving me. And didn't I fall right into her trap? Wasn't I the total jackass? Here I was, thinking that she was making me play the lover to get money for my picture. And all she really wanted were those pictures so she could break us up."

"You think she sent the pictures?" The notion wasn't a complete surprise. She had weighed the possibility many times. He was telling her things she already knew; only now she was beginning to see them in a different light. Before she had just followed the obvious evidence. Why wouldn't he want Catherine? Wasn't she more attractive? More fashionable? More Hollywood? But why would Catherine have wanted him? She had no shortage of admirers. She had chosen Padraig just to take him away from Jennifer. And she might have sent the pictures so that there would be no doubt about her victory.

Suddenly, Padraig made sense. Neither Catherine nor Peter had wanted her new husband in the family, much less as a partner in the business. They had tried for a prenuptial agreement and, when that failed, for a marital agreement. And when neither she nor Padraig showed much interest in who might end up owning what, they had tried to kill him. Jennifer had come to believe that he was the true target of the automobile crash. It was only afterward that her sister had taken a serious interest in producing the movies that Pegasus would distribute. That decision had put Catherine into bed with her husband. And then what had Catherine done? Had she tried to cover up Padraig's indiscretion? Had she done anything to reassure her sister? No, she had documented the seamy affair in pictures. It was even worse than that. She had hired the photographer in advance. This hadn't been an accidental moment of weakness. She had carefully planned to bring him down in full view of his wife. What other reason could there be but to destroy the marriage?

When she looked up, Padraig was pacing back and forth between the sofa and the huge industrial window that looked out onto the narrow street.

"What are you saying, Padraig? That none of this was your fault?

"Oh, it was all my fault," he answered with irony in his tone. "But it wasn't the fault that you're talking about. You think I'm guilty of lust, but my real crime was stupidity. Your sister and your partner played me out and then pulled me back in like a yo-yo. First they fix the brakes, and I'm thinking that sure as hell you're going to leave me. And then they come at me with money. More money than I ever could have raised on my own. And all I have to do is take down your sister's pants. And, sweet Jesus, didn't I fall right into it. I thought, Screw the lady so she can brag that she's had the great lover of the big screen. Who cares? I'll make my movie, and it will make money for their company, and then maybe they'll leave Jennie and me alone. But you know what? It wasn't just me, and it wasn't just money. It was hatred, darlin'. They hate me, for sure. But someone hates you, too. Someone was out to trash us no matter how much it cost."

She was staring at him, spellbound, when the doorbell sounded. Slowly, Jennifer got up from the sofa and walked past him to the intercom. "It's me, Henry," a voice said filling the room. Jennifer didn't answer. She just pushed the button.

"Henry?" Padraig asked.

"Henry Harris," she responded. "The lawyer handling my—our—divorce. He's bringing over the document you wanted to sign."

Padraig nodded. Jennifer sat, but instead of returning to his place on the sofa, Padraig walked around the coffee table and sat close to her. "You know," he began, "I don't want to sign this thing. That's why I've been delaying. It's not that you're not entitled, and there's nothing I want to contest. It's just that this is the surrender document, and God, how I hate to surrender."

"I don't want your surrender," Jennifer answered. "I just want my life back."

Padraig sighed. "That's exactly what I *don't* want. I don't want my old life back. It was just a game. Fakery. Seduction. Pretense. A big image on the screen and not a bit of light inside. All special effects. None of it real. With you, darlin', it was a new life, with honest words and true feelings. I really was somebody. With you I had a chance. That's what I want. A new life. Not the old one back again."

There was a knock on the door. Jennifer hesitated for an instant, then braced herself and crossed the room to let Henry Harris in.

He was all spit and polish, a chalk-stripe suit magnificently tailored to fit his youthful, well-sculptured frame. Henry shook Padraig's hand firmly, showed his best smile, and introduced himself. He looked around, spotted Jennifer's desk in the office area of her loft, crossed to it, and spread out the papers from his briefcase. "Mr. O'Connell, this incorporates all the changes that your attorney requested. The wording is a bit different, but I'm sure you'll find that the substance is—"

"Lend me your pen," Padraig said, stepping up beside him.

Harris looked from Padraig to Jennifer, then back to Padraig. "I always advise my clients to read these things before signing," he said, but he uncapped his fountain pen and handed it to Padraig.

"Do your clients have that much time to waste?" Padraig asked as he tossed through the pages to find his signature line.

"Padraig, take it with you," Jennifer said. "Another day or two doesn't matter. Make sure you agree with everything."

"Why? You've read it, haven't you? There isn't anything in here that takes advantage of me, is there?"

"No," Jennifer told him softly.

He found the line marked for his signature. He signed with a flourish and then handed the document to Jennifer. "You're free, darlin'. Peter and Catherine get what they want. And you and I get . . ." He touched the edge of the divorce agreement. "We get this, which isn't really what either of us want." He stopped at the coffee table and tossed down his drink. Then he crossed to the door and let himself out.

They heard his footsteps fading in the hallway. "Not the worst person I've ever met," Henry allowed.

"No, certainly not the worst."

The lawyer went back to the desk, gesturing for Jennifer to join him. "All it needs now is your signature. Then I'll take it back to the office and handle the filing." He offered the same pen that Padraig had just used.

"Not now, Henry. I want to read it over a few times."

He looked surprised, so she explained. "As Padraig said, neither of us are getting what we really want."

Padraig and Catherine traveled to Hollywood for the premiere of their first movie and walked down the red carpet arm in arm with the film's small cast. The actor playing the obsessive older man wasn't really recognized by the crowd, and the young girl he was lusting after had yet to make a name. Padraig gathered most of the applause, and Catherine, in a plunging décolletage, was easily the most photographed. They partied at the bar of the Mondrian until the reviews came in, then partied longer when they read the critics' raves. Padraig's little movie was an artistic triumph, assuring that it would be picked up by nearly all the exhibitors. They were heady with success over the weekend at his beach house.

He was returning to Ireland for the final scenes of the boy-and-his-dog epic. The filming would end at the same moment as the money, which meant that he would need still more funding for editing and music. "Another ten million will absolutely lock it up," he had told Catherine as she was dressing for her return to New York. When they parted at the airport, he suggested that $15 million was probably more realistic.

Catherine's stopover in New York was another publicity triumph. She was on the board of a small but important East Side gallery that was hosting the American debut of an important Israeli painter. New York society was on hand for the opening, then scattered to half a dozen very private supper parties. Catherine made them all, changing her gown between each event, her attire more sensational and revealing as the hour grew later. She was on the late-night news of two networks and had two different photos on the society page of the *Times*.

She came into the office like Cleopatra returning to Egypt, trailed by junior executives and secretaries who wrote furiously to keep up with her dictated instructions. Behind them trailed security guards who had been pressed into carrying her luggage. She set up dinners with television producers who were delivering their shows over the satellite network, and with the chairman of a computer company that was using the satellites for data traffic. When all her arrangements were completed, she called Peter Barnes to let him know that she was in and wanted to see him. Jennifer got word thirdhand through Peter's secretary.

"A triumph," Catherine announced, tossing the newspaper reviews onto the conference table. "Three of the major exhibitors have agreed to take it as a downlink from our satellites. That adds up to over a thousand screens."

Peter and Jennifer offered their congratulations and added praise for her success at the gallery opening. "Too bad we can't carry fine art on the network," Peter teased. "That would be another business that you could get us into."

But Catherine quickly got to the additional funding for Padraig. The figure caused Jennifer's jaw to drop and nearly sent Peter into shock. "Out of the question," he said the instant he recovered. "The plan is to find a buyer who might give us fifty cents on the dollar for all we've invested. We don't want to go any further into the hole."

Catherine snapped that he was being shortsighted. The production company, she claimed, was a hot property. The new film, coming on the heels of this success, was bound to be big at the box office. "Why should we take a loss so that a studio can come in and skim off the profits?"

They argued well into the evening, Catherine moving from one justification to the next while Peter dug in his heels and fell back on their original decision. Jennifer listened, asked for clarifications, and commented. She never stated her own preference. When it came to a vote, she joined with Peter in denying any more money to the Irish film. Catherine left in a huff but promised to carry the company's decision to Padraig.

"You were on the fence," Peter said to Jennifer when they sat down to an early dinner at a small Italian restaurant. "For a while, I thought you wanted to pull O'Connell's coals out of the fire."

Jennifer dismissed the idea and restated her commitment to their plan. But then she shared the details of her last meeting with her husband. "Tell me, Peter," she said in conclusion. "If Padraig had nothing to do with my auto accident, would you still have reason for hating him?"

He nodded. "Because he took advantage of you."

"Is that what you believe? Why do both you and Catherine think that anyone who shows an interest in me must be after my money?"

"I don't think anything of the kind," he protested. "I just think that you deserve better."

They paused while the waiter took their orders, and sat in silence while the wine was being poured. But as soon as they were by themselves, Jennifer took up the topic again.

"Do you remember, in Cannes, when I first met Padraig?"

Peter nodded. He remembered the film festival very well.

"You and Catherine were both thrilled that I was mingling with the beautiful people. Catherine was overjoyed that someone with the dash of Padraig O'Connell was paying attention to me."

"Of course. You were working too hard. We were happy to see you enjoying yourself."

"Was that it? Or were you happy that someone was finally paying attention to the ugly duckling?"

He was speechless for a moment. Then he laughed out the words "ugly duckling," making them sound preposterous. "Jennifer, you're anything but an ugly duckling."

"I know I'm reasonably attractive," she said factually. "But there are two of us. Catherine is glamorous, fashionable, witty, popular . . . all the things I'm not. So when you look at the Pegan sisters, she's queen of the barnyard and I'm the ugly duckling. And I must admit that it gets to me. Particularly when my closest friends decide that they have to protect me from fortune hunters. As if anyone who shows an interest in me must be out for money."

"That's not true," Peter said.

"No? Then why did you both turn against Padraig the instant he got serious about me? All of a sudden you weren't thrilled to see me out with the beautiful people, enjoying myself. My God, you even hired detectives."

"Jennifer, you own forty percent of the stock in a major corporation. Protecting you isn't an intrusion into your life. It's a business necessity."

"You weren't protecting me, Peter. You were trying to keep me away from a man I was falling in love with. You just assumed that all a celebrity like Padraig could see in me was forty percent of the stock."

"We checked him out, Jennifer, and what we found wasn't encouraging. He wasn't going to get his next movie, he was broke, in debt, and trying to get into producing. The man was desperate for money."

Jennifer sneered. "He was still broke, in debt, and trying to get into producing when Catherine took an interest in him, but I haven't noticed you trying to break them up. How much of our money have they made off with? Eighty million? Next to that, all he ever got from me was pocket change."

They waited anxiously while the waiter placed their dinners before them. Neither of them even looked at the food.

Peter resumed immediately. "It's not at all the same. Padraig was pursuing you. Catherine, on the other hand, went after him to make use of his connections."

"Sure," she said scornfully. "I've seen pictures of his connections."

"She also wanted to show you that it was the money he was after. That he'd drop you in an instant if he could get the money somewhere else."

Jennifer sighed and lifted her fork but kept it hovering above her plate. "Why do I think that a loving sister would try to hide that fact? Do you think she was really doing me a favor by breaking up my marriage?"

"I thought it was an outrageous idea," he answered. "I was against it."

"But?"

"But I can't control Catherine, any more than I can control you. I thought it was a mistake for her to get involved with him. I thought it was a mistake to keep him on to finish his great Irish epic."

Jennifer had to admit that there was consistency in Peter's actions. He seemed to hate O'Connell no matter which of the sisters was involved with him. But still, Peter couldn't see the possibility that Padraig had ever loved her. And she had to believe that her husband's interest hadn't been entirely in her money.

They ate in silence, but both pushed their plates away half full. While they were waiting for their coffee, Jennifer dropped her bomb.

"I think I'm going to invest in Padraig's movie."

Peter's face sank. "Jesus," he said, shaking his head.

"Not company money," Jennifer clarified. "I'm going to make a private investment. I'll lend him my personal money. At interest. Strictly a business venture."

"Don't," Peter told her. "You'll never get it back. There are preferred creditors. When this project bellies up—and it will—there won't be anything left to pay you."

"I'm betting he'll be able to pull it off," Jennifer answered.

He studied her for several seconds. "You're still in love with him, aren't you?"

"I'm not sure. Sometimes I think I am. I know I miss him."

"Miss him how?"

Jennifer smiled. "I don't think you can use your questions this time, Peter, because I'm not going to try to answer. The thing is, I think he's still in love with me."

"He needs money," Peter warned.

"That's what you think, isn't it? If anyone falls in love with the ugly duckling, it must be because he needs her money."

"You're not an ugly duckling," he snapped back. Then he glanced around the room and found that he was drawing attention from the nearby tables. In a softer voice he wondered, "What the hell has that guy got? How did he get such mindless devotion from you and your sister?"

"Now isn't that a coincidence," Jennifer said. "That's the very question that Padraig asked about you."

She regretted the comment as soon as it was out of her mouth. She could tell that she had hurt him, and he handled the check in pained silence. Outside, he got her a taxi, which she accepted though she generally used the subway. She mumbled an apology as he was showing her into the cab, but he closed the door before she finished. All the way down the West Side she kept berating herself. Peter hadn't done anything except look out for her interests, which he'd been doing as long as she had known him.

Nonetheless, his loyalty didn't exonerate him. Someone had ordered the brakes cut on Padraig's car, and Peter had to be a prime suspect. Whether it was to protect her, or his own privileged status, he was one of the few people she knew with the clout to track an enemy to the ends of the earth and the determination to destroy him. And there was no doubt that he hated Padraig. She could see it in his eyes every time her husband's name was mentioned.

When she reached her loft, she saw the divorce agreement on her desk, exactly where it had been placed when she had refused to sign it. She wasn't planning to reread it. She had read it in each of its redrafts and knew she could probably recite pages of it from memory. She understood exactly what it meant. What held her back was the thought that Padraig had planted, probably unintentionally. Neither of them were getting what they wanted. Peter and Catherine were the winners. Once she signed it, she and Padraig lost what they had both cherished—each other.

Maybe she and her husband should talk before she cut the last ties that bound them. Up to now, all the conversation had been bridged through attorneys who were completely indifferent to their feelings and their futures, who were obsessed with words instead of the people speaking them.

She thumbed her Rolodex and looked at Padraig's phone number in Ireland. Maybe she should respond to the emotions he had made so obvious during his visit. She lifted the phone, but then set it down again. The fact was that he and her sister had hurt her terribly. She wasn't sure that she had it in her to forgive.

SIXTEEN

GIVEN HIS loyal fans, and the crowd of camp followers that had gathered around his first production effort, Padraig's rift with Catherine would have automatically made all the tabloids. What elevated it to the front pages of serious dailies, and earned it fifteen seconds on the evening television news, were the public location of the breakup and the hilarious details of their spat. Not since James Cagney crushed a breakfast grapefruit in the face of Mae Clarke had the industry found so much to write about.

They had begun fighting the moment Catherine returned from New York with the news that there would be no more money from Pegasus Satellite Services. Padraig, according to gossip columnists, had suggested that Catherine put up her own money, and she had responded that she had already invested her whole career in Padraig O'Connell and that there was nothing more to give.

The filming had wrapped up without enough money to pay shipping costs back to California, or to redeem the surety bonds from the communities they had invaded. Padraig had returned to Hollywood to arrange financing for his postfilming costs. Catherine had gone back to New York in her last effort to borrow the money. She had flown out to the coast empty-handed to meet the actor, who had just been turned down by all the legitimate financiers. His best offer had been money equal to 15 percent of the total production investment for a 50 percent interest in the film. It had been offered on a take-it-or-leave-it basis. Padraig's only visible alternative was to sell the footage to a studio for fifty cents on the dollar. To ease his embarrassment, they had promised him an executive producer's card in the titles.

He took Catherine to lunch at Le Dome. He still had two credit cards that would go through, and he insisted that it was important to put on a show of strength for the deal makers who used the restaurant as a personal stock exchange.

They made a grand entrance, Padraig in a clan cravat and Catherine in a bare-midriff pantsuit. They stopped at every table along the way to shake hands, laugh cordially, and demonstrate their confidence. "I hear you need money," someone whispered to Padraig.

"You're damn right I need money. I always need money. But I'm not selling even one second of my picture," he said.

"What's this about funding difficulties?" someone asked Catherine. Her response was a wry smile. "I spend more on cosmetics than you've ever spent on a movie," she answered.

They took an obvious table and ordered a cocktail and an appetizer they could split. Their attitude fairly shouted that if Padraig's picture was in trouble, he and his angel certainly weren't worried. The suggestion was that if some lab owner or film editor wanted to offer his services against a percentage of the box office, they might be persuaded to entertain the idea.

But their nonchalance disappeared over the main course. Twice Padraig was seen to throw down his fork and yell that something or other was "out of the question" or simply "unacceptable." Catherine was heard to raise her voice with "Use your head, Padraig. This isn't a screenplay, this is real!" As dessert was being served, Catherine jumped up, apparently on the verge of tears, and rushed to the powder room. When she returned, people who had already paid their checks stayed pinned to their seats to see how the luncheon would wrap up.

They weren't disappointed. While eating the chocolate truffle cake, Catherine had suddenly snapped in a raised voice, "How can you say that? It's simply not true!" Padraig had responded, "How would you know? You were out with the lighting crew."

At which point Catherine had lifted her dessert plate, weighted it for a second in the palm of her hand, then smashed it into Padraig's face.

The actor did his best take, letting the chocolate and whipped cream run down his chin while he ceremoniously folded his napkin and scraped the mousse out of his eyes. For her part, Catherine took her time folding her napkin and gathering her purse. She finished her coffee, took a final sip of her water, got up and left. She reached the front step just in time to run into the photographers and television crews that had rushed to cover the event.

Catherine's comment was that Padraig was too used to getting his way with women who were probably brain-dead to begin with. Padraig told reporters that Catherine's artistic judgment came from painting by the numbers. There was little doubt that their torrid personal relationship and dazzling business partnership had come to an end. Catherine made a great show of processing her six bags of California clothing through ticketing, then caught the red-eye back to New York. Padraig went directly to his beach house and was seen sitting on his deck with a bottle of Scotch. He didn't return phone calls.

In the morning Catherine flashed through the Pegasus reception area in a neat-as-a-pin business suit, her face as fresh and rested as if she were returning from a spa rather than the infamous overnight flight from California. She made a visit to her sister's office, where she told Jennifer how lucky they were to be rid of O'Connell. "He frustrates directors, infuriates actors, and thinks a budget is some sort of record that he has to surpass." Catherine detailed the pleasure she had felt at grinding a pie into his "heroic face," and swore that her partnership with him was over. "I went to bat for him every time he promised to get things under control," she lamented, detailing the amount of funding she had brought to his efforts. "And then the bastard has the nerve to blame me for his own failure."

Jennifer found herself laughing at her sister's rage. "Seems to me that you both got what you deserved. You screwed me over and then he screwed you over. What could be fairer?"

"No, that's not what happened," Catherine corrected. "He screwed you over. But I got even. Padraig O'Connell is going down in flames, his movie shot out from under him. Believe me, he's finished in Hollywood. We're going to get most of our money back, and then we're going to leave the bastard for dead."

She was even more confident when she got to Peter's office. "Someone's going to pick up that film for pocket change and make a killing," she explained. "I think it ought to be us. If Pegasus buys it, we can offset our part of the loss and stick Padraig with his. What do you think?"

He answered with a question. "Did Jennifer tell you that she's planning to lend Padraig the money he needs to finish?"

Catherine's face fell. "For God's sake! That little fool. He'll take her to the cleaners."

"That's about what I told her," Peter said. "It's a bad investment. But she thinks I'm biased. According to her, I'm the one who tampered with the brakes on Padraig's car and hired the man who broke into your apartment."

"What?" Catherine looked amazed.

"She also thinks I made a second attempt at Padraig when his helicopter went down. It strikes her as too much of a coincidence that I arrived there the day before."

Catherine rose slowly and wandered to the windows. He watched her as she stared out for a moment and then came back to the conference table. "Peter . . ." she began hesitantly, "I think that Jennifer may need some help. Medical, psychiatric, whatever."

He said nothing, but his expression showed she had his full attention.

"I think she's terribly . . . confused. Somehow Padraig comes through all this as her unblemished hero. You and I are the enemies?"

He nodded. "Maybe she has reasons. You and I never wanted to see her and Padraig together."

"True, but her reasons go back a long way. Jennifer has this obsession that I'm out to ruin her life. She's had it since we were children. Now she hates me for proving that Padraig was just after her money."

"You chose a rather heavy-handed way of making your point," he reminded her. "From her viewpoint, you stole her husband."

She nodded. It was certainly true that Jennifer had every right to be furious with her. "But this goes further," she said. Then she said, "Peter, I think Jennifer was behind the attempt on my life?"

"Why would you think that?" he questioned.

"For the same reasons that the police suspect her. The man worked in her gym, waited tables at her favorite coffee shop, and lived in her building. It's just not credible that she never spoke to him and didn't even remember seeing him."

"It happens in the city. I don't know my next-door neighbor. I think the police understand those things."

"But there's something the police don't know. This isn't the first time that Jennifer tried to kill me. Several years ago, when we were diving in Belize, she tried to pull out my air hose. And she had much less reason then for wanting me dead than she does now."

He was flabbergasted. "She tried to kill you?"

Catherine nodded gravely. "She denied it. Even implied that I was reaching for her air hose. And, to be truthful, we were swimming very close to each other and it was confusing. But I know what I saw. There was no doubt in my mind that she wanted to rip the air line off my tank."

Peter took off his glasses and dangled them from his finger-tips. "I've always felt the undercurrent between you and Jenni-fer. Maybe even a little jealousy, although I have no idea what either of you could be jealous of. You're both so talented, both such attractive people. But . . . murder. I simply can't believe it."

"I don't want to believe it, either," Catherine said. "But I no longer go to Jennifer's apartment, and I don't have her over to my place unless someone else is there. So I guess, deep down, I know that it's true."

Peter stood, paused thoughtfully, and walked to a window. "I can't believe what's happened to us," he said, shaking his head slowly. "I always thought that when I left the company you and Jennifer would be a perfect management team, despite your differences."

"Left the company?" Catherine was shocked. "What are you talking about?"

"My resignation. I've been thinking about it for some time. My work here is pretty well finished." He refitted his glasses.

"You can't! Not now. You've never been more needed than you are now."

"No," he answered calmly. "Lately, I've simply been in the way. I've made an enemy of Jennifer by trying to stop her from bringing in Padraig O'Connell. And I've made an enemy of you by blocking any more funding for Padraig's company. Pegasus is your company, and I should be working for you and Jennifer. The fact is that I'm still working for your father. That has to stop."

"But not now," Catherine pleaded. "You can't walk out of here and leave me in partnership with someone who wants to kill me."

"I don't believe Jennifer is capable of that. As for the business problems, the two of you will work them out."

Catherine was becoming frantic. "The two of us? You just said that she's going to fund Padraig. That means there will be two of them against me."

"I can't solve that problem. It's not a business problem. It's a personal problem that involves you and your sister. I blame myself because I should have nipped it in the bud. That's what your father would have done, but I'm not your father. I'm a hired manager, and that doesn't give me any right to get involved in your personal affairs."

"You can't go now," Catherine persisted.

"I'll give it another month," he said. "But I'm not going to come between you and your sister, and I'm not going to take sides. If you ask me, I'll tell you what I think. That gives you and Jennifer a month to decide what the real issues are."

Padraig O'Connell smiled when he heard that Jennifer was on the line. He took a sip of water and cleared his throat before he picked up the phone, then answered with his most charming Irish lilt. "And to what do I owe the pleasure?"

"A business proposition," Jennifer said, making no attempt to match his cordial tone. "I want to lend you some money at a very high interest rate. Say, nine percent."

"I can get eight from a bank," he answered.

"I'm not a bank."

"True," he said. "And as you probably know already, the only thing the bank will give me is a home mortgage. So I guess I'll pay you nine." Then he asked how much she was planning on lending him.

"How much do you need?"

He purred for a few seconds. "Would ten million be out of the question?"

"It would. I've done my homework, and it looks as if you need five."

"Five? That wouldn't get me back to even."

Jennifer laughed. "I'm not proposing to pay your bar bill. Just editing and music. If we make a profit, then you can get back to even."

"Done," he announced. "Where do I sign?"

"The paperwork will come by overnight messenger. The check will follow as soon as I get the signed note."

"Jennifer," he said before she could hang up, "thank you. I've made a great many mistakes recently, but you weren't one of them."

The phone clicked dead in his hand.

Jennifer still hadn't signed the divorce agreement. In fact, she hadn't touched it since her attorney had left it on her desk. She had been happy with Padraig in their brief time together. And it wasn't simply that she had enjoyed the moments of celebrity that came from holding his hand. Padraig had given her a new vision of herself. When she saw herself reflected in his eyes, she was a totally different person than she was used to seeing in mirrors.

He made her aware of her beauty. She had always thought that she was as plain as water next to her glamorous sister. Catherine's face glowed with vitality and her smile was rapturous, while Jennifer was bland and serious. But Padraig had dismissed the superficial beauty and glamour surrounding him as being nothing more than decoration. He had seemed enthralled at the truth of Jennifer's appearance.

He had brought out her personality. Jennifer had often thought she was socially inadequate. Catherine moved confidently among the world's cultural and charitable leaders, while Jennifer was alone, curled up with a book. Yet Padraig seemed to find everything she said interesting and talked to her with the certainty that she knew and appreciated what he was saying.

He had given her love. Jennifer had no idea what Catherine felt in the arms of a man, but she had always suspected that it must be more intoxicating and fulfilling than anything she had experienced. Her adult affairs had been few, never earthshaking, and usually boring. Each had ended in mutual unspoken admissions of lack of interest. But Padraig had brought her to the heights of ecstasy and, just as important, had seemed to travel with her every step of the way. Not only was she capable of being loved, but she was an exciting and provocative lover herself.

She had harbored few illusions about Padraig. No one would ever take the place in his heart that he had reserved for himself. No one would ever claim his undivided attention or win his unwavering loyalty. He would never settle into a quiet, comfortable relationship with one woman because there was no woman who could fill all his needs. But a single piece of Padraig O'Connell was more exciting and more satisfying than the whole of any other man she had known. By signing the divorce document, she would lose even that small piece.

And yet she couldn't just forgive. He had wounded her terribly and then abandoned her for a public celebration with another woman. He must have known how deeply she was hurt by the publicity he generated with Catherine on his arm. He had to understand how painful it was for her to sit through meetings where his business venture with her sister was discussed. He had left her to suffer without an apology or even a word of explanation. All he had offered was a hint that he hadn't been given a choice, and that what he had done had been necessary to save his new career.

She had reasons to love him and more reasons to hate him, but she felt neither. Instead, she felt curiosity. Had he ever really loved her? Did he really intend to hurt her? Of all the things he had said to her, which had been true and which had been lies? Could they ever be together again, or was the tear in their relationship too wide and too ragged to ever be repaired?

Jennifer couldn't even explain why she was offering the money he needed. She felt sure that she wasn't simply trying to buy her way back into his affections. She had no intentions of using the debt to dominate him or embarrass him. Nor was it the simple business deal that she pretended. It was, as Peter had warned her, a bad investment. The odds were that she wouldn't get her money back. But on the other hand, she didn't want Padraig to sink just because Peter and her sister had opened the seacocks in the bilge. If his movie failed, it should be because he had made a bad movie, not because Catherine and Peter didn't like him and couldn't trust him.

So, did she love him or hate him? The truth was that she really didn't know. And that was why she was now the one dragging her feet on their divorce, and probably why she was the only investor who had come to his rescue. She simply had to know what was left between Padraig and herself, and she needed time to find out.

SEVENTEEN

JENNIFER THOUGHT she recognized the voice that called up from the lobby the next evening. "FedEx. An overnight letter for Jennifer Pegan."

"Who's it from?"

She listened to paper shuffling. "O'Connell, from West Hollywood, California. Signature required."

Jennifer remembered the note that Padraig was to sign and return. She buzzed the messenger into the building, then waited idly until her doorbell rang. "FedEx," the voice repeated when she asked. She looked through the peephole and saw an express envelope blocking her view of the person. She hooked the chain and unlocked the deadbolt. Padraig's face appeared in the crack of the door.

"I'm not sure whether I give you the package first or you have to sign first," he said. "So I'll give you the clipboard and keep the package, and then we can swap when you're finished signing."

Despite herself, Jennifer had to laugh. Who but Padraig would deliver an overnight package personally? She closed the door and unlocked the chain. He burst into the room with his familiar joyous gait. He had staged a miraculous recovery from the whipped dog that had dragged his tail in on his last visit.

"Are you crazy . . ." she started to ask, but then she answered her own question. "Yes, of course you are. Why would there be any doubt?"

"I need only a moment of your time," he said, handing her

the envelope. She kept her eyes on him as she tore it open. On top was the loan note, duly signed and notarized. Below it was a publicity photo of Padraig, posed in the blazer and golf shirt generally worn by his international spy character. He had signed it, "To my favorite ex-wife, with love, Padraig."

"I had a few hundred of these made up," he explained. "Ex-wives are an important faction in my fan club."

"I won't have the check until tomorrow," she said, still standing in her foyer. She had made no gesture to invite him inside.

"Then I'll wait until tomorrow. Okay with you if I sleep here?"

"Not a chance," she answered.

"I didn't mean in your bed. Just a pillow and the use of one of your sofas."

"That's what I thought you meant when I said there wasn't a chance."

"Well, perhaps a cup of tea then. That's substandard hospitality even for ex-husbands."

Jennifer smiled. "Okay, tea. Or if you'd rather a nip of your Scotch . . ."

"God, but you're clairvoyant! You can see to the bottom of my soul."

"The bottle is right where you left it, so you can fix it yourself," Jennifer said. Then she added, "And by the way, Padraig, you don't have any soul."

He returned from her bar with two drinks over ice.

"None for me," Jennifer said forcefully.

He looked disappointed. Then he said, "Well, we'll just have to make lemonade out of the lemons." He poured her drink into his and set the empty glass back on the bar. As he was crossing to join her in the living room, he noticed the familiar document still waiting on the desk where he had signed it. He went to it and flipped through to the signature page. The line for her signature was still blank.

"You really ought to sign this," he told her. "Unless, of course, you'd like to reconsider."

"I'm saving it for the divorce party," she answered. "We're going to have champagne and a cake."

He tasted his drink, nodded his approval, then took a bigger sip. "Would you like me to jump out of the cake?"

"Sorry," she said. "I've already hired a skunk."

"Ouch!" Padraig winced. "You've left powder burns and bloodstains. But, I truly have been something of a . . ." He paused, grasping for the right word.

"Prick," Jennifer suggested.

He nodded vigorously. "Yes, exactly the word I was looking for." But then he set down his glass. "On a less humiliating note, I came all this way not to hurry your check but simply to thank you in person. The truth is that I was going down for the third time with your sister's foot planted firmly on the top of my head. I had no place to turn. And of all the people who might have helped me, you were the last one I expected to hear from."

Jennifer nodded. "You're welcome," she answered.

He sipped again, giving drink to his courage. "As I have said often to others and tried to tell you, you are the very best person who has ever entered my life. And, ironically, the one I treated most unfairly. I'm going to wait until the critics see my film, and if they give it the reviews I think it will deserve, I'm going to dedicate it to you. That won't repay my debt, which is far larger than the amount written on this note. But it will be public acknowledgment that I've been an awful . . . what was the word?"

"Prick," Jennifer supplied.

"Yes, yes. Of course." He downed the drink. "So, I'll see you tomorrow. Where and when do you suggest?"

She thought for a moment, knowing that she didn't want him walking into her office. That would kick off a new round of rumors, and new pressures to bear. "Here, tomorrow morning at eleven."

"Eleven it shall be." He was already on his way to the door. But he stopped just before she closed it behind him. "Oh, if you're planning lunch, could we dispense with the dessert? I've had quite enough sweets for a while."

She laughed, and was still laughing when she heard the elevator going down.

Catherine and Peter tried to convince Jennifer not to support Padraig. Peter's argument was the all too familiar charge that Padraig had tried to kill her. "I don't know how he made the arrangements from the States, or how he switched the attempt from Ireland to Italy," he admitted. "But he was the one with the motive, and he was the one with the opportunity."

Catherine made the case that he had betrayed Jennifer for the money from Pegasus. "It was a simple test. What did he want? You, or an unlimited bankroll for his new career? He snapped at the money. He nearly bit my fingers off to get it. And when I couldn't raise any more for him, he dropped me just the way he dropped you."

But Jennifer wasn't listening. She had heard it all and put her own interpretation on events. For years she had lived in the shadow of her sister. Then Padraig had come along and bathed her in light. Someone had tried to kill him. Maybe a Hollywood rival. Maybe her mentor, who didn't want to lose his control over her. Possibly even her jealous sister. It was Peter who had built up the evidence to make Padraig look guilty. And when that didn't split her from her husband, it was Catherine who lured him away.

Certainly Padraig had betrayed her. That was something she still wasn't able to forgive. But the betrayal wasn't his idea. That had been engineered by Peter's charges and Catherine's money. He had failed her, but stronger men than he would have collapsed under less temptation.

The money she was lending him? Of course she understood that it wasn't just a financial investment. She was spending it to keep his dream alive, and hoping that, in the process, she might keep her own dreams alive as well. As soon as the bank messenger delivered the check from her personal account, she canceled her meetings and took the subway downtown.

Padraig was a few minutes late, pleading the difficulties of getting a taxi. He accepted a cup of coffee, sat with his knees crossed, and told her about the phone calls he had made after leaving her the day before. An Academy Award–winning composer had agreed to do an original score using traditional Irish instruments. A special-effects guru had taken on the task of extending the panoramic scene that had been cut short by the helicopter incident. He had succeeded in hiring "the best film editor in the business." When Jennifer handed him the check, he never looked at the amount. "This makes it all possible," he said as he folded it into his shirt pocket. "You've saved my life."

"Use it well," Jennifer said, referring to the money.

"Up until now I've used it poorly," Padraig answered, referring to his life. "Carelessly might be a better word. Or maybe I should say selfishly. I'd like to turn things around." Then he added, with a hint of sadness, "With you I would have had a chance."

She decided to answer him. "I had a chance with you, too. Our whirlwind marriage was good for me. I felt I was really beginning to live."

Padraig raised his eyes. "Oh, I wish you hadn't said that. It makes what I destroyed even more beautiful, and that makes my sin that much blacker."

He finished his coffee, stood slowly, and reached out for her hand. "We both know I don't deserve your kindness, but you've given me that anyway. Maybe someday you'll extend your forgiveness, which I deserve even less."

"I still haven't signed the divorce papers," Jennifer said, as if that were the answer to his question.

"Sign them, darlin', so you'll be rid of me. Then you can get back to your life."

"There isn't really that much to get back to," Jennifer told him.

They stood in silence, staring at each other, each waiting to hear words that neither could manage to speak. It was Padraig who finally broke through. "Jennifer, if I thought there was any chance for us, any chance at all, I'd be on my knees."

She managed a thin smile. "You're not the kind of man who looks good on his knees."

Padraig gestured at the divorce papers. "If you haven't signed those by the time I finish the picture, I'll take it as encouragement."

"I can always sign the damn papers," she answered.

He phoned her when he got back to Hollywood, then began phoning her every evening to report on the day's work, "just to keep you informed of the status of your investment," as he put it. "You should hear the music," he began one evening. "A tin whistle and a flat drum. The whistle is searching for a new beginning, and the drum is counting out the years. It's a frail moment of hope despite the weight of time grinding the people into dust." He spent nearly an hour talking continuously about musical motifs and their fit into his story line. He hummed and tapped the rhythm on the telephone handset while Jennifer listened quietly. "Are you still there, darlin'?" he finally asked.

"I'm still here."

"Well then, I must be boring you to tears or driving you to madness with my singing. So I'll run along. Talk to you soon!"

"You should see the helicopter shots," he began on another call. "They've worked miracles with their computers. They take a bit of footage of the lad running through the shell bursts, and they turn it around so you see it from another angle. Or they mate the boy to the background of another sequence. And just like that, you've got magnificent footage that we never shot, or locations that we never visited."

One night he asked her to come out to California. "We've got the editing and the special effects coming together, and we're adding in the music. It's something I can't describe. You have to see it for yourself, darlin'. There's no way that I can tell you about it."

She hesitated, but turned down the invitation. The decision she had to make about her future was hers and hers alone. If she met Padraig on his turf, it might become his decision. She couldn't let that happen to her.

When she hung up, she thought of the divorce papers, still unread and unsigned. Her attorneys called two or three times a week to see if they were ready for the court. "Is there something wrong with it? Anything that you don't understand?" Henry Harris kept prompting. She always told them no, then endured a moment of silence that seemed to be asking her why, if everything was in order, she hadn't signed. And there were the daily calls from her sister and frequent comments by Peter, always referring to "the danger to Pegasus" of leaving Padraig's status undefined. "We need either the marital agreement or the divorce," they kept telling her. "You've got to do something."

But she had decided not to sign. Not yet, at any rate. So she might as well return the document to her lawyer. But she didn't see it on the desk, and when she searched the drawers, it wasn't there. She went through her bedroom, where she often read late into the night. Maybe she had brought it to bed. She still couldn't find it. Then she went through the files in her office. There was no trace of the agreement.

"Well, technically," the lawyer explained, "we're back to square one. Naturally, we have copies, but that's the only one that O'Connell signed. So it's out of your hands. We need to get Padraig's agreement all over again."

"What good would it be to anyone?" Jennifer questioned. She didn't usually misplace things, and she was always careful about papers that she put out in the trash. She suspected theft.

The lawyer shrugged. "Your husband, of course, would want to get his hands on it if he was thinking about changing his mind."

"Padraig's in California," she answered.

"Is there anyone else who might want to stop the divorce from going through?"

She could think of no one.

"Or someone who might want to make the divorce official? Forge your signature or get you to sign it unintentionally with a lot of routine papers?" Her thoughts went instantly to Peter and Catherine. But she dismissed the idea. That wouldn't do them any good as long as she was around to deny her signature.

It was two days later, when someone tried to break into her apartment during the middle of the night, that Jennifer began to suspect she might not be around to contest her signature.

Her building, an old printing loft, had fire stairs at each end with the freight elevator in the center. Her apartment occupied the entire top floor and was entered via the elevator landing. For security, she could set the elevator at night not to ascend to her floor. Each of the stairs served as an entrance to the smaller apartments on the floors. But they were sealed off with an iron gate below her floor.

She woke up in the middle of the night to a strange sound, a soft electrical humming in the hallway outside her bedroom door. She slipped out of bed and into her robe and walked sleepily into the hallway to investigate. She had no thought of danger, other than the possibility of a leaking pipe or a failed electrical circuit, so she was stunned by the sight of a dim flickering light under the sealed fire door. She stepped quietly to the door to investigate, ready to scream if someone was outside. It was then that she saw the unused doorknob turning slowly. Right before her eyes, the point of a drill bit whirled slowly through the lock assembly, carving a spiral shaving of metal that fell down on her carpet.

Her scream was piercing as she backed away toward her living room. The humming sound of the drill motor stopped. Shadows passed through the light that seeped under the door. As Jennifer reached for another breath, she heard a loud crash. The door and even the frame trembled under the impact of someone hurling his body against the door from the other side. Long painted-over seams cracked like glass. The lock and doorknob bent inward. There was another crash, and again the door trembled, but once again it held.

Jennifer got to her phone and quickly punched in the three-digit code that dialed her alarm company. The emergency lights placed inconspicuously throughout the apartment snapped on. A siren began to warble at a shrill pitch.

She stood frozen at the end of the hall, staring at the damaged door, expecting that it would burst open at any second. But there was no more movement against it. The light she had noticed underneath seemed to have faded into darkness.

She buzzed the police up as soon as the first squad car arrived, and took a moment to get dressed before the detectives came onto the scene. Ten minutes after that, Peter arrived, having been called by the security service as one of Jennifer's designated contacts. She fell into his arms instinctively, seeing the protector she had always known rather than the enemy who had perhaps conspired against her husband. "God, it was awful," she kept repeating. "I've never been so frightened. Just standing there, watching someone saw through the door to get to me . . ."

"It's over. You'll be okay," he comforted. "Probably a burglar who thought you were away."

But as she thought about it, she knew that wasn't the case. A common thief would have run the instant she screamed. This person had made two attempts to break down the door after she screamed. It was Jennifer he wanted.

The police were baffled. Nothing added up. The burglar, if that's what he was, had drilled through the hinges of the gate on the stairs below. With the noise of the drill, he had risked detection. And if it had been a random break-in, why not hit one of the apartments below the gate that closed off the fire stairs? It seemed certain that Jennifer's apartment was a carefully selected target.

But if the intruder knew the apartment, why would he choose the door next to her bedroom? There was an equally accessible door at the other side of the building, opening into her kitchen and office area. Why drill where she might hear it when it was just as easy to drill where she probably wouldn't hear anything?

And then another question: Why drill at all? Once he had gotten through the gate, the intruder had easy access to the roof. Then he could walk a few steps to the skylight over the living room. A glass cutter and a bit of sticky tape to lift out the pane, and a person could get into the apartment with nothing more sophisticated than a ten-foot length of clothesline. Someone had been smart enough to single out an apartment filled with valuables, then cut their way up the deserted fire stairs. And yet that same person had been dumb enough to try drilling through a metal door that was right outside her bedroom.

There was one more factor that aroused police suspicions. Jennifer's name and address turned up a still active file that connected her with the attempted murder of her sister. She was the one who lived in the same building with her sister's assailant and frequented at least two of his workplaces. It seemed strange that a potential perpetrator had suddenly become a victim; or that two sisters living in different parts of the city would be victimized in roughly the same way within a few months. Of course it could be a coincidence. But it was just as likely that there was some connection.

The next morning, Catherine rushed into Jennifer's office with a shower of sympathy. "How awful . . . how terrifying! Did you have any idea? Do the police have any clues?"

Jennifer mentioned that she suspected someone had been in her apartment before. She told Catherine about the missing divorce document.

Catherine saw the same possibilities that the attorneys had raised. Could someone have stolen the document to delay the divorce? And if that same person had succeeded in killing her before she was divorced, then the beneficiary would obviously be—

"Padraig," Jennifer said, finishing her sister's thought. "Peter was hinting at the same thing. Who benefits if I die while I'm still married to Padraig O'Connell? It's the same conclusion the two of you jumped to when I had the auto accident. It has to be

Padraig, that conscienceless, moneygrubbing monster who's making a fool out of Jennifer. Why else would he be paying any attention to her if he wasn't after her money?"

Catherine was offended. "I wasn't thinking anything like that. It's just that it certainly would be convenient for him. But of course it could be someone else." Then she asked the question that Jennifer had been struggling with: "Who else might it be?"

That was where Jennifer's theories fell apart. Peter and Catherine were the last people who would want her to die before the divorce went through. Nothing would frighten them more than the prospect of Padraig O'Connell in their boardroom. So, who else was there? One of the legion of Padraig's enemies? Not likely. He was highly visible in Hollywood, where he was completing his film. Anyone with a score to settle would take care of it out on the Coast. And why would one of his enemies want to harm her? She and Padraig hadn't been together in months. Who could possibly know that she had lent him a bit of money or that she was still hesitating over their divorce?

Padraig called her seconds after Catherine had left her office. "Jesus, but someone has it in for you girls."

"It may just be a coincidence," she tried, but he would hear none of it.

"Coincidence, my arse! Someone broke in on your sister a few months ago, and now this. There's a lunatic out there somewhere with a terrible grudge against the two of you."

"If you try to tell me that it's Peter Barnes—" she started, but he interrupted.

"I'm not trying to tell you anything, although I wouldn't mind stretching that bastard on the rack or holding his feet into a fire. I'll bet he could tell a story or two. But I don't care about him. It's you that worries me. Why don't you come out here where you can see the results of your loan? You'd love the movie that's coming together, and while you're here, I could keep an eye on you."

"Not yet, Padraig. I'm not ready to spend that much time together."

"Look, I'll move out of the beach house so you can move in. And I'll hire round-the-clock security people. When you come to Hollywood to see the film, you'll be in a dark theater. You won't even know I'm there."

She had to laugh at the outrageous offer. Then she realized that she hadn't laughed at anything since the last time he was in her apartment. "Tempting," she said, "but I'm busy here. And I won't let myself be driven off. There are decisions I have to make, and I want to be sure I make them for the right reasons."

"Well, if you can't come here, then I'll go there. I'll sleep outside your door."

"You have a picture to finish. I have all the security I need."

He started back into his argument for her to come to California. He promised to get Sylvester Stallone as her bodyguard.

"Goodbye, Padraig," she said to cut him off, and hung up.

Peter stopped by to see how she was surviving the day. She could stay in his apartment, he said. He could easily move into his club. And the company's security force would assign additional people. They could put a woman inside the apartment with her and guards outside the door, on the roof, and in the lobby.

"I'm not frightened," she lied. "I have no problems with going back to my apartment once they fix my door and put a new gate on the fire stairs."

"That's being taken care of," he promised. He didn't tell her that he had already made arrangements with the security firm for a guard on the roof, one in the elevator, and one in each of the stairwells.

Who had tried to get to her, Jennifer wondered. And why? She posed the questions over and over again and tried any number of answers. But in the end, it always came up Padraig. He was the one with the most to gain. As long as she stuck to the concerns of the business and followed the money motive, Padraig was the only name that fit.

But suppose money had nothing to do with it. Suppose the intruder had no interest in who ran Pegasus, or whether the movie was finished or was sold. What if the reason for the attack was as irrational as the attack itself? What if madness was the only motive? Then it was her sister who jumped to the top of the list.

Her sister? Unthinkable. And yet it was the only scenario that she could explain to herself. She was fairly certain that Catherine had once come close to killing her. They had become tangled while diving in Belize, and she was sure that her sister had grabbed for her air hose. Catherine had, of course, said it was the other way around. She had accused Jennifer of trying to tear out her air supply. But that was Catherine's bizarre gift: She could turn the truth to fit any scenario.

And now Catherine was frightened. She suspected Jennifer of hiring the man who had come within a few inches of hurling her off her balcony. Why wouldn't Catherine strike back? Maybe just to frighten her and show that two could play the violence game. Or maybe to kill her and put an end to their lifelong competition.

It should be unthinkable. But it was the only solution she could believe. Far more logical than the suggestion that Padraig O'Connell, who seemed truly penitent, had reached all the way from California to harm her.

When Padraig called that night to satisfy himself that she was safe, Jennifer asked straight out whether it could have been her sister. "You know Catherine well. You've shared secrets with her. Is it possible that she could want me dead?"

"Jay-sus, but that's a frightening thought," he answered. "There's no doubt she would love to see me join the faithful departed. But you? I really don't think so. I know that she can be . . . how can I put this tactfully?"

"A cunt," Jennifer said.

"Yes. That's tactful enough. And possibly the most self-centered woman on earth. And she told me a hundred times how much you get on her nerves, which I naturally find impossible to believe."

"Padraig, please, just tell me."

His tone changed. "Well, she's absolutely certain that you hired someone to kill her. But I think her reaction is more fear than vengeance. She's more afraid that you'll try again than she is determined to get back at you. So I'd have to say no. I don't believe that Catherine would ever try to kill you."

EIGHTEEN

THE POLICE were back at Catherine's house, but this time just the two detectives, without the usual army of forensics experts. In the past they had brought people who measured the height of her balcony railings, cut pile from the bedroom carpet, ran tests on the electrical connections of her alarm system, and looked for traces of blood in her bathtub. She had lost patience with their meticulous investigation of her story, as if they were determined to disprove any alternative explanation of the events. "He attacked me in the bedroom," she had repeated over and over again, then detailed everything she could remember about the struggle until the intruder was dead at her feet in the kitchen. If they wanted to run any more tests, she had threatened, they would have to come back with a court order. But the two detectives had promised that there would be no more forensics. Just a few questions that they hoped would "wrap things up." They accepted coffee and sat with her in her den.

"This will be a bit difficult for you," one of the men began, "but can you think of any reason why your sister might want to have you killed?"

"My sister?" Catherine was almost laughing.

"I know it probably sounds incredible," the other detective interjected.

Catherine shook her head. "No, not incredible at all. I'm laughing because you seem to think that it would be the furthest thing from my mind. But I've thought of little else since that night."

Carefully and accurately, she explained the details of the business arrangement she shared with Jennifer. Jennifer would vault into the limelight if anything happened to Catherine, not to mention instantly becoming about $5 billion richer. But they knew all that. The operations and worth of Pegasus were public record.

She listened while they reviewed the coincidences of the intruder living in Jennifer's building and working in her rehabilitation center. While they flipped the pages of their notebooks, she reminded them that Will Ferris had also worked in a coffee shop that Jennifer frequented. But all that had been known within hours of the break-in. Why were they focusing on it now?

"Because we went through your sister's telephone records and found a call placed from her home to Will Ferris's apartment," one of the detectives told her. "One call isn't terribly significant by itself. They were both members of a tenant's committee. But your sister said that she had never heard the man's name, and that doesn't seem likely since she called him."

Catherine shifted to the edge of her chair. "She knew him?"

"So it seems."

Then the second detective took over. "We also went through the checks at the restaurant where Ferris worked. There were two checks within three months of your attack where her credit card was used and Ferris was the waiter credited with the tip. Again, people don't always remember waiters. But your sister was positive she had never seen the man before. Actually, he had waited on her a week earlier."

Should she tell them? Catherine thought. Should she tell them about all the times when Jennifer had lied about her, stolen from her, even tried to kill her? They were looking for motives in the business relationship that the two sisters shared. They didn't have even a clue what Jennifer's real motive would be. But could they understand? Was there any way to make them see her sister's insane jealousy? Could they possibly believe how Jennifer had hovered around her like an angel of death ever since they were children? They wondered whether there was any reason why she might want to see Catherine dead. There were a thousand reasons, starting with a blinded doll in a yellow dress. All of them were much more important than money.

"Your sister is married to Padraig O'Connell, the actor?" the first detective asked, taking his turn in the interview.

"Yes, although they're in the process of a divorce."

"And you have a business relationship with Mr. O'Connell?"

"I do, but again that's in the process of being terminated." She explained briefly that she was a co-owner of Leprechaun Productions but was planning to sell her interest. "It hasn't been a happy experience."

Now the other detective cleared his throat. "Is that what you and Mr. O'Connell argued about in a Hollywood restaurant?"

"Yes," she said, concealing her surprise that policemen were up on Hollywood scandals. "We have differences over how the company spends its money."

"Did your sister resent your business relationship with her husband?"

Catherine thought of a dozen ways to explain the strain that O'Connell had caused. It wasn't just the business relationship that Jennifer resented. It was the personal relationship that had driven Jennifer to threaten her. But she kept to the facts. "Yes, she was very upset that I was involved with O'Connell."

"Could she have blamed you for the failure of her marriage?"

"She could, but she also blamed her husband."

The detectives paused to review their notes. "Where is all this leading?" Catherine asked impatiently.

One of the men sighed and slipped his notebook into his pocket. "Just one more question: Do you have any idea who might have tried to break into your sister's apartment?"

"None at all," Catherine answered.

"No one comes to mind who might have a grudge against both you and your sister? Because you won't believe the odds against two sisters suffering break-ins at two different locations. Statistically, it's likely that there's a connection of some sort."

Again Catherine explained that she and her sister co-owned a large business venture. "I suppose anyone who has a problem with Pegasus might want to take it out on us."

They seemed satisfied as they finished their coffee. They rose together and saw themselves to the door with Catherine trailing at their heels. At the last minute one of them turned back to her. "Oh, we'd appreciate it if you wouldn't talk to your sister about this interview."

"You suspect her, don't you?"

They looked at each other. Then the detective admitted, "She certainly is a suspect."

Catherine nodded slowly. At long last, people were beginning to understand her sister.

Padraig had been working furiously and driving his associates at his own frantic pace. His film, titled *Inheritance*, was nearly finished, and he was determined to meet the deadline for its first screening. Not that the date had been dictated by higher authority and set in stone. It was just that the coffers filled by Jennifer's loan were almost empty. He couldn't afford to run over by even one more day.

He had seen the entire film in segments, out of order and in various stages of completion. Some parts he had viewed while the special effects were in progress, others before the music score had been mixed in. He wasn't sure of the artistic impact of his work. He could reorder the scenes in his mind and mentally hum the music. He could imagine how the effects would work and how one bit of dialogue would evoke an earlier theme. But the finished project existed only fleetingly in his mind, and its quality soared and according plummeted more to his mood than to objective criteria. "It's going to be great," his coworkers kept reassuring him. But he knew that even the biggest flops were great until the the first screening, when a picture left the hands of the craftsmen and tried to fly with its own wings.

The event would be small. Just Padraig, his partners, and a

few key production associates. None of the cast would be invited. All actors would do was moan over scenes that had been cut or dialogue that was truncated. No sound people or special effects artists. Inevitably, they wanted to fix imagined defects in their own contributions. And certainly not studio heads or screen owners. A hundred defects that could be fixed or at least glossed over would become apparent at the first screening. There was no point in sharing these with the buyers.

He called Catherine with the date. She should fly out the night before the screening, which would be the morning after. They would look at the film, spend a few hours discussing what they had seen, and then look at it again. She was excited by the prospect. "How is it?" she begged.

"We won't know until we look at it," he snapped back.

Catherine promised to extend the invitation to Peter.

Then Padraig called Jennifer. "I'm ready to repay your loan," he announced.

"Really!" She hadn't been following his progress and was taken by surprise.

"Not in money, mind you. It will be a few months before the cash registers start ringing. But in artistic beauty. The movie is assembled and ready for showing. I want you to see it."

Jennifer bubbled with enthusiasm. "The music works the way you thought it would?"

"Like a dream. A wonderful dream. Listen to the music and you understand the story. You know exactly how to feel about the things you're seeing."

"And the effects? All that you hoped for?"

"More. These people lift the story right off the film. They make things happen that you couldn't even imagine, much less stage."

She promised to be there. "You said it would be dark and that I wouldn't even know you were in the room. But I think, as I watch it, I also want to see the expression on your face."

Catherine balked when she learned that she would be in the

same suite as her sister. "For God's sake, Peter," she whined, "the police have all but told me that Jennifer hired my killer. With her so close, I might die in my sleep."

Peter told her again that he couldn't believe that Jennifer would harm anyone. And she countered with all the hard evidence that the police had amassed. She told him about the telephone records and Jennifer's tips to Will Ferris at his restaurant. "I used to be wary of Jennifer. I always tried to keep a cautious eye. But now I'm terrified. I asked you if we should be getting her help and you laughed at the idea. Now I'm telling you. Jennifer is right at the edge, maybe even over the top if she really tried to have me killed. She belongs in a hospital, not at a Hollywood screening."

Her hysteria was so apparent that Peter had to take her seriously. "You really believe that Jennifer tried to kill you? That she'd try again?"

"I believe the police. And I know things about her that they haven't even guessed. Yes, I think she tried to kill me. And until she gets some help, I'll be damned if I'll give her another chance."

Peter agreed to change the arrangements. He put each sister in a separate hotel, and he promised not to tell either Catherine or Jennifer where the other was staying.

Peter went out to the Coast a day early. He had been disappointed in the failure of his investigators to find the photographer who had taken the damning pictures. Someone, he reasoned, had to be bragging about photos of Padraig O'Connell in the altogether. But, as the detectives explained, they had pretty much covered all the photographers. They were now working on the private detectives, who would be much more reticent to talk about their work.

"Do you have any idea how many private investigators there are out here?" one of the investigators told him. "Almost as many as out-of-work screenwriters. They must all keep busy following each other's wives."

"Put more men on it," Peter urged. "People's lives are in danger until we find out who hired the photographer."

He drove past Padraig's beach house, convinced himself that there was no one home, and then drove down the driveway. He figured that there were alarms, so he didn't go to the doorway or climb up on the deck. But just by walking around the property, he was able to figure how the photos were probably taken.

Padraig's bedroom opened out onto a walkway that connected with the deck overlooking the beach. The photographer could have climbed to the deck and then gone around to the walkway. There he could literally press his nose against the glass slider. Or he might have parked up on the road, then walked halfway down the hill. From there he could see into the bedroom and take his pictures with a telephoto lens.

The only problem Peter could think of as he looked up at the house was that there was a drape drawn across the glass door. With the drape closed, there was no way to see into the room. So, he wondered, why wasn't the drape drawn when Catherine and Padraig were in bed together? Were they just careless? Or did one of them want to be seen and photographed? Maybe they wanted the light from the stars and the sound of the crashing sea. But maybe the event had been staged to destroy Jennifer's marriage. He needed to know for certain who had hired the photographer.

The first screening was held in the bunkerlike offices of the film editor, with Peter between the two sisters and Padraig sitting by himself. They were in a basement screening room, a theater with three rows of couches built to seat a dozen people. The lights lowered, and a visual countdown filled the screen while the sound system crackled and hissed. When the numbers got down to zero, the screen went black.

Then, in the darkness, came the distant sound of a tin whistle blowing a soft, lazy dirge. Slowly, a landscape came out of the darkness, a rolling countryside in early morning, the trees still outlines and the green grass nearly black. In a long shot, the camera panned the pastoral setting, finding the detail of morning. A lamb stirred and staggered to its feet. A light appeared in a window. There was a trace of smoke from a sod fire in a hearth. The camera searched and found peace everywhere.

Suddenly the flat drum began to beat, its pounding rising over the tin whistle melody. Simultaneously, the camera caught distant headlights moving along the meandering hillside. In an instant, the mood went from serenity to urgency.

The car came closer, but still in the long shot so the headlights were simply dots jumping out from the enormous background. At last it emerged from the mist, a 1920s English touring car with its roof up and the curtains pulled down. It turned from the main road onto a side road, where a two-story farmhouse came into view, and killed its lights while rolling. The drum went still. The whistle died. An unseen dog began barking. Three men jumped out and walked purposefully to the house. They were all in long coats. One wore a fedora and the other two caps. They went straight in through the front door.

Lights were on inside the house. There were voices, and then a few shouts raised in argument. Suddenly the door burst open. The three men came out, walking a man who was still in his nightshirt between them. They steered him into the car, and then they backed out onto the road. The headlights came on as the car lurched and drove away.

Then came the first cut, to a window on the second floor of the house. A boy looked out, his nose pressed to the glass, his breath creating a fog. A dog's face, tongue panting, jumped up beside his. Across the scene came a simple white title, *Inheritance*. The small audience settled back into the sofas.

The movie ran nearly three hours, the sequence shot from the helicopters taking fifteen minutes by itself. It ended with a close-up of the dog walking to a grave, circling it briefly, and then lying down on top of it. The camera pulled back slowly, eventually losing the grave site as a detail in the much wider panorama, a duplicate of the opening scene. Then there was a fade-out, ending in the last breathy tone from the tin whistle.

The lights came up on tearstained faces and a long moment of silence.

"Wow!" Jennifer said, finally breaking the spell, and then the gathering applauded as if they might call the actors back for an encore.

Padraig turned from his front-row seat, obviously touched by what he had just seen. Peter leaned forward and said to him, "I'm glad you stayed on." Then he said to Catherine, "It looks as if we have a hit on our hands."

"What do you think?" Padraig asked the film editor, who answered, "Too long. We've got to trim at least ten minutes. Maybe more." Padraig nodded.

"We have to do better with timing the breaks for television," another voice offered. "We want commercial breaks coming during suspense to bring people back."

Another nod from Padraig.

"But, overall," the editor rejoined, "a nice story beautifully told. It's going to be one hell of a premiere."

They saw it again an hour later. Peter thought he saw much more the second time and enjoyed the experience more. Catherine was thrilled and accepted congratulations from all corners as if she were responsible for the artistry. "We're going to get our money back," she said to Peter in an I-told-you-so cadence. "This is going to turn into a major profit center."

"You may be right," he conceded. And he admitted to himself that he may have misjudged O'Connell. The man was still a bastard, but his artistry was genuine.

Jennifer remained behind when the others left for the airport. Then she joined Padraig and his entourage for a modest celebration at a club frequented by studio executives. The party was intentionally understated but still loud enough to announce their success. The studios, Padraig reasoned, would front some of the costs of satellite distribution just to buy into the new era.

"Stay for a few days," he begged her when they were finally

alone. "Move into the beach house. I'll move out. Or stay at your hotel if that suits you. The important thing is that we have a lot to talk about. We have much more between us than the success of the picture."

Jennifer was tempted, and she hesitated. "Maybe for a day," she finally conceded, pleading that she had left too many tasks unfinished back in New York. Padraig promised to drop everything so they could have a full day together. He took her for a drive up the coastal highway to Santa Barbara and a small inn that looked out over the straits toward Santa Cruz Island. They sat on a porch under an umbrella, sipped lemonade, and chatted idly about the movie until Padraig moved the conversation to the important issues.

"Can we try again, Jennifer? Do you think we'd have a chance?"

"I don't know," she said as if she hadn't given the possibility a thought. But in fact she had been thinking of little else. She knew she would enjoy being back in his company. But there were two issues that she had to work through.

The most important question was why he had married her in the first place. Had he truly found her attractive? He had said apologetically that his initial intention was nothing more than a one-night stand in Cannes. But she liked the idea that of all the bedroom bunnies who had been available, he had been drawn to her. And then he had said he found her real, a delightful departure from the perpetual sales pitch that he lived in. She wanted to believe that.

He had never mentioned an interest in her wealth, but Jennifer knew it must have been a factor. He was trying to launch a new career in an expensive sector of the industry without any financial backing. It would be poetic if he had fallen in love with a peasant girl, but that was unrealistic. He wouldn't even have been looking in places where there wasn't any money.

But what had been the deciding factor: Had he truly been taken by her? Or, as Catherine and Peter suspected, was her wealth the only thing he could find attractive? Was she really the ugly duckling who needed to fend off any compliment as obviously insincere; or had she grown into the swan, elegant and beautiful in her own way, who could be perfectly confident of suitors' intentions.

The next question was why had he traded her for Catherine. Was it a simple matter of easier access to more money? Or was it the more attractive sister, at home in his world and a much greater asset on his arm? If it had been his idea, then his betrayal had been total. He had come for money and found it in a more attractive package. But if it had been Catherine's idea, then Padraig wouldn't be nearly as guilty. Catherine could have made it very plain that Pegasus would never tolerate him as Jennifer's husband. The tampered brakes were clear proof of how far she and Peter were willing to go. She could have persuaded him that a business relationship was his only source of capital, and that she would be the overseeing partner. Under that weight, he might crumble even if he did truly love her.

His question still hung in the air? Could they possibly get back together? Would she even consider trying a fresh start?

"I really don't know," Jennifer said again. "I don't understand why you wanted me in the first place. I'm not sure why you abandoned me. And I have no idea why you want me back. I'm not sure whether I blame you or Catherine. She's easier to hate than you are. But you're harder to believe."

He managed a smile. "I suppose I am a habitual liar," he admitted cheerfully. "There's no reason why you should believe me." But then he launched into his own version of events, taking on her questions one at a time. It was her freshness and her honesty that had attracted him. And when he had learned that the trade-show hostess was actually one of the richest women in the world, he had found her even more exciting. "Even I couldn't get away with pretending that your wealth wasn't attractive, but with you it was an added inducement, not the first feature."

Why had he left her? Because her Pegasus partners wanted him out. Badly enough to hire someone to kill him. Badly enough to buy his fledgling production company out from under him if he didn't do things their way. "It wasn't as if I had a choice. Nobody asked would I prefer to remain independent in the bosom of my wife. It was take it or leave it. Either Pegasus bought in, with Catherine as my overseer, or I could expect even more accidents." Did she know, he wondered, that Catherine had even tried to regulate his personal spending, down to deciding how much he was allowed to spend for his office furnishings?

And why did he want her back? Because *Inheritance* was going to give him a new start, and he wanted to spend his reclaimed life with Jennifer. "It's you I love, darlin', and I think you still have some feelings for me, too. We were happy together, and I think we can be happy again."

It was everything Jennifer wanted to hear. And for that reason she was suspicious. Did he really love her, or her money? Did Peter really try to kill him, or was Peter the only man whom she could actually trust? And, most important, was Catherine simply greedy for even more success, or was she a devil who had to be destroyed?

They were back to small talk for the rest of the day. Padraig waited in his car while she checked out of her hotel, and then drove her to the airport. As they were parting, he asked, "What can I do to make you give us another chance?"

"Give me time, Padraig, there are a lot of questions that I have to answer for myself."

"All the time you want," he said. "But can we talk in the meantime? Can we spend some time together?"

She paused to think. "I'm not moving out here, if that's what you mean. And I'm not inviting you back into my apartment."

"There are other places, like the inn we were at today. Places on the East Coast as well. I need a chance to do some courting, darlin'. Otherwise, some dull money manager will make off with you."

He brushed a goodbye kiss softly across her cheek. "We'll talk, Padraig," she promised. "You're probably the only one who can answer all my questions."

NINETEEN

PADRAIG CAME up with a place where they could be together without seeming to move back in with each other. "It's called Pennobquit. It's an island off the Maine coast."

Jennifer didn't know how to react. She had never heard of the place, and it sounded even more primitive than French Guiana. "Padraig, I need more time, not a change in scenery. I don't think moving to an uninhabited island is going to help."

"It's just a chance to get away from everything else," he pleaded. "Your satellites, my film, your sister, all the things that confuse us. We can take a boat out of Camden and get lost in the Acadian islands. Nobody lives on Pennobquit. But I hear it's a rocky beach on one end and a sheer cliff on the other."

"But if nobody lives there . . . " she objected. It seemed logical that if the place was so attractive, someone would have discovered it before Padraig.

"There's a cove where we can anchor. We can use the boat as our cottage and have the island as our garden. The sea . . . the rocky shore . . . it should be beautiful. And we can wander around for as long as we want with no fear of coming across a tourist or even catching a glimpse of a television news report. We can talk, Jennifer. For hours at end."

She found the idea appealing. Maybe, with all the distractions of their lives put aside, they could figure out whether or not they belonged together. But she also saw the danger. Once she became captive to his charms, he could probably talk her into anything. She didn't want to find them reconciled until she was comfortable with his answers to her questions.

"Padraig, there's so much going on here—" she started, trying to build a foundation for her excuse.

"What?" he demanded. "For the love of God, lass, what's more important than the two of us? My movie will survive with the editors. And your satellites aren't going to tumble out of orbit. The world will be the same a week from now. But you and I don't have to be. We can decide how we ought to be living."

She put him off. "Out of the question," she said finally. But in the middle of her business day, she pulled up a map of the Maine coast on her computer and kept enlarging the detail until she found Pennobquit Island.

It was dead south of Harwood Island, in Blue Hill Bay, due west of Bass Harbor, all places she had never heard of. There was Camden to the west, and Mount Desert Island to the east, and nothing but rocks in the immediate vicinity. Jennifer couldn't find anything appealing in the terrain or any reason to go there.

The next day Padraig sent her a picture of the boat. It was a forty-eight-foot trawler, fitted out as a luxury yacht. There were private cabins fore and aft, each with a queen-size bed and a private head and shower. Between was a raised helm, a very complete galley, and a great room with lounges and a pop-up table. She could, he indicated, have all the privacy she wanted. But they could meet on the decks for the long talks that they needed, and go ashore to do all the exploring they could handle.

"I won't press it if it makes you uncomfortable," he wrote in an attachment. "But it is kind of a middle ground between my beach house and your loft. Kind of a Vienna for signing our peace treaty."

Uncomfortable? She found it terrifying. Out of touch with the world and alone with a man who Peter still believed had tried to kill her. A week with no one to talk to except the man who had abandoned her and left her to suffer in silence. But still, she found it intriguing. They would never solve their problems if they met only during the intervals that their separate business affairs allowed. They needed to get away if he was ever to explain where her sister now stood in his life. She needed time to listen and quiet to think if she was ever going to be able to believe him.

She returned an e-mail, telling him to make the arrangements and hire the boat. She couldn't spare a week, but she could take a long weekend. An hour later, a messenger showed up at her door with a bouquet of flowers. The note said that three days wasn't long enough, but that Padraig would take even a minute if that was all she could give him. Rumors about the flowers passed from office to office faster than if they had been broadcast by one of the company's satellites.

Peter was the first to raise concerns. "Meet him anywhere," he told her. "But in a reasonably public place. How are you going to get away from him on an island?"

She wasn't afraid of Padraig, Jennifer answered. He had never harmed her. And then she asked if Peter still thought that the only thing Padraig found attractive about her was her money. "I'm not Daddy's little girl anymore, Peter. I'm a grown woman, able to make my own decisions. You don't have to watch over me anymore."

He nodded in acknowledgment. All he could add was "I guess I like watching over you."

Catherine telephoned to say how much she had come to detest O'Connell. "I showed you what he was after," she said. "And that's still what he's after. He knows that Peter and I want to pull out, and he's looking for another banker."

Even though she had heard it before, Jennifer still felt the sting. "Sure. What else could he possibly find in me? Particularly now that he's been to the mountain with you."

"Damn you, Jennifer! Stop wallowing in your self-pity and use your head. You're nobody's ugly duckling. But that doesn't mean that Padraig O'Connell isn't the big bad wolf. He's a liar and a con man. You shouldn't meet him on a public street, much less on some desolate island in Maine. Why do you think he wants to get you alone?"

"Maybe to seduce me," Jennifer said.

"Oh, for God's sake," Catherine answered.

The two police detectives called ahead and arrived at Jennifer's apartment precisely on time. She led them into her living room and made them comfortable around her coffee table, one on either side of the small director's chair she pulled up for herself. She assumed that they had come to discuss the intruder who had tried to drill through her door. She was surprised when the first thing they brought up was her relationship with Will Ferris.

"I thought we covered that," she said irritably. "I told you I never met the man."

"Then you never called him on the telephone?" the man to her right asked.

"Of course not."

"But his number was in last month's listing of your local calls. You phoned him from this apartment." The officer offered her a copy of her local exchange's printout.

She glanced at it and didn't understand it but decided not to ask. "If his number is in there, it has to be a mistake. I never called anyone by that name. At least not knowingly."

The other detective set copies of restaurant receipts on the table. Jennifer looked and then showed surprise. "That's my signature." She looked closer. They were credit-card receipts she had signed at Peaches coffee shop.

"You wrote in a tip for the waiter. Server eleven." He pointed to the waiter notation on each of the slips. "Server eleven was Will Ferris."

Jennifer seemed bewildered.

"This one," the policeman went on, "was just four days before the break-in at your sister's apartment. So Ferris was standing right in front of you while he waited on your table."

"Maybe he was," she conceded. "But I couldn't tell you right now who waited on me at lunch today. It's just not the kind of thing I notice."

The detective retrieved his copies of the receipts. Before Jennifer could compose herself, his partner took over. "Your sister went into business with your husband, didn't she?"

She nodded but then added, "It was company business. We were both involved."

"But your sister was working closely with him. She was the one in day-to-day contact."

Jennifer agreed, but she didn't mention just how close that contact had been.

"How did you feel about that?" he continued.

She looked from one to the other. "It was a business arrangement," she snapped. But she guessed they knew exactly how she felt. Enraged, defeated, embarrassed, vengeful, and murderous. She stood abruptly. "Look, I don't want to talk any further about this. If you have more questions, call my attorney."

"Do you need an attorney?" one of them asked.

"Am I suspected of something?" she countered.

"You might be charged," the other said casually.

"Charged with what?"

"Hindering an investigation. You haven't been very helpful regarding your relationship with Will Ferris."

"Then charge me. My lawyer always knows where to reach me." She went to her desk and found the two policemen standing when she returned. "Here's his card. Henry Harris."

She began to tremble as soon as they left, and rushed to the bar for a drink that might calm her. The police, it was obvious, were nibbling at the edges of the truth. Maybe they already knew the true nature of her relationship with Catherine. There were countless witnesses to their years of simmering hatred. Catherine herself could have provided details. They probably knew Jennifer was lying when she said that her sister's relationship with her husband was "just business." And what if they had the pictures? That would be all the proof they would need of her motive for murder.

What should she do? There was no place she could run to. Even Padraig's barren rock on the Maine coast wouldn't be far enough. And yet she couldn't just sit around and wait to be arrested.

She thought of calling Harris and began rehearsing what she might say. "Henry, I think I'm going to be charged with attempted murder!" But that would only begin a probe on his part and lead to more questions that she didn't want to answer. She thought of Padraig but dismissed the idea instantly. She wasn't yet sure that she could trust him. Would he rally to her interests, Catherine's, or only to his own? And, of course, she thought of Peter. Except she had just told him that she no longer needed his protection and that he should stay out of her affairs.

She began to feel the loneliness that had been part of her adult life. She was off by herself amid events rushing by that she couldn't control. She needed help, and there was no one she could turn to. The prospect of escaping with Padraig to a desolate island suddenly became attractive.

Padraig came east two days before their trip to make the arrangements. He stopped by her loft, bringing a fantastic bouquet of flowers. "I won't be here to enjoy them," she protested, but he argued that a few hours of enjoyment was all that was to be expected from cut flowers. He gave her a list of personal items that she might need, including seasickness pills and insect repellent. "Just precautions. I've arranged flat seas and ordered the entire island dusted with Agent Orange. All the bugs will be suicidal."

Finally, he produced an elaborately wrapped gift that he urged her to open. She eyed it suspiciously, guessing that it might be a provocative nightgown or some other toy suggestive of his true intentions. "You said there are two cabins on this boat," she reminded him.

"And you can have both of them," he answered. Then he gestured impatiently toward the package. "Open it. It won't explode."

She did, with exaggerated care, and took out a set of inflatable water wings. "In case you decide to leave early," he explained.

Jennifer laughed hysterically while Padraig struggled with the air valve and exhausted himself blowing up the toy. Then she told him, "You know, the only time I laugh anymore is when I'm with you." She leaned in to him and kissed his cheek. She didn't pull away when he turned his face so that their lips were touching.

He was the one who pulled back abruptly. "Now, now, we mustn't let ourselves be distracted. There's work to do." He handed her the water wings. "Wear these when you get into Camden. That way I'll be sure to recognize you." And then he was gone, leaving Jennifer staring at the door he had closed behind him and thinking that maybe she should pack a sexy nightgown just in case.

PART FOUR

TWENTY

It was obvious that she had to die. And it really had nothing to do with hatred. You could look at it as self-defense. Without a doubt, she was the one who had planned the break-in at my apartment. If it weren't for the security system, I probably would have been killed right where I was standing.

Or maybe it was the only ending left to either of us. She had taken Padraig away from me, or at least that's what she was trying to do. And that was the pattern of our entire lives. Whatever one had, the other wanted. She had copied my drawings, taken my toys, and stolen the recognition that I earned. She had moved in on my boyfriends and horned in on my business achievements. I really had no hope of having a life of my own as long as my sister was looking over my shoulder and breathing down my neck. There was little doubt that one of us would have to go.

I think that's why she tried to have me killed. Like me, she understood that there wasn't room for both of us. It was as simple as that. It had nothing to do with a psychopathic personality. It was simply a solution to a lifelong problem that wasn't going to go away.

That's why this boat trip Padraig came up with was so appealing. It provided the perfect opportunity as well as the perfect alibi. Think about it. We were going to be hundreds of miles apart and completely out of touch with each other. One of us on a rock that was precisely in the middle of nowhere. The other in Manhattan. How could anything that happened to one of us possibly be blamed on the other? Oh, I'd know what happened. And, of course, my dear sister would find out in the end.

Of course I knew it was wrong. One person is not supposed to wish evil on another, much less pull the trigger. So we can forget all that nonsense about insanity and my not knowing the difference between right and wrong. I knew. I knew it was a crime and that if I got caught, I could spend the rest of my life in prison.

But what you have to understand is that there was no other way. I simply had no choice. Ever since we were children, she has been edging her way into my life. Now she was trying to take it over completely.

Inheritance *was my picture. I put up the money to keep it alive. Padraig had told me several times that he was going to dedicate the film to me. But my sister walked into the screening as if she owned the place. You can't imagine how it feels to see yourself being elbowed out of your own achievements.*

You can just imagine the premiere, can't you? Padraig steps out of the car and then reaches back in to help his lady out. And out comes my sister, smiling and waving at the television cameras. And what would I do? Come in the second limo and sneak in behind the crowd as if I'm just a friend of the family?

Padraig was mine, as any sensible person would have known. But with her around, I never could be sure. He told me he loved me, and I suppose I knew it was true. But at the same time, he was still seeing a lot of my sister. So how could I be sure he wasn't saying the same things to her? Maybe he was telling her that he needed to keep me around for business reasons, just until the movie began returning money. Maybe he had promised her that he'd drop me as soon as he could so that they could be together forever. I assumed that he was stringing her along. But it could have been the other way around. After all, he was an actor. He won the Academy Award.

And Pegasus was mine. Everyone knew that I was the brains behind the business. Peter certainly knew it. But she turned him against me, until Peter was using all his muscle to keep Padraig and me apart. What did Peter care? There was plenty of money for him whether Padraig left or stayed. In fact, he probably would have made more once Leprechaun blossomed. But he fought it to the end just to drive Padraig out of my life. Who do you suppose put him up to that?

In the final analysis, it was my sister or me. Together we would have self-destructed. And she knew that as well as I did. She tried to have me killed, didn't she? So I struck first, in order to reclaim the life she had stolen and save the life she was determined to destroy.

Call it a crime, if you must. But it's not insane hatred, and it's not the mind of a brooding psychopath. It's simply a case of doing what has to be done and letting the chips fall where they may.

TWENTY-ONE

PADRAIG HADN'T expected the crowd. He knew that Camden, with its picturesque harbor, weathered white houses, picket fences, and boutique stores was a summer tourist mecca. But he hadn't figured on the foliage. Fall, on any civilized calendar, was still a month away. But in Maine the leaves begin to turn in late summer, weeks before the procession of color would work its way down the Appalachians during October and November. The foliage followers had already arrived, and the streets were packed.

He was pleased, for a change, to go unnoticed behind a disguise of sunglasses and a soft, floppy hat. The bland rental car wouldn't attract any attention. Of course, he'd be recognized as soon as he stepped into the yacht agency to claim his trawler and the hired captain. And, as always, the word would spread until half the town and most of the tourists were pressed to the glass outside the office. But they had no advance warning. None of the arrangements had been made using his name. In his telephone conversations with the broker, he had been careful not to use his signature brogue. Just another businessman planning to get away for a few days.

He turned off the main street to the drive that headed to the piers, and crept along behind tourists until he reached the broker's sign. Then he stepped out of the car, pulled the brim of the hat down over his face, and sauntered along the pier. He could see the boat, a white-hulled trawler with sparkling brightwork around the doors and windows. The name, *Maineman*, was painted across the transom, with Camden listed as the port of registry. He paused momentarily to take her in and wonder what impression she would make on Jennifer, who, he remembered, had done some yachting with Peter Barnes. He guessed she would appreciate the boat's businesslike lines. He noticed the inflatable dinghy sitting on the rails atop the afterquarters, its small outboard already mounted. And the boom out from the mast that would lift the dinghy into the water. That would give them easy passage from the boat to the beach. He stepped inside and went to the secretary's desk, still wearing his hat and sunglasses.

"Mr. Pegan," he said softly. "I believe I have a charter waiting."

The woman never looked up but simply flipped through the pile of charter contracts on her desk. "Mr. Cashen would be handling that," she said, settling on one of the documents.

"Yes, that's his name. Cashen," he agreed happily.

She rose. "Come with me," she said, and led him down a hallway to the back of the building. There was one office, not overly large and housing only one desk. The sign on the door said HOWARD V. CASHEN, which struck Padraig as unnecessary, since there was no one else to confuse him with. The man in the office got up and offered his hand. Padraig took off the hat and folded the sunglasses into his pocket. The broker's eyes and the secretary's eyes widened at the same instant. His expression turned from business to pleasure. Her mouth dropped open and stayed that way until she covered it with the back of her hand.

"That explains," Cashen said after dismissing the dumbstruck secretary and gesturing Padraig into a chair, "why all the correspondence came from a third party."

"Is that a problem?" Padraig asked.

"Not now. Not since I understand your reason for confidentiality." Cashen was amused. "I suppose you have to go through this sort of thing all the time."

He pulled his records and consulted them as he explained how the boat had been provisioned. Diesel fuel and freshwater tanks had been filled. The holding tank had been drained and freshened, the bilge pump checked, all plumbing lines tested, all toilets, showers, and faucets exercised. The engine had been checked out, electronics and navigation systems verified. "She's in tip-top condition. Thoroughly seaworthy," Cashen concluded. Padraig marveled at the sizable dollar figure that was at the bottom of his page.

Then he got into the galley provisioning. There were fresh eggs, bacon, and sausages for the breakfasts, as well as cold cereals and bake-and-serve muffins. A variety of microwave meals for the lunches, along with several servings of cold finger foods. And for the dinners, there were steaks, chops, and fresh fish that could be done on a grill hung out from the stern cockpit, and half a dozen kinds of fruits and vegetables. For all this, together with the hefty stores of champagne, gin, single malt, and beer that had been locked in the liquor cabinet, and the variety of wines in the wine rack, there was another surprising sum of money due.

And, of course, there was a fee for the captain who would take Padraig and the yacht on the thirty-mile trip from Camden to Blue Hill, where Jennifer was scheduled to come aboard. She planned to be chartered up on Friday morning to a small airport on the water where Padraig would pick her up. With the complicated rock formations and the challenging navigation behind them, the captain would then depart, leaving it to his passengers to make the short trip out into Blue Hill Bay and anchor off Pennobquit Island. For three hours at sea and one simple docking, the captain was making more than one of Padraig's stuntmen.

"So," Cashen totaled on a small pocket calculator, "it comes to an additional three thousand, two hundred dollars. And your check allowed for three thousand in provisioning."

Padraig reached into his pocket and peeled off two hundred in cash. The broker swept it up, then passed Padraig an empty logbook. "I wonder if I might have your autograph?"

The captain turned out to be anything but a yacht officer.

Padraig was expecting a Nordic figure, painfully shaved, in officer's cap and uniform jacket. Instead, he got a short, bushy type with three days' growth of beard, who wore jeans and a checkered sports shirt. He came without a title and identified himself only as Mike. He took a quick tour of the trawler, sneered at the small, ornate wheel and the computerlike navigation display, and started the engine. Padraig dragged his own duffel aboard, the broker threw off the lines, and the *Maineman* backed out of its slip.

It got cold the instant they cleared the breakwater. Along with the early foliage season came early frost, and an onshore breeze chilled by passage over the Labrador Current. They could expect the days to be pleasant and the nights to be raw. "Hope ya hahve somethin' a bit heavier than that," Mike said, nodding at Padraig's golf shirt.

Padraig was immediately thankful that he had requested a captain. The chart was a confusing pattern of deep blues and glaring yellows indicating safe passages and dangerous shoals. The passages were pockmarked with small islands, which he could see were really rocky spikes, and with X's indicating rocks that lurked just below a low tide. Most of the thirty-mile passage was filled with hazards that could tear the bottom out of a ship. Yet Mike had both engines pushed to cruise, scarcely referred to the chart, and hadn't bothered to turn on the navigation electronics. "Plenty of water," he said when Padraig commented on the proximity of stone walls rising up out of the sea. Then he tore the filter off a cigarette and struck a wooden match with his thumbnail.

The view was truly beautiful. The water was black and clear, nearly the color of the rocks it washed against. The trawler plowed through with pulsating crashes, throwing out a salty white spray. Huge clouds climbed in towers high into the sky. And on the shoreline, the bright green grass was topped by reds, oranges, and yellows in the trees.

"When is the young lady joining you?" Mike asked to show Padraig that he knew exactly what he was up to.

"Tomorrow morning. She's flying up from New York."

"That's nice!" Mike observed. Then he added, "You actah fellas certainly lead excitin' lives."

"You don't know the half of it," Padraig answered.

They cruised to the east above North Haven Island, then turned to the south to move around Deer Isle. The weather picked up a bit and the spray began hitting the windows as they moved out toward open water. "Blowing a bit," Padraig said, trying to sound like a seafarer.

"Nothin' like wintah," Mike answered. "Then it's the waves that are bangin' on the windahs."

Padraig was happy that he hadn't waited another week.

Peter made one last try to keep Jennifer from going. He walked into her office unannounced and stretched into the chair across from her desk. He beat around the bush with a few questions about the state of the network and took her through some traffic figures that she had already seen. Only when she shuffled impatiently did he get to his message.

"I'm really uncomfortable with this trip you're taking, and I wish you'd reconsider." He saw she was about to interrupt him, so he rushed his words. "There are hundreds of places that you and Padraig can meet to talk things out. It doesn't have to be on a deserted island out of communication with the rest of the world. Have dinner in a private dining room. Or take a buggy ride through Central Park. Someplace where you're not alone."

"The whole idea is to be alone. To get away from everything—and everyone—else."

He felt chastised. He was most likely the "everyone" she was talking about. Catherine had given up after her initial protests. "I don't care what she does," she had finally conceded.

But Peter did care. He had still not shaken the idea that it was O'Connell who had arranged Jennifer's accident. And he had no doubts about the motive. Peter had documented to the penny exactly how much the man had taken from the two sisters.

There was hardly a scenario where *Inheritance* could return even seventy-five cents on the dollar. Their chances of being repaid were nonexistent.

"Suppose you have another accident," he tried hesitantly. He knew he was touching a subject that would drive Jennifer into rage. "Who's going to know about it? And when someone learns about it, how are they going to get to you? You were in a hospital last time in less than an hour. There is no hospital where he's taking you. There may not even be a place to land a helicopter."

"What kind of accident do you have in mind?" she responded sarcastically. "We won't have a car, if that's what you're worried about."

He snapped back, "You're at sea without a captain, for God's sake. Anything could happen."

"We'll be anchored about a hundred feet from shore. It's probably a lot safer than taking a carriage ride through Central Park. Catherine will be in more danger if she steps out on her balcony."

"Unexpected things happen very quickly on boats!" he reminded her. And then he killed his argument by adding, "Particularly when the other guy in the boat is distracted."

She rolled her eyes. "Please, Peter, I have a lot of things to finish up before I leave."

He looked at her. "Please, I'm begging you. Don't go!"

Jennifer was taken back. Peter, begging? That wasn't the man she had known for the past ten years. He would disagree. He would argue. But he would never put his feelings into his case. He stood or fell with the facts. He never whined or complained. He never begged.

"Why are you doing this?" Jennifer asked. "You know I have to see this through."

"Why do you have to see it through? You already know how badly it can end. You don't have to give him another chance to . . . to hurt you."

"I have to give myself another chance," she answered. "Padraig can have a hundred more lives, with me or without me. But he's the only life I have. He's the only one who cares about me."

"I care about you. I always have, and I always will."

She heard him clearly, but she wasn't prepared for his meaning. Of course he cared about her. He had promised her father that he would, just as he had promised to take care of Catherine. But he didn't understand. It wasn't her physical health at issue, or even the fortune that he had helped to build. What needed caring for now was simply her. Her self-image, her temperament, her vision of a future. Her need to love someone more than herself, and to be loved by someone in return. Her freedom and her individuality. All the things that could never take root as the poor little rich girl living in the shadow of a famous sister.

Peter meant to keep her safe, and she appreciated that. But being safe wasn't enough. A bird was safe in a cage, and it was exactly the cage that she had to smash. Peter couldn't help. He had built the cage to keep her safe. Catherine had slammed the door to keep her rival from flying out into the open air. She had to escape from both of them.

"Thank you," she said. "I really do appreciate your concern. But this is a chance I have to take."

He thought of what else he might say. And there was nothing. At least nothing that was believable, or that might make a difference. When he was walking back to his own office, he prayed that he might be wrong. Perhaps he had been totally wrong about Padraig O'Connell. Perhaps, after wallowing through his weakness and greed, the man was ready for a serious relationship. He hoped so, although the thought of Jennifer lying in Padraig O'Connell's embrace was more than he could bear.

She was the only passenger in the twin-turbo charter that cut diagonally across Connecticut and broke out over the water at the base of Cape Cod. She picked out the towers of Boston ahead on her left and Provincetown off to her right. Minutes later and she was out over the Gulf of Maine with the million-island coastline coming into view.

Jennifer had no illusions about what was ahead for her. Padraig would wear his contrition like a bloodstained bandage. He would douse her in flattery while pouring on his Irish charm and lightning wit, all in his thickest and most lovable brogue. The temptation to cave in, especially while bobbing at sea in the shelter of a lonely island, would be strong indeed.

But she was determined to exact a price. Padraig would have to explain, to her satisfaction, exactly what Catherine meant to him. He would have to convince her that Catherine was no longer a factor in any of his business or personal equations, and that he could be committed, as she was, to putting an end to her sister's domination. Whether intentionally or not, he had bored into their area of vulnerability and played the two sisters against each other in whatever combination it took to keep the cash flowing. All that was going to end.

She looked down at the islands that were passing below, remote, uninhabited outposts of the continent reaching out into the North Atlantic. Peter's anxieties came back to her. This was not a place where she could easily be rescued. But it suited her purposes exactly. She was just going to have to take her chances.

The plane was losing altitude and beginning a wide turn in toward the mainland. She heard the flaps lower and the landing gear snap into place. Mount Desert Island stretched out to the right, and Blue Hill Bay was under the left wing. Seconds later she was bouncing across the runway of a small executive airport that never could have handled a larger airplane.

Padraig was waiting, jaunty in an open windbreaker and officer's cap, to take her garment bag and lead her to his car. He was chatting instantly, describing the boat like an old salt in terms he had picked up from Mike. Then he was into their voyage through the rocky passage and out into Blue Hill Bay. In his telling, Mike did little more than make the coffee. And the scenery! They were driving through the glorious fall colors, but he insisted that they looked different when seen from the water. "It's a heavenly place, darlin'. If it were any prettier, it would need a pearly gate." His banter was incessant, a nervous flow delivered in his excited tenor voice. It was almost as if he was afraid to let her get a word in.

He turned down a gravel path toward a shed that sagged on splintered pilings and seemed about to topple into the sea. Then he was out of the car and rushing up a wobbly gangplank, her baggage in hand. Jennifer took in the setting. It was as pretty as Padraig had described. But, as Peter had warned, it was also desolate, close to the edge of the earth. She followed Padraig into the shed, trying to keep her balance.

They came out the other side onto a narrow pier and Jennifer got her first glimpse of the trawler. Suddenly she felt very secure. It was a big boat, high out of the water, with seafaring lines. She stepped quickly across the dock, thankful that she was wearing sneakers, and nearly leaped aboard. To her mind, the boat was far less likely to sink than the building and its pier.

"Welcome aboard," Padraig said, rendering her a snappy salute. "May I show you to the admiral's quarters." He led her through a sliding door into the main saloon.

"Wow!" Jennifer said.

"Wow, indeed," he answered. "Hardly the hold of a slaver!" There was a sofa covered in forest-green sailcloth down one side of the space and matching armchairs facing in from the other side. A wide cocktail table was in the middle. Between the two chairs was a built-in entertainment center with a television, CD player, and sound system. The wooden brightwork, polished deck, and forest-green furniture gave the cabin the feeling of a posh men's club. Forward, on the port side, was a galley that compared favorably with her own kitchen. More compact, to be sure, but just as well equipped. To the right was the captain's chair, raised up like a bar stool behind a steering wheel and a bank of electronic gauges and screens.

"And your quarters," Padraig said, gesturing to steps that descended at the aft end of the cabin. He stepped back so that she could go ahead.

"Wow again!"

There was a queen-size island bed with night tables, a full

closet, and a door to her private head. Inside, there was a full-stall shower, not just the hand sprayer she had used on Peter's sailboat.

"You like it?" he asked anxiously.

" 'Hardly the hold of a slaver,' " Jennifer quoted.

The bedspread and the curtains were patterns of astrological maps in deep blues and silver. Masculine, perhaps, but neutral enough to serve any woman's taste. There was enough drawer space for one of Catherine's wardrobes.

"And," Padraig pointed out, "a sturdy lock on the door, just in case you stoke fires in my loins."

"I brought a pistol," she answered.

"Thoughtful," he said. Then he explained that his cabin was in the bow, as far away as it could be without being in the water. "Why don't you unpack and freshen up. Then, when you're ready, we'll take her to sea."

She looked at the lock after he left and decided she wouldn't need it. Padraig seemed as nervous as an adolescent on a first date. Nothing so far had been intimidating to her. Her job, she thought, would be to quiet him down so that they could talk seriously. Only then might the lock come in handy.

Peter was late getting to his office. He had been on the phone with the aircraft company that chartered executive jets to Pegasus, awaiting confirmation that Jennifer's plane had landed safely. He had breathed a sigh of relief that he knew was unnecessary. Both Jennifer and Catherine flew all over the world, commercially and in executive aircraft. He had never worried about them before. Besides, the flight was the least dangerous part of Jennifer's journey. There was no reason to feel relief. His anxiety was just beginning.

Padraig had been an escape artist when it came to signing documents. The agreement he had cavalierly offered to sign was still lost somewhere in the legal processes. The divorce agreement he had signed had never been filed. At this moment, Padraig would have a husband's claim on ownership of Pegasus should anything happen to his wife.

And what might happen? A sinking that only Padraig would survive? That wasn't likely. Peter knew the kind of boat they were aboard and doubted it could be sunk, at least not without allowing enough time to escape in the tender. An explosion, then? The boat would blow up while Padraig was ashore; he would find only smoldering wreckage with no trace of his wife. Probably not. Even a small-town police force in Maine would find that suspicious, and as an investigation could easily trace the exact location and cause of an explosion. A swimming accident? That was likely. Jennifer loved to swim and Padraig didn't. So, she went swimming over the side and took a cramp in the cold water. Credible, especially if they found an unmarked drowned body.

But then he caught himself. Jennifer felt safe, and she was no fool. She had done her own investigating of the auto accident and had found good evidence to show that Padraig wasn't to blame. More to the point, she had been alone with him on many occasions since, and nothing had happened to her. When someone had tried to break into her apartment, Padraig had been in Hollywood.

Peter had to admit to himself that his fears of foul play were really a by-product of his loathing for O'Connell. He hated the thought of the egotistical actor being with either of the sisters. He had tried to keep Jennifer away from him, to no avail. He had advised Catherine to take whatever financial loss was involved in order to be rid of him. She had refused. Both of them had decided to trust Padraig.

But there was a difference between his concern for Jennifer and his concern for Catherine. Peter was beginning to admit to himself what he had suspected for years. He was in love with Jennifer. It was a feeling he had suppressed for the sake of Pegasus, to remain impartial between the two heiress daughters. When he had noticed her interest, he had closed his eyes and turned away. And then, when he admitted his interest, she was

the one who had ignored the signals. But now, with all his promises to their father fulfilled, he was planning to leave the company. And once he left, he would be free to announce his feelings
and pursue them with all his strength.

That, he tried to tell himself, was the reason he was frightened. He was terrified that the liaison on the lonely coast would
bring Jennifer and Padraig back together, that Peter would lose
the woman he was just beginning to hope for. He knew it was
unworthy of him to try and stop her from finding happiness,
even if he wasn't part of it. But no matter how he tried, he
couldn't rid himself of the fear that Padraig was dangerous and
that something awful was about to happen to Jennifer.

He was lost in thought when his secretary broke in to announce a phone call. A Mr. Redmond was calling from Los Angeles. Redmond? Peter had to search his memory for the name.
Of course! Phil Redmond, the security company's man in Los
Angeles.

"Good morning, Phil. You're up early."

"Well, I wanted to get to you first thing. We finally came
across the photographer you were looking for. Like you predicted, he couldn't keep action photos of Padraig O'Connell a
secret forever. He did a bit of blabbing, and he happened to be
talking to one of his colleagues that we'd interviewed. The man
remembered our interest and called me last night to suggest a
price. He wanted ten thousand just for fingering the guy. We
settled for three."

"Who is he? Peter snapped.

"Turns out to be a Beverly Hills private detective. Photography is just a sideline, but he's gotten pretty good at it. Padraig
O'Connell isn't the only star in his portfolio."

"Phil, I don't care about the detective. What I need to know
is who hired him."

"Oh, Miss Pegan. Your boss."

"There are two Miss Pegans. Both of them are my boss."

"Jesus, I don't know. Is it important?"

"Life and death, and right at this moment."

"Sorry. I'll get back to you right away."

Peter found himself holding a dead phone. He set it down slowly as his mind began to whirl. Catherine, he thought. Why would she hire someone to photograph her with Padraig? To prove to her sister that Padraig was unfaithful? Why? She had already delivered that message to Jennifer, and she probably could have caught the bastard with any number of other women. That just didn't make sense. And then to send the photos to her sister: Why would she want to court her sister's hatred and fire up her anger? What could she possibly hope to gain?

So it had to be Jennifer. It wasn't impossible that she would want her husband followed, particularly after the evidence that he might have been involved in her accident. She would have gotten the photos of his philandering and then been enraged when she discovered that he was cheating with her sister. And then . . . the rest made sense. Then, in her anger, she could have remembered the out-of-work actor who lived in her building and trained in her gym. It was Jennifer who wanted Catherine thrown from the building. It was Jennifer who wanted revenge.

But there were holes in the case, and he wanted to find them. Who had tried to break into Jennifer's loft? It had to be one of the players, and it certainly wasn't Jennifer. Unless it was coincidental, just another New York break-in that had nothing to do with the attempt on Catherine's life.

But either way, whether Catherine had ordered the photos or Jennifer had gotten them as part of checking up on her husband, Padraig wasn't involved. His only crime was switching from one sister to the other to follow the money.

Then Peter had another thought. Suppose it was Jennifer who had prompted the rendezvous. She had tried to get even with her sister. Maybe now it was Padraig's turn.

The dockmaster threw off the lines, and with a soft gurgle, the *Maineman* eased back from the dock. Jennifer, in jeans and a sweater, was out on deck, taking in the docking lines and coiling them for storage. Padraig, up on the flying bridge, pushed one engine forward, swinging the bow around to the bay. A minute later Jennifer was by his side, high atop the trawler, ghosting out into a flat sea.

"Is this something you learned in your adventure films?" she teased.

"Heavens, no. I never drove any of those boats. My double did. All I did was pose while they tossed a bucket of water in my face."

"So, when did you become a yachtsman?"

"Yesterday, as a matter of fact. I took a lesson from Captain Bligh on the way over from Camden. Seems easy enough. Just move these things frontward and backward to make the boat move, and turn the wheel to aim it where you want to go." He reached into his shirt pocket and pulled out a crumpled piece of paper. "I made some crib notes for anchoring. You'll have to read them to me when we get there."

She was laughing again. No one but Padraig would set out to sea with crib notes.

They were heading south, into a channel between two stone islands. There was a fishing shed hanging off the edge of one of them, long abandoned, with its roof holed and its windows blown out. Jennifer sighed as they passed it. "I was hoping that was the place you were taking me to."

"Much too luxurious! You and I are stripping away the frills and extras. We're getting back to nature."

Now she could take in the fall colors along the shoreline, reflected as abstracts in the edge of the sea. Beautiful! But she couldn't let herself be seduced. She had to keep a clear head.

They passed between the islands and the bay opened up in front of them. The tiny villages, grouped around moored workboats, grew smaller behind them.

Peter rushed out of his office, ordering his secretary to forward the expected call to Catherine's office. She was already on the phone, so he paced impatiently around her conference table until she finished and hung up.

"What's the matter?" she demanded.

"Catherine, did you hire the detective who took those pictures?"

She looked confused. "The photos of Padraig . . . and . . ."

"You," he filled in for her. "The ones that Jennifer got in the mail."

"No. Of course not. Did Jennifer tell you that?"

"No one told me. That's why I'm asking."

She laughed. "That's ridiculous. Why would I want my picture taken in such an unflattering pose?"

"To break up your sister's marriage," he challenged.

"Peter, my sister's marriage was already broken up, as the photos clearly showed."

He turned back to his pacing. "If it wasn't you . . ."

Catherine came around her desk. "Then what?"

Peter stopped abruptly. "Do you know where they were meeting? The name of the charter company? The boat? Anything?"

She was shaking her head. "No! Why would I know? Jennifer didn't invite me along."

Should he believe her? What she said made sense. There was no reason to have herself followed and photographed, and certainly no need to send the pictures to her sister. That would be a mindless act of cruelty.

It had to be Jennifer. And if she was the one striking back, then it was Padraig O'Connell who was in danger. Not that Peter cared about O'Connell, but he did care about Jennifer. Somehow he would have to find her and save her from herself.

Catherine's secretary broke in. There was a call for Peter. He picked up the telephone on the conference table.

"Phil here," the Los Angeles detective said.

"Go ahead," Peter snapped.

"Catherine Pegan. She told him she wanted pictures, and she told him where and when. Only this is the crazy part. The photographer didn't know who the guy was until he printed the negatives. Then he saw a chance to make some real money, so he took the photos to Padraig O'Connell. O'Connell bought the prints and the negatives."

Peter held the phone for a second and then reached out and drew Catherine near. "Phil, I want you to repeat that word for word. There's someone here with me who needs to hear it."

He gave the phone to Catherine, who put it up to her ear. For a moment her face was expressionless. Then her lips tightened and the color drained from her cheeks. "That's a lie!" she suddenly snapped, and slammed down the phone. She and Peter were inches apart, Peter staring into her face, but she turned away from eye contact.

"Catherine . . . why? You and Padraig?"

She pulled away from him. "None of that is true. Not one word of it. They're all lies, and I know exactly who planted them. That's the way she is. She's just covering up because she tried to kill me. It was Jennifer who hired that creep, and all this is part of her scheme."

"It was your check. You hired the detective," Peter reminded her. "Why Catherine? Why would you set out to destroy your sister? And for what? You have everything. What more could you want?"

"My sister," Catherine scoffed. "Always my sister. Why do people always believe her? Well, she's lying again. She tried to kill me, and all I'm doing is protecting myself. Ask Padraig. He knows what a conniving little bitch she is. That's why he's on my side. That's why he's helping me."

"Helping you?" Jesus, was that what Padraig was doing? Helping Catherine get even with her sister? "Catherine, where are they? What's the name of that boat."

She turned away and went back to her desk. "I don't want to talk about it anymore. You'll see. Padraig will tell you that I'm right. It's Jennifer who did all this. She hired the photographer. She . . ." She stammered to a confused end, then she picked up one of the papers on her desk and began reading it as if nothing had happened. She was back to work, as always. Everything was normal.

Peter flew through the door to her outer office. He ordered one secretary to get the airline on the phone. "Find out where they took Jennifer yesterday and how long it will take them to get me there." He wheeled to face another of the young women. "I need you to go through all Catherine's correspondence for the past month. Find anything on a boat-charter company someplace in Maine. Get it to me on my cell phone, or on the plane if I'm in the air." Then he added, "And call for a doctor. Tell them that Catherine has been taken ill."

He rushed into the hallway, nearly knocking over a mail boy, and ran to Jennifer's office. Jennifer's secretary jumped up, frightened, as he confronted her. "Did Jennifer have any correspondence about a boat in Maine? Anything about a charter or a vacation trip? A number where she can be reached?" He was pounding the questions so furiously that the girl wilted back against the wall, her hands to her mouth. Peter got a hold of himself. In a calmer tone, he apologized and asked her to sit down. Then he called the other secretaries to her desk and went through his questions carefully. "Someone must remember something," he said to all of them. "We have to find her."

"Okay, you're dead in the water," Jennifer called from the foredeck. Padraig hit the anchor-release button on the console. Like magic, the anchor dropped from the pulpit and plunged into the water, dragging the rattling chain behind it. A gauge counted the length of anchor chain that was being let out. "About seven times the depth of the water," Mike had told him. "Then pull in just enough to make sure she's set, and let it back out again."

Jennifer watched the proceedings from the pulpit. In her days of racing with Peter, they had anchored often. But it had always been a hand operation by the crew members at the bow. She had never seen it done automatically by an amateur on the flying bridge.

Padraig studied the depth indicator, and when enough chain was out, he engaged the anchor windlass. Then he waited as the boat moved away, powered by the wind and the tide. It drifted for several minutes until the chain finally stiffened. The sea began running by as the boat held still.

"By George, we've done it," he called down to Jennifer.

"Are you sure?" she called back.

"Of course not. But we'll keep taking bearings, and if we're still here by nightfall, we can call it a success."

They worked together, attaching the hoist to the dinghy and then putting the inflatable over the side. Padraig scampered down the ladder and stepped tenderly across. He started the outboard, ran a circle around *Maineman*, and then headed over to Pennobquit's stony beach. He had promised to reconnoiter the island before he brought Jennifer ashore.

"What could be over there?" she had asked, dismissing his caution as unnecessary.

"Cannibals," he answered seriously. "They might let me go, but they could never resist a tasty dish like you."

She watched him secure the dinghy, wave back to her, and then disappear into the brush. Jennifer was mildly disappointed. She had come for a serious discussion. She had no interest in requalifying as a Camp Fire girl.

He returned in less than an hour, bubbling with enthusiasm. There were campgrounds with lean-tos and stone fireplaces. There was a captured pond on the other side, shallow so that it probably heated a bit in the sun. And the view from the cliff edge was spectacular.

"Could you rustle us up a bit of lunch?" he asked. "I think the microwave is self-explanatory. And maybe a nip of Scotch." Then he went to his cabin to put on dry clothes. The spray in the dinghy had soaked through his trousers.

Jennifer quickly selected a packaged quiche from the cabinets in the galley. In the ice chest, she found the makings of a salad, and the liquor cabinet yielded a fifth of Padraig's favorite malt. Then she started through the drawers, looking for the silverware and serving utensils. It was in the first drawer that she saw the folder with the charter contract. She almost had the drawer closed when she spotted the name hand-lettered on the folder: Catherine Pegan.

She glanced around quickly. Padraig was still down a level in his forward cabin, the door shut. She could hear him humming as he dressed. She opened the folder. There was a list of provisions signed for by Padraig. She dug deeper and found the contract, signed by the broker in one place. The signature next to it was Catherine's, a flourish Jennifer had seen thousands of times in her adult life. And then, pinned to the contract, was a copy of the check. It was Catherine's check, again with her signature. Jennifer pushed the papers back into the drawer and eased it closed. Quickly, she located the silverware and had the place settings in her hand when Padraig came up to the galley.

"Quiche?" he said, picking up the package. "Real men—"

"You stocked it," she interrupted. She took a knife and began preparing the salad.

Padraig read the directions and popped the paper tray into the microwave. Then he was back to his description of the wonders of Pennobquit. He was making it sound as inviting as Capri.

Jennifer was nodding, smiling when it was called for, and frowning when Padraig seemed concerned. But she wasn't listening. While he ate, drank, and held court, she was facing up to the reality that she had found in the drawer.

This wasn't just Padraig's idea. It was Catherine's as well. She had arranged the boat, picked the location, and paid the cost. Yet she claimed that Padraig had turned on her just as he had on Jennifer. It was never love. It was always the money, she had charged. She would stay with him in Leprechaun Productions just long enough to get her money back. Then, according to Catherine, she would cut the lying bastard off at the legs.

Then why had she made the arrangements and paid the costs

out of her personal account? What was she hoping to gain?

And Padraig had insisted that there had never been anything between Catherine and him. He had simply let himself be seduced by his desperation for money. Now, if Jennifer believed him, he was truly repentant.

Then why was he sharing his personal life with Catherine and letting her finance his reconciliation?

The trip was a lie, and she was the one being lied to. But why? What were the two of them scheming?

Once again it was Peter's warning that she remembered. As of this moment, Padraig was her husband and heir to a good part of her fortune. And then she understood. She was all alone with the one person who had the most to gain by her death. And he had lied to her and conspired with her sister to get her here.

Jennifer was suddenly certain that she was about to have another accident.

"West Trenton, Maine," the pilot said while Peter was stepping aboard. "It's a small strip right at the causeway to Mount Desert Island. We had to look it up ourselves."

"And from there?" Peter asked.

The pilot shrugged. "Someone picked her up in a car. No one told me where they were going. I'm supposed to go back for her on Sunday night."

So that's where they had to be. Someplace close to Mount Desert Island. Otherwise why pick such an obscure airport.

They had found the charter-company arrangements in Catherine's desktop folder. The secretary who called had given Peter a company name and an address in Camden. Then she had called back to tell him they had found the check entered in her checkbook. Peter had called and spoken to the rental agent. "Yes sir, Padraig O'Connell himself. I tell you, my girl nearly wet her pants. Handsome fella! Gave me his autograph."

He described the boat and gave Peter its radio call letters. Then he remembered that a charter captain had taken O'Connell to Blue Hill. "Guess that's where he was setting out from. But I have no idea where he was headed."

"Some obscure island off the coast," Peter told him.

"Not much help theyuh. Has to be a couple of thousand of those."

Then Jennifer's office telephoned with nothing to report. She had left no record of her arrangements, nor any way that she could be reached. All they knew was that she was due back on Monday.

Peter had contacted the Coast Guard but had found an unsympathetic day officer. "Mister, we're not in the business of tracking down girlfriends. If the yacht is in trouble, we'll go get it. Or if there's a crime reported. But we don't have the right to butt into a private party." Peter was then kicked up the chain of command. "I have good reason to believe that a woman aboard that boat is in great danger," he explained. The officer responded that it sounded like a police matter. "If the police call us for assistance, we'll cast off in a minute. But without a boat in physical danger, and no federal crime in progress—"

Peter had begged. Of course he would contact the police. But there was no time to lose. Something in his voice rang true, because the officer promised unofficially to have his patrol flights look for the trawler in the vicinity of Mount Desert Island. "But," he warned, "it's a big area with lots of coves. And most of the boats up here are workboats. So I can't promise we'll find her."

Peter tried to relax but found himself pinned to the edge of the seat. He recognized the cape off to his right, and Boston bathed in the light from the sun that was settling in the west. It would be dark by the time he found the spot where Jennifer had boarded the *Maineman,* and there was little chance of finding the boat at night. But at least he could get into position and enlist the help that he needed. Then he would be ready to go out and find her. He had stood in a doorway once and watched a friend die in a burning building. But not this time! This time he was going to rush into the fire.

Padraig had wanted to motor over to the island, but Jennifer had used every excuse. She had been slow clearing up their simple lunch. Then she had pleaded weariness from her trip and gone to her cabin for a nap. This time she had used the lock, and had settled into the bed with two pillows so that her head was up and her eyes fixed on the door. There was no chance of her sleeping, but she needed to get away from his continuous chatter so she could think. Padraig had maneuvered her to a place where no one could save her. If she was going to make it through the next two days, she would have to do it on her own.

When she came back up to the saloon, Padraig was on deck, looking patiently across at Pennobquit Island. Instead of joining him, Jennifer made a point of busying herself in the galley, pretending to be enthusiastic over the evening meal. He came in, hoping to hurry her along so they could still get over to the island before dark. The pots and dishes were chattering in her hands, and nothing she said sounded natural.

"Jennifer, darlin', you seem distraught. Dinner is no problem. I don't give a damn what we eat."

"I want things nice," she lied, and then she dropped a plate of vegetables on the deck. The plate bounced and rolled, leaving a trail of zucchini slices. She bent to pick them up, then jumped when his hand came down on top of hers.

"What is it?" he asked. She thought he seemed suspicious rather than concerned.

"We came out here to see if we had a future, not to explore an island," she snapped at him.

He stayed on his knees, helping her clean up the mess. "Whatever you want," he assured her. "We can take a glass of wine up to the flybridge. And we can talk until the sun comes up. The island will still be there tomorrow."

But his expression had changed. His eyes were narrower, and the signature smile had disappeared from his lips. The nervous chatter was gone. He was talking softly and trying to sound reassuring.

He knows, Jennifer thought. He knows that I've found out why he brought me here. At that moment it seemed that her best chance to make it through the night was to convince him that she had no suspicions whatsoever.

They climbed up to the flybridge with a bottle of wine and glasses and watched the sky redden to the west. Jennifer used the moment to press her first question: Had he ever really loved her?

He swore that he had. "Not at first, of course. No, at first it was strictly a matter of money. You had it and I needed it."

"Just money?" she asked as though it were a dirty word.

"Oh, it's never just money. Not for me, anyway. With me it was my life. Things were falling apart on me, darlin', and I was frightened out of my wits."

He explained the miserable ending of his career that was staring him in the face. He was middle-aged, playing the role of a youthful hero, and there were these young Turks snapping at his ass. "Kids just out of film school and illiterate punks who had decided that they were actors. There wasn't one of them who could play the butler in a high school play. And they were all sitting around in their black shirts, smoking their dope, and talking about bringing in one of their studs to replace me. So, the future looked bleak, Jennie, darlin'. There was nothing left for me. Maybe doing a few walk-ons or playing some pathetic fool in a television series. No, it wasn't just money that I needed. I needed to save my life."

He admitted that their first meeting hadn't been as romantic as he had often painted it. It had been no accident when he walked in on her at the trade show. Letting her drive through the mountains had been the most frightening experience of his life. The car he had given her had been no money down. "All I made was the first payment. We were two months behind when the damn thing went over the cliff." And his exit from the hotel in Cannes had been carefully staged. He had lurked behind a pillar while the desk clerk explained his departure, and then he had paraded his entourage across the lobby, knowing she would see him.

"What a fool," Jennifer derided herself. "I should have known."

"Now, don't be thinking that way," he consoled her. "Theater is about making people see what isn't there and believe what isn't true. And I'm damn good at my craft."

She asked him about her auto accident, and he took on a brooding expression while he weighed his answer. "Hardest thing I ever did," he finally admitted. "You see, by then I was truly taken by you. I had already called the whole thing off once, and I damn near called it off again."

That had been his plan right from the beginning. Marry her, then arrange for her to have an accident. He had made the arrangements in his best French, paying half the cost in cash up front and promising the rest after the accident. It had been all set up for Ireland. But when the time came, he couldn't go through with it. For the first time since his adolescence, he had truly fallen in love. "There were mornings, darlin', when I'd just lie in bed and watch you sleep, hoping you'd wake up so I'd be there when you first opened your eyes."

But then the real cost of launching Leprechaun had become apparent. Her checking account wouldn't even come close. He needed total access to limitless funding. "That was the moment of truth. Was I going to remain an important man in the movie business? Or was I going to settle down with a lovely young girl and enjoy my newfound bliss? It wasn't an easy choice. But I just couldn't stop being Padraig O'Connell the famous actor." He shook his head slowly. "It was the wrong choice, of course. But I'd probably make the same decision over again. Fame is an opiate. Not many of us can kick the habit."

"So then it was you."

He nodded slowly. "My needing the car was just an alibi. I called the garage and told them I'd be using it so it would look like I was the one who was supposed to go over the cliff. But I want you to know that when you walked out of that room, I was on my feet and after you. I got downstairs just in time to see you spin out onto the street. Another few seconds and I would have stopped you. And then, when I saw you in that hospital, pale, dead, with those hoses keeping you breathing, I was horrified. I knew I had destroyed the most wonderful thing that ever happened to me."

Jennifer had heard enough truth for one night. Peter had been right when he blamed Padraig for cutting the brakes. And she had been right in thinking of herself as the ugly duckling. The only thing that Padraig had seen in her was money. They watched the sun set, and then each of them found a private place, Jennifer on the sofa in the saloon and Padraig outside, pacing the deck in the darkness.

She tried to look at ease, sitting with her legs drawn up and turning through the pages of a magazine. But her thoughts were racing. He had confessed that he was after her money and had talked freely about attempted murder. Unburdening himself of his guilt, perhaps, but in the process sticking his neck in a noose. She realized that the only reason he had spoken so candidly was that he knew it would never matter. She was the only one he was telling, and she would never tell anyone else: more proof that she wasn't going to make it back.

She had to get away. But how? She couldn't coax him ashore and then escape in the trawler. Padraig had the ignition key in his pocket. She could swim to Pennobquit. But it would be only a matter of time before he found her. You could stand on one end of the island and see the other. So it had to be the inflatable dinghy.

It wasn't a certain escape. She wasn't sure she knew how to operate the boat, although an outboard couldn't be too complicated. She had no idea how much fuel it carried or how far it would take her. But she could head back up the bay as far as the boat would go and swim to whatever land was nearest to her. Without the dinghy, Padraig wouldn't be able to get ashore and would have no way to find her.

When? It had to be right now. Tonight. She had no idea of Padraig's plans, but she guessed she was supposed to die in an accident on the island. Probably a fall from the cliff. She had succeeded in stalling for the entire afternoon, but if she refused to go ashore with him in the morning, he would know for certain that she was on to his murderous intent. And then what? A blow to the head and her body tossed into the dinghy so she could be carried to the island and dropped from the cliff. No matter how she looked at it, time was against her. It had to be tonight.

She made a mental list of the things she would need. Some matches in a plastic bag so she could light a signal fire wherever she landed. A knife to cut twigs, or maybe even use in self-defense. A bottle of water and a few of the frozen breakfast bars. A length of twine to tie her supplies to her leg if she had to swim ashore. That was all she could carry.

Jennifer watched Padraig walking the deck down the port side that faced the island. She went to the galley and put on a pot of tea as her excuse for being there. Then she assembled what she needed and sealed her things in a kitchen bag. She had just slipped the bag under her belt when he came inside.

"I put a kettle on," she said innocently. "You make some tea while I go below for a minute." She walked past him and down the steps to her stateroom. He seemed more interested in the kettle than in her. Jennifer hid her supplies under the pillows, flushed the toilet, and went back up to the saloon.

"Chilly outside," Padraig said, explaining why he was setting the teacups on the saloon table. He sat in one of the chairs. Jennifer went back to her place on the sofa. "But the sky is clear," he went on. "Tomorrow will be a great day for exploring the island. We can look around in the morning, then maybe take a swim in the pond."

She nodded. "Sounds great!" And then, to cover the panic that she was sure was giving her away, she continued the conversation from earlier. "You found you had feelings for me, and you came into New York every weekend to help me recover. So we had a second chance to make it together. But then you took up with Catherine . . ." She left the statement hanging so that it begged for an explanation.

"Your sister is quite a woman," he began. "Drawn to the limelight like a moth to a flame. She knows it will burn her into ashes, but still she can't resist."

"That's what you said about yourself," Jennifer reminded him.

He nodded. "Sad but true. Catherine and I were made for each other by the devil. It's a marriage made in hell. But still a marriage. She had all the money I would ever need, and I had the movie industry, the world's biggest and brightest stage. She had to be a player, and she was willing to spend everything to have the world as her audience."

Jennifer was puzzled. "She was already a celebrity."

"Ahh," he said. "But she has this magic mirror that she looks in every day. She asks, 'Am I the fairest of them all?' But there was always a movie star to edge her out. She couldn't stand it! She had to hear the mirror say that she was certainly the fairest.

"Then one day she asked her question, and the mirror said, 'No, Catherine. Your sister, Jennifer, is the fairest of them all. Look how Padraig O'Connell worships her.' And at that point, darlin', you and I were dead. Catherine came to Hollywood with an armful of poison apples."

"But if you knew all this—"

"Don't try to understand," he said, answering the question he knew she was asking. "Only a moth understands the allure of the flame. To sane people, like yourself, risking everything for vanity makes no sense at all.

"But your sister was willing to put it all on the line. And I have to tell you, she was dazzling. More glamorous than the stars. Smarter than the producers. With more money than the studios. She came in like a vision, and people simply sighed and fell down. It was like Marilyn in the old days, making kings and presidents tremble. Or like the Japanese when they arrived with more money than the Hollywood tycoons had ever imagined. Within a week, she was a force to be dealt with. And there was

I, a fading actor suddenly reborn in her aura, with people who wouldn't buy me lunch suddenly wanting to invest millions. I may have been falling in love with you, Jennifer, but the fact is that you never had a chance."

Jennifer went to the galley and returned with more tea.

"I knew Catherine hated me," she said as she poured. "But I didn't try to kill her. I swear I wasn't the one who hired that actor."

"Of course you weren't." He laughed as she sat back down. "How could it have been you? The truth is that it was me."

"You? It can't be. You just told me that Catherine was your rebirth. You were living in her aura—"

"True. But I was paying a terrible price. My God, but she can be an awful bitch. She was grinding my face in the mud. Humiliating me in front of my friends. She had used me just long enough to get into Hollywood and to make sure that your face would never pop up again in her magic mirror. The thing about Catherine is that she suffers no rivals. She destroys them lest they distract from her magnificence."

"But how? You were out in Hollywood. And he was struggling in New York."

"Now, try to be kind, Jennifer. I may be past my prime, but people still recognize me. Particularly aspiring young actors. It was Will Ferris who spotted me at that health club. And he made two passes at me. First just to introduce himself and to wonder if there was anything I could do to help his career. I gave him the standard answer: Send a picture to my agent. Then, a couple days later, he sprang at me in your doorway. Just wanted to let me know that if there were anything he could do to work with me—absolutely anything. When actresses say that, it's an invitation to take them to bed. With actors, they're covering their bases on the chance you might be gay. He was a pathetic little twit, but I did ask for his card and promise that I'd look for something. As I was leaving him, he called after me: 'Remember, Mr. O'Connell . . . anything.' "

"Even murder?" Padraig had to be exaggerating, Jennifer

thought. Even desperate people didn't hire themselves out as killers.

"Even murder," Padraig answered, "and the price was quite reasonable. Pocket change to keep him solvent. A small part in my next film. Maybe two brief appearances and a couple of lines. There isn't an aspiring actor in the world who wouldn't kill for that kind of opportunity. I placed the call from a public phone at Kennedy Airport, using a stage voice and giving a fake name. The money was cash, your cash, as a matter of fact. He would never turn on me, because I really would have given him the part. But even if he wanted to, there was no way he could turn the deal back to me. And then, of course, the idiot got himself killed, so I was never in any danger."

"But Catherine was still alive," Jennifer reminded him.

"True. That's what you get for dealing with amateurs. A whack on the head and he could have thrown the body over at his leisure. Instead, he tried to drag her kicking and screaming out onto the balcony." Padraig sighed and shook his head in despair. "Amateurs," he repeated sadly.

There was one more question, but she couldn't ask it. Why, after having tried to kill Catherine, did he get back together with her? She couldn't ask, because she wasn't supposed to know that Catherine had been his partner in planning their trip. Catherine was his accomplice in the murder he was about to commit. Her murder. And to ask the question would be to hurry the moment of execution.

Peter found the wobbly shed on the water's edge deserted. "If she got aboard in Blue Hill, it would have been here," the town's only police officer explained. "The other docks are for fish and lobstah."

"It was here," Peter said. He had heard from the hired captain who had brought the trawler over from Camden. This was the dock. "Can we talk to the owner?" he asked.

"Not really. He's been dead for quite a while."

"Well, who runs this place?"

"His daughter, I suppose.

"Where can I find her?"

"In Boston. Works for a big company down there."

The pier, it seemed, was just there: a convenience for anyone who wanted to use it until the channel filled with silt or the building collapsed. "I'm going to need a boat," Peter said, "and someone who knows how to run it."

The policeman nodded. "Plenty of boats available. Nothin' fancy like that trawler you're lookin' for, but lots of good seaworthy workin' boats. I can probably set somethin' up for yuh."

They drove to a four-building town across the gravel road from the water. There were a dozen boats bobbing in the darkness. The officer knocked on a door, greeted a young man in his underwear, still in his teens, who was trying desperately to grow a beard to go with his long, unkempt hair. "Kevin, here, knows the area good as anyone. Got a nice seaworthy dory."

Peter shook hands and then followed Kevin into a single large room that held his bed, his stove, his fishing gear, and his office. "Make yerself at home," Kevin offered, and then he disappeared into the bathroom to get dressed. Peter remained standing in the middle of the room. That was about as comfortable as he was going to get.

He helped carry supplies down to the dock, where a big, open boat was tied up. Then he watched while the young man poured cans of diesel oil into an exposed tank in the center of the boat. "I can get us some sandwiches," Kevin said. Peter peeled two tens from his wallet, and Kevin promised to be back in an hour.

An hour, Peter thought. There wasn't much sense in leaving now. They would do better waiting until near sunrise, and then be out in the bay when the sun came up. But an hour was an eternity when Jennifer was out there someplace with a man who was planning to kill her.

———

Jennifer sat on the edge of her bunk, as alert as she had ever been. Her cabin door was closed and locked, but light from the saloon leaked through the louvered panel. She had come below as soon as she had cleared away the tea. Padraig had embraced her, kissed her cheek, and then gone forward to his own stateroom. The small twelve-volt lamp in the saloon was to serve as their night-light.

She could see out onto the afterdeck through the portholes that were high up above her bed. The deck and the railings were clearly illuminated by the single anchor light that burned on the stern. She could see the line from the inflatable dinghy tied to the cleat just inches away.

She had put on her bathing suit, a one-piece sports model that was ideal for swimming. Over it she wore jeans and a windbreaker, and her sneakers with no socks. She planned to keep the sneakers on, so that if she had to swim, she would have them for land. Her supplies were jammed into the pocket of her windbreaker, tied to a string that was fastened around her ankle. There was no sound aboard the boat. Padraig was certainly asleep by now at the other end of the trawler. It was time!

But she wasn't ready. The boat had swung at its anchor, and as she looked out from the portholes, she couldn't find Pennobquit. It was apparently overcast—there was no starlight on the water—so she had no reference to give her a heading. She had pulled open the hatch in her overhead so she could see straight up. She couldn't find any familiar pattern of stars. When she pulled away in the dinghy, she wouldn't know whether she was heading back in toward land, or out into the open sea. She'd have to wait a bit longer, until it was closer to sunrise. She would need at least a small trace of light to get her bearings.

Another problem was that she couldn't decide on her best escape route. If she stood on her bed, she could get her head and shoulders through the hatch. But just barely. Then it would be a struggle to pull herself up. She would probably bang against the hatch and the deck, which would make noise. And there was a good chance that she might get stuck halfway through.

The other route was to leave her cabin and go up into the saloon. That would mean going toward Padraig, but she could do that quietly and, if he was sleeping, without disturbing him. She could ease open the sliding door out to the deck with a minimum of noise and then be over the rail and into the dinghy. But if Padraig was awake, watching just as she was, even the slightest sound would bring him up into the saloon.

Both routes had their dangers. Neither was attractive. But she had to escape. Waiting for a better opportunity didn't make sense.

Then there was the engine. It had to start on the first try. When she got into the boat, she would take the mooring line with her and drift a few feet away. If the engine started, she would be on her way before he even made it up on deck. But if it coughed and sputtered, she would be a prisoner in the boat, probably in the glare of the trawler's spotlight; and she might not know which direction to swim.

She waited an hour, counting the minutes on her wristwatch. She was about to start forward into the saloon when a distant sound stopped her. She listened carefully. A door closed ahead in the bow. She heard the toilet pump running. Padraig had gotten up. She sat down and began counting off another fifteen minutes. She also changed her mind about her escape route. If she had gone forward a few seconds earlier, Padraig would have caught her. She decided to go up through the hatch.

She slid it open again. Then she stuffed the blanket and pillows into her empty duffel and pulled it up onto the bed. By standing on it, she could give herself another two feet of height. And if her hips were tight in the hatch opening, she would have something to stand on to give her additional leverage. She stuck her head out into the night air and looked around. There were no stars, and she still couldn't find Pennobquit. But she could see her way to the dinghy clearly in the glow of the anchor light. She pulled back down and thrust her hands up ahead of her. She had to wiggle as her head, surrounded by her arms, squeezed through. But then she could stand up quite easily atop the duffel.

She almost smiled at the ironic advantage of being a bit flat-chested.

With her hands on the deck, she was able to push herself up higher and felt the supply bag in her jacket pocket squeeze through. She kicked off from the duffel and launched herself up with her hands. But her hips jammed into the opening like a cork in a wine bottle. For a moment she seemed trapped. But bending forward pulled her butt through, and wiggling from side to side cleared her hips. She turned her body until she was sitting on the deck with just her feet hanging down through the hatch.

She froze, listening carefully. There was a breeze, and the sound of waves lapping on the side. But she couldn't hear any movement in the saloon. Carefully, she lifted her feet, swirled around, and dropped them silently on the deck. She leaned out so she could see the narrow part of the deck that led forward, past the sliding door, and up to the bow. Padraig was still inside, probably down in his cabin. She stood and swung her leg over the rail. Then she was on the steps down to the swim platform. She held her breath as she worked the knot that secured the dinghy. Then she stepped carefully aboard. The dinghy rocked under her but settled when she was able to squat on the thwart. She reached back to the engine and touched the starter switch. Nothing happened.

She blinked into the darkness but wasn't able to make out the controls. Why hadn't she thought of a flashlight? One lever seemed to be a shift lever. She moved it slowly until she found the middle position that was probably neutral. Then she noticed a valve on the line from the gas can and moved it open. A quick glance told her that she had already drifted a boat length away from the trawler. Jennifer hit the starter switch again. This time the engine growled noisily, shaking the dinghy as it tried to start.

It turned over again and again with a grinding noise that seemed deafening in the still night, but it wouldn't catch. And then light flashed through the forward portholes, followed by a blast of light from the galley.

In a panic, she forced herself to study the switches, now visible in the light from the trawler. The gas line was turned off, and she twisted the valve open. At that instant, the saloon door rattled open, and Padraig was out on the deck, screaming, "Jennifer. Where are you going?" He ran aft.

She touched the starter again, and once more the engine cranked. "Catch, dammit," she yelled to herself. She pushed harder on the starter button, as if that could make a difference. But there was still no ignition.

Padraig was swinging over the rail, his shadow spreading over the flickering light in the water. Jennifer glanced at him, but her attention was on the engine. She never saw him reach down and lift the end of her mooring line out of the water. She still thought she was free until she felt her drift being checked. When she looked up, she saw Padraig hauling the dinghy back toward the trawler.

She tossed forward and began working the knot that secured the line to the inflatable. It was almost free when his hand locked down on hers. "It won't start without these, I'm afraid." In his other hand he held the two spark plugs that he had taken from the engine. Then he was reaching out to her. "Come on up here, darlin'. You'll catch your death of cold sitting out there like that."

There were any number of things she could have done. Use her leverage when she had her feet on the swim platform and pull him past her and into the water. Knee him the instant she was aboard, then push him over. Or even pick up the small oar that was on the bottom of the inflatable and swing it like a weapon. But her defeat was total. She felt ridiculous for her pathetic attempt to escape. She let herself be helped up the ladder and pushed back over the railing.

Padraig saw the cord that came from her jacket pocket, and he pulled out the kitchen bag with her survival things. "Oh, dear God, girl, where did you think these toys would get you?"

"Away," she answered.

He shook his head in despair. Then he took her arm. "Come inside and let me fix you a cup of tea." As she stepped into the cabin, she saw the first trace of morning, barely bright enough to mark the eastern horizon. If she had made her escape, she could have easily found her way home.

Jennifer sat silently on the edge of the sofa while he set a steaming mug of tea in front of her. "Drink that. It will warm you."

She stared at the mug but didn't reach for it. "You're going to kill me, aren't you?"

He didn't look at her, just kept squeezing the slice of lime into his tea. "How did you find out?"

"The charter papers are in the drawer. Signed by my sister. The check is hers."

He nodded. "The idea is hers, too. With your piece of the pie, we have control over both companies. We can get rid of your friend Peter and become king and queen of the universe. The movies. The distribution. Everything between the story idea and the theater. And then all the television after that."

"Wouldn't it be easier to give me a chance to buy in?" she suggested.

"Ahh, that was my very thought. But I'm hopelessly romantic. Your sister thought you could be dangerous to our enterprise. After all, you'd still own half of Pegasus. But I think the thing she was really afraid of was that your picture might pop up again in her magic mirror. She sensed my fondness for you. She knew that sooner or later the two of us would be cheating on her. So I suppose you could say that my love was your death sentence, although that would probably be too operatic for today's audience."

"How?" Jennifer asked.

He squinted. "How . . ."

"How are you going to kill me?"

"Painlessly, darlin'. In a way you won't even know it's happening."

"A bullet in the back of my head, maybe while I'm kneeling with my hands tied behind my back."

"Oh, don't be thinking that way, lass. I have a gun, but I have no intention of using it. I'm not sure I'd know how." Then he chuckled. "Terrible thing for a secret agent to admit, isn't it."

"Well, how then? Maybe a knife blade across my throat so you can watch me bleed to death?"

"No! No knives and no guns." He seemed annoyed that she would even suggest such things. "While I was over on the island, I found myself a very stout walking stick, and I planned to slip behind you while we were looking out from the cliff and deliver one clean blow to the head. You'd go dark instantly. You'd never feel yourself falling onto the rocks below. And, of course, your wounds from hitting the ground would disguise the blow of my stick. So it would just be an accident."

"But there would still be evidence. Someone would find your bloody club and would know it was my blood on it."

He nodded. "Would you believe I had thought about that one? And I decided that given your terrible tragedy, the natural thing for me to do would be to light a fire to attract help. I thought the stick could be part of the fire."

"And now that I know, and won't turn my back on you for an instant . . ."

"I suppose things will get a little messy."

Jennifer forced a laugh. "Messy? If you come near me, I'll claw your face open. I'll bite and kick. You'll look like you've been in a catfight. And you won't be able to shoot me. How could you explain a bullet wound if your story is that I fell accidentally?"

Padraig drew a heavy breath. "I hope you won't make this difficult, darlin'. There's no pleasure in this for me. It's just that it has to be done. Especially now that you know the whole sordid story."

Jennifer's mind was driving, trying desperately for a chance to stay alive. "Padraig, what if I offered you the same deal? You and I could own it all. And we wouldn't have to kill anyone. My sister is crazy. We could have her put away. I'd have her power of attorney, and you and I could have everything."

He chuckled. "We're a pair, aren't we. I thought much the

same thing when I prompted that poor actor to put an end to her. But Jennifer, we both have to face the facts. Your sister is the celebrity. She's the one who fills the house and sells all the tickets. With her, everything is twice as sensational! Twice as big! You and I could do just fine. But Catherine and I can run it all."

He stood. "The sun is coming up, so we should get going. Is there anything you need to do first? Use the bathroom or something?"

She slid across the sofa and went down the steps to her cabin.

Padraig called after her. "And please, Jennifer, don't lock yourself in or hide under the bed. It will just make everything more difficult for both of us."

The trace of light in the east was their signal to cast off. Peter took in the lines and jumped down into the bow of the launch. Kevin backed the engine and threw the tiller over. The boat swung out, giving him room to put the engine ahead and turn the bow out to sea.

They began slowly, and Peter was impatient to pick up speed. But even when the throttle was pushed all the way forward, not much changed. The engine's pitch went up a note or two, and the boat struggled to add a few more knots. But she certainly wasn't a speedboat. The big dory ran even in the water, carving an elegant wake without any attempt to lift up and skim over the water. She was certainly a workboat, and she was used to being paid by the hour.

Kevin showed no sense of urgency, either. With the engine set, he settled back with an arm wrapped over the tiller. Like a horse, the boat knew its way out into the bay without any annoying tugs on the reins.

Peter stared ahead, straining through the binoculars that came with the boat. They were blurred and impossible to focus. He set them aside and scanned as best he could. There was a blinking light somewhere ahead. He couldn't guess how far. And there was a red light off the port bow. He guessed that it was a channel marker or a warning of land close aboard.

The eastern sky lightened. Suddenly he could make out the dark silhouette of an island behind the red light, and then another island off to the right. "Kevin," he called back. "Are we okay?"

"Yup."

At least he was awake. "Can we get any more speed out of this thing?"

"Nope."

But they were making decent speed. Peter saw the islands moving by on each side as the boat split the channel. And with the sunrise, he could see the opening into the bay ahead. There were small rocky islands piercing the water off to the right.

"Should we check those out?" Peter asked.

"Not likely to find anything," Kevin answered. "It would take a good captain to work his way through theyuh. Newcomers usually keep to the deep water."

"Where then?"

Kevin pointed ahead. "Out a ways. Couple of islands out theyuh that are safe anchorages for weekenders. Some of 'em even have state pahks."

"Okay," Peter agreed. He hated to pass any cove or inlet without peeking in, but he had no choice. The young man made his living in these waters, and Peter didn't want to second-guess him.

"*Maineman*," Kevin volunteered, "is a big white trawluh. We see her around here during the summuh. Rides high in the watah. If she's here, we won't miss her."

Peter found his confidence in the scruffy captain growing. He knew what they were looking for, which was more than he could say for himself.

As the sun got up a bit in the sky, the small pink ball grew larger and turned into blinding white light. It was hard to see, but Kevin kept plowing ahead. To his mind it didn't matter. There would be nothing to see until they got there.

They were out more than an hour when Peter first noticed a shape ahead. Kevin saw him squinting. "That's Pennobquit," he said. "If I was runnin' off with a lady, that's where I'd take her."

"How far?" Peter asked.

"Half hour. Not much more!"

Padraig led Jennifer out on deck and then aft to the dinghy. He had it tied up close and had already been aboard to replace the spark plugs. He stood behind her as she climbed over the rail and then helped her down to the boat. She didn't resist when he eased her into the bow. Then he took the line and stepped in at the stern.

She tried again. "You don't have to do this. It's not too late to turn back." Padraig didn't seem to notice the sound of her voice. He set the engine controls and then pushed the starter. The little outboard broke into a pleasing buzz. As soon as he moved the shift lever, they were on their way to the island.

"Padraig, this isn't a movie. It's real. In real life, murderers get caught. And they rot in prison."

He glanced at her. "It isn't my idea, girl. I don't like it a bit. But there isn't another way."

"There is! We can go back together and tell Catherine that I'm buying in. You can tell her that you want to be with me, and I'll tell her that I don't give a damn what she sees in her magic mirror. What can she do?"

"Take away Leprechaun," he said. "She and Peter can toss me out on my arse. I'd be looking for work while Catherine was taking bows for our films. Can't you just see her, up on the stage, thanking all the little people for her Oscar? And me playing the butler in a stupid sitcom."

"It wouldn't happen. Peter and I could warn her that if she dropped you, she wouldn't get another cent out of Pegasus. She'd have to go along."

"Peter," he mocked. "Jaysus help me if I ever have to count

on that one. He'd be only too happy to kick my arse out the door."

"But he—"

"Jennie, darlin', don't you think I've been through this a million times. Don't you know that if I could start all over again, I'd never have put either of us in this predicament? But here we are. Rotten as it is, this is my only chance."

The bow scraped on the beach, and Padraig quickly killed the engine. Jennifer bounded out of the boat and ran inland as fast as her feet could carry her. O'Connell took his time pulling the boat ashore and tying the mooring line securely. Then he tipped the engine up and patiently disconnected the spark-plug leads. He used a wipe cloth to grasp the plugs as he twisted them out.

When he walked inland, he headed directly to a small clump of brush. There he retrieved his "cane," a widening branch with the joint of another branch broken off at its head. With the narrow end on the ground, the top came up to his waist. It was more like a baseball bat than a walking stick.

Padraig started up the hill toward the park area with its lean-tos and fire pits. That was the only area that offered any sort of hiding place. And if she wasn't there, he would certainly be able to spot her; the campground was near the cliff and afforded a view of the whole island. "Jennie," he called ahead. "Please don't make this hard on yourself. It's not as if either of us have a choice."

There was no answer, not that he expected one. He walked up the hill turning left and right to see where she was hiding. When he did spot her, Padraig couldn't believe what he was seeing. Jennifer was in her bathing suit, sitting on a curved boulder. As he watched, she pushed herself off and slid into the sea. A second later, she bobbed up and began stroking back out to the trawler.

"Oh, sweet Jaysus," he snapped, and he ran back down to the dinghy. "Jennifer," he screamed at the top of his lungs. "Come back. You'll never make it." But just in the few strokes that he watched, he knew she had a chance. She was swimming powerfully, propelled by a steady kick. In the light seas, she was moving very quickly.

He fumbled with the plugs as he replaced them. The alignment had to be perfect, and in his hurry, he made two false starts. Then one of the electrical connectors proved balky and wouldn't snap into position. He needed his pocketknife to make the hookup. He pushed the dinghy out before he untied the line, then had to pull it back to climb aboard. By the time the engine started, Jennifer was more than halfway to the trawler. She was still swimming with a strong stroke.

But she was numb from the cold. The icy water that first stung her skin had now taken away most of her feeling. Her muscles were generating their own heat, but she could feel cramping in her lower back and her thighs. Her arms, which had carried her much farther in the warm waters off French Guiana, were beginning to feel heavy. She knew she was losing strength.

Padraig could see her in the water, and he knew he was closing the gap. Even with its small engine, the inflatable was a fast boat, skimming across the surface rather than plowing through. He guessed they would reach the trawler at about the same time, and thought he would have little trouble overpowering her and bringing her back. But still, he picked up the small paddle, wielding it like a hatchet.

"There she is!" Kevin was pointing out over the port bow.

Peter squinted. Pennobquit loomed ahead, its coastline a series of craggy rocks. But he couldn't make out detail. Just a shape against the dark water. "Where? I'm not picking it up."

Kevin had moved the tiller and was pointing straight over the bow. "Dead ahead. You can see her stern around that rock. In the cove."

Peter began to make it out. The white hull contrasted against the dark stone. And then it was clear. He could see the windows in the pilothouse. As best he could make out, there was nobody on deck. No hint of movement aboard. But the boat was still there, still riding at anchor. Whatever Padraig was doing hadn't been completed; otherwise he would be bringing the boat back into port.

Then Peter saw the dinghy, although at first he had no idea what it was. Some sort of boat with one person aboard, leaving a small wake behind. Suddenly, he focused in on the *one* person. There should be two of them. For a sick instant, he thought he might be too late.

Jennifer was still short of her goal when she heard the engine behind her. She didn't look back. The cramps were tightening her limbs and the cold was making it difficult for her to breathe. If she stopped swimming, she might never start again.

Twenty strokes more, she told herself. Count them. Nineteen, eighteen . . . She was shivering violently, beginning to feel delirious, just as if she were wracked with fever. She had to keep her mind working as well as her body.

The buzzing engine was louder. Now she could hear the sound of the flat-bottomed boat bouncing on the water. How far behind? Twenty yards? Fifteen? Keep swimming. Count the strokes. Ten . . . nine . . . eight . . .

"Jennifer . . ." It was Padraig calling behind her. How far? Just a few feet.

She reached for the swim platform, and it was just beyond her fingertips. One more stroke. Her hand was on the trawler. She grabbed the ladder to the swim platform and nearly floated aboard.

But she couldn't stop, not even to take a breath. She had to make it up the ladder and over the rail before the sound of the outboard overwhelmed her. Two steps . . . one step . . . her hand was on the rail when Padraig's grip locked around her ankle.

He was trying to do everything at once. Kill the engine, tie the bow line, and keep Jennifer from escaping. She was able to kick free and spin herself over the rail. Padraig scampered aboard right at her heels. But he stopped suddenly. With the outboard quieted, he was aware of a new sound. A droning engine. There was a boat approaching.

He leaned out just enough to look past the bow. He saw a wooden dory, its hull colorless, with two people aboard. For just an instant, he was frozen in panic. Then he bounded over the rail and made after Jennifer.

She had gotten to the sliding door, pushed it open, and made it inside. She was within an inch of pulling it all the way closed when Padraig got hold of the outside handle. They struggled like arm wrestlers, the door sliding back and forth. But with his weight alone, Padraig had the advantage, and Jennifer was exhausted. She found herself falling backward. She let go of the handle to try for her cabin. It was no escape, but it would be one last barrier between them.

Padraig's arm cut her off. He caught her around the neck and pulled her back outside. He could still get rid of her. A blow to the head and drop her over the side. He kept hold of her with one arm while he searched his jacket pockets with the other. Jennifer struggled but had no energy to put up a credible fight. In a second he had retrieved the nine-millimeter automatic he had brought aboard, holding it by the barrel so he could use the handle like a hammer. But at that moment the dory appeared, turning around the opposite side and across the stern. He saw Peter leap the gap between the boat and the swim platform. Now Padraig's purpose changed from getting rid of Jennifer to saving himself. He pulled her in front of him like a shield and backed toward the foredeck.

Peter was over the stern rail instantly and rushing forward. Padraig turned the gun in his hand and aimed while he struggled with Jennifer. Peter came up the narrow side deck next to the saloon. He saw the gun but never hesitated. Padraig fired, three quick shots. Peter stopped as if he had run into a wall and dropped to his knees. His eyes widened, more in surprise than in pain.

O'Connell steadied his aim for the finishing shot. But then he caught a glimpse of Kevin moving forward along the other side. He panned the gun over and fired. His wild shot shattered the pilothouse window.

Padraig moved to his left, over to the other side to find a clear shot. And then there was movement to his right. Peter was back on his feet and coming at him, unsteadily but still quickly. Now he wheeled the gun to his right.

Jennifer suddenly had his arm. Her two hands were locked around his wrist, pushing the muzzle of the gun up in the air. Then Peter's hands clasped on top of Jennifer's. Padraig let go of Jennifer and tried to point the gun back into Peter's face, but Peter had all his weight behind his grip, and instead the muzzle was slowly turning on Padraig. They fought until the automatic was pressed against Padraig's head. Jennifer reached up and tried to rip the gun out of his hand, and Kevin moved in from the other side.

Then Padraig stopped struggling and left the pistol exactly where it was aimed. "Forgive me, darlin'," he said to Jennifer. And then he pulled the trigger.

His face contorted, and a spray of gore flew over the side. Peter lost his grip and fell back in horror. Jennifer screamed. O'Connell crumpled through the railing and dropped into the sea.

Peter and Jennifer both stood looking at where he had been. Neither went to the edge to look after the body that came to rest just beneath the surface.

Kevin was the first to move. He started to the rail but then stopped. "Wasn't that . . ." He gestured toward the water while he searched for a name. "You know, the secret agent, the one who's always saving the world."

"Padraig O'Connell," Jennifer filled in.

Kevin squinted. "No, that's not it . . . the English spy—what's his name?"

Peter had been hit twice, the first shot through his thigh, and the second, aimed higher by the pistol's recoil, through his shoulder. Kevin, who had once saved a crewman who lost an arm in a winch gear, worked on both wounds. He pressed towels against the entrance and exit wounds in the shoulder and tied a tourniquet to slow the bleeding from the leg wound. Then he tuned the radio to tell the Coast Guard that there was an emergency aboard *Maineman* and give the position. He and Jennifer hobbled Peter into the saloon, where he stretched out on the sofa. Jennifer brought a blanket to keep him warm, and Kevin contributed a large glass of Padraig's favorite Scotch.

The young seaman had little problem jumping the ignition to start the trawler's engines. Then he took his own boat in tow, weighed anchor, and headed back up the bay to Blue Hill. They were under way only a few minutes when they heard the distant beat of helicopter rotors, and seconds later a Coast Guard medic was lowered aboard *Maineman*. The medic redid Kevin's first aid, injected Peter with a painkiller, and started a drip flowing into his arm. There was no need to haul him up into the chopper. He was doing fine, and the boat would have him ashore soon enough.

Jennifer sat beside him, holding his hand until the narcotic took effect. Then Peter slumped against her shoulder and dozed off peacefully.

Kevin then grilled the medic. "You know those English spy movies—what's the name of the hero? The secret agent who always gets the girl?"

"Oh yeah," the medic said. "I know who you're talking about." But he couldn't remember the name.

Peter spent two days in a Bangor hospital with Jennifer at his side. Kevin came for a visit on the second afternoon and announced that he knew the name of the movie star. "Padraig O'Connell," he said. He showed them a front-page photo of O'Connell. The story, on the obituary page, called his death "A suicide, while yachting with friends near Mount Desert Island, Maine."

Peter was flown down to New York where he spent another week in a hospital: minor surgery to remove the bullet still lodged in his leg, and a few days for observation. When he finally returned to his apartment, Jennifer had it well stocked, with fresh flowers in all the vases. "Who sent the flowers?" he asked. "I don't have any friends."

"Yes you do," she answered. "They're all from me."

She begged him to reconsider his resignation from Pegasus Satellite Services. Peter refused. He'd stay long enough to complete the buyout of Leprechaun Productions, and to bring in replacements for Catherine's marketing roles. But then he was determined to leave, "to pursue other interests."

"What other interests?" Jennifer demanded.

"You," he said. "I went back into the fire to get you, and I'm not going to lose you. I don't want to be in business with you, Jennifer. I want to be in love with you."

EPILOGUE

Padraig O'Connell was our last rivalry, and our most bitter. It wasn't just the devotion of a man that was at issue. It was all that went with it. Padraig was celebrity and glamour. He was television interviews, magazine covers, Academy Award walk-ons, and even royal invitations. He was everything important in life. We both wanted him desperately.

Think about it. If Jennifer would scheme to get my drawings, my doll, and my boyfriends, there was no limit to how far she would go to get Padraig. And she was clever. You had to give her credit. Look at the way she connived to get the Serini glass vase from our father. Or the way she spoiled my "Man of the Year" award.

Of course, Padraig was taken with her first. In the beginning, all he was after was money, and my sister was the easier mark. God, she was so desperate she would have settled for any man, and here was a world celebrity paying attention to her. She grabbed him with both hands and held on for dear life.

She was shameless, following him all over the world. And that business about loving to drive sports cars, that was just her way of stringing him along. Padraig had her money, which was all he ever wanted from her. But he couldn't get away. Jennifer popped up wherever he went.

You don't think he really wanted to marry her? That was her idea. She probably threatened him: No more money without a wedding ring. I'll bet he was drunk when she got him to stand up in front of the clergyman.

I didn't think much of him at first. Just a fortune hunter, as far as I was concerned. The only reason I paid any attention to him was to keep Jennifer from making even more of a fool of herself.

I wasn't really surprised when he came on to me the way he did. After all, I was much more bankable in Hollywood than my sister. And I was offering easier access to much more money. The surprising thing was how quickly he fell in love with me. I mean, Padraig could have any woman in the world just by snapping his fingers. But he went absolutely mad over me. It was flattering. And I enjoyed moving in his circles. Before I knew it, I was in love with him, too.

I think that was what drove Jennifer over the edge. All her life she had been taking from me and then lying to cover up. Like the vase. I had just as much right to it as she did, but she stole it out from under me. And then, when I accidentally dropped it, she acted as if I had done it on purpose. So now she got this insane idea that I had stolen Padraig from her. It was her turn to break something of mine. That was why she decided to kill Padraig. Oh, sure, she was furious with him for choosing me over her. But her real reason was to get back at me.

I did what I could to keep it from happening. I even arranged for someone to break into her apartment. Not to hurt her, just to warn her to leave her hands off Padraig and show her that she wouldn't be safe if anything happened to him. But it didn't work.

Jennifer had tried to have me killed. Now she was going after Padraig. And no one would believe me. I told Peter, and he only laughed at me. He wouldn't believe that Jennifer would hurt anyone. Even Padraig wouldn't take me seriously. He still had a soft spot for her.

So, in the end, that's what it came down to. It was up to me to stop her, just as it had always been. That's when I told Padraig that Jennifer had to have an accident.

He was furious with me. He said I was imagining things. He even implied that I was the one who was crazy. But even he had to face the facts. He and I were a great team, ready to take on the world, and all Jennifer could do was ruin everything. He might be willing to risk his life, but I wasn't going to risk mine. So if he couldn't do this one thing for us, if our life together meant that little to him, then he could forget about his company and his movies. I'd pull out and take my interests elsewhere.

That's why I arranged the boat trip. I thought it was a perfect way for him to take her by surprise. But it looks as if Jennifer beat us to it. She was the one who took Padraig by surprise.

Ironic, isn't it, how unfair life can be? Jennifer was always trying to destroy me, and you'd think that in the end, she'd pay the price. Instead, she got her way once again.

She killed Padraig just as she planned. She paid me back for breaking her damn vase, and for breaking her leg and for all the other things she imagined I had done intentionally. And then she put me in here.

This is her final vengeance. She was the one who convinced the judge that I was a psychopath. That's how she got herself appointed my guardian and had me committed here. Big favor! I'd rather face the charge of conspiracy to commit murder. At least then I'd be able to tell about all the things she's done to me since we were little children.

She's out there now, running my company and living my life. She must get great joy out of knowing that she's taken everything from me. But she can't have Padraig. And she can't have me. I'm not going to become her next Serini vase, on display for all her friends to look at. A conversation piece so that everyone can sympathize with her for having such an evil sister and praise her for being so good to me. I'd rather be smashed into pieces than give her the satisfaction.

The bedsheet twists into a perfect rope, and the sprinkler pipe is strong enough to hold my weight. So when you come in here tomorrow and find me hanging, it won't be suicide. It will be my final triumph over Jennifer. The vase will have slipped through my fingers.